Here We
Go Again

ALSO BY ALISON COCHRUN

Kiss Her Once for Me
The Charm Offensive

Here We Go Again

— A NOVEL —

Alison Cochrun

ATRIA PAPERBACK

New York London Toronto Sydney New Delhi

ATRIA
PAPERBACK

An Imprint of Simon & Schuster, LLC
1230 Avenue of the Americas
New York, NY 10020

First Atria Paperback edition April 2024

ATRIA PAPERBACK and colophon are trademarks of Simon & Schuster, LLC

Simon & Schuster: Celebrating 100 Years of Publishing in 2024

For information about special discounts for bulk purchases, please contact Simon & Schuster Special Sales at 1-866-506-1949 or business@simonandschuster.com.

The Simon & Schuster Speakers Bureau can bring authors to your live event. For more information or to book an event, contact the Simon & Schuster Speakers Bureau at 1-866-248-3049 or visit our website at www.simonspeakers.com.

Manufactured in the United States of America

1 3 5 7 9 10 8 6 4 2

Library of Congress Cataloging-in-Publication Data
Names: Cochrun, Alison, author.
Title: Here we go again / by Alison Cochrun.
Description: First Atria Paperback edition. | New York :
Atria Paperbacks, 2024.
Identifiers: LCCN 2023044317 (print) | LCCN 2023044318 (ebook) |
ISBN 9781668021194 (trade paperback) |
ISBN 9781668021200 (ebook)
Subjects: LCGFT: Romance fiction. | Lesbian fiction. |
Humorous fiction. | Novels.
Classification: LCC PS3603.O2933 H47 2024 (print) |
LCC PS3603.O2933 (ebook) | DDC 813/.6--dc23/eng/20231004
LC record available at https://lccn.loc.gov/2023044317
LC ebook record available at https://lccn.loc.gov/2023044318

ISBN 978-1-6680-2119-4
ISBN 978-1-6680-2120-0 (ebook)

Author's Note

Dear readers,

   This book contains references to an off-page death of a parent due to overdose, and it includes the on-page death of a parental figure. Please be gentle with yourselves and take care.

With love,
Alison

For all the queer educators out there.
You save lives simply by showing up.

And for every queer teenager who became
a little too attached to their English teacher.

A ship in harbor is safe, but that is not what ships are built for.

—John A. Shedd

Yes, I've been brokenhearted
Blue since the day we parted

—ABBA

Vista Summit, Washington

Chapter One

LOGAN

As she stands in the middle of an Applebee's being dumped by a woman she didn't realize she was dating, Logan Maletis has a realization: this is all Death's fault.

The way that hunchbacked skeleton holding a sickle and crunching its way over carnage had stared up at her from the tarot card with accusation in its eyes . . .

She should've known better than to let a sixteen-year-old with a septum piercing read her future.

But it was the last week of school, and most of her sophomores were done with their end-of-year projects and were now signing yearbooks or staring blankly at TikTok. After working a sixty-hour week, grading 150 final essays, and dragging at least a dozen seniors, kicking and screaming, across the finish line so they could graduate on time, Logan was too exhausted to consider why it might be a bad idea.

And Ariella Soto was so proud of her hand-painted tarot cards, so eager to show her English teacher her newfound skills of divination, and Logan couldn't say no to that kind of earnestness.

So, Logan sat in a too-small desk across from her student and put her fate in those intensely manicured hands.

"Tarot doesn't predict your future, Maletis," Ariella had explained in her best woo-woo voice. "It's best used as a tool for introspection and self-reflection."

That seemed so much worse.

"Ask the cards a question."

She'd overheard Ariella reading her classmates' fortunes, sophomores who asked questions like, *Where should I apply for college?* and *What should I do with my life?* Those same students had gathered around to watch Maletis's reading, and she couldn't exactly ask a real question, like *Will I ever move out of my dad's house?* or *What should I do with my life?* Instead, she closed her eyes and leaned into the theatrics. That's her role at Vista Summit High School. She's the fun teacher. The cool teacher. The teacher who doesn't take anything too seriously. "Am I going to have an awesome summer?"

Ariella tutted disapprovingly and the rest of the class snickered. "You're supposed to ask an open-ended question, like you make us do in seminar."

Logan made a show of considering thoughtfully. "*What* awesome things should I do this summer?"

More adolescent laughter.

Ariella rolled her eyes at the rephrased question but flipped the first card anyway, and there was that skeletal bastard smirking up at Logan over a bloodred background. The death card. Logan's first thought was *Joe*, and she tensed uncomfortably in the tiny desk.

"It doesn't mean literal death, Maletis. Don't look so freaked," Ariella reassured her. "It's a metaphorical death, usually. An ending."

Again, she thought of Joe, but she kept her smile broad for her students. "Like . . . the end of a school year . . . ?"

"Or perhaps the end of an important phase in your life," Ariella said in the same mystical tone. "The end of your adolescence, perhaps?"

"I'm thirty-two."

Her students laughed, but Ariella stared at her as though her heavy eyeliner allowed her to see directly into Logan's soul.

Ariella continued, "Or, it's possible it's referring to the end of a relationship. . . ."

At this, Logan relaxed a little. The boys made low *oooo* noises, and Waverly Hsu singsonged, "*Maletis has a girlfriend*," over and over again.

"*Maletis and Schaffer sitting in a tree*," Darius Lincoln added. "*K-i-s-s-i-n-g.*"

That was what she loved about working with sixteen-year-olds; at turns, they watched both *Euphoria* and *SpongeBob*, tried to snort aspirin in the back of your classroom, and sang ridiculous nursery rhymes like innocent children at recess. They were goofy and weird, which meant she could be goofy and weird, too.

"Something in your life will come to an end, Maletis," Ariella decreed, bringing the room back under her spell, and filling Logan with unexpected dread, "prompting a period of newfound self-awareness."

• • •

Didn't predict the future, her ass.

Because here she is, three days later and two hours into summer vacation, facing the end of a relationship she didn't know existed, while she tries to enjoy her Tipsy Leprechaun. And it's *definitely* Death's fault.

"This just isn't working," the tiny white woman holding a Captain Bahama Mama tells her.

"*This* . . . meaning . . . *us?*"

"I'm sorry to do it like this," Schaffer shouts over the sound of two dozen teachers celebrating their freedom with watered-down cocktails and half-priced apps.

"But it seems best to have a clean break before summer," Schaffer continues at a loud volume, alerting the gossipy counseling department that something dramatic is happening within earshot. Several of her colleagues turn to watch the scene unfold.

Teaching high school is often an exercise in humiliation, but this is a bit much, even for her.

It isn't the dumping itself she takes issue with. She's been dumped *many times*. In fact, she's been dumped in this exact Applebee's at least twice.

No, she takes issue with the fact that they're surrounded by their hetero coworkers on all sides. The social studies teachers-slash-football coaches who were distracted by a Mariners' game playing on the flat-screens are now attuned to this conversation. Sanderson and her crew of mean girls with their Pinterest-perfect classrooms are now ignoring their shared nachos to leer at the scene. Even her principal is doing a bad job feigning disinterest as he goes to town on a chicken wing.

Not that she really cares what her coworkers think of her. Most of them made up their minds about her when she started this job eight years ago.

Hell, at least half of them made up their minds about her when she started at Vista Summit High School as a ninth grader *eighteen* years ago.

But as the only openly queer teachers in their conservative small town, it would be nice if people weren't staring at them like they're a couple on *The Ultimatum*.

"Doesn't a clean break seem best?" Hannah Schaffer asks in response to Logan's blank stare. At least, Logan is pretty sure her first name is Hannah.

Like, *90 percent certain*.

It's definitely Hannah, and not Anna or Heather or Hayley.

Probably.

It's not Logan's fault she's fuzzy on the first name of her current casual-workplace-acquaintance-with-benefits. Most teachers at Vista Summit go exclusively by their last names as a byproduct of working at a school run by dude bros who once played Vista sports and then became teacher-coaches so they could revel in those glory days forever. At work, she's never *Logan*. She's Maletis. And the tiny blond with the pink drink is only ever referred to as *Schaffer*. Except in Logan's phone, where her contact still reads "New Science Teacher" followed by a winky face emoji.

And you can't get dumped by a woman whose contact is still a generic descriptor. Logan has dozens of ambiguous contacts in her phone—*Cute Coffee Shop Girl* and *Emily Hinge* and *Hot Butch from Tinder*—and none of those fleeting hookups ended with a breakup. They ended the *respectable* way: with a mutual fizzling out and absolutely no need for a serious conversation.

She doesn't really *do* serious.

But Probably-Hannah Definitely-Schaffer seems hell-bent on having a serious conversation in this Applebee's. "It can't come as a surprise that I'm ending things."

"It really can," she grumbles into her drink. And is Sanderson . . . *holding up her phone?* Is she recording this atrocity? Logan fights to keep her stance casual and her face impassive. You can't be hurt over the end of a relationship you didn't know you were in.

"I mean, we can't keep pretending we don't have problems," Schaffer continues. "Things haven't been good between us for a while now."

A while now? Logan scans her romantic history with this science teacher and tries to find any evidence that might justify the use of *a while*. From that first drunken makeout after a staff happy hour, Logan had made it clear they were keeping it casual. Late night *U up?* texts and never sleeping over. It wasn't exactly the stuff that Nora Ephron films were made of. And it started . . . *what?* A month ago? Two months, tops.

So, yeah, Logan is surprised. And confused. And quite frankly, a little nauseous from this green drink.

"Look, you're a fun time," Probably-Hannah says. "But I think we should end things before either of us gets hurt."

As if she would ever let herself care enough to get hurt. "You're probably right," she agrees in an attempt to expedite this postmortem on a fake relationship and get back to celebrating the start of summer. "Thanks for the talk. Now, if you don't mind, I'm going to—"

Her evasive maneuvering is swiftly ignored. "I just think we're in different places in our lives. You still live with your dad and you're in your *thirties*."

She says *thirties* like it's a terminal diagnosis. Logan should've known better than to hook up with a zillenial who thought Mary-Kate and Ashley were three people. Like most of the young teachers at Vista Summit High School, Schaffer lives in Portland, a forty-minute drive across the river. And she's very self-righteous about it. "It's tragic the way your quality of life starts to decline at the ripe old age of thirty-two," Logan snarks.

"You're literally always complaining about your back, and you get sick every time you eat cheese," she points out.

Fair point, Schaffer.

Hannah looks her up and down with an expression of barely concealed revulsion, and Logan wonders if Sanderson captured that on her phone, too. "What's your plan, Logan?"

She considers this in the same way she considered what question to ask the tarot cards. "Well, I was probably going to order some mozzarella sticks, maybe switch to beer—"

"What is your plan for your *life*?" Schaffer interrupts. "Are you going to live with your dad in this disgusting town forever?"

She feels that question wedge itself deep into her chest. *The end of your adolescence, perhaps?*

"Vista Summit isn't disgusting," Logan says reflexively. Sure, the historically red voting trends in Vista Summit are abominable.

And the lack of openly queer people is less than ideal for a single lesbian.

And there's the smell. From the paper mill up the river. So, in the literal sense, Vista Summit is *technically* disgusting, at least in odor.

And okay *fine*. Their current mayor is a former rodeo clown and current flat-earther who ran on a platform of bringing Chick-fil-A to town (a promise he still hasn't made good on after seven years in office). And yes, she's known most of these people her whole life, and they're all a bunch of busybodies who've kept receipts on every mistake she's made since she was in OshKosh B'gosh.

But . . . the town is right along the gorgeous Columbia River, and on clear days there is a staggering view of Mount Hood and the Gorge. There are ungoverned trees and open spaces, boundless green and hiking trails in every direction, so many ways to escape into nature where there are no walls and no rules and no one to judge her. Of course, she'd dreamed of escaping for real as a kid—of fleeing this suffocating small town for a life of adventure, a list of places she wanted to see written on notebook paper, carried around in her childhood best friend's pocket.

But childhood dreams, like childhood best friends, aren't meant to last. So, she stayed. And she's fine staying.

"I'm not sure my life plans are any of your business," she snaps at Schaffer. "Like, we were just hanging out, and if you're done hanging out, that's cool, but I don't think we need to make it a whole thing."

"*Just hanging out?*" Probably-Hannah repeats slowly. "For four months, we've just been hanging out?"

Logan's indifference falters for a minute. *Four months?*

No. It hasn't been that long.

Has it?

"Four months?" she repeats. Had she really let it go on for that long? She usually knows better than that. Leave before you get left, because everyone leaves eventually. Logan isn't the kind of woman people stick around for.

"Yes, four months. Did you forget to take your meds again this morning or something?"

And against all odds, Schaffer *does* manage to hurt her. Logan blinks back any signs of real emotion and juts out her jaw. "Look, I made it clear that this was casual from the beginning," she says, "and it's not my fault if you fell tit-over-clit in love with me."

Probably-Hannah screws her fists to her hips and glares up at her. "Tell me something, Maletis. What's my name?"

The entire Applebee's has gone suspiciously quiet, and she gets the impression even the servers are watching this public flogging unfold. Sanderson is still holding up her phone. "Schaffer," Logan answers with unearned confidence.

"My *first* name."

Kristen fucking Stewart. Logan's eyes dart around Applebee's searching for a hint or an escape hatch or a deus ex fucking machina, but everyone in this room seems firmly poised against her, mocking her the same way the Death card had. She swallows. "It's . . . Hannah."

Hopefully-Hannah stares at her in stunned silence. And then she throws her Captain Bahama Mama directly into Logan's face.

Logan closes her eyes and feels the pink sugar drink splash across her face, up into her hair. It drips down onto her favorite button-up shirt, the one with pineapples on it.

"I should've listened when everyone told me not to waste my time on an apathetic asshole who doesn't care about anyone or anything," Definitely-Not-Hannah seethes.

And Logan pretends *that* doesn't hurt at all.

• • •

Not for the first time in her life, Logan flees the Vista Summit Applebee's in disgrace.

It's starting to rain as she storms through the parking lot, but it hardly matters since she already has Malibu and Captain Morgan all over her. Her bra is filled with sticky liquid that drips down her torso with each step.

She throws herself into her rust-orange Volkswagen Passat and searches for something to clean herself off with. But her car only contains empty Red Bull cans and Starbucks breakfast sandwich wrappers and paperbacks with dog-eared pages. She's not shoving Roxane Gay down her shirt.

An apathetic asshole who doesn't care about anyone or anything.

She wonders how long it will take for the entire town to hear the story of her Applebee's humiliation. Perhaps Sanderson will upload the video to the town website to make it easier. Logan finds a single dirty hiking sock under the passenger seat and wedges that between her boobs to soak up the drink.

Something hot and frantic and terrifyingly tear-like builds up in her chest. There is no use crying over spilled garbage alcohol, and there is definitely no use crying over Not-Hannah.

It takes one . . . two . . . *three* tries for the car to start, and she fumbles for the tangled cord of her tape deck aux and plugs in her phone, pressing shuffle on her Summer Jams playlist. "Our Last Summer" from the *Mamma Mia* soundtrack starts playing at an unholy decibel.

I can still recall, our last summer . . .

She begins to back out of her parking spot as Colin Firth's tragic bleating is cut off by the robotic voice of a Siri notification. "New message from JoJo DelGoGo rainbow emoji," the default male Siri voice informs her, changing tone slightly as it reads the text from Joe: "Happy last day of school," the message begins. "I don't want to spoil this most sacred of days, but it would seem I've had a bit of a fall. I've tried to reassure my nurses that I'm fine, but they've insisted on bringing me back to Evergreen Pines because I might have, perhaps, broken my foot? You know how I feel about this godforsaken place. Could you please come by this evening?"

A bit of a fall.

Back to Evergreen Pines.

Broken my foot.

Joe.

Her hands clench around the steering wheel. Smirking skeletons and carnage and a blood-red background. She wishes she could be more apathetic about this, but her entire body feels like it has turned to stone. She's thinking about Joe and the Death card and endings, and not about the fact that she's still backing out of her parking spot when there's a screech of metal on metal as she whips toward the steering wheel. She slams on the brakes, but it's too late.

She hit something.

Specifically, she hit another car.

More specifically—she looks in her rearview mirror—she hit a gray Toyota Corolla.

Shit on a fucking biscuit. Logan watches in horror as the driver of the Toyota flies out of the car like a bat out of Ann Taylor Loft. In the name of Shay Mitchell's Instagram, *no.* Not her. *Anyone* but her.

Three-inch heels and black nylons, a gray pencil skirt and a cardigan with polka dots buttoned all the way up to her throat, all of it drenched in the brown liquid of an iced latte.

Who the hell teaches in three-inch heels?

Rosemary Hale, that's who.

Of all the people she could've rear-ended, it had to be Hale. No one in this town keeps receipts better than her.

In the rearview mirror, Hale touches her pale pink fingernails to the wet splotch on her stomach like a soldier in a movie groping at a fatal bullet hole. Hale hasn't updated her hairstyle since the sixth grade, so her pale blond hair is scraped back in its usual severe French braid, which swings like a pendulum as she shakes her head in horror. Her pasty-white skin has gone a splotchy red and purple. "You hit my car!" Hale shrieks.

And Ruby fucking Rose. She had. She'd been publicly ridiculed and dumped, Joe was injured, and she'd rear-ended the shit out of her childhood best friend turned nemesis's car.

Colin Firth still warbles from the speakers. *Our last summer.*

Logan glances at Hale in the rearview mirror again, and for a moment, she sees a flash of the young girl she once cared about more than anything. That earnest, imaginative, brave girl. Then Hale stamps her foot, and all Logan sees is the woman that girl became and the destruction she herself has created.

This is probably Death's fault, too.

Chapter Two

ROSEMARY

Rosemary Hale doesn't want to stab a man with a Pilot V5 pen, but she will, if it comes to that.

Her fingers grip tighter around the purple grading pen as she chokes out the words: "I don't understand . . . are you *firing me*? In an Applebee's?"

"Not firing." Principal Miller holds up both hands defensively, as if he's the victim in this ambush over chicken wings. He's got BBQ sauce on his fingers. It almost looks like blood. "We're laying you off with the hopes of rehiring you in the fall once the district has more accurate enrollment numbers."

"How is that any different than *firing me*?"

Before anyone ends up impaled by fine point, Rosemary tries to take a four-count breath like Erin taught her. Inhale for four. Hold for four. Exhale for four. But the restaurant is blaring yacht-rock and gauche wall to gauche wall is stuffed with people, and she's overwhelmed by the smell of deep-fried food and the feeling of the vinyl barstool against her legs and the sound of "Rosanna" by Toto, and the encroaching realization that she's unemployed, so she only gets to three on the inhale before she screeches, "But I went to Yale! And Columbia!" Because her panic has eclipsed all rational thought.

Stop panicking. She tries to take another deep breath. Panic is for the unprepared, and she's always prepared for everything.

Except, well, this.

When she got the email from her boss in the middle of sixth period asking for a last-minute meeting after school, Rosemary hadn't thought much of it. Miller often insisted on meetings that could've been emails, and this particular email—rife with typos, random ellipses, and bright blue Comic Sans—asked if the meeting could take place at Applebee's, because the principal didn't want to miss any of the traditional staff happy hour that takes place every year as soon as the final bell rings on the last day of school.

Rosemary never goes to the staff happy hours, but she also never ignores orders from her boss, even if he does sometimes wear flip-flops to work. So, she drove to Applebee's against her better judgment. She thought maybe he wanted to congratulate her on her 98 percent testing rate on the Advanced Placement exams, or commend her impeccable zero-failures rate, or celebrate her students who placed at the National Speech & Debate Tournament. Or maybe Principal Miller wanted to pick her brain about the curriculum she created and piloted for the English Department this year, so they could get a jump-start on next year's rollout.

Whatever it was, it was something *good*. Bad things didn't happen at Applebee's.

Except now she's being fired at a literal party, while all her co-workers get drunk on neon cocktails.

"I know you're one smart cookie," Miller says. "You are one of the best students Vista Summit has ever produced. Perfect SAT scores, National Merit Scholar, Valedictorian, early acceptance to Yale . . ."

She bristles at the idea that she was *produced* by this shit heap of a town—that the town itself deserves any credit for her adolescent accomplishments. The only thing Vista Summit did was inspire her to get as far away as possible.

"We never thought our golden girl would come back home," he continues, "and we're so lucky to have a teacher like you working at Vista Summit."

Her grip loosens on the pen. "Then why the hell are you firing me?"

Miller flinches at her directness. He's never been one for confrontation—or any form of leadership. Before he white-man failed his way into the principalship, he'd been her ninth-grade pre-calculus teacher. Or, more accurately, she'd taught herself precalculus in the back of his classroom while he chatted with the basketball boys and participated in the time-honored tradition of lazy teachers everywhere: movie Fridays. Rosemary still has no idea how the movie *October Sky* was supposed to teach them calculus, but she's seen it approximately twenty times. (She did like Laura Dern's character, though.)

"Again, Hale, this isn't a firing."

"But—" Her brain snaps, crackles, and pops as she tries to come up with some argument to save her job, save herself. She *is* this job. "But I was Washington State Teacher of the Year!"

"You were a Washington State Teacher of the Year *finalist*," Miller corrects.

"Are you firing me because I'm gay?" She's death-gripping the pen again. "Because I swear, I'll have the ACLU up your ass so fast—"

Miller makes a consternated face as he stares down at her manicured pink fingernails. "Wait, you're gay?" She can see his brain trying to puzzle through how she fits into his stereotype of what a lesbian can be.

"None of this is about your skills as an educator or you as an individual. We simply don't have money in the budget, and you're the ELA teacher with the least seniority."

She squeezes her eyes shut because she'll be damned if she lets Dave Miller see her cry.

Four years. For four years, she's given everything she has to this school, this job, her students. Seventy-hour workweeks and debate tournaments every weekend from November to March. Spending every lunch period helping seniors with their college essays; wearing a wrist brace to bed every night from grading-induced carpal tunnel and a mouth guard for stressed-induced teeth grinding. Caring so much about every kid in her classroom, she doesn't have the capacity for anything else.

She doesn't date, doesn't have time for friends . . . teaching is her whole life. It's safe, it's structured, and it's a place where she has total control. Competency is the perfect antidote to anxiety. She doesn't know who she is if she's not a teacher.

Rosemary opens her eyes again and catches Miller's gaze wandering over to where several coaches have lined up tequila shots, their attention fixed on a conversation across the bar. Rosemary spots a familiar figure insouciantly leaning against a high-top table. A tornado of short, dark brown hair and an embarrassment of long limbs standing there without a care in the world. Logan Maletis is talking to Rhiannon Schaffer—or, more accurately, Rhiannon is talking to Logan while Logan's attention wanders around the restaurant as if searching for the next interesting thing. Applebee's is now playing "Dreams" by Fleetwood Mac, and Rosemary feels the past slam against her chest.

Thirteen years old in this same Applebee's, a shared platter of nachos and dreams of the adventures they'd have when they could finally flee this town. The places she'd see and the stories she'd tell and the books she'd one day write.

But that was a long time ago. A different version of herself. A *very* different version of Logan Maletis.

Miller sighs wistfully as the coaches knock back their second shot, and Rosemary yanks her focus back to her boss. She is the only thing standing between him and a summer of day-drinking, and she won't step aside easily. "What about my summer school class?"

Miller sucks on his teeth before answering. "The district has decided to give the summer class to Peterson."

"Peterson? Peterson! You're giving my class to Peterson? A football coach?"

"It's not your class, Hale. It's—"

"I wrote the proposal, I secured the grant funding, I created the entire fucking syllabus." She jabs the pen down on the table to emphasize each point.

"Calm down," Miller warns, glancing around the restaurant like he's worried someone might overhear him getting scolded by a petite woman in a cardigan. But no one in Applebee's is paying them an ounce of attention.

"Calm down? What am I supposed to do with my summer if I'm not teaching this class?" She already had it all mapped out: weekday mornings in a sunny classroom teaching composition; afternoons grading papers on an outdoor patio while sipping iced coffee; creating lesson plans and definitely not thinking about Logan Maletis or forgotten dreams or her complete lack of a life outside her job.

"You could always work on your little stories," he tries. "You were always winning those writing contests as a kid. Do you still write?"

"No, because I'm not a kid anymore," she growls under her breath.

"Then take a break," Miller says, like it's that simple. "It's summer."

"Take a break," she echoes, because it's actually not simple at all.

"When was the last time you took a vacation?"

She blinks in surprise at the question. "I—I went to that equitable grading practices conference in Cincinnati last fall."

"I said *vacation*, not work trip."

She scoffs. Did he expect her to recall some excursion where she sat by a pool sipping an umbrella-garnished cocktail? Ridiculous. She doesn't own a swimsuit, and she hates open-toed shoes and unnecessary sun exposure. Besides, she doesn't drink, and she doesn't do idle time, but she can't explain any of this to a man who currently has BBQ sauce on his chin.

Miller sighs and his gaze once again wanders to the coaches. "Look, I should really get to the party and start celebrating with the staff. You know . . . for morale, and stuff."

"Sure. *Morale.*" Rosemary demurely slides off her barstool. Or, more aptly, she slides as demurely as a five-foot-one woman in a pencil skirt and three-inch heels can manage. She is walking out of this Applebee's with her dignity intact.

"You're an incredible teacher, Hale," he says, even as he's mentally already shooting bottom-shelf tequila with his bros. "We're going to do everything we can to hire you back in the fall. In the meantime, try to relax this summer."

• • •

Relax?

She stomps out of Applebee's, each step accompanied by the sharp clack of her heels on the pavement.

Relax? Principal Flip-Flops wants her to relax while her career— *her life*—hangs in the balance?

Like hell she will.

Her hands shake with fury as she fumbles for her car keys. She's not going to waste time relaxing. She'll update her résumé and apply for a teaching job at a *better* school. She'll get a PhD in educational leadership and steal Miller's job. She'll publish several academic articles on pedagogy, frame them, and mail them to Miller's house.

She'll tear out that one wall in her condo that makes her feel uneasy, and she'll finally replace her bedroom carpet with hardwood floors, and she'll train for a marathon, and the absolute last thing she'll do for the next ten weeks is sit around with her *thoughts.*

But right now, she's going home so she can cry in peace. She's going to unzip the top of her skirt, take off her heels, and let her feet sink into her plush white rug. She'll make herself some cold brew and she'll water her plants and click on her Roomba, and she won't let herself think about any of this at all.

"Siri," she says as soon as she's in her car. "Play 'Bitch.'"

"Playing 'Bitch' by Meredith Brooks," Siri repeats. The car fills with the opening guitar strings Rosemary memorized long ago. Listening to this song became part of her first-date routine back in New York after the third woman in a row ended a date by calling her emotionally closed-off.

"But you are a little emotionally closed off," her mother had helpfully pointed out during a post-date phone call.

"Of course I am! But I don't think it's a polite thing to tell someone on a first date!"

So, before her next date, she listened to "Bitch" on repeat for thirty minutes, screaming the lyrics to herself.

Incidentally, she never developed a second-date routine.

And then she moved back to Vista Summit and stopped dating altogether.

Still, she listens to "Bitch" whenever she feels the intense need to rage, because raging is so much safer than the alternative: the untethered spiral of anxiety that spools out whenever she loses control.

And *this*. Losing her job. She hasn't felt this out of control in four years.

As Meredith Brooks reaches the crescendo of her musical manifesto, Rosemary sing-screams along. She grabs a mostly melted iced coffee from the center console and takes a drink and rage, rage, rages.

She's shouting about being someone's hell when the song cuts off and the dash screen flashes with an incoming call. Joseph Delgado.

"Joe?" she snaps as soon as the call connects, her voice raw. "Are you okay? What's wrong?"

"Don't freak out," he starts, "but I've had another little fall."

Unemployment is suddenly the furthest thing from her mind.

"Joe! What have I told you about trying to go to the bathroom without your walker!"

"Nothing is broken," the deep voice insists through the speakers. "Nothing *major*."

"Where are you right now? I'll be there in five."

"You're freaking out," he says calmly. "The fall wasn't that bad. But I'm back at Evergreen Pines, and—"

She jerks the car into reverse and pulls out of her parking spot. "I'm on my way."

She takes another frantic sip of her iced latte just as she sees a flash of orange bumper out of the corner of her eye.

Between Joe and the coffee and the layoff-induced rage, she doesn't react quickly enough. There's a sickening crunch, a lurch. She slams on her brakes harder than necessary, and her right hand instinctively flies out to protect some invisible person in the passenger seat. As her hand flings forward, her iced latte jerks sideway, and she feels the cold sensation all down her chest before she realizes what's happening. Sticky iced coffee saturates her cardigan, drips down her stomach, and pools into a puddle in her crotch.

She sits there, stunned. Then she bolts out of the car, her rage all funneled toward a new source.

An orange Volkswagen Passat smashed against her driver's-side rear door. Because *of course*.

Only Logan Maletis would hit her car while she was driving ten miles per hour. The bumper of the rusted Passat is snug against the back of Rosemary's now dented car, but Logan's crime against emissions appears to be perfectly intact.

Rosemary looks around at the wreckage of her car—the wreckage of her life—and comes to two conclusions.

One: bad things do happen at Applebee's.

And two: she's going to kill Logan Maletis.

Chapter Three

ROSEMARY

The driver's-side door opens with an ancient groan, and a leg swings out of the car, checkered Vans landing on the damp asphalt with a thud. The white squares on the Vans have all been colored in with a rainbow pattern that blurs slightly in the rain.

What kind of thirty-two-year-old woman draws on her shoes?

Logan Maletis, that's who.

Rosemary tries to take another set of four deep breaths, but then she looks at her crushed car, and the oxygen hiccups in her throat.

The rest of Logan finally follows her shoes: long limbs, denim overalls covered in bleach stains; one of her tropical shirts, which she seems to think are appropriate for every occasion; a white T-shirt that's drenched in pink liquid. Was she drinking *alcohol* while driving?

Her long face is framed by thick, chestnut-brown hair chopped bluntly at her shoulders, and a giant smirk slashes across her expression.

As a rule, Rosemary doesn't look at Logan's face. Too many memories live in those features. But she can tell her smirk is one of perfectly calm indifference. Rosemary's anxiety spikes and she clenches her fists, her long nails digging in sharply.

Returning to Vista Summit four years ago had been the smart

thing to do. Logical. Safe. After everything that happened in New York, it made sense to be closer to her mom—to return to a town the size of a fishbowl, where things are predictable and contained. That didn't mean coming home again wasn't hard, and coming home to find Logan Maletis not only still lived in Vista Summit but worked at the high school where Rosemary had just accepted a job, was a level of poetic injustice Rosemary still isn't ready to unpack.

"You hit my car!" Rosemary shouts.

Logan tilts her head to the side and studies the place where their vehicles have melded together. "Huh," she says. Rosemary can barely hear it over the sound of the *Mamma Mia* soundtrack blasting through her open car door.

I can still recall, our last summer . . .

Rosemary can still recall her last summer with Logan Maletis by her side, and she's *still* pissed as hell about it, eighteen years later.

"Huh?" Rosemary echoes. "*Huh!* Look at my car! It's like the set piece in an *Avengers* movie."

Logan steps closer to the wreckage. "Nah. That's a scratch. I think you can just buff that out."

"*Buff it out?* You smashed into me!"

Logan rolls her hazel eyes. "It was an accident."

"You *accidentally* didn't look behind you when you were backing up?"

"Look, it takes two to fender-bender," Logan retorts, "and you clearly weren't paying attention either."

Rosemary presses her tongue to the roof of her mouth and tries not to scream. She's not about to admit that she was distracted by the phone call with Joe and the destruction of her life plan and all of the fury barely suppressing her anxiety. Especially not to Logan. "Except *you* backed into *me*. So you're the one at fault."

"Fault?" Logan puffs out an infuriating breath of air. "I did you a favor, honestly. A gray Corolla? Could you have chosen a more boring car?"

"We can't all drive quirky Volkswagens like some manic pixie dream girl in a movie written by a man."

Logan makes her classic I-Hate-Rosemary face. It involves scrunching up her long, beak-like nose and twisting her mouth into a repulsed snarl, as if she smells something foul. Rosemary looks away from that face and her eyes fall on the back seat of the Passat. Through the window covered in dog-nose smudges, she can see the chaos tornado-fire of Logan's life. Food wrappers, stacks of student papers (some graded, some not), and *so many books*. An entire mobile library's worth of paperbacks with bent covers and dog-eared pages.

"Oh, well, now I understand why you hit me. You were trying to see through this Jenga tower of emotionally abused literature."

"You are," Logan starts, exhaling theatrically, "the worst."

Rosemary holds her posture perfectly straight. Dignity, dammit! "Can we please just exchange insurance information so we don't have to talk to each other for the next ten weeks?"

Logan stands there with one hip cocked to the side and says nothing.

"You *do* have insurance, don't you?"

When Logan *still* doesn't reply or reach for her wallet, Rosemary feels the anxiety break through her rage barrier and all of her worries come spilling out like pieces of paper from an overturned file cabinet. What if Logan doesn't have insurance? What is her deductible for an uninsured driver? What if her car is *totaled*? How will she be able to afford a new car now that she's lost her job?

She lost her job. Holy shit. She has another paycheck coming in July, but then what?

What if she doesn't get rehired?

What if she can't find another teaching job?

What if she can no longer do the only thing she's any good at?

What if right now, ten minutes across town, Joe is dying in Evergreen Pines from the gangrene on his foot, and she's not there with him because she's here, bickering with Logan over something as foolish as a dent in her car? What if—

"Hale!" Logan's voice cuts through the mental noise, and Rosemary looks up to find Logan standing close to her, her smirk replaced by a worried frown. Her left hand is reaching out toward Rosemary's arm, like she might try to comfort her the way she used to do, when they were kids. When Rosemary's anxiety got out of control like this.

The past slams into her again.

Rosemary is eleven years old, seized by loss and grief, moving across the country for a fresh start with her mom, terrified of not knowing anyone in school. But there is Logan, standing at the bus stop on the first day of sixth grade: a skinny girl with bushy brown hair and bruised knees who flashes a bucktoothed smile when she sees Rosemary for the first time.

She's twelve, lying on the summer grass with a friend who feels like the missing half of her soul, staring up at the stars and sharing their dreams; the sound of Logan's laugh like a song she can't stop listening to on repeat.

She's thirteen, always reaching for Logan's hand, always holding on too tight, struggling to understand how any friendship could feel so enormous inside her.

She's fourteen, in a garden at a pool party, making an epic mistake and losing that friendship forever.

She's eighteen, packing up her mother's Subaru so she could leave this town; leave Logan and the memory of her behind.

She's twenty-eight, coming home again to realize she can never truly escape Logan Maletis.

She is thirty-two, crashing into Logan. Always crashing into her. Three years of friendship, four years of hating each other, ten years of not talking, and then *this*. Arguing in department meetings and glaring at each other in the hallways and fighting in an Applebee's parking lot.

And how absurd is it that after *everything*, Rosemary wishes Logan would reach out and touch her arm. She still grieves their lost friendship, still sometimes imagines finding a way to stitch them back together again. But Logan made it clear as soon as Rosemary returned to Vista Summit that she was picking up their relationship exactly where they left it in that dark garden at fourteen. It is a bruised and bloody mess of a relationship, a gaping wound they can't stop poking.

So, no, Logan doesn't comfort her. Her hand never makes it to Rosemary's arm. It flies into one of the many pockets of her overalls and pulls out a wallet held together with duct tape. "Don't shit a brick, Hale." Logan snorts. "Of course I have insurance."

Rosemary shakes off the images of the past and shoves all those thoughts and feelings back into their file folders. She snatches the insurance card from Logan's grubby hand. "I can't help it if every time I see you, Maletis, I fear for my life."

LOGAN

"You hit Rosemary with your car?" Joe asks as soon as she rounds the corner into his room at Evergreen Pines Rehab Facility.

She throws herself down on the plastic chair beside his hospital bed with a *harrumph*. "How did you hear about that already?"

"My nurse is Kelsey Tanner, and she heard about it from her hairdresser's boyfriend, who saw the whole thing in the Applebee's parking lot."

"I hate this town."

"Yet you refuse to leave." Joe raises a grizzled eyebrow at her. "Please tell me you weren't aiming for Rosemary. Attempted vehicular manslaughter is taking your little feud a step too far."

"I didn't hit *her*. I hit her car. And it was really more of a tap. And if that tap happened to injure Hale's brittle bones, well . . . that's just an unexpected perk."

"Thirty-two is a little old for a mortal enemy."

"Not if that enemy is Rosemary Hale." She folds her arms across her chest. "Remember how she used to correct all our teachers back in school, except for you? Well, she still does that, but with our co-workers in reply-all emails. And she's always bringing essays to staff meetings so she can grade them in her lap. Like, *we get it*. You teach AP. You're very important."

Joe opens his mouth, but Logan plows on. "And remember that time junior year when she made Ivy Tsu cry after the regional debate competition because Ivy used the wrong color pen? I think she made everyone on the Speech and Debate team cry at least once. She was a little despot in Mary Janes."

Joe smirks up at her from his bed. "Did she ever make *you* cry?"

So, so many times.

"No, because I don't care what Hale thinks of me."

Joe scrunches his face in an exaggerated expression of skepticism, and Logan thinks about Hale in that parking lot, snarled into knots with anxiety. She thinks about her overwhelming urge to comfort her, like she used to. "Look, enough about Satan's stepdaughter. Let's talk about you. You look like shit, by the way."

He does a mock bow in his bed. "Thank you, darling. I call this chemo chic." He flourishes his hands. "Also, you seem to have a sock inside your bra, so let's not cast aspersions."

She pulls out the sock and waves it dismissively. "You broke your foot? Did you try to poop without your walker again?"

"No, I broke it while salsa dancing with Antonio Banderas."

"Don't strain your groin trying to be funny, old man."

He holds up one wrinkled middle finger and shoves it in her face. "I'm not old."

Technically, he's right. Joe Delgado is only sixty-four, but a long battle with pancreatic cancer has aged him like a time-lapse video. The Mr. Delgado of her memories had been larger than life in every way. Tall, with broad shoulders and a booming voice, his thick black hair was always too long and too messy, but in a way that just made sense for his personality, like he was too brilliant to waste time on something as commonplace as hygiene. A mad scientist, but his science was syntax and diction. He always spoke in animated gestures with hands the size of baseball mitts; his dark brown eyes sparkled whenever he talked about Toni Morrison or iambic pentameter, coordinating conjunctions or Gabriel García Márquez. "El gran poder existe en la fuerza irresistible del amor."

For almost thirty years, he taught ninth grade English and AP Literature and coached the Speech and Debate team at Vista Summit High School. He'd raised two generations of kids in this town. He'd definitely raised her.

She started ninth grade as a social pariah. Outed at the end of the summer, she went into high school as the lesbian with no friends and a mom who left her for another family. She thought she'd never belong, but there he was. Joseph Delgado, a beloved openly gay teacher at an aggressively conservative high school. He had a pride flag above the projector screen and a decorative scarf around his neck, and he never apologized for being exactly who he was: a gay son of Mexican immigrants who loved teaching young people how to empower themselves through reading and writing.

Mr. Delgado was the first adult who ever truly made Logan feel *okay*. Okay for being gay. Okay for having ADHD and a brain that worked a little differently. He helped her harness the creative chaos of her mind. He got her to join the Speech and Debate team.

He nurtured her love of books.

He helped her get into college.

She became an English teacher because of him. When she first started working at Vista Summit High School, they'd meet at Rochelle's for milkshakes on Fridays after work, to debrief the week, and he would give her advice on how to connect with the students she couldn't reach and on the department politics she could never understand. They'd grade papers together at Java Jump on Saturday mornings. They'd talk pedagogy in the living room of his old Victorian house off Main Street while Van Morrison spun on the record player.

He was her teacher, her role model, her surrogate parent. Her mentor, her coworker, her best friend.

And then, two days before his sixtieth birthday, he got the diagnosis. The doctors said they caught it early enough; they'd attack it aggressively. Surgery to remove the tumors. A year of rewatching *Gilmore Girls* during chemo, vomiting for days after each round. Watching that mad scientist hair fall out strand by strand. Adopting him a cancer dog because Logan didn't know how else to help.

Remission and relapse. A clinical trial that took forty pounds and his ability to sleep. Surgery to remove the whole pancreas. Insulin injections that made him sick. More chemo.

The first fall, which broke his ankle and put him in rehab for three months. So much physical therapy. Selling his house because he couldn't get up the stairs anymore.

The cancer coming back. In his liver this time.

After all that, the man in this hospital bed under the unflattering fluorescent lighting of Evergreen Pines isn't larger than life. He's too small, almost hollow-looking. His brown skin and his handsome face sags with new wrinkles. Clutching his beige blanket, his hands look like shrunken husks. She hates seeing him here, in this sterile room with vomit-colored walls, without his books or his vinyls or his dog. Evergreen Pines has a strict pet policy, and Odysseus has to go stay with some nice lesbians who own a farm a few towns over whenever Joe's in rehab.

"Stop looking at me like that," Joe barks.

"Like what?"

"Like I'm Colin Craven from *The Secret Garden*."

She huffs. "I never read *The Secret Garden*. I don't fuck with hetero books."

"No, you just fuck with every queer woman in a thirty-mile radius."

"Ouch." She clutches her chest in mock-hurt, even as the words actually leave a sting.

"I heard about what happened with Rhiannon, too."

"Wait. Is *that* her name?"

"There's a video, you know." Joe grabs his ancient Android phone off the bedstand and hands it to her. "At least ten teachers sent it to me. . . ."

"Fucking Sanderson, that masochistic dick." Logan opens the video, but the quality is terrible on Joe's phone, and quite frankly, she doesn't need to relive it.

"So, you heard her call me an apathetic asshole who doesn't care about anyone or anything?" she asks, fiddling with the buckle on her overalls.

Joe fixes those insightful eyes on her. "I think we both know you care far too much about everything."

She shifts uncomfortably, feeling too seen. The plastic chair groans beneath her.

"I didn't know you were dating anyone," Joe says, mercifully changing the topic.

"Neither did I."

"Oh, Logan." Joe heaves a sigh, which quickly turns into a cough. "Not again."

"What do you mean *again*?"

Joe reaches for the handkerchief in the pocket of the wool cardigan he's wearing over his hospital gown. Through it all, he's never compromised on his professorial fashion sense. "I mean, this isn't the first time you've found yourself in a relationship without realizing it. The same thing happened with what's-her-name? The barista in Portland?"

"Ari. But that wasn't my fault!"

"It's never your fault."

"She U-Hauled! We were in a casual, *open* relationship, and then she was shopping for trips for two to Tulum for spring break!"

"And then there was that tattoo artist who didn't renew their lease because they thought you were moving in together."

"An innocent miscommunication."

"And the fifth-grade teacher—"

"Okay, that's enough examples. I see what you're doing. Focusing on my love life instead of dealing with whatever new health thing you've got going on." She waves her hand in a circle in front of his face. "I invented that kind of emotional avoidance."

Joe coughs twice into his handkerchief. "Face it, Logan. You're a fuckboy."

"Tegan and fucking Sara, who taught you the term *fuckboy*?"

"I'm not that old," he manages before dissolving into a full-on hacking fit. She reaches for the water bottle on the bed tray and extends the bendy straw toward his mouth. "Oh, stop!" He swats at her. "I can still drink water without assistance."

"You never settled down with one person, and no one called you a *fuckboy*."

A grimace of pain appears in the corner of Joe's mouth, the new wrinkles in his forehead deepening. "Maybe I want to prevent you from making my mistakes." He pulls out his handkerchief and blows his nose. "Which brings me back to Rosemary . . ."

There isn't an eyeroll big enough for that sloppy segue, but Logan tries anyway. "Why would we *ever* need to talk about Rosemary Hale?"

"I always thought you girls would bury the hatchet."

"Hale *definitely* keeps maps of where she put them."

He shifts against his pillows. "But you used to be best friends. Why do you hate her so much?"

"Because of her entire personality," Logan answers. She doesn't want to go into the rest. The past: the pool party, the game of spin the bottle, the dark garden, Jake McCandie. Now: Hale showing her up at staff meetings, making everything look so easy, reminding Logan of all the ways she falls short.

But Joe keeps staring at her with the full weight of his old-man insightfulness. "But you have so much in common."

"Hale and I have nothing in common!"

"You are both high school English teachers at your alma mater. . . ."

"Yes, but I became a teacher because I genuinely care about helping reluctant learners develop confidence and a passion for school! Hale became a teacher because she gets off on bossing people around. She never once struggled with school, so of course she chose to do it forever."

Logan has a theory. There are two types of high school teachers: the teachers who had such a great time in high school that they never wanted to leave, and teachers who were so miserable in high school they came back to try to make things a little better for the next generation. Hale is the first kind; Joseph Delgado was the second.

"I know you've always had a soft spot for her because you can't resist taking in strays, but Hale is a rigid, controlling, sanctimonious little shit."

Joe clears his throat as his gaze settles on something over Logan's right shoulder.

Behind her, someone clicks their tongue. Logan doesn't turn around. She doesn't have to. There's only one person in Vista Summit who uses condescending tongue-clicks as her weapon of choice. "I said her name three times, didn't I?"

The tap-tap of pointy heels, and then Hale is standing at the end of Joe's bed. Hale smells like vanilla body lotion, the same scent she's worn since middle school. As a consequence, Logan has experienced not one but two panic attacks inside a Bath and Body Works.

"What is she doing here?" Hale asks in that condescending voice that always makes Logan feel like a student again, like she forgot to do the homework and the teacher is making an example out of her for the rest of the class.

"Rosemary," Joe says affectionately. "I asked both of you girls to come here, actually."

Hale huffs, and Logan gets a whiff of her mouthwash. Artificial spearmint and neuroses. She's changed into clean clothes, but it's just another skirt and cardigan that fits her like a straitjacket.

Joe takes another labored breath. "There's something I need to tell you. . . ."

"You're back in diapers, aren't you?" Logan grimaces. "I sure as shit won't be the one to change them."

Joe grimaces, then speaks. "I'm dying, girls."

Chapter Four

ROSEMARY

Dying.

Rosemary takes a sharp breath and steadies herself against the hospital bed frame. She tries to stanch the anxiety already building in her chest, but it's useless. *Dying.*

"Elton fucking John, you're such a melodramatic queen!" Logan makes a goose-like honking sound that seems to be a laugh. She leans back in her chair and kicks her checkered Vans up onto his beige blankets.

"Fuck you, Logan Maletis." Joe coughs a few times, and Rosemary hurries to the other side of the bed to adjust his pillows. "I *am* dying."

"What else is new?" Logan asks with that flippant smirk. "You've been dying for four years."

"But now I'm *dying* dying. I've got mets."

"What are mets?"

"Hell if I know, but my doctors won't shut up about them."

Rosemary looks down at Joe and notices he's spilled some water on his chin. "Metastases," she explains, discreetly drying his chin on the arm of her clean cardigan. "It means the cancer has spread beyond your liver now."

"Always the star pupil," Joe says, tenderly putting a hand on hers. "Ten gold stars, Rosie, darling."

Logan glares up at her from the other side of the bed. "Oh, so you're an oncologist now?"

She presses her tongue to the roof of her mouth before she can say anything unkind. She wishes she'd been the one to get here first, that she'd had time to talk privately with Joe about his fall and his broken foot, about how he is *really* doing, about these supposed mets. But she had to call her insurance company to report the accident; she had to call Mickey's Mechanic to set up an appointment; she had to race back to her condo to change her coffee-stained clothes.

Logan is sitting there still covered in now-crusty pink liquid.

"Where are the mets?" Rosemary asks, focusing all her attention on Joe.

He sighs. "They're everywhere, girls. In my bones. I'm too weak for more chemo, and apparently, you can't survive with cancer in every damn part of your body."

"I mean, not with that attitude," Logan says.

Joe laughs. Overhead, the fluorescent lights flicker and hum, and Rosemary presses her cool fingertips to both temples like that will somehow help her incipient anxiety migraine. Logan always gets to be the fun one. She's the one who brings Joe Tillamook cheeseburgers from Burgerville when he's in the hospital, even though he's not supposed to eat them since his Whipple procedure. Logan gets to be the one who watches Netflix with him, the one who impulsively buys him a dog, the one who sneaks him out of rehab for milkshakes.

Rosemary is the one who drives him to all of his appointments; the one who picks up all his prescriptions; the one who helped him sell his house; the one who moved him into assisted living.

Nearly everyone in Vista Summit between the ages of twenty-two and fifty-two has Joe to thank for their understanding of the semicolon and their appreciation for the themes in *Frankenstein*, and when he first got diagnosed with pancreatic cancer, the town banded together to support him. Bake sales to raise money for his medical procedures and meal-trains and an Excel spreadsheet with volunteer time slots, so Joe was never alone when he was in the hospital. Rosemary had just moved back home, and she baked brownies and cooked lasagna and sat beside him every Tuesday from five to eight, reading the new Isabel Allende aloud to him.

But the community support began to taper off during his second round of chemo. Soon, there were no casseroles, and no baked goods to help with the medical bills; the chair next to his bed was often empty. The people of Vista Summit had been happy to rally around Joe when it seemed like a cure was imminent, but the longer his battle went on, the less anyone seemed to care. Except for Rosemary.

Except for, inexplicably, Logan Maletis.

Metastases in his bones. She swallows around the anxiety lump in her throat and tries to focus. "What's the treatment plan?"

"There is no treatment plan," Joe answers with unnerving calm. "My oncologist says I've got three months, at best. I'm just hoping to make it through one last summer."

"No treatment plan?" Rosemary echoes, staring at the wrinkled face of the man who cultivated her love of literature and nurtured her writing; the man who cared about her at a time in her life when no one else did. How can she possibly be calm about this? "That's unacceptable. Logan, tell him that's unacceptable."

Logan fiddles with the clasp on her overalls. "It's his life." She shrugs.

"Like hell it is." Her brain swirls around solutions and miracle cures and next steps. Could they get more Herceptin with his current insurance? Could she find another clinical trial?

"Girls," he says again, like they are still an indistinguishable pair, inseparable even though they've been separated for so long. Like they're still the fourteen-years-olds who walked into his classroom two decades ago. "You know I adore you both, and I appreciate your stubbornness, Rosie, but my death is *mine*. I get to set the terms, and I don't want to die fighting. I want to die as high as a kite—so fucking high, I can't even spell mets."

Rosemary presses her tongue to the roof of her mouth. "Cancer isn't funny."

"Out of the three of us, I'm the only one dying from it, so it's funny if I say it's funny. What did I teach you in AP Lit?"

"You can't combine two independent clauses with a comma?" Logan guesses.

"That comedy and tragedy are arbitrary genre distinctions," Rosemary answers, like she's back in the front row of his classroom, raising her hand at every question. And Logan makes a barfing noise like she's still stuck in the backroom of his classroom, mocking everything Rosemary did. Logan Maletis always makes her feel fourteen again in the worst kind of way.

"That's right. The only difference between a Shakespearean comedy and a Shakespearean tragedy," he continues in his resonant lecture voice, "is that one ends with marriage and the other ends with death."

"That's somewhat of an oversimplification of Frye's genre classifications—"

"We're not in a Shakespearean play," Logan cuts in.

"Aren't we?" Joe asks with a tilt of his head.

"I didn't hit her with my car on purpose!" Logan flails. "I am *not* the Iago!"

Rosemary tunes her out. Cancer in his bones. No treatment plan. *One last summer*. She feels nauseous, but that's how she always feels at Evergreen Pines. The whole place smells like bleach and wet towels, and the lights wash everything out in a sallow, sickly glow, and Joe always looks so pitiful, tucked under cheap blankets in a khaki-colored room.

He's dying. She crouches down beside him and clasps one leathery hand between both of hers. "I'm so sorry, Joe."

Logan shakes her head in denial. "If you're dying for realsies, where in the name of Phoebe Bridgers is your family?" she asks, like she hasn't been paying attention at all the past four years.

"Dead, mostly," Joe answers. "It's just my brother and his family outside Houston."

Logan scoffs. "And why isn't your brother here?"

Joe chuckles. "I'm so happy you girls grew up in a generation where the answer to that question isn't obvious."

"Ah. Homophobe?"

Joe nods. "Homophobe."

Logan makes a clucking sound and turns her head toward the window where Joe has a magnificent view of the parking lot, and Rosemary breaks her rule, just for one minute. She studies Logan's face in profile, trying to get some sense of the emotions behind that neutral mask.

She'd been so expressive when they were young: round cheeks that scrunched up to her eyes when she smiled; gawky limbs that moved like wet noodles when she spoke excitedly; a big beak-like nose that started too high on her face, giant teeth, and bushy eyebrows. Eleven years old, with a dead dad, in a new town, completely petrified. But then she saw Logan standing at the bus stop with her baggy shorts, a chaotic bird's nest of dark brown hair on her head. Rosemary couldn't look away.

Now, Logan's face is mostly sharp angles and symmetrical features used for smirking or flirting. Somewhere over the course of the last two decades, she learned how to carry her limbs, but she never got braces, so she still has a terrible overbite from childhood. Her two front teeth stick out, so her upper lip can never fully close around them, making her perpetually on the verge of saying something. Or kissing someone.

This version of Logan is beautiful, and Logan absolutely knows it. Everyone who's ever met her knows it. That's why women fall at her feet, even though they all know she's going to trample them beneath her ugly shoes.

But Rosemary preferred Logan better when her awkward features telegraphed every emotion. Because here they are. Joe is dying, and Logan looks like it's just a scratch on her car; like she's going to tell Joe to just buff it out.

"I've mostly made my peace with dying, my family be damned," Joe says into the quiet of the room. Logan tears her gaze away from the window, and Rosemary tears her gaze away from Logan.

"What do you need from us, Joe?" Logan asks with a tone as unmoved as her expression. "Why did you ask us both to come?"

Rosemary reaches out for Joe's hand. "Yes, tell us what you need," she adds. "What can we do for you?"

Joe exhales. "Well. You could drive me to Maine."

"Like, Main Street?"

"Like, Maine the state."

Logan erupts in wild laughter. When Joe doesn't crack a smile, her expression sobers again. "Wait. Are you serious right now?"

"I have a cottage in Maine, on the water outside Bar Harbor," he says. This is news to Rosemary, and based on the flicker of feeling in Logan's face, it's news to her, too. "I want to return there. I want to see that old cottage by the sea and the Atlantic Ocean. That's my dying wish."

"Your dying wish?" Logan snorts. "You're truly *such* a theatrical queen."

He makes a flourishing gesture, like he is flipping an invisible scarf over his shoulder, and the past slams into her again. Rosemary is back there, on the first day of high school. Feeling so small, so afraid, so terribly alone since she'd lost her best friend that summer. She walked into her first-period English class, and she immediately felt at ease.

Joe was in his midforties then, noticeably handsome, with grays speckling his thick, black hair. His dark eyes crinkled in the corners as he smiled and somehow greeted each student by name, even though it was the first day of school. She would learn later that he always memorized his rosters in August, a habit she would adopt, too.

He wore a navy sweater with patches on the elbows and a bright silk scarf, which he tossed theatrically over one shoulder when the bell rang. "Good morning, my children," he'd greeted almost musically. "Welcome to high school."

And he'd meant it. He treated each student like they were *his*. When he found out Rosemary usually spent her lunch period crying in the bathroom, he invited her to eat in his classroom instead. And when he found out she liked to write little stories, he encouraged her to keep at it. And when he began to suspect she was like him, he didn't push it or say a damn word about it until she was ready to come out to him senior year.

At Yale, she still sent him every creative writing assignment, every A paper, every short story she managed to get published online, because Joseph Delgado never stopped caring about his children.

"I'm not joking," Joe says now. "I don't want to die in some sterile hospice facility. I want to die in that cottage. I want to die in Maine, near the ocean."

She can hear in his voice how serious he is—it's the voice he used when lecturing about Romantic-era poetry or the Harlem Renaissance or active verbs. "Okay," she says, squeezing his hand as tight as she can. "I can fly to Maine with you."

He shakes his head. "No, no. I want to drive. I'd like to see a little more of this country before I go."

Logan visibly balks. "I'm not sure you'd survive a cross-country road trip, old man. You broke your foot trying to go to the bathroom."

"No one said anything about surviving, asshole." Joe takes a slow breath. "Look. I'm fully aware that I might die on the road between here and Maine, but it would be worth it for the chance to see that place one more time."

"I can show you the ocean right now. On Google Images." Logan pulls out her phone. "You don't need to suffer in a car."

"Think about what you're asking," Rosemary says. "I-I don't think I could drive you to your death, Joe."

1

He shakes his head. "Then don't think about it that way. Think of it as just a fun vacation." He attempts a smile, but it quickly dissolves into a cough. He grips his old handkerchief, the hand-embroidered one with the initials RSP in the corner. She's always been too polite to ask, but she wonders whose possession Joe has always clung to so desperately.

"Where is your sense of spontaneity and adventure, girls?" he manages when the coughing is under control.

Rosemary watches the way that question works its way across Logan's features, solidifying into a stubborn expression Rosemary knows so well. Logan was always the adventurous one—the one who pushed them to go higher, faster, past every boundary. The one who dared Rosemary to swipe a Butterfinger from the Quick-E-Mart, the one who made them jump from the tallest rock into Tarren Lake, the one who used to dream about their future together when they finally escaped this horrible town. The Logan Maletis she'd known in middle school was an immovable force, all kinetic potential and unchecked yearning and sparkling wit.

When Rosemary moved back to Vista Summit four years ago, she wondered how that version of Logan could ever lead to *this* version: thirty-two years old and still stuck in this small town that had been too cramped for her even at eleven.

"Let's say I did agree to drive you . . . ," Logan begins, swiping at her top lip with her tongue as she thinks. "How would that even work?"

"I have faith the two of you could figure out how to transport a dying man across the country."

"The two of us?" For the first time since she arrived at Evergreen Pines, Logan looks directly at Rosemary. Her hazel eyes still burn with the passion of her eleven-year-old self.

"I want you both to drive me," Joe clarifies. "We'll drive to Maine, all three of us. That's why I asked you here."

Now Rosemary is the one who laughs. "The two of us? In a car? For *three thousand miles*?"

Joe's chapped lips curl into another smile. "Sounds like a dream."

"You know we literally got in an accident today? She smashed my car."

"Our cars were smashed together," Logan clarifies. "There's been no admission of fault."

"Car accident aside," he says diplomatically, "I wouldn't trust anyone else to drive me across the country."

"Then you'd better settle for Delta Airlines' basic economy," Logan tells him, but Rosemary's brain is stuck on Joe's question. When was the last time she truly did something spontaneous? She thinks about that sweltering day in August their last summer together, when Logan convinced her to strip down to her underwear and swim in Tarren Lake, just the two of them. They'd been hiking all day in the heat, passing a single water bottle between them, their fingers brushing every time, their mouths occupying the same small piece of plastic. The cool water felt like sin against her bare skin.

She could drive Joe to Maine. Even as her anxiety branches out like a spider's web of what-ifs, her brain cobbles together a makeshift itinerary. She suddenly has ten weeks off, an entire summer spread out before her. She could do this.

"Please, girls," Joe begs. "Don't let me die in this beige room."

Rosemary knows in the pit of her stomach she won't. She glances over at Logan, whose face is still impassive. "Please, Logan. Bury those hatchets," Joe says quietly, like it's only the two of them in this moment, and Rosemary is intruding on something deeply private. "Do it for me. Because you care about me."

Logan reaches for her sunglasses, even though it's still raining outside. The reflective tint of her aviators hides her expression entirely as she says, "Haven't you heard, Joe? I'm an apathetic asshole who doesn't care about anyone."

Chapter Five

ROSEMARY

"Have you ever changed an adult diaper before?"

"Good morning to you, too," her mother grumbles as she lets herself into Rosemary's apartment. She's wearing her Scooby Doo scrubs, and she has a spare key in one hand, a coffee carrier in the other, and a bag of bagels clenched between her teeth.

"What am I talking about?" Rosemary says, mostly to herself. "You're a nurse. Of course you know how to change an adult diaper. Can you teach me?"

Andrea Hale drops everything onto the midcentury modern coffee table in front of her daughter with an unceremonious *thunk*. "Last week it was learning Portuguese on Duolingo, and this week it's geriatric incontinence. Kids these days . . ."

Rosemary snatches her Americano from the drink carrier and goes back to her bullet journal where she's taking notes on how to convert a vehicle so it's wheelchair accessible. Her hand is starting to ache from gripping the pen too tightly, but she ignores it. "I'm doing research."

"I'm only fifty-six. And sure, sometimes when I sneeze, a little pee comes out, but that's what happens when you have a baby. I'm still a few years from diap—" Her mother cuts off as she seems to notice the supplies spread out across the living room. The wireless printer, the label maker, the laminator, the three-hole punch, the open binder full of color-coded tabs. "Is that a laminated map of I-80?"

"It is," she answers without looking up.

"What, exactly, are you researching?"

"How to transport a dying man from Washington to Maine."

"Okay, let's set down the washi tape for a minute." Andrea has to pry the bullet journal from Rosemary's clawlike fingers. "Why would you need to medically transport someone to Maine?"

Rosemary closes her eyes and sees Joe's desperate expression under those ghoulish fluorescents. *Please, Rosemary. You have to convince her,* he said after Logan so cavalierly walked away.

It's my dying wish.

The grief and loss and fear creep up her throat just thinking about it, but she washes those feelings down with a gulp of scalding-hot Americano. Right now, she has to focus on what she can control, and that's this. Her research. Her binder and her itinerary.

She finally looks up and sees the familiar concern in her mother's face. "Joe is dying," she explains. "The doctors give him three months, and he wants me to drive him to Bar Harbor, Maine, before he dies."

"And you're actually considering doing it?" Her mom glances around the room again, and Rosemary sees her living room through her mother's eyes: the detritus of another hyperfixation. "Did you stay up all night working on this?" her mom asks carefully.

It's only then that she notices the sting of exhaustion in the back of her eyes. "Mom, it's Joe." Her voice cracks over his name.

Her mom slowly lowers herself into the wingback chair across from her daughter. "I know Joe is important to you, but this is a lot to ask of a former student. . . ."

"Joe isn't just my former teacher. He's—" She bites down.

He was there for me when you couldn't be. The thought cuts through her exhaustion.

She knows Andrea did the best she could with what she had, and growing up, they didn't have much. Years of therapy helped Rosemary accept this.

Andrea Hale believed love was moving her eleven-year-old daughter across the country where nothing would ever remind her of the dad she lost; love was never talking about loss at all; love was working double shifts at the hospital so she could put food on the table, clothes on Rosemary's back, money in her college fund. Andrea wasn't around for family dinners, or movie nights on the couch, or heart-to-hearts; she didn't take Rosemary shopping for homecoming dresses or ask her about her day or hug her more than a few times a year.

So, most days, instead of going home to an empty house after school, Rosemary went to Mr. Delgado's classroom. When she struggled with her anxiety, when she struggled to manage her stress, when she began questioning her sexuality, her mom wasn't the adult she turned to for emotional support.

Until her life in New York fell apart and she came running back home. Now, she and her mom have Saturday morning bagels and Thursday dinners and the occasional impromptu check-in on her mental health. She appreciates these small gestures, but none of them can change the fact that they're two women with the same pale eyes and pale hair who don't really understand each other. Her mother was never going to *get* the way Rosemary's brain worked. And while she didn't bat an eye at the idea that Rosemary liked women, Andrea can't fathom why Rosemary doesn't ever *date* women. Why she seems to have no interest in dating or intimacy or (heaven forbid) sex.

In Andrea's defense, Rosemary doesn't really know why she has no interest in those things, either.

"Honey," Andrea starts in her best trying-to-be-a-mother tone. "I'm not sure this is the healthiest thing for you right now."

"I'm totally healthy."

Her mother clicks her tongue, trying to censor herself. A family trait. "But what about . . . don't you have summer school?"

Rosemary glances down at the calluses and ink stains on her fingers. "I-I got laid off, actually."

"What?" Her mother is out of the wingback chair and beside Rosemary on the couch before she can blink. "Oh, honey. No. I know what that job means to you."

The burn of tears joins the exhaustion in her eyes. She takes another swig of her Americano. "So, the timing is perfect, really. I have the summer off, which means I can do this for Joe."

Another tongue click.

"It's his dying wish, Mom."

Andrea sighs, and then puts a hand on Rosemary's shoulder. It looks awkwardly out of place there. "Is this about your fath—?"

"This isn't about Malcolm," she snaps. "This is about Joe. About honoring Joe, who gave his whole life to the young people in this ungrateful town and never got the thanks he deserved."

She feels her mom's fingers briefly tense, then relax, through the wool layer of her cowl-neck house sweater. "Okay. You feel this is something you need to do. I can respect that. But, honey, you can't drive Mr. Delgado three thousand miles by yourself."

Rosemary stares at her binder, at the plan that's beginning to take shape. "No. I won't be doing it by myself."

LOGAN

She wakes up to Shania Twain.

In some households, nine on a Saturday morning might be a little early for a nineties country kitchen dance party, but not in Antonio Maletis's house. It's one of the many reasons she shouldn't be living with her dad anymore.

She tunnels down deep into her sheets and tries to fall back to sleep, despite the way Shania is loudly listing the things that don't impress her much. As long as Logan stays asleep, she doesn't have to accept the reality of the last twenty-four hours.

But reality refuses to be ignored. It's in the pounding music and a pounding headache, and the fact that she is so miserably hungover.

The details of last night are a bit fuzzy, but she remembers taking an Uber to Five Bar on Main Street, alternating whiskey shots and hazy IPAs, scrolling through Tinder until she found a hookup only ten miles away. Another Uber to a stranger's house.

Impulsive and reckless and borderline self-destructive? Sure.

But as she pressed herself against a woman who didn't expect Logan to learn her name in the back seat of a Kia Sonata parked in a suburban driveway while her kids slept inside the house, Logan could shut out all the noise in her head. She could let the lust and pleasure override all the other too-big feelings in her chest. In that dark car, she couldn't think about Joe Delgado and the Tarot Card of Death.

She couldn't think about Not-Hannah and all of her shortcomings eternally documented in a sharable video file.

She couldn't think about Rosemary Hale and smashing the absolute shit out of her car.

She couldn't think about being *left*.

Except the problem with trying to outrun her feelings with sex and alcohol is that they always catch up with her again. When she's finally alone, and there's nothing left to distract her from the thoughts inside her head. Logan scrubs her hands up and down over her face and groans. The only thing worse than the whiskey hangover is the bad-decision hangover, and she's staring down the barrel of so many bad decisions at the moment.

Shania is done dismissing rocket scientists and Brad Pitt, and now Faith Hill croons from the other side of the paper-thin walls. *I don't want another heartbreak. I don't need another turn to cry.*

Logan does an inelegant flop off the bed and directly into a pile of washed-but-never-put-away laundry. Her entire bedroom—the same bedroom she slept in her whole childhood—is like the photo from a brochure on how to deal with your ADHD teenager. Stacks of old papers to grade on the desk and dresser, Post-its with her half-baked scribbles stuck to every surface, cans of empty Red Bull and mason jars with cold brew crusted to the bottom, twinkle lights strung across the ceiling, posters of Mia Hamm and Panic! At The Disco and *Grease* she never bothered to take down from middle school.

How does life get so off course? Faith wonders. Logan stifles an IPA burp, pulls on a pair of sweatpants, a sports bra, and a tank top that at least smells clean.

"She finally rises!" her dad declares as she enters the kitchen. He is mid-twirl, singing Faith into a slotted spoon while wearing a kimono that shows far too much dad thigh for Logan's taste.

"Must we do this"—she waves a hand in the direction of his cooking dance routine—"so early in the morning?"

Her dad does another twirl. "It's not early, Chicken." *Chicken* is the nickname her dad gave her at four years old. As in, *running around like a . . .* "I've been up for hours." He uses his spoon to point to the water, four ibuprofen, and slow-release Adderall waiting for her on the counter.

"Bully for you." She gags down the meds and pours herself a mug of coffee.

"No, bully for *you*. I'm making homemade loukoumades."

This news improves her mood considerably. The Greek, honey-glazed donuts can cure almost anything, including the impending death of mentor-figures and chronic poor decision-making. Antonio Maletis—the man who gave Logan her bushy eyebrows, her nose, and her penchant for the dramatic—finishes rolling the balls of dough and does something with his pelvis that Logan should not have to witness when the Spotify playlist changes to some Jo Dee Messina.

There is so much to love about being Greek, loukoumades being at the very top of that list, tied with spanakopita, Greek meatballs, and lamb gyros. She loves her perpetual olive complexion, even during gloomy Pacific Northwest winters, and she loves that everyone on her dad's side of the family is just as loud as she is. But growing up in the Greek Orthodox Church had been less than delightful, for both Logan and her dad.

Despite the kimono and the Shania Twain and stereotypes to the contrary, her dad is, unfortunately, heterosexual, and intent on remaining that way. But Antonio Maletis loves show tunes and espadrilles and baking baklava with his mother, and in the nineties, in a conservative church that *still* rejects LGBTQIA+ people, those things were enough to condemn him as a "funny boy," even if he attended mass every Sunday, sang in the church choir, and married Sophie Haralambopoulous, a good Greek girl, at twenty-three.

So, when Logan came out to her dad at fourteen and refused to ever go back to church, it wasn't hard for Antonio to walk away from that part of his Greek heritage. It took her papou a decade or so to come around to the idea of having a lesbian granddaughter, but her dad embraced it instantly, kept the delicious food, and ditched the religious trauma.

Sophie Haralambopoulous, on the other hand, doesn't even know her daughter is gay. She's in Vermont with her new family and knows absolutely shit all about Logan. Period. And that's why Logan still lives with her dad, despite what Rhiannon Schaffer thinks. He's the one who stayed. And she can't leave him. Not the way Sophie did.

"What's up, Chicken?" her dad asks, tapping her head with the slotted spoon. "You seem far away this morning."

She takes her black coffee over to the breakfast nook and curls into a chair like a cat. "Joe is dying."

Antonio makes a comforting *hmm* sound as he preps the donuts. "I know. He's been sick for a long time now."

"No, like, he's *dying*. Soon. At least, that's what he says. You know he's dramatic as hell."

"Oh, Logan." Her dad drops the spoon and his dough balls and comes across the kitchen to reach for her. "I am so sorry to hear that. I know how much he means to you."

Her dad's pity hug makes her feel itchy, and she shakes him off. "I'm sure he's fine. The doctors are always predicting his death, and the bastard just keeps on kicking."

"Yes, but his quality of life . . ." Antonio shakes his head. "I can't imagine being in and out of hospitals and rehab centers all the time."

Please, girls. Don't let me die in this beige room.

She tries drowning her feelings in a drink of coffee, but when it comes to accomplices in emotional subterfuge, coffee has nothing on whiskey. "Last night," she starts, "Joe asked me to drive him to Bar Harbor."

"Is that the new cowboy bar off highway 40?"

"Dad."

Antonio puts his hands on his hips and cocks his head to the side. "Joe asked you to drive him to Bar Harbor, Maine? *Why?*"

She fights to keep the indifference in her voice and wins. "Apparently, he has a house there, and he wants to drive across the country so he can . . . uh, die . . . there."

"And he asked you to *drive* him? Does he need my airline miles?"

"I think the drive is part of it for him. He wants to have one last adventure."

Her dad looks at her with such tenderness, it hurts somewhere in the back of her throat. "Sounds like someone else I know."

Logan laughs like it's funny. "I haven't exactly lived a life of adventure."

She used to dream of living one, though. She wanted to see the world and kept a list of all the most amazing-sounding places. The Andes Mountains of Peru, Patagonia, the Atacama Desert. Hike the Himalayas in Nepal and snorkel in Australia and see the Northern Lights in Iceland or Sweden or Svalbard. She wanted to climb every mountain, ford every stream, follow every rainbow. She wanted to buy a cabin in the woods or a little house on a lake and live among the trees.

Instead, she went to college fifteen minutes away at Washington State University's Vancouver campus. She never moved out of her childhood bedroom, never got a passport, and never followed any rainbows. Now, all she sees is the distance between her dad's house on Juniper Lane, and the high school on the other side of town. But at least there are mountains and streams and rainbows and so many damn trees right here.

And why would she waste her income on rent when her dad lives alone in a spacious house he's already paid off and has two extra bedrooms? Aside from the obvious Shania Twain, dad thighs, needing to get-fingered-in-a-Kia-Sonata reasons.

"I think this road trip could actually be good for you," her dad declares as he returns to his vat of crackling oil. He slides in his thermometer and studies it with his tongue poking out the left side of his mouth.

"I'm not going to do it."

He gasps. "Why not? You have the whole summer off!"

"I can't."

"You *can*."

She gives her dad her most withering, teenagery sigh. "He wants me and Hale to do it together. He wants both of us to drive him to Maine."

Her dad winces as a splash of oil catches his arm while ladling in the bits of dough. "He wants you and Rosemary to drive him across the country *together*? Doesn't he realize you'll all be dead before you reach the Idaho border?"

"I think the Oxy is turning his brain to mush. That's why I said no."

Her dad eyes her across the kitchen. "I'm sorry that Rosemary hurt you," he says in his gentlest voice.

"I don't care about Hale enough to be hurt by her."

Her dad clucks as he begins fishing the now-cooked donuts out of the fryer. "I seem to remember some pretty big Rosemary-themed fits back in high school." He takes on an unflattering mimicry. "Dad, Rosemary set the curve in chemistry, and I think she cheats. Dad, Rosemary poisoned my cookies. Dad, Rosemary tripped me in the cafeteria! Dad, Rosemary is still dating Jake McCandie!"

Logan holds up a single finger of protest. "While I can admit Rosemary never cheated on any test, she definitely put laxatives in those cookies. Why else would she have given me cookies at the state-qualifying debate tournament?"

"Because she was a sweet, socially misunderstood young woman?"

"It's definitely not that."

He waves his hand like he's about to pull a rabbit out of the deep fryer. "And now all I ever hear is, *Rosemary insulted me at a staff meeting, Rosemary thinks her job is more important than everyone else's, Rosemary wears pantyhose.*"

"Yes, well, I'm hoping she gets a yeast infection."

"Do you remember when you girls used to play Barbies for hours?"

"It was middle school, Dad. We didn't play Barbies. We dressed them up and wrote their character backstories."

Antonio leans back against the sink and stares right through her attempts at apathy. "I think you should do it," he says firmly. "I think you and Rosemary should drive Joe to Maine."

"Oh, so you *want* me to commit first-degree murder?"

"I want you to get out of this one Taco Bell town."

She hears Rhiannon Schaffer, asking if she's going to stay in this disgusting town forever. Joe, asking about her sense of spontaneity and adventure. A list of places she hasn't seen and a tarot card about endings. "But don't you need me here, Dad?"

"I love having you here. But no, Chicken. I don't need you."

Neither of them speaks for a minute as Antonio fries another batch of the donuts and Alexa switches from Martina McBride and Tricia Yearwood. "She's In Love with the Boy."

No amount of coffee or whiskey could quell the ache inside her that always comes from hearing this song. As girls, she and Hale would jump on her bed and sing it into hairbrushes and water bottles, and secretly, in her head, Logan would change the lyrics.

She's in love with the girl.

"Alexa, stop!" Logan barks. Her dad turns to face her again.

"I think you should do this, Chicken," he says firmly. "I think you *need* to do it."

While her dad finishes his baking, Logan pulls out her phone. She types Vista Summit, Washington, and Bar Harbor, Maine, into Google Maps, and thinks about all the new places between here and there.

The sound of the doorbell echoes through the house. "Who the fuck rings the doorbell at nine thirty on a Saturday?"

Logan strops out of the kitchen and when she wrenches open the front door, she finds her answer. Hale, standing there with two coffees from Java Jump and a binder tucked under her arm.

She's wearing a pleated skirt, a frilly shirt with some kind of silk neckerchief, nylons, and a pair of three-inch black heels. On a *Saturday*. Before *noon*. In *June*.

Logan wants to tell Hale to fuck right off—that whatever demented impulse led her to this doorstep should be promptly squashed. But then Hale stares up at her, purple bags framing her pale blue eyes and pale blond lashes, her pink mouth turned down into the perfect frown. She looks sad, and there it is again, that buried instinct to comfort this person from her past. Logan wants to make Hale smile and laugh and tell fantastical stories like she did as a kid.

In a moment of weakness, Logan hesitates.

"I have a proposition for you," Hale blurts, her cheeks flushing pink.

Then, she thrusts one cup forward. "But first, I brought you coffee."

Chapter Six

ROSEMARY

Rosemary stands in front of the Maletis household and considers her odds.

There's about a 50 percent chance Logan can still be bribed with white chocolate mochas, a 17 percent chance Antonio will chase her away with a broom, and a 92 percent Logan will laugh in her face once she sees the contents of this binder.

Still, she has no choice but to try.

Rosemary shifts the binder under her arm and tries to work up the courage to move. It's just a short paved walkway through the grass up to the front porch. Ten steps, tops.

She can take these ten steps, past the tire swing suspended on a rope from the thickest branch of the oak tree out front where they used to sit with their knees pressed together, spinning in dizzy circles. Up onto the porch where Logan used to wait every morning until Rosemary walked past, so they could finish the journey to the bus stop at the end of the street together. The porch where they sat outside on warm summer nights just staring at the stars.

The memories crowd her, filling in the spaces between her ribs like a too-heavy meal. It was only three years of friendship, an entire lifetime ago. Why does it feel like she is still grieving that loss? She inhales four times, takes the ten steps, and rings the doorbell.

Something loud thumps inside, then heavy footsteps, then the door opens violently to reveal Logan, wearing a pair of gray sweatpants low on her hips and a Nike tank top that drapes low beneath her armpits, revealing the sides of her orange sports bra. Her features immediately revert to Rosemary-face. And Rosemary didn't consider the possibility that Logan could slam the door closed before she even gets the chance to laugh at her.

So, she relies on the only asset she has: the white chocolate mocha. She thrusts it toward Logan, babbling incoherently at the woman who used to keep all of her secrets.

Logan studies the cup, and her nose un-scrunches itself. She reaches for the coffee, taking a long, skeptical drink. "Why are you at my house?" she finally asks.

"I—I was hoping we could talk." She winces at the hesitation in her voice. She hasn't felt this nervous in front of Logan since she was eleven, since that first day when they sat next to each other on the bus, and Rosemary was certain that as soon as she opened her mouth, this cool, magnetic girl would get bored and choose someone else to ride next to every morning and afternoon.

"Please, Logan. We need to talk about Joe."

Logan's mouth twitches.

"Maybe I could come in—?" Rosemary tries, just as Antonio shouts from inside the house, "Alexa! Play Shania Twain, dammit!"

Alexa chirps, "Playing songs by Shania Twain," before the song "You're Still the One" blares through the house. Logan shouts over her shoulder, "Can you turn that down!" and it's exactly the kind of chaos Rosemary remembers growing up in this house, back when she was invited to Maletis family dinners.

Antonio Maletis appears behind his daughter wearing an indecent feathery robe. "Who's here?" he asks before he peers around Logan's shoulder and smiles. "Well, if it isn't Rosemary Hale!"

Logan mumbles in protest as her dad leans forward to kiss Rosemary on both cheeks. He smells like lavender face cream and honey. "It's good to see you, Mr. Maletis," she says politely, as if she didn't duck behind a display of LaCroix when she saw him in the Safeway the other day.

"Were your ears burning, darling?" Antonio asks. "Because we were just talking about you."

"All terrible things, I assume," Rosemary says. Antonio laughs. Logan glowers.

"I've missed you, Rosemary," he says wistfully.

"No, you haven't," Logan snaps.

"You look incredible," Antonio continues, "please tell me your skin-care routine."

"She feeds off the souls of children."

"Surely not." He *tsks*.

"No, it's just CeraVe."

"You know, I just made loukoumades, so if you wanted to come inside and—"

Logan finally edges her dad out of the way, steps onto the porch, and closes the front door behind her. "Fine, Hale. Talk."

Her mind flashes through all her arguments and talking points, but her mouth somehow supersedes all of her logic, cuts right to the quick of it before Logan can run away. "I think we should drive Joe to Maine."

There's a twitch in the corner of Logan's mouth, but she covers it with a laugh. "Shit biscuits, how hard did I hit you with my car?"

"Is that an admission of fault?"

"Never." Logan takes a few steps forward and slumps down onto the porch steps. "Hale, we can't drive him."

Rosemary carefully sits down a safe distance from her. "If you would just look at my binder—"

"I don't need to look at your binder to know this is a terrible idea."

"I don't have terrible ideas."

Logan shakes her head, and her frizzy brown curls bob and weave around her face. "You clearly haven't thought this through."

"I stayed up all night making a binder, so yes, I have."

"We'd be in a car together for days. We'd have to stay in hotels together for a week!"

"Five nights."

"What?"

Rosemary flips to the binder tab labeled *Itinerary*. "I've charted a course that only takes six days, five nights, staying in cities that have good hospitals in case Joe needs medical attention. We stop in Twin Falls, Idaho; Cheyenne, Wyoming; Des Moines, Iowa; Cleveland, Ohio; and then Worcester, Massachusetts before finishing out the last stretch to Bar Harbor."

"All the most boring cities in the country, then?" Logan snips. "The problem with a road trip is that we'd have to drive back."

"I've considered that." Rosemary flips to a new tab. "And I've come up with several alternative propositions so we wouldn't have to spend an additional five nights together returning to Vista Summit."

Logan is quiet for a moment as she takes another drink of her mocha. "I'm still stuck on the part where *you* would willingly spend five days trapped with *me*?"

"It's Joe," she says with a small shrug.

Logan still looks unmoved, and Rosemary knows she has to give her more if she's going to convince her of this plan.

She takes a deep breath and swivels her knees toward Logan. "Joe is the reason I became a teacher. I was miserable in high school."

Logan snorts in disbelief. "Yeah, right. You had perfect grades, got into the perfect college. Everything came so easily to you."

"Nothing ever comes easily to me," Rosemary confesses, and the smirk vanishes from Logan's face. "I had perfect grades because I thought I had to be perfect to be worthy. I obsessed over every assignment, stayed up all night studying, took too many AP classes and forced myself to be the best in all of them. I wasn't eating, wasn't sleeping . . . sophomore year, my hair started to fall out from the stress. And it felt like none of my teachers cared how sick I was making myself. They all held me up as this model student. Except Joe."

She only pauses long enough to swallow. If she stops talking for too long, she'll realize she's being vulnerable with the person most likely to use it against her. "Joe was the only teacher who really *saw* me. The only teacher who cared about me as a person, not a test-taking machine. So, I decided to become a teacher because I wanted to be that for someone else. To be the adult who cares. And this trip to Maine is a chance for me to give back to Joe everything he's given me."

All of her emotional honesty hangs in the air between them like an awkward perfume. Logan doesn't say anything, doesn't visibly react to this confession. She takes another long drink of her mocha and stares out at the weeds in the yard. Then, finally: "Okay, let me see this freakazoid binder of yours."

With one tug, Logan pulls the binder out of Rosemary's hands. Rosemary sits there in awkward silence, watching Logan flip through the different subsections, the laminated pages, the Post-it Notes in the margins with Rosemary's cursive asking questions like, "supine?" and "moving him into the wheelchair?" and "what do we do with the poop?"

"As far as I can tell, there are just two things your binder doesn't account for," Logan declares after several minutes.

Rosemary bristles. "The car, I know." She smooths out her navy shirt like she can smooth out the wrinkles in the plan. "I need to find a vehicle that's wheelchair accessible and has a large enough back seat so Joe can rest comfortably for long stretches of time, but I've researched rental cars, and they're either too expensive or booked out months in advance."

Logan closes her eyes and tilts her head back. "I think I have a car."

"*Yours?*" Rosemary makes an unflattering sound and tries to hide it with another drink. "We can't drive your car across the country. And my car is in the shop since *you* hit it. Besides, both are too small for—"

"I wasn't talking about my car. One of my ex-girlfriend's ex-girlfriends has a van she converted for her cuddle business."

"Her . . . cuddle business?"

"Don't be judgmental. She had this mobile cuddle business, kind of like a mobile dog groomer. The back seat folds down into a queen-sized bed, but there are still seat belts and everything. I think I could convince her to sell it to me."

"She doesn't need it for . . . cuddling?"

"No. Professional cuddling didn't survive the pandemic."

"I'm shocked."

"She's been trying to sell the van since her business went under, but she hasn't had any takers. I could probably get it for less than a thousand."

Rosemary nods carefully, afraid to assume what this means. "So . . . you'll do it, then? You'll help me drive him to Maine?"

"I don't know . . ."

"What's holding you back?"

"The second thing."

"Excuse me?"

"The second thing your binder fails to take into account," Logan says.

"Which is . . . ?"

Logan turns her head so she is staring directly at Rosemary, those hazel eyes burning. "How the hell are we going to drive to Maine without killing each other?"

LOGAN

They are definitely going to kill each other.

"What is that?" Hale shrieks.

"What?" Logan yawns. It's six in the morning, and Hale is already worked into a snit. They haven't even made it out of the driveway.

"That!"

Logan follows her outstretched finger toward the van they're about to drive across the country. "That's the car, Hale."

"*That* is the car?" Angry spit gathers in the corners of her mouth. "And it didn't occur to you that driving that across middle America might be a problem?"

Logan studies the van. Sure, it is on the older side, but Robin assured her it's in good shape, and she'd taken it in to get serviced earlier in the week, per Hale's insistence.

Plus, she'd purchased five air fresheners to cover up the smell of mold and patchouli.

"What's wrong with it, exactly?"

Hale strops forward, her heels smacking against the concrete. Apparently, she is going to drive eight hours today in heels. "*That* is what's wrong with it." She slams her hand against the logo painted on the side of the van.

The words *The Queer Cuddler* are painted in swooping letters over a giant rainbow.

Oh. *That*.

"That was the name of her business. The Queer Cuddler."

Hale takes in a sharp breath through her flared nostrils. "Yes, I gathered as much. Why the hell is it still painted on the side of the van?"

"Why wouldn't it be?"

Hale does a slow, judgmental strut around the vehicle, shaking her head in a particularly violent fashion when she gets to the back. Which means she probably noticed the "Gayest Ride in Town" bumper sticker.

"Are you starting to understand why I might be upset right now?" Hale hisses.

"I am," Logan's dad says from the front porch where he is sipping coffee, ready to see them off. Andrea Hale is beside him in her Smurf scrubs, looking equally bemused.

"Why does it matter if it says a bunch of gay stuff on it?"

"Because we're driving through *Iowa*!"

"I'm pretty sure there are gays in Iowa."

"That's not the point. It's a little naïve to think we won't get any reactions driving this van through 'Don't Say Gay' states."

"Are you afraid people might think you're gay by association?" Logan relishes in the way Hale's mouth puckers like a cat's ass-hole. "That's not . . . I'm a . . . Of course not," she sputters. "But queer and trans people are hurt for a lot less than this, especially Black and brown queer people. We might have a lot of privilege. We're white and straight passing—"

"You're not straight passing, you're straight," Logan can't help but correct.

Hale blinks erratically. "But did you even consider Joe's safety when you chose this . . . *gay mobile*?"

She obviously had not, and she suddenly feels like a total asshole for it. Vista Summit wasn't the best place to grow up a lesbian in the mid-aughts, but she's never truly felt unsafe. She's not sure if Joe can say the same thing.

"We should paint over the logo when we get the chance." Hale turns back to her mom's Subaru Forrester and begins unloading her bags from the trunk. *Seven*. That's the number of heavy-looking items Hale pulls from the trunk.

Not for the first time in the past week, Logan wonders how the hell she ended up here, agreeing to this ridiculous scheme. But deep down, she knows. It's because Hale sat on her front porch and let herself be vulnerable. For the first time in years, that perfect veneer slipped a little, and Hale sounded like that earnest, honest girl she'd once loved.

Hearing Hale talk about how Joe changed her life reminded Logan that she wouldn't be a teacher without him, either.

Before Joe, Logan only had teachers who saw her as a nuisance. The kid who couldn't sit still, the kid who blurted in class, the kid who lost all her homework. The kid who wasn't living up to her potential.

Joe saw *her*. He saw the way her brain worked, and instead of trying to fix it, he celebrated it. He taught her how to harness her passion and creativity, and he believed in her when no other teacher ever had. She became a teacher because she wanted to help a new generation of neurodivergent teens learn to love their brains, too.

If she and Hale had that in common, then maybe they could put aside their differences for a man like Joseph Delgado.

Of course that was before she learned Hale packed seven bags. She reaches for the nearest suitcase and tries to lift it, but it weighs as much as Hale does. "Why did you pack so much?"

"At least one of us has to be prepared!"

"Prepared? You're wearing heels and a dress!"

Hale clicks her tongue. "I'm sorry, should I be dressed like a middle-aged insurance adjuster on a golf course in Hawaii?"

Logan looks down at her tropical shirt (this one dotted with parrots), her basketball shorts, and her Birkenstocks. She almost laughs at Hale's attempt at humor. "This feels like a normal road trip outfit."

Hale gestures to her own slim frame. "So does this."

"A wool frock?"

Hale tilts her head like a confused bird. Logan wishes she didn't find the gesture oddly endearing. "This is organic cotton," Hale corrects with that same earnestness as before. "I got it from ModCloth."

Hale almost looks self-conscious about the dress as she smooths out imaginary creases in the fabric. "It's . . . cute," Logan tries as she starts hauling Hale's heavy luggage into the back of the van. Hale glares suspiciously at the compliment.

"Don't worry, Princess, you just stand there. I'll take care of all the manual labor."

"Girls!" her dad raises his voice from the porch. "If you fight with each other like this while driving, you're both going to end up dead on the side of the road. And I am not going to fly coach to Ohio just so I can identify your bodies. Is that understood?"

"Yes, sir," Hale mutters, looking properly ashamed.

Logan puts on her sunglasses. "We've got to get going."

A prolonged series of goodbyes takes place, in which her dad pulls her in close, squeezes her tight, and whispers, "You deserve an adventure, Chicken."

She refuses to think about the fact that she's leaving him, that he'll be alone. She kisses him on the cheek, adjusts her duffle over her shoulder, and turns to Hale.

"Okay, Captain. What's the plan?"

Hale hands her a laminated schedule with their driving directions for the day broken down into two-hour shifts, with planned stops for the bathroom and gas.

Rosemary: *Vista Summit to Boardman.*
Logan: *Boardman to La Grande.*
Rosemary: *La Grande to Ontario.*
Logan: *Ontario to Twin Falls.*

The amount of work and forethought Hale put into this trip in such a short amount of time is impressive. Logan could never wrap her brain around organizing a trip like this.

Logan looks up and sees Hale struggling to boost all measly five feet of herself into the driver's seat of the van, her heels slipping on the running board, the back of her cotton dress riding up so Logan gets a peek at slender thighs and the hem of her white cotton underwear. Without thinking, Logan steps closer and places a hand on Hale's back before she falls. The fabric of the dress is smooth against Logan's skin, and she catches another whiff of vanilla and peppermint. It makes her dizzy.

"Let go of me," Hale snaps. "I can get into the van by myself."

Logan pulls her hand away, and Hale slips again before climbing behind the driver's seat. And oh yeah.

There's no chance of either of them surviving the next six days.

Vista Summit, Washington to Twin Falls, Idaho

Chapter Seven

LOGAN

A complete inventory of the luggage Rosemary Hale packed for a weeklong road trip: two large, four-wheeled rolling suitcases (rose-colored with plastic sides), presumably stuffed with every article of clothing she owns; one red cooler, filled with a variety of nutritious snacks and cans of LaCroix; a literal picnic basket with nonperishables, including enough gourmet crackers, almonds, and dried figs to make at least six charcuterie boards; a silk pillow; a first aid kit big enough to fit Hale herself; an emergency roadside kit; a *wireless printer*.

"In case we need to make adjustments to the itinerary," Hale explains as she puts on her seat belt. "My travel laminating machine is in my large bag."

"They're both large," Logan corrects. She packed a normal-sized duffle bag with enough pairs of underwear to get her to Maine, where she can do laundry, and a backpack with six paperbacks, various electronics chargers, and a few snacks purchased from the 7-Eleven the night before. It's only five nights until Maine. Then, once they get Joe settled, Logan will try to sell the van to someone else, or, worst-case scenario, they'll donate it to the nearest Habitat for Humanity, and they will both fly home *separately* from there.

"Why did you pack so much food?" Logan asks as Hale spends five minutes adjusting her mirrors and the driver's seat and the steering wheel and then her mirrors again.

"So we're not tempted to eat drive-through the entire time."

"Isn't that the fun of being on a road trip?"

"If you enjoy acid-reflux, I suppose." Hale clicks her tongue. Maybe Logan won't kill her, but there's a high probability she will cut out her tongue. Dangle it from the rearview mirror like a talisman for good luck. "What food did you pack?"

Logan pulls out a bag of Funyuns.

"You absolutely will not be eating those in my car."

"Oh, so this is your Gay Mobile?" She doesn't care that it's six thirty in the morning: Logan opens that bag of Funyuns. "And no fighting with me while driving, remember?"

Hale huffs as she shoves the Gay Mobile into drive.

It took them six days to prepare for this trip, and they were the longest days of Logan's life. The first week of summer vacation is usually sacred. She sleeps in until noon. She spends an entire day playing *Tears of the Kingdom* while eating pizza pockets and microwave taquitos. She gets outside, hiking in the Gorge with the trees and the mountains and the river. She gets high on edibles and watches the sunset with her dad.

Except this past week she substituted sleeping in with seven a.m. emails from Hale delineating the day's task list. She exchanged video games for learning how to change Joe's diaper while he screamed at her about the indignity. She outfitted the van with a makeshift wheelchair ramp and an adjust strap above the sliding door, and she spent all her sunsets inside Joe's apartment in the assisted living facility, packing up the stuff he cares about and donating the rest. He doesn't intend to return to Vista Summit. She argued with oncologists who insisted this road trip was a terrible idea, and she ignored the nurses who handed her brochures about end-of-life care.

"It's my end-of-life," Joe complained, "and I get to decide how much I care."

Hale signed his discharge papers. Logan lifted the heavy boxes. Because they were doing this.

They were *really* doing this.

Now, they pull up to Evergreen Pines for the last time. Joe is already out front in a wheelchair, his broken foot in a blue cast half-hidden by his brown corduroy pants. An angry-faced nurse stands behind him, and at his feet are the belongings he chose to keep: his record player, his collection of vinyls, a box of books, a Pendleton blanket.

"Sweet Walt-Whitman-at-a-log-cabin-retreat-with-Abe." Joe whistles as Logan climbs out of the van. "That's the gayest thing I've ever seen."

"Do you like it?" Logan does a flourishing gesture toward the logo even though she's terrified she's made a horrible mistake.

"Honey, it's exactly the vehicle I would have chosen for my death road trip."

Logan turns to Hale. "See? He likes it."

"It's not a death road trip." Hale falls out of the tall van and twists her heel on the curb. "What is that?" she asks as she straightens herself, her tone again accusing.

"What's what?" Joe asks innocently.

"That." She is pointing at a dog.

"This is Odysseus," Joe answers, gesturing to the all-black, monstrous mutt at his feet. "My cancer dog. You remember Odysseus."

"Of course we do," Logan coos. She crouches down as the dog lumbers over for scratches. "And he remembers me too. Yes, I'm the one who rescued you from that horrible place. How's my little Odie doing?"

"Yes, I remember Odysseus," Hale says through tight teeth. "But I am confused as to why he's here."

When Joe first started chemo, Logan had felt so helpless, so ill-equipped to provide the kind of emotional support he was going to need. So, she did the only thing she could think of: she went to the nearest animal shelter and bought him a six-month-old dog. A dog would have the emotional intelligence she lacked.

When Joe saw the black fur ball with the floppy ears and giant paws, he said the dog reminded him of Argos from *The Odyssey*: Odysseus's loyal dog, who remembers him even after his twenty-year journey away from home, and then promptly dies upon his return. Logan insisted he couldn't name the rescue after a dog who is most famous for dying. So he named the dog Odysseus instead.

The animal shelter promised Odie would be forty pounds, at most. He's now ninety pounds of pure muscle. He has the body of a jaguar and the face of a baby otter.

"Why wouldn't he be here?" Joe asks Hale. "He's my dog. He's coming with us."

Hale turns a cute shade of purple. "And it didn't occur to you to mention him at any point over the course of the past week of planning for this trip?"

Joe frowns at her. "I figured you knew he was coming. Rosie, dear, did you think I was going to give away my dog on Facebook Marketplace like I did my reclining chair? And he's technically a service dog."

"Technically, he's not," Logan corrects, letting Odysseus lick her eyeballs. "He failed his final exam."

"Standardized testing is bullshit," Joe says. "And it's not Odysseus's fault that he ate all those Costco hotdogs."

Hale taps the toe of her heels against the sidewalk. "You want to travel across the country with a fraudulent service dog?"

"Not fraudulent. More . . . unlicensed."

"That makes him a fake service dog."

"But he's of service to *me*." Joe clutches his chest. "My dog is not a negotiable part of your two-hundred-page itinerary."

The dog whimpers at Hale like he *knows* she's trying to leave him behind. She switches topics. "And this record player really isn't practical for a road trip."

"Says the woman who packed a wireless printer." Logan hoists the outdated technology into the back of the van. Then she discovers the giant bag of dog food hiding behind Joe's wheelchair and lifts that, too.

"I want to die in Maine," Joe ruminates wistfully, "staring at the ocean, listening to my Van Morrison records with my favorite blanket and my dog curled up at my feet."

Hale begins massaging her temples. "Please tell me you also packed useful things, like clothes and diapers and your medications?"

Joe makes a scandalized face. "Please do not discuss my diapers in mixed company, Rosemary."

"He has all that stuff," the nurse says as she hands Hale a large black medical bag. "We got permission from his doctor to get refills of all his prescriptions to last three months, and we packed extra diapers, extra—"

It's clear from Joe's souring expression that he doesn't want to sit here thinking about all the various accouterments needed to keep him alive. He packed his dog; he packed his records. He is ready to get in a car and drive.

Logan thinks about yesterday when she stayed late at Evergreen Pines watching *Family Feud* with Joe. "Are you sure you want to do this?" she'd asked him, as a woman screamed *We're gonna play, Steve!* on the TV. "You can still change your mind and stay here. Evergreen Pines can make you extremely comfortable for this last part."

And he looked her dead in the eye with a grimace of pain twisting his mouth. "I spent my whole life choosing comfort. In my death, I want to choose something else."

"Enough chitchat," Logan blurts now, interrupting the nurse and her unending list of death supplies. "Are you ready to Thelma and Louise this shit?"

Joe beams at her. "Does that make me a Mexican Brad Pitt?"

"There are some sexual connotations there that I'm quite un-comfortable with, but if you want to be Brad Pitt, you can be Brad Pitt. It's your death trip."

"It's not a death trip!" Hale stamps her little foot.

"Chill, Thelma." Logan picks up the vinyls and the books and loads them into the back of the van. "Or I'll drive us off a cliff just to spite you."

ROSEMARY

"The speed limit is seventy."

"I am aware."

"You're going fifty-five, though."

Rosemary arches her back. "I'm being safe."

"People are honking."

"Probably because I am driving an enormous blue van with the words 'The Queer Cuddler' painted on the side."

"I think it's because you're driving dangerously slow on a freeway. My yiayia drives faster than this, and she's eighty."

Rosemary grips the steering wheel tighter. "If you think your constant taunts will convince me to speed, you will be sorely disap-pointed."

They've barely started down I-84 East through Oregon, and Rosemary's ready to admit this is the worst idea she's ever had. All the laminated maps and first aid training couldn't adequately pre-pare her for spending five days trapped in a car with Logan Maletis. Not to mention the toddler horse masquerading as a dog stinking up the back seat, who barks at every single car they pass like he's protecting his territory.

Getting Joe into the car had been a feat of herculean strength and saintlike patience. Even with the wheelchair ramp and the assist strap above the sliding side door, it was a ten-minute ordeal of seesawing his body onto the reclined back seat. Joe screamed about his pride the entire time, and Odysseus drooled on her Saint Laurent heels.

Rosemary tries to focus on the beautiful view out the driver's-side window, the Columbia River Gorge, dappled in the sunlight of early summer. She tries to focus on her deep breathing and on her perfectly structured itinerary.

But Logan is like a mosquito bite you know you shouldn't scratch but can't ignore. She chomps loudly on a Funyun, and Rosemary feels the sound in the back of her teeth. "Can you please desist with that abominable crunching?"

"Calm your tits," Logan says, masticating with her mouth wide open. Bits of chip spray onto the dashboard in front of her. "It's breakfast time. I have to eat."

"Fascinating." Joe whistles from the back seat. "Absolutely fascinating."

Rosemary has to push herself up off the seat to look at him in the rearview mirror. The back seat is reclined to a forty-five-degree angle, with pillows propped behind Joe's head, and his legs stretched out in front of him. With his Pendleton blanket and his dog curled up beside him, he looks almost cozy, but Rosemary sees the sadistic twinkle in his eye. "What's fascinating?"

"This. The two of you. Two adult women reverting back to who they were at fourteen due to their unresolved conflict from that time."

Logan crumples up her Funyun bag and chucks it in Joe's face. "Don't psychoanalyze us, old man. We're taking you on your death trip. Please allow us to repress in peace."

"It's not a death trip," Rosemary insists. "And I'm not repressed."

Logan kicks up her long, tan legs and props them on the dashboard. "I, for one, am happy to let my past trauma resurface at unexpected times. It's like a never-ending game of emotional Whac-a-Mole."

In the rearview mirror, Rosemary sees Joe smile. "I spent thirty years of my life with teenagers, and while I'm grateful for every minute of my career as a teacher, I would rather not spend this trip with bickering children."

Rosemary bites down on her jaw until she feels the pain radiate back to her ears. She doesn't want to behave like a child. She doesn't want to fight with Logan at all. The truth is, she would give anything to *talk* to Logan. She's the only other person who might understand what it means to Rosemary to lose Joe.

But Logan is hell-bent on not understanding her at all.

"I'm sorry, Joe."

"Thank you, Rosie dear. Now please take this exit."

Rosemary glances to the right to see the upcoming green sign for Exit 22. "What?"

"Get off the freeway. Right here."

Joe says this so casually, as if he's not impulsively derailing everything. "But we're already six minutes behind schedule."

"Rosemary," Joe says, less casually. "Pull over the damn car!"

"Pull over the damn car!" Logan echoes, and Rosemary panics, jerks the wheel to the right. The van pitches sideways as the wheels crunch over white lines and slide into the exit lane at the last possible second. Thankfully, no other cars exited I-84 at that precise moment. She slams on the brakes when they reach the stop sign at the end of the off-ramp.

"What the hell?" Rosemary bleats. Her heart is skittering in her chest and her palms are damp around the steering wheel.

"Are you okay?" Logan flips around in her seat and there is nothing impassive about the expression of terror on her face. "Are you in pain? Do you need to get out of the car?"

Rosemary presses a hand to her chest to feel her heartbeat against her ribs and stares at the concerned crinkle of Logan's bushy eyebrows, the first sign that she truly cares.

"What I need," Joe says, casual again, "is for us to take a brief detour."

Rosemary puts on the hazard lights and turns to face Joe, too. "A detour? No. Absolutely not," she says as Joe nods his head in confirmation. "You have a copy of the itinerary. We'll stop to use the bathroom in seventy-five minutes and not before."

Joe thoughtfully strokes Odysseus's ear. "I didn't agree to that."

"Excuse me?"

"I didn't agree to your itinerary," he says. "My death trip has detours."

It's not a death trip, she wants to scream. She can't think of it that way. If she thinks about the fact that all that's waiting for them at the end of this hellish journey is saying goodbye to Joe, she won't be able to put one foot in front of the other, one mile marker behind the next.

"I'm dying, Rosemary," Joe says breathlessly. "Are you really going to deny me a small detour?"

Logan throws her head back and laughs. "You're really going to milk that for all it's worth, aren't you?"

Rosemary takes four deep breaths and clicks off the hazard lights. "Which way?"

"Right," Joe says, and Rosemary turns right.

Chapter Eight

ROSEMARY

They take a winding road through the trees that climbs drastically until it curves into a parking lot, and Rosemary realizes where they are as a familiar shape comes into view. It's a giant circular building made out of gray sandstone, with a darker gray dome reflecting atop it in the sunlight, the grandiosity entirely out of place in the middle of the woods. The building is surrounded by retaining walls, and Rosemary is immediately struck by a memory: Logan, thirteen, limbs stretched out like saltwater taffy, climbing up onto the retaining wall, balancing herself precariously as Rosemary begged her to come down.

"The Vista House." Logan braces her hands on the dashboard and leans forward. "Damn, I haven't been here in forever."

Odysseus flings himself at the window with excitement, too, as Rosemary reluctantly pulls into a handicap parking space. "Why are we here, Joe?"

Logan doesn't wait for an explanation. She grabs the red dog leash off the floor and hops out of the car. "Come on, buddy. You need to get out and stretch your legs."

"It's been forty-five minutes!" Rosemary shouts as she does an elegant slide out of the driver's seat. When she comes around the passenger side, Logan is hooking the dog leash around the door handle. Then she climbs into the back of the van to begin the arduous process of getting Joe out of his comfortable lounge position and back into his wheelchair. The last thing she wants is to make Joe feel like a burden, because he's not. He never could be. So she doesn't complain as they transfer him. Neither does Logan.

After a few clumsy moments, they help Joe into his wheelchair, and Logan grabs the leash again, taking off up the path toward Vista House.

"I know you're mad at me," Joe says as she pushes his wheelchair over uneven cobblestones.

"I'm not mad at you."

"Yet I can't help but notice that you seem tense."

"When, in the past eighteen years, have you seen me *not* tense?"

Both his wheelchair and her heels get stuck in a groove, and she has to wiggle them free. "That's what I'm saying, Rosie, darling. You seem tense, even by your standards."

"I'm not."

She realizes she's clenching her jaw again and tries to relax it. "I just . . . I want to do this for you, Joe. Get you to Maine. You've done so much for me—so much for *so many people*—and I want to make sure you get your wish."

"Part of my wish involves stopping at the Vista House."

"Okay, but the quickest, safest way to get you to Maine is to plan our stops so you're not getting in and out of the van unnecessarily and risking another fall." *Or worse.*

"Who said I wanted safe?"

"You do want to get to Maine *alive?*"

Joe grunts as she gets his wheelchair stuck on another paver. "I do. But I don't want to be so fixated on getting there that I miss this."

They reach the edge of the retaining wall and the Columbia River

Gorge spills out in front of them. A blue, serpentine river disappearing on the horizons both east and west. Green hills hug the river's north and boundaries, and the early morning sky is the palest, clearest blue, a proper Pacific Northwest June day. Sunny, with a few columns of clouds to remind you how rare it is.

"How could I miss the chance to say goodbye to this?" Joe asks.

Rosemary swallows. It's almost painfully beautiful. She spent her early childhood in Western Massachusetts, her college years in Connecticut and New York, and a summer touring ten European countries after undergrad, but this is still her favorite view in the world. Other places aren't this green. Or they aren't this many shades of green. They don't have this many hills or mountains or topographical variety. Every time she travels, she's always surprised to discover how many places in the world are just flat. It always makes her feel ironically claustrophobic.

There is nothing better than seeing the trees and hills out an airplane window as she lands in Portland.

When was the last time she hiked into these hills to see this view? They're on the other side of the river from home. If she looks northwest, she can see Vista Summit, but it looks like an insignificant speck from here. She turns her head east, the path of their drive, and catches Joe staring up at her with an appraising eyebrow furrow.

"Are you sure that prominent tendon in your neck doesn't have less to do with detours and more to do with our car companion?"

"You mean the dog?"

"I do not."

Rosemary scans the circular path, and there's Logan, climbing up on the retaining wall with a red dog leash in her hand. A volunteer materializes to scold her into getting down. "Why Logan?" Rosemary wonders aloud.

"Because," Joe answers. "It has to be you and Logan."

"Cryptic."

"I could ask you the same thing, you know. Why Logan?"

"Why do I hate her? Joe, it's fairly obvious."

"Why did you used to love her?"

That question hits her like a punch to her throat. Why had she loved Logan when they were girls? She hadn't meant to. God, she'd tried so hard *not* to.

But Logan was the first kid she'd seen since her dad died and her mother packed their bags and moved them to a tiny town three thousand miles away. And she fell in love with her because Logan said hi first, asked to sit next to her on the bus, brushed their shoulders together as she excitedly talked about a summer camping trip she'd taken to Crater Lake.

Because Logan was everything she *wasn't*: tall and loud and goofy; brave and unfiltered, quick to laughter, quicker to tears, every big feeling worn boldly on the outside. The kind of girl who foolishly climbed on retaining walls for the thrill of it. For all of middle school, Rosemary wanted to *be* Logan. She certainly didn't want to be herself.

And at some point, those feelings twisted into something she wasn't ready to deal with at fourteen. She no longer wanted to simply *be* Logan; she wanted to be *with* her. The love grew into something beyond the intense bond of female friendship.

Rosemary's still not ready to deal with it. She doesn't want to scrutinize why she was able to love someone so deeply at fourteen but hasn't managed to feel that way since.

But she can't explain all of this to Joe. She shares most things with him, but eleven-year-old Logan is best left tucked away in the deepest file cabinet in her heart. Instead, she says, "I hate Logan because she treats people like Barbie dolls and tosses them aside as soon as she gets bored with them."

"Maybe she's just afraid of being tossed aside first."

She thinks about the sleepovers where Logan would wake up in the middle of the night in tears, calling out for her mom. "She's reckless with other people's feelings, Joe."

"Reckless with your feelings?" he asks with another deft arch of his eyebrow.

Even *she* doesn't touch that file cabinet. "We could've hired a nurse, you know. Someone else who could have done this trip with us."

He shakes his head. "Like I said. It had to be both of you."

At that moment, Logan bounds over to them. It's hard to say who has bigger dog energy: Logan or the actual dog. "Can you fucking believe how lucky we are?" Logan shouts. "To live in a place this fucking gorgeous?"

She throws back her head and makes a show of taking a deep breath through her nose. Rosemary watches her chest expand and collapse. "Is there anything better than a sunny day in the Pacific Northwest?"

When Logan looks down at Joe again, she has a huge, goofy grin on her face. "Have you finished saying goodbye to this place, Joe?"

He looks out at the Gorge—at this river, these trees and mountains, that patch of blue sky—one last time.

"Goodbye," Joe whispers. Rosemary feels the fist slam all the way down into her stomach, but she takes that feeling and files it away too. She glances over at Logan, and for a second, she thinks there are tears in the other woman's eyes. But Logan is already putting her sunglasses back on.

• • •

They're at a complete standstill.

I-84 East is down to one lane just outside La Grande, and all Rosemary can see over the steering wheel is brake lights. The minivan three cars ahead of them seems to have turned off its engine entirely, the bearded driver climbing out onto the freeway to do lunges. According to Google, a wildfire jumped its barricade and got too close to the freeway, stopping traffic until they can maintain it again.

"This"—Rosemary pokes a finger at the windshield—"is why we don't do detours!"

"Come on, Hale," Logan says through a mouthful of double cheeseburger. "We don't know that we would've avoided this traffic if we didn't stop."

Logan has both bare feet dangling out the passenger window and a McDonald's bag in her lap. Rosemary tries to set that bag on fire with her eyes. McDonald's added another twelve minutes to their drive, on top of the detour and the precious time lost in this traffic. Still, she is grateful for the planned stop in La Grande. At least it means she's behind the wheel again. She didn't enjoy handing control over to Logan for two hours.

Rosemary tries to take another set of deep breaths—four in total, holding each one in for four seconds, like her therapist always insists—but she immediately chokes on a rancid odor.

"Does it smell like skunk in here?"

Logan stops feeding Odysseus french fries and takes a big whiff. "Uh, I don't think that's skunk. . . ."

"I don't smell anything," Joe says from the back seat, and Rosemary hears him exhale heavily. The rancid scent intensifies.

She turns around. "Joe! Are you smoking weed?"

"No." Joe exhales again and smoke fills the back seat.

"Joe!" she shrieks. "You cannot smoke weed!"

"Of course I can." He draws the joint back to his mouth demonstratively. "See?"

"You know that's not what I meant!"

"It's legal," he says with a shrug.

"But it won't be when we get to Idaho!"

"Honey, we aren't getting to Idaho anytime soon. Besides, I have a prescription."

"That won't assuage the cops if we get pulled over and they find you getting lit in the back seat!"

"No one says *lit* anymore," Logan contributes to this ongoing disaster.

Joe pouts. "Rosemary, are you really going to deny a dying man his sole comfort?"

"Yes!" she shouts, perhaps louder than necessary. Odysseus barks in response. Logan gives him another fry. "Is it even safe to smoke in a confined space with Odysseus?"

"Of course," Joe says. He reaches over and pops open the back window. "Probably."

"If she's going to keep squawking, I'm going to need a hit too."

Logan swivels toward Joe with an outstretched hand, and Rosemary quickly smacks it away. "Absolutely not! You have to be able to drive! We still have another four hours, at least!"

Logan rubs her hand as if Rosemary injured her. "Fine." Then, to Joe: "I'll smoke a joint with you when we get to the hotel."

"No, you won't! No one is smoking weed on this road trip! This is a drug-free trip!"

"I have an entire duffle bag of controlled substances," Joe points out.

"That's different." Her teeth are starting to hurt again. "Those are for your pain management."

Joe twirls the joint between his fingers like a baton. "So is this. I hate to disappoint you, Rosie dear, but this isn't some *Tuesdays with Morrie* shit. I'm not some noble old man who's going to share the meaning of life with you as he dies." Joe lifts the joint to his lips again. "I'm not dying to help you solve some problem in your life. I'm just going to die. And I would like to be high while that happens."

"But—"

"Why are you going full Nancy Reagan over a tiny amount of legal, *medicinal* weed?" Logan asks in the most condescending way possible.

"B-because," Rosemary flusters. She can sense both Joe with his weed and Logan with her fries staring at her.

"Does this have anything to do with the fact that you don't drink?" Logan asks.

Rosemary's shoulders tighten. "How do you know I don't drink?"

"Um, because at every staff party, you make a big deal of ordering only water, and you stand in the corner silently judging the rest of us."

"I'm not judging."

"I feel a bit judged at the moment," Joe puffs.

"Why don't you drink?" Logan presses, but there's something surprising in her tone. Logan doesn't sound mocking; she sounds genuinely curious. Her face has softened again, too. Rosemary finds it infuriating.

"I'm not sure what makes you think you're entitled to details about my personal life. Does this usually work for you? You just waggle your attractive eyebrows and women do and say whatever you want?"

"Yes," Logan answers simply. "You think my eyebrows are attractive?"

Heat crawls up the back of her neck. "Oh, don't pretend to be modest. You know you have sexy eyebrows."

"Sexy? Wow, that escalated quickly. I didn't even know eyebrows could be attractive, and now mine have been upgraded to sexy?"

"See?" Rosemary strangles the steering wheel in her hands. "This is why I would never tell you anything real about myself. I'm just a punch line to you."

"You're not a punch line, Hale. You're a puzzle." She can feel Logan's golden eyes burning into the side of her face. Rosemary glances at her sideways and finds that same soft, open expression. It reminds her of the Logan she used to know, and for a brief moment, it almost feels possible to get back to those girls they used to be. Maybe under the layers of sarcasm and feigned apathy, her Logan is still in there somewhere.

"You're squabbling again, and I'm bored with it," Joe blurts from the back. "Do you girls know what would make this traffic infinitely more tolerable? Van Morrison."

Logan's gaze finally shifts away from Rosemary. She clears her throat. "Some Van in the van," she says blithely. "I'm on it."

Within seconds, she's cued up "Caravan" on her phone and plugged into some elaborate tape-deck aux hookup.

"Apt," Joe says with an approving head nod.

"Very apt," Logan agrees. She tilts her chair back, and Odysseus takes this as an invitation to climb into her lap. All ninety pounds of him.

"It's actually not as ugly out here as I thought it would be," Logan says, staring out at the rolling brown hills of Eastern Oregon over the dog's head.

Rosemary forces herself to relax her shoulders again. "It reminds me of Steinbeck."

"They remind me of butts," Logan says. "Don't the hills kind of look like butts?"

"Or ball sacks," Joe chimes in as he exhales puffs of smoke.

"Or boobs. Look." Logan points at one particularly boob-like hill. "That cluster of bushes is the areola, and that rock is the nipple."

Rosemary takes four, four-count breaths and thanks the travel gods that traffic is starting to move again.

At least one fire has been contained.

Chapter Nine

LOGAN

"Well, this is definitely a murder hotel."

Hale swallows and stares at the hotel through the windshield from the passenger seat. "This . . . this can't be it." She scrambles for her phone in the dark, and when it lights up, Logan can see her tense, puckered mouth. "This can't be our hotel for the night."

"I'm pretty sure this entire state is just Nazis and ski resorts, and this place sure as shit ain't a ski resort." Logan *really* should've thought through the Queer Cuddler thing. Or considered Joe's safety, like, *at all*. She's truly such an asshole.

"'The Stag's Head Inn,'" Hale reads off the screen. She glances up at the neon sign in front of them, and although it's missing several crucial letters, it's clearly supposed to read "Stag's Head Inn."

"This is *not* what it looked like in the photos."

"Did you read the reviews?"

"Logan Katarina Maletis," Hale says like she's being choked. "I don't stop to use a public restroom without reading the reviews! Of course I read the reviews! They said this was a modest, affordable hotel in a safe location with comfortable beds, perfect for travelers passing through Twin Falls."

Logan points out the driver's-side window. "That giant banner in front of the pawn shop that says 'Get Guns Here' is making me feel *super* safe."

"I don't understand! The website said nothing about the hotel being attached to a liquor store!"

"Shocked they didn't boast about that amenity."

"Your jokes aren't helping!" Hale starts massaging her temples and taking her intense breaths, and Logan swallows her flippant response.

"Joking is my flawed coping mechanism," she said. "I'm not trying to make things worse."

"But you are. What are we going to do? We can't stay here for the night. Can we stay here?"

Logan shifts her gaze between the guns and the booze. Her capacity to deal with this situation died around their twelfth hour in the car. Everything took so much longer than expected, and Hale refused to sing Shania, even though Logan would bet anything she still remembers all the words. And whenever it was her turn to choose the music, she put on the audiobook of *Persuasion*.

The only highlight of the day was the stop at Vista House. When she's surrounded by trees, it's so much easier to *breathe*. To stand still. To quiet the chaos of her brain. To just . . . exist.

"What are we going to do?" Hale squawks again.

Joe, who's been snoring since dinner, suddenly jerks awake. "Where are we?"

"Nowhere worth mentioning. I'm finding us another hotel." Hale's sharp nails click clack against her iPhone screen for a few minutes before she screams. "How are there no vacancies anywhere in Twin Falls, Idaho!" Several more violent thumb jabs. "Oh. It looks like there's a . . . *knife and gun expo* in town this weekend."

Logan barks out a deranged laugh.

"It's almost eleven o'clock at night, and I'm so tired, and there's nowhere else to stay!" Hale shouts, her arms flying around like panicked acrobats. "I fucked this up! It was my job to secure our lodging, and I booked us a murder hotel!"

Hale is about to snap. All the telltale signs are there. Teeth? Grinding. Fists? Clenched. Creepy throat tendon? Bulging creepily. Logan knows this version of Hale. She knows the way a minor inconvenience can become a catastrophe in Hale's mind, and how a small mistake can avalanche into a spiral of panic. Every misstep is a fuckup, and every fuckup is a sign of a great moral failing.

Hale can't just let herself be a flawed human. She never could.

Logan flashes back to their conversation on the front porch. *I thought I had to be perfect to be worthy.* The thing is, Hale is perfect at most things. Her brain is like ten supercomputers all going at the same time, solving problems before Logan even knows the problems exist. As kids, Hale could conjure entire stories like spells at the snap of her fingers, write books from nothing but her overactive imagination. It made Logan feel special to be allowed into that magnificent mind.

Hale is brilliant, hardworking, and hyperfocused—everything Logan is not. But sometimes, the supercomputers go a little haywire. Sometimes, Hale's anxiety gets the best of her.

Logan used to be the only one who could help Hale in those moments. There was a time when Logan would see the twitch in her left eye and the puckering of her mouth, and she would make a silly face to break the tension. Or she'd bust out the choreography to "Bye Bye Bye" until Hale was laughing too hard to remember why she was melting down. Logan would grab her by the hand and drag her into the woods, so nature could smooth the rough edges of her mind, because Hale loved open spaces and trees as much as Logan did.

But that was twenty years ago, before the pool party and all the unforgiveable things that unfolded between them. Now, Logan is the one who makes Hale's eye twitch. And most of the time, she enjoys it.

Except right now, in this terrifying parking lot, Logan almost reaches for Hale. She almost opens Spotify, almost presses play on "Bye Bye Bye" and does the dance they spent most of sixth grade memorizing. She feels an overwhelming need to bring Hale back from the brink of whatever mental black hole she's about to fall into. To comfort her.

"What's wrong with our current hotel?" Joe grumbles from under his blanket. Logan realizes she has started reaching for Hale, her hand hovering between them over the center console.

"Nothing," she says, shoving her hands under her thighs. "Assuming you're angling to be hate-crimed on this road trip."

"We should've painted over the logo," Hale grumbles.

"I know," Logan admits.

Someone who moves like he's three platypuses inside a trench coat stumbles closer to the van, but then Odysseus lunges at the window and barks like a maniac, and the trench coat platypuses stagger backward and disappear into the night. She grabs the seat beneath her. "We should just stay here. There's nowhere else to go, and we're all too tired to keep driving. We'll be safe for one night. Odysseus will protect us. He loves unjustified violence."

Hale does a slow head bob of acceptance. "Yeah, okay. Okay. You go inside and check us in."

"You're going to send the *lesbian* inside? Hell no. You go. You're straight."

Joe starts to protest in the back, but he's drowned out by Hale's loud stammering. "I'm—I mean—You're *tall*. You should go."

"What does being tall have to do with anything?"

"You can protect yourself! I'm dainty!"

Joe curses loudly before things devolve into another screaming match. "Girls, why don't we all go inside together?"

Which is how they find themselves, ten minutes later, in the lobby of the Stag's Head Inn: a tall woman, a short woman, an old man in a wheelchair, and a dog, surrounded by the absolute weirdest assortment of shit because they didn't feel safe leaving any belongings in the car. They had to press a buzzer to be let inside, and the inn really lived up to its moniker, re: the number of heads mounted on the walls.

The white man behind the check-in counter is wearing a T-shirt that somehow simultaneously praises fly fishing and insults his wife. He has a humorless face and a questionable mustache. He studies them with a look Logan has seen before. She does not like this look.

"Checking in," Hale squeaks, "reservation for Hale."

The man pulls out an honest-to-God ledger. There is no computer. "Two rooms. Adjoining. One with a king bed. One with two queens."

"For my two queens," Joe says in the gayest way possible. Logan elbows him.

The man peers over the counter, his unsmiling mouth barely visible through the 'stache. "You didn't mention you'd have a dog."

Hale cringes, and Logan knows she'll beat herself up for that oversight as she falls asleep tonight. Odysseus pulls back a leg and begins licking his groin. "Is . . . is it okay if we have a dog?"

The man sucks on his teeth. "Gonna have to charge you fifty bucks more."

Hale nods emphatically. "Of course."

Joe is bankrolling this whole misguided adventure, so Hale hands over his credit card.

The man eyes Hale for a beat too long, then lets his eyes slide over to Logan. "What are you?" He points at them with his Bic pen. "Sisters? Friends?"

Tig fucking Notaro. If she had a dollar for every time she's been asked that question while in public with another woman. "Sisters!" Hale blurts before Logan can answer.

Logan flashes the man her biggest smile. "Yep. Sisters." Then she sells it by putting a sisterly arm around Hale's shoulder and giving her a noogie with the other hand.

Hale looks mutinous but brushes aside the flyaways in her hair and tries to smile. Hale shakes beneath Logan's arm—maybe from exhaustion, maybe from anxiety, maybe from the carcasses being used as décor—and Logan leaves her arm there for a minute, waiting for Hale's shoulders to relax.

The man points out the dark front windows to where the van is parked, the words *The Queer Cuddler* spotlighted by the parking lot floodlights. "That your car?"

"No," Logan and Hale say in unison, but not before Joe trills, "Yes!"

The man sucks on his teeth again, and Logan assesses whether she could take this fifty-year-old hotel clerk in a fight, if it came down to that.

"My daughter is trans," he says, and it takes Logan a second to register that he didn't respond to the Gay Mobile with something homophobic. "She brought her girlfriend home for Memorial Day Weekend. This is her."

The man reaches for a cheap picture frame on his desk with a photo of a young girl in a Boise State jersey, her cheeks punctuated with blue and orange paint, and her long brown hair pulled into a high ponytail. "She's studying to be a lawyer. I'm real proud of her."

Hale seems to be as frozen in shock as Logan is, but Joe smoothly responds, "She's beautiful. And so lucky to have you as a father."

The man beams beneath his plentiful mustache, and it's then that Logan notices a "Protect Trans Kids" sticker pinned to a bulletin board behind the counter. Suddenly, she sees The Stag's Head Inn in a new light. Sure, the location isn't great, but she can see through an open archway that the liquor store is more like a quaint bar that happens to sell liquor bottles to-go. And the heads mounted to the wall aren't great, but the rest of the lobby is cozy, if dated, with wood beams and a large stone fireplace. And this man who loves fly fishing more than his wife, at least according to his shirt, also loves his trans daughter so damn much, that he starts talking about her to the first guests who might be queer.

"You know what? I'm gonna go ahead and remove that fifty-dollar pet fee." The man winks at Joe. He reaches for two old-fashioned hotel keys, and Logan checks his name tag before choking on a disbelieving laugh.

"Thanks, Homer. For everything."

The man named Homer smiles sweetly at her, and she feels like she's on one hell of an odyssey.

And she doesn't realize she still has an arm around Hale's shoulder until Hale roughly shakes it off and reaches for the room key.

ROSEMARY

As she stands under the hot shower water in a hotel where they narrowly avoided getting shanked in the parking lot, all Rosemary can think about is Logan's arm around her shoulder.

The way it settled there, stayed there, like her arm remembered their past so easily. Logan often draped her arm around Rosemary like that when they were young. Jokingly, whenever Rosemary said something funny. Protectively, whenever Jennifer Platt or the other mean girls teased her about her compulsive need to answer every question a teacher asked, correctly and first. Encouragingly, whenever she wanted to convince Rosemary to do something reckless. Lovingly, whenever it was just the two of them.

Rosemary thoroughly scrubs her arms and legs like she can scrub away those memories along with the feeling of Logan's skin.

"Holy Dickensian antihero, what are you wearing?" Logan blurts when Rosemary steps out of the hotel bathroom.

She gestures to her pajamas. "This is a sleep dress, and I'll defend it with my life."

She's always cold and hates having her legs restricted while she sleeps. Discovering that Land's End makes long-sleeved flannel night-gowns was a godsend for her anxiety-induced insomnia. She owns this sleep dress in four colors.

"It has *frills*. You look like you're about to be visited by the Ghost of Christmas Past."

Logan is her Ghost of Middle School Crushes Past, and that is so much worse than anything Ebenezer had to deal with. She's sprawled out on her hotel bed, scrolling through TikTok, based on the annoying bursts of sound that change every thirty seconds. She's wearing a "Read Banned Books" T-shirt and a pair of TomboyX underwear and absolutely nothing else. Rosemary looks anywhere but at Logan's long, naked legs. She pulls out her pink toiletries bag—pink for skin care—and begins her nighttime routine of lotions, moisturizers, and serums in front of the mirror.

There's something calming about the regimen, about slipping into the same steps she performs every night in her own home. Change is difficult for her, but this routine anchors her to the familiar. It helps her forget that she's here, in a strange hotel. That Joe is sleeping in the adjoining room with a baby monitor by his bed in case he needs anything in the night. That Logan will be sleeping in the adjacent bed.

She gets lost in her skin-care routine, then switches to her hair-care routine (purple bag). When her hair is dry enough, she twists it into a French braid and climbs into bed with her silk pillow. It's after one in the morning, and even though every inch of her body is exhausted from the long day of driving, her brain is amped up. She pulls out a copy of a new Elizabeth Acevedo book she wants to teach next year, but then she remembers she got laid off, and she can't seem to focus on the words.

From the other bed, Logan scoffs. "We get it. You're smart. Now put away that boring-ass book and fall asleep watching TikTok like the rest of us. I won't tell anyone."

"You shouldn't use screens in the hour before bed." Rosemary drapes the book across her stomach. Her skin feels itchy beneath her sleep dress. "And those videos will destroy your attention span."

"That inattentive ship has already sailed."

Rosemary tries to read her book again, but after ten minutes, she realizes she's been staring at the same page the whole time. She puts down the book and clicks off the light beside her bed. She fluffs her pillow and tries to get comfortable, but she's too keenly aware of Logan, ten feet away, still on her phone. "For how much longer do you intend to watch those videos?"

"Christ on a cracker," Logan huffs. "Dangle your prepositions, you robot."

Logan plugs her phone into its charger and rolls over. The hotel room is dark except for the glow of red alarm clock numbers and parking lot lights filtering through the curtains.

"Hale?" Logan asks into the dark. Rosemary isn't sure why, but she holds her breath. "Don't pretend you're asleep. I can hear your anxiety."

She sighs. "What?"

Logan goes quiet again, and Rosemary counts her heartbeats while she waits. "You . . . you did a good job, choosing this hotel for the night."

Rosemary waits for the *but*, for the punch line, for the underhanded compliment, but it never comes.

"You did a good job planning this whole trip, okay? So go easy on yourself."

Rosemary has no idea what to do with this unexpected kindness. "At least we didn't get murdered," she says back. For a moment tonight, Logan's arm was around her shoulder, and it felt like they were on the same team again.

"Don't count your murder eggs before they hatch," Logan groans into her pillow. "I still fully plan to kill you in your sleep."

Twin Falls, Idaho to Cheyenne, Wyoming

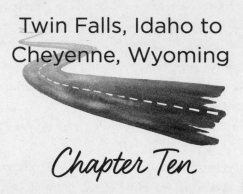

Chapter Ten

ROSEMARY

Logan doesn't murder Rosemary in her sleep, but she looks on the verge of homicide the next morning as they pack up the van for another day of driving.

"It's so fucking early," Logan moans. She's wearing her sunglasses and holding a thermos of terrible hotel coffee, leaning against the van like a tortured teen.

"It's seven. This is a perfectly reasonable time to get on the road." Rosemary hugs the binder tightly against her chest. "It's a nine-hour drive to Cheyenne, and I don't want to get off schedule like we did yesterday."

"Can we stop in Yellowstone?" Joe squints up at her in the early morning sun.

"No . . . Yellowstone is not on the way to Cheyenne. It's in a completely different part of the state."

"The Grand Tetons, then."

Logan giggles into her thermos. "Grand *Teet*-tons."

Rosemary squeezes the binder like a stress ball. "No, we won't be going out of our way to see any mountains that look like butts or boobs or ball sacks."

"Whoa. Hale just said ball sack." Logan clutches her chest. "Am I still sleeping?"

She ignores that. "There will be no detours at all today. We are going to Cheyenne, and *straight* to Cheyenne."

"Come on, Hale. Can't we stop and see some cool shit along the way?"

"Yes." Joe nods. "I would like to see some *cool shit* before I die."

"Too bad. Now, everyone. Get in the van."

"Someone needs to take Odie to use the bathroom in that patch of grass over there." Joe points to the tiniest patch of green beside the hotel.

Logan puts her finger on her nose. "Not it."

Rosemary rolls her eyes. "Damn dog."

Logan starts humming the tune to "Cruella De Vil."

If she doesn't scare you, no evil thing will.

Rosemary snatches up the red leash and drags Odysseus over to the grass, where he sniffs every individual blade before choosing the perfect place to relieve himself. She stomps back over to the van and finds Joe and Logan are talking in hushed tones. They stop as soon as she approaches.

"What?"

"We're conspiring to rescue the 101 Dalmatians from your evil lair," Logan answers without missing a beat.

Rosemary rolls her eyes again. "I'm on first shift."

• • •

Twin Falls looks perfectly normal in the daylight, a flat town with all the regular fast-food options but not nearly enough trees for Rosemary's liking.

Rosemary plugs the directions into her phone and sets it carefully in the dashboard holder she bought for the drive.

"We have to go south for a bit before we can go east," she

explains. "We'll take I-84 toward Salt Lake City and then get onto I-80, which will take us as far as Illinois. Then it's I-90 all the way to Maine. It's pretty much a straight shot from here."

"Cate fucking Blanchett, even your driving directions are *straight*." Logan grabs her hoodie and shoves it behind her head as Rosemary navigates their way back to I-84.

"Okay, I have to ask . . ." Joe begins delicately. "Logan, is there a reason you seem to believe Rosemary is a heterosexual?"

Rosemary's body flushes hot, then cold, then goes completely numb. She doesn't want to have this conversation. Not while trapped in this claustrophobic van.

Logan snorts into her sweatshirt pillow. "Because Hale *is* straight. Look at her dress."

She glances down to see the Ralph Lauren floral midi-dress she put on this morning. She loves this dress. The fabric doesn't irritate her skin, and it's tight against her subtle curves in a way that makes her feel secure. Like a hug from her clothes. She owns this dress in three different patterns and she incorporates them into her wardrobe rotation every summer.

It's like her vanilla lotion or her Essie's Ballet Slippers nail polish or her French braid. It's one less decision she has to make every day, one less source of anxiety.

And she resents the idea that wearing this dress somehow makes her *less* gay.

Feeling returns to her hands and she flexes her fingers like a falcon's talons perfectly poised at ten and two. "Actually, I'm not straight," she spits out. "I'm a lesbian."

Those three syllables conjure the panic she felt the first time she said them aloud, bursting into Joe's classroom one morning during spring of her senior year. Four years of agony and confusion, feelings she tried to ignore by dating boys, feelings she psychoanalyzed each night as she fell asleep, before finally saying that word and feeling like it fit as perfectly as her favorite pair of shoes. *Lesbian*.

Logan cackles in the passenger seat. "Wow, Hale. You do still have a sense of humor."

She clenches her jaw as tight as her hands on the steering wheel. "I'm not joking."

"She's not joking," Joe echoes. "And you should know better than to think queerness is supposed to look a certain way."

Logan—who is wearing a backward baseball hat over her greasy, unwashed hair, and a pair of shorts she definitely bought in the men's section at Target—flops her mouth open and closed in shock. "Wait, are you being serious?" She sits up in her seat and cranks her head to look at Joe, then Rosemary in rapid succession. "*You* are gay?"

Slowly, Rosemary nods once in affirmation.

"Since when?" Logan explodes.

"Since . . . always. I think that's how it works. . . ."

Logan whips around to Joe again. "And you knew about this?"

Rosemary watches in the rearview mirror as Joe flips his invisible scarf. "Not to brag, but I was the first person she told."

"People know! Students know! Other teachers know! Your dad definitely knows!" Rosemary explodes. "I'm out, and I'm not exactly hiding my gayness."

"But—" Logan's mouth gapes open and closed a few more times. "But I didn't know."

"That's because you're oblivious and self-obsessed! You don't care about other people!"

For the first time in twenty years, Logan doesn't have a snappy rejoinder at the ready. She sits there, stroking Odysseus's floppy ears, unnervingly quiet. Rosemary refocuses on the road in front of her until Logan eventually breaks her silence.

"You're really, actually gay?"

"Yes."

Logan lapses into another round of stupefied silence. Then, in the same way that Rosemary can always sense incoming rain from the subtlest shift in barometric pressure, she can *feel* Logan's mouth stretching into a smirk even as her gaze remains fixed ahead.

Through that infuriating smirk, Logan finally says, "So is *that* why you kissed me at the pool party?"

• • •

There had been two kisses, actually. Rosemary remembers them both perfectly.

The first was an exhibitionist one performed for horny eighth grade boys who thought it would be funny to see two girls kiss. It was a joke. A laugh. Usually, you were allowed to re-spin the bottle if it landed on a girl instead of a boy.

Rosemary hadn't wanted to play Spin the Bottle in the first place. She'd been lured into Jennifer Platt's bonus room by Jake McCandie, and she caved under the pressure and spun the bottle when it was her turn.

Only it hadn't landed on Jake McCandie like he had planned. It landed squarely on Logan, sitting across from her in the circle. Logan, who had red Popsicle juice on her chin.

"*Oooo*," the boys all moaned, elbowing each other excitedly.

"Spin again," Jake ordered.

"No, you have to kiss whoever the bottle lands on," Jennifer Platt said with complete authority. She had an in-ground pool and a Nokia cell phone. Whatever Jennifer Platt said was law.

Rosemary *couldn't* kiss Logan. Logan was her best friend, and a girl. . . . so why couldn't she stop staring at the sticky red juice on Logan's face?

Suddenly Logan—amid Jake's protests and the other boys' catcalls and the other girls' expressions of revulsion—rolled her eyes and crawled forward. Her butt stuck into the air, the giant T-shirt she wore over her bathing suit opening around her throat so Rosemary could see all the way down the front. Rosemary's heart jumped into her throat. Logan closed her eyes and leaned in.

Rosemary was too shocked to even close her eyes when Logan's mouth pecked hers.

The briefest connection, the loudest smacking sound. Over before Rosemary could register it.

The room erupted in noise, but Rosemary couldn't hear it over the sound of her heartbeat roaring like the ocean in her ears.

"Lesbians," Jennifer Platt muttered under her breath. *That*, Rosemary heard. Across the circle, Jake McCandie pouted.

Only Greta Le defended them. "You made them do it! That was messed up."

"Those are the rules of Spin the Bottle. And no one forced Logan," Jennifer taunted. "She wanted to do it. She *liked* it."

Logan just rolled her eyes again, like she truly didn't care what anyone else thought.

"Rosemary didn't like it," Jake cut in. He turned to face her with earnest eyes. "Did you?"

She felt like the bottle, spinning on the carpet in the bonus room, unsure of where to land.

"No," she finally croaked. "No, I didn't like it."

But the second kiss.

The sun was starting to set on the pool party, and everyone had gone around the front of the house to play Sardines in the cul-de-sac, but Rosemary stayed behind to pick up the paper plates on the lawn for Mrs. Platt.

"Hey," Logan said, coming up behind her with another Popsicle in hand. She said *hey* like the kiss had never happened, like their lips had never touched. Like Rosemary had dreamed the entire thing.

But if it were a dream, why could she still feel the phantom imprint of Logan's lips on hers? Why did she still feel hot prickles of shame down her spine?

"Why did you kiss me?" Rosemary asked, shoving an abandoned hotdog into a Hefty bag.

Logan shrugged like she always did. "To shut everyone up. It's just a game. It's not like it's a big deal."

Rosemary glanced down at her hands. She wasn't sure why, but there was a tingling in her fingertips. "It was my first kiss."

"Duh, Rosie. I know," Logan said casually. "Mine too."

"That . . . that wasn't how I expected my first kiss would be."

She wasn't sure how she thought her first kiss would be, exactly, but she didn't expect Logan's face close to hers, a sticky chin, soft skin beneath her T-shirt.

"Come on." Logan reached for Rosemary's hand. Her fingers were as sticky as her chin, and she dragged Rosemary along the side of the house, to a little garden in the shadows where the summer air smelled sweet. Logan sat down in the dirt and pulled Rosemary down with her.

"Rosemary," she said, and it took Rosemary a second to realize Logan was reaching out to touch a plant with little green leaves beside them. *Rosemary*. Or, at the very least, something that resembled it.

"How did you think your first kiss would be?" Logan asked when they were completely alone.

"I don't know," she mumbled, hoping it was dark enough to hide her blush this time. "I guess I thought it would be romantic. Private. With a . . . a boy I liked."

"Well, I can't do anything about the boy part, but we like each other, right?"

And they did, back then. Rosemary liked Logan so much, sometimes she thought her body couldn't contain their friendship, like it wasn't big enough for all the feelings she had for this other girl.

"And this is private." Logan gestured to the little bit of garden. "You can pretend I'm a boy if you want. Do you want a redo first kiss?" Logan asked so innocently, it took Rosemary a minute to understand what Logan was offering. To kiss her, in the dark, where no one was watching.

Logan plucked part of the plant-rosemary off the branch and reached over to tuck it into girl-Rosemary's braid. Logan's face was so close, having moved in to touch Rosemary's hair, and with her fingers already brushing the back of Rosemary's throat, it wasn't hard to follow the gesture to its natural conclusion.

To tilt her head forward and to find Logan's Popsicle mouth.

That time, she closed her eyes. That time, it was a graze, not a peck. It was the skim of soft skin against soft skin. Logan's soft fingers and her soft mouth.

And all the panic that usually ran rampant through her brain quieted to make room for a new feeling inside her chest. Logan opened her mouth. Logan's tongue sweeping against her tongue. Rosemary hesitantly kissing her back.

It was the entire universe, that feeling in her chest. It was galaxies and infinity.

The kiss gathered inside her, made her feel brave, the way Logan always made her feel brave.

The kiss felt like math, like variables and equations spilling out in front of her, and if she kept kissing Logan, eventually she would understand what they all added up to.

So, she kept kissing Logan. Kept touching her. Her skin was so soft, and her mouth tasted like sugar, and Rosemary didn't understand *why*. She just knew she had to keep kissing Logan.

But then Logan pulled away, and the universe inside her chest became a black hole, a vacuum of nothingness. Logan's Popsicle-red mouth twisted into a strange smile Rosemary would later call a smirk. "Ha!" Logan said smugly. "I knew you liked it during Spin the Bottle!"

She looked triumphant and, in that moment, more than ever before, Rosemary didn't understand. She barely registered the faint sound of voices approaching.

Logan stood up then. The backs of her bare legs were covered in bark dust as she walked away, leaving Rosemary sitting in the dirt with a plant in her hair, humiliated and alone.

• • •

There were three kisses, actually, if you count the one with Jake McCandie right after. Rosemary pulled him into that same garden, pushed her lips against his, and hoped she'd feel an ounce of what she'd felt kissing her best friend.

She hadn't felt anything at all.

Chapter Eleven

ROSEMARY

She's dreaming about popsicles and pop bottles when she's startled awake by an explosion.

She has no idea how long she's been asleep, but it takes her brain a second to realize the loud *pop* isn't part of her dreams. She jerks upright in the passenger seat and sees Logan wrestling the steering wheel like she's trying to ride a wild bull. The Gay Mobile rattles violently. Logan curses. Joe screams. Odysseus barks.

Rosemary's heart is in her throat. "What's going on?"

"We blew a tire!" Logan grits through her teeth as she manages to guide the car onto the shoulder. The van slows down, and the shaking subsides to a gentle sway as they come to a complete stop. They've kicked up a storm cloud's worth of dust that obscures everything around them.

The combination of sleepiness and adrenaline makes her feel disoriented. Rosemary tries to remember where they are. Logan took over driving back in Ogden, where she made them stop to get In-N-Out. Rosemary closed her eyes, only for a minute, but must have fallen asleep.

And now they're stranded on the side of the road.

Rosemary swivels to face Logan in a panic. "You blew a tire!"

"Yes, I *intentionally* blew out one of our tires," Logan says dryly. She hits the hazard lights but leaves the keys in the ignition, even though the feeble air-conditioning does little to combat the excruciating heat of the van. Based on the position of the sun overhead, Rosemary slept for quite a while, and the windshield is like a magnified glass burning ants. "I'm the villain you think I am, Hale."

"It's because of your *speeding*!" Rosemary screeches, but Logan is already climbing out of the driver's seat and carefully making her way around the back of the van.

Still half-asleep, Rosemary hesitates, and then opens the passenger-side door.

"Wait!" Joe shouts. "Don't leave me here by myself! I want to know what's going on!"

Rosemary opens the sliding door so Joe can hear the unholy sound that escapes her mouth when she sees the rear passenger-side tire sliced into absolute ribbons. Odysseus barks twice and then lunges out of the open door, and Rosemary stumbles to catch his leash before he runs into traffic. "What are we going to do?"

Logan simply puts her hands on her hips. "I guess we're going to learn how to change a tire," she says. Her calm sets Rosemary's teeth on edge. They're on the side of a freeway. Cars are rushing by at eighty miles per hour, and she's trying to contain a dog that weighs almost as much as her, and they have a *flat tire*. On day two.

They'll have to call a tow truck.

They'll have to buy a new tire.

They'll be horribly behind schedule.

Her anxiety twists in on itself like a double helix. "This isn't funny, Logan!"

Logan cocks her head to the side and studies the remains of the tire. "I promise I'm not laughing. There is a spare tire, right?"

Rosemary tries to take a deep breath, but her lungs are thick with exhaustion and dust, and she chokes on it. "You didn't make sure we had a spare tire before we left?"

"Chill your bill. I'm like eighty-two-percent sure we have one."
Logan walks around to the back of the car and opens the back of the
van. Rosemary fights to keep Odysseus away from the road while
Logan rustles around for a minute, taking out their belongings and
dumping them on the gravel shoulder for the world to see. "Aha!"
she finally declares when she pulls up the floor flap to reveal the
secret compartment underneath. "A spare!"

She clumsily pulls the tire out from the trunk and drops it to the
ground, rolling it toward Rosemary. "Now. All we have to do is learn
how to change a tire."

"I know how to change a tire!" Joe shouts from inside the van.
"You need a jack!"

"Awesome!" Logan maintains that same unflappable calm. "What's
a jack?"

Rosemary huffs and shoves the dog's leash in Logan's face. At
least one of them had the sense to pack a roadside emergency kit.
She hunts around for the bright yellow jack, along with one of those
bolt remover things the internet said she would need in this situation.

"Okay. Step one!" Joe tries to explain blindly. "You need to get
the car up on the jack."

Rosemary's patience is already frayed, so she pulls out her
phone to google how to change a tire, and that's when she notices
the weather widget on her home screen. It's ninety-two degrees in
Kanab, Utah.

But that . . .

That can't be right.

Her phone also says it's a little after two in the afternoon, which
means they shouldn't be in Utah anymore. They should have entered Wyoming hours ago. Joe is shouting directions at Logan,
who is hunched down in the gravel trying to position the car jack
while holding the dog leash and shouting things back, but Rosemary tunes them both out. She finally takes in the full picture of

their surroundings. The freeway is bracketed by plateaus of red rock, stretches of scrub brush fields, desert.

They're in the fucking desert.

It's true she's never been to Wyoming before, but she's pretty sure it doesn't look like Mars. Logan does a triumphant dance once she gets the car raised on the jack. "Where are we?" Rosemary demands, and the dance quickly desists. Logan's expression is unreadable from behind her sunglasses.

She clenches her teeth and speaks through the jaw pain. "Where. The fuck. Are we?"

Logan stands up and wipes her dirty hands on the front of her tropical shirt. "Don't freak out," Logan starts, "but we took a little detour."

"You did *what*?"

Logan's arm flails toward the van. "It was Joe's idea!"

"Oh, very classy," Joe calls back. "Throw the dying man under the Gay Mobile!"

Rosemary spins around and sees Joe looking fake innocent beneath his Pendleton blanket. "Joseph Miguel Delgado," she hisses. "Where are we going?"

He coughs into his handkerchief like he's trying to remind her he's enfeebled. "The Grand Canyon."

She has no problem yelling at an enfeebled man. "The Grand Canyon in *Arizona*?"

"Pretty sure there's only one," Logan pipes in.

Rosemary's jaw is about to crack from clenching it so tightly. "That is not a detour. That's a thousand miles in the *wrong direction*!"

Logan tries to insert herself between Rosemary and Joe. "Come on, Hale. He's never seen the Grand Canyon before, and he wants to see some cool shit before he dies. I mean, look at that face."

Joe quickly arranges his features into something both pitiful and angelic.

"How could I say no to that face?"

"Because the Grand Canyon is *south*, and we're supposed to be driving *east*! We're supposed to be in Wyoming! I made a binder! I mapped out our entire journey!"

"I think there's a lesson to be learned here about overpreparing."

Rosemary is going to strangle Logan. For real this time.

She lunges, but Odysseus thinks it's a game, so he leaps up onto her, paws landing painfully against her chest so he can lick her face. She screams on the side of the road in Kanab, Utah.

"No fighting while we're driving!" Logan tells her when she stops.

"We're not driving! Because you got a flat tire!"

Logan grimaces. "Yes, okay. Fair point. But come on, Hale. It's an adventure!"

"Turn us around. We're going to Cheyenne."

Logan pushes her sunglasses up into her bun and has the audacity to say, "No. No, we're not turning around."

"But the binder!"

"Fuck your binder!"

"Rosie, sweetheart," Joe coaxes. "It's the Grand Canyon. I need to see it. We all need to see it."

He sounds so earnest, and for the first time, his pleading expression doesn't look like a performance. Even amid all her anxiety, Rosemary finds her heart aching for Joe.

"Then why didn't you just say that when you asked us to take you on this ridiculous trip?"

"Because you would've said no," he says plainly.

Rosemary opens her mouth to argue again, then closes it around another scream. He's right. Driving him to Maine is one thing, but if Joe had said he wanted her to go to the Grand Canyon with Logan Maletis, she would have refused.

She stares at the streaks of dirt down Logan's loud tropical shirt. Then she stares down at her own floral dress, two reddish-brown paw prints perfectly imprinted on her boobs.

She's not overprepared. She is completely and totally out of her depth.

"Can you even find a hotel at the Grand Canyon at the last minute when the entire country is on summer vacation?"

Joe holds up a Booking.com reservation on his phone. "Done! And look. It's pet-friendly!"

Her brain is already trying to recalculate routes and driving distances and how much more time she'll have to spend with Logan thanks to this little detour. "Out of my way," she snaps, shouldering Logan aside and dropping to her knees in the dirt. She starts muscling the lug nuts off the destroyed tire.

"Does this mean—" Logan starts.

"Please shut up, Maletis, and just help me change this fucking tire."

• • •

It's a little after nine when they finally pull into the town of Tusayan, and Rosemary feels dead behind the wheel. *Five hundred miles in the wrong direction.* Two hours spent at a run-down mechanic to get a new tire. Her brain keeps spiraling around those numbers, and she feels like at any second she could burst into tears. Or vomit.

No one else seems to be faring any better. Joe's been asleep since they entered Arizona, Logan is hangry and covered in dirt, and Odysseus keeps pacing around the back seat like Rosemary's anxiety is contagious. Everything smells like dirty dog and burnt rubber, and their Southwest-themed hotel shines like an oasis in the dark. She's so relieved, she could cry.

That is, until she sees the room Joe and Logan booked for the night. Room *singular.*

It's one hotel room with two queen beds and nothing else.

"What is this?"

Logan drops her duffle bag onto the bed closest to the door. "Home sweet home."

"You only booked one room?"

"There was only one room available," Joe says groggily as he rolls himself over to the second bed.

And that's it. It's official. These two clowns are definitely conspiring to push her toward a full mental breakdown. They're like the idiots who opened the bag of winds in *The Odyssey* and blew everyone completely off course for ten years.

"And what is the sleeping arrangement supposed to be?"

It's clear Logan didn't actually think that piece through as she rubs a hand up and down the back of her neck. "Well, uh, Joe and Odie will sleep in that bed." She points to the one by the window. "And then—"

"You can sleep on the floor?"

Logan's mouth hangs open even more than usual for a minute before she snaps it closed. At which point Odysseus leaps onto the closest bed and rolls his filthy body up and down the duvet. "Stop! Down! You mangy dog! You're getting everything dirty!"

The dog ignores her. Logan hums a few bars of "Cruella De Vil" again before she takes charge. "Odie. Off." She snaps her fingers, and the dog jumps off the bed and plants his butt on Logan's rainbow Vans.

Rosemary is going to cry and vomit at the same time, actually. "I can't handle this. I'm getting in the shower."

"Great!" Logan grabs Joe's bags and brings them over to his bed. "Take Odie with you."

"Excuse me?"

"You're right. He's gross. Take him into the shower with you and get him cleaned off."

"Fuck you" is her reasonable response to this absurd request.

Logan shrugs. "Okay. Then let him get his dog dirt all over your silk pillowcase."

Rosemary takes four breaths and contemplates her options: get on the next plane out of Arizona, strangle Logan with the cord of her travel label maker, shower with a *dog*. But then Joe starts coughing out of sheer exhaustion from an entire day in the car, and she remembers why she's here, at the Grand Canyon. It's all for Joe.

Which is how she finds herself standing naked in the bathroom with a dog staring up at her ten minutes later.

"Okay, dog." She points to the bathtub-shower combo. "In."

The dog cocks his head to the side like he doesn't understand her command. *Does* he understand? She knows fuck-all about dogs.

She turns on the hot water and tries again. "Dog. In. Get in the shower."

He still doesn't move, but his giant tongue slides out the front of his open mouth. It makes him look like Logan. She tries getting in first. "Come, dog. *Come*."

"You might have to pick him up!" Logan shouts from the other side of the bathroom door.

Odysseus looks like a single-headed Cerberus. There is no way she can lift him.

"Odysseus, *please*."

She's not sure if it's the use of his name or the magic word, but the dog suddenly, calmly obeys.

But as soon as the shower water hits his fur, Odysseus begins thrashing around, trying to make his escape. "No! No!" She closes the shower curtain and hopes he'll think the flimsy vinyl is impenetrable.

"Stay. Stay. Good boy."

She stands under the lukewarm water and tries to wet her hair as quickly as she can. Every few seconds, the dog paws at the shower curtain, and she shouts, "No! Stay!"

When the shouting loses its effect, she switches to gentle coaxing while trying to lather her hydrating shampoo into her hair. "Come on, sweet baby boy. Don't do that! Don't go anywhere. Isn't this fun? Aren't we having fun together?"

Then she switches to washing him, and the brown water that

drips off his fur, and the black hair that comes off on her hands, make her gag.

"Stay, stay, stay," she chants like a prayer. Or a Taylor Swift song. And it works for a bit.

But then she accidentally gets a splash of water in his floppy ears, and he absolutely loses his shit. He bucks around like a mechanical bull and bursts through the shower curtain like the fucking Kool-Aid man.

Rosemary screams. Odysseus barks as he runs agitated circles around the bathroom. She shuts off the water and launches herself out of the shower.

"Odysseus, no! Stop!" She nearly slips when she tries to tackle the dog with a towel. "Come here! Come here! Help me!"

She's not sure what possesses her to cry out for help, but one minute, she's catapulting her naked ass after a dog, and the next, the bathroom door is opening, and Logan is standing there, staring at that naked ass with her mouth wide open.

Chapter Twelve

LOGAN

Hale is naked.

There are other things happening—a maniacal dog covered in soap is thrashing around a hotel bathroom while a dying man zonked out on oxycodone is snoring—but Logan's brain is stuck on the naked part. For approximately three seconds.

Then Hale manages to cover herself with a towel just as Odysseus bursts out of the bathroom. He leaps over suitcases and jumps onto their queen bed, rolling around so there's soapy water on the pillows and blankets.

But again, Logan has tunnel vision, and that tunnel is homed in on Hale's dripping wet legs beneath the hem of the towel, her exposed collarbone, and her birdlike neck. Ropes of wet hair falling over her pale, smooth shoulders, delicate like the petals of a white rose. Logan can't remember the last time she saw Hale's hair out of its braid, the way it frames her pretty face.

Demi fucking Lovato, she's so, so pretty.

Hale steps out of the bathroom in a cloud of vanilla-scented steam, and Logan feels fourteen again, on uneven ground as her feelings for her best friend began dangerously shifting. Holding her breath while Hale changed into pajamas at sleepovers; the way something as innocent as brushing Hale's hair—an act she'd done a hundred times—suddenly felt wrong. Watching the way her blond tendrils pooled in the delicate dip between her shoulder blades when they went swimming at the lake.

The way a simple touch that had always meant nothing suddenly meant everything. Confusion and shame and an inexplicable flutter in her rib cage every time she made Hale laugh. You weren't supposed to feel that way about your best friend. You weren't supposed to fall asleep counting the pale lashes against her cheeks.

You weren't supposed to kiss your friend at a pool party and screw up the only perfect thing you'd ever had.

And *Janelle fucking Monáe*, after all these years, it turns out Hale is gay too. What is she supposed to do with that information?

"Why are you staring at me like that?" Hale asks in a quiet voice.

The innocent confusion in her voice ends Logan's nudity-induced stupor. "I'm not."

"Could you please just get the dog?"

Logan pivots, and with one sharp command, Odie lays down on the floor with his head bowed shamefully. She grabs an extra towel from the bathroom and starts drying him off, a peace offering for Hale.

But when she looks over at Hale again, she isn't appeased. She's sobbing.

"Oh shit." She scrambles away from Odie. "What did I do?"

"Nothing." Hale snivels. "And also, *everything*. All I want is to repay Joe for everything he's done for me, but I have *you* here. And you mock me relentlessly, and you conspire with Joe behind my back to take us five hundred miles in the wrong direction, and you make me shower with a dog, and you don't respect the binder."

"I mean, it's a three-ring binder from Target. . . ."

Hale cries harder, and her pale face reddens like the Southwest rocks. Logan stands awkwardly close, once again paralyzed by her need to reach out for this person.

"I'm already so tired! I can't make spontaneous detours and impulsive changes in the plans! I need a schedule! I need a routine! Or else I . . . I spiral into what-ifs and the uncertainty just . . ."

Hale doesn't have to finish that sentence. Logan knows what happens when Hale's anxiety doesn't have routine and consistency and control. Deep down, Hale is still that scared little girl who lost her dad and abruptly moved across the country and always needed to know what was coming next. Hale's done a good job hiding that girl behind pencil skirts and high-collared shirts—behind her perfect work ethic and her perfect Pinterest classroom and her perfect face—all of which give off the illusion of a woman who is always in control.

But in this moment, Hale is stripped of the illusion. No braid and no heels and nothing to hide behind. Just . . . vulnerability.

And Logan can't help but reach out for her this time. Just the gentle pressure of fingers on forearm.

"I know you need routine," Logan says. "But I want the same thing you do. To give back to Joe what he's given to me. I'm not *trying* to piss you off."

Hale chokes on a sob.

"Okay, I'm not trying to piss you off most of the time. I'm just trying to make Joe happy."

Hale glances up at her through tearstained lashes, and then cuts her gaze over to Joe, sleeping soundly in his bed. She looks back at Logan, down at those fingers resting against Hale's pale white skin. Logan feels rammed through with unexpected guilt. It's her fault Hale is crying half-naked in this hotel room. She *knows* how Hale's anxiety works, yet she's done nothing to accommodate it and everything to make it worse. She drove them five hundred miles in the wrong direction, for Shay Mitchell's sake. Logan let herself get fooled by the perfect veneer, assuming the little girl was gone.

"I know you are," Hale finally says, "I think maybe we're just too different."

Logan isn't sure why those words hurt so damn badly, but they do. Hale reaches for a hotel tissue and wipes her face. Logan lets her fingers fall away. "Do you mind . . . turning around? I need to change."

Logan turns around and she tries not to hold her breath while Hale slips into her sleep dress.

ROSEMARY

"Moondance" is playing, and when Rosemary opens her eyes, she sees the moon is still shining through the window in the pitch-black of the room.

She sits up in bed and tries to orient herself. She's in an unfamiliar hotel room, and there's a dog curled up at her feet and a person curled up against her side. She has no idea where Van Morrison is coming from.

"Hale, I swear on Shay Mitchell's legs, if you don't turn off that alarm right now—" rasps a voice across the room.

"Rise and shine, girlies!" says the voice in bed next to her, and she remembers now, climbing into Joe's bed and sleeping on the edge of the mattress all night because it seemed safer than sleeping beside Logan.

"Fuck you, Joseph Delgado!" Logan grunts. She attempts to throw a pillow in the dark, and it lands on the dog's head. "It's three thirty in the morning, you dick!"

"*I know*," Joe singsongs cheerfully. "We better get going or we're going to be late."

After fifteen more minutes of yelling and cursing and throwing things, they're in the hotel parking lot, groggy as hell, trying to load into the Gay Mobile without any reason as to why. They each have a cup of horrible hotel coffee Rosemary fetched from the lobby. She was shocked to see so many other tourists up and moving.

"Where are we going and why are we going there at this ungodly hour?" Logan bemoans as they get Joe into the back seat.

"Faith, Logan. Have faith in me."

Logan makes a half-asleep sound of dissent. Rosemary has no faith to speak of.

The weather app says it's going to be 104 today, but predawn, it's a cool 70, and Rosemary feels more awake with the desert breeze on her bare skin, so she drives as Logan complains in the passenger seat with Odysseus sitting in her lap like a horse who thinks he's a cat.

In the back, Joe is the most excited she's seen him in four years—the most *alive*—so she doesn't question his directions when he tells her to take Highway 64 toward the national park.

As they near the entrance, the traffic thickens, throngs of other tourists making the same inexplicable pilgrimage. The sky is a muted predawn blue by the time they pull into a handicapped parking stop near Mather Point along with hundreds of other people.

Logan takes Odysseus's leash, and Rosemary helps Joe toward a paved path.

They weave through the crowds, follow the path through a curve, and *oh*. There's the Grand Canyon. Just right there.

Families have gathered around in unruly clusters, but Logan elbows her way up to the railing, carving out a spot for the three of them.

It's just *right there*. A huge hole in the earth, endless rock highlighted and blurred by shadow and the rising sun.

"Oh," Logan says in hushed awe.

"*Oh* is right," Joe whispers, as if this moment is too sacred for his full volume.

Rosemary didn't expect it to be quite so . . . grand. She's seen pictures. She thought she knew. But pictures don't capture the sweep of it, the *feel* of it, like being on top of the world and on a different planet at the same time. On the other side of the canyon, the North Rim burns bright orange and neon yellow as the caverns below remain an unsolved mystery in the dark.

Joe points to the right, where the sun edges over the rocks, lighting up the canyon piece by piece. Golden spotlights reveal the grays and browns, yellows and reds of the rock below, layers stacked on layers. It's like nothing she's ever seen before.

The fire fades and the sky turns light blue, pale purple, shocking pink. The sun reaches new crevices one at a time, and there's green sagebrush, deep orange and gold, white clouds streaked over a blue sky.

It's sublime—there is no better word for it—and it stirs something she can't quite name. Surrender, maybe, to a force she could never control.

No one speaks for a long time. Even Odysseus seems to know this morning is holy.

Rosemary watches the sunrise reflected on Joe's face for a minute. The golden glow warms his brown eyes and catches the glisten of tears streaming down his cheeks. His mouth is open around a quiet gasp of wonder. It's just as magical as watching the sunrise itself.

He looks the way Rosemary remembers from the first day of high school, so overwhelmed by the raw potential of the students in front of him.

"This," Joe exhales. "I needed to see this before I die."

Rosemary shifts her gaze to Logan and is startled to discover she's crying, too.

"Shut up!" Logan grumbles, caught in the act. She tries, and fails, to brush away the tears with the back of her hand, and then hides her eyes behind her sunglasses instead. "I'm only human."

"You know what we need . . . ," Joe starts, but Logan already has her phone out. Van Morrison starts playing "Into the Mystic."

"Apt," Joe croaks around a sob.

"Very apt," Rosemary agrees. There are tears gathering in the back of her throat, but she holds them back. She tries to file these too-big feelings away so she can look at them later, when she's alone. She already let Logan see her cry once on this trip.

But no matter how hard she tries, the feelings keep popping back up, like trying to hold a beach ball under the surface of a pool.

"I-I was wrong," she says when the song ends. "About this detour. We . . . we had to come here." The sun is a little higher now,
and the dried-out path of the Colorado River becomes visible in the
depths of the canyon. "This . . . this was worth going five hundred
miles in the wrong direction."

Chapter Thirteen

LOGAN

The Grand Canyon is cool shit.

She'd expected it to be one of those things that's overhyped and overrated and ultimately disappointing, like the *Mona Lisa* or the Colosseum or the Leaning Tower of Pisa. Not that Logan has ever *seen* those things herself, but she's heard they don't live up to the image in your head.

But now she's here, standing on the edge of something so far beyond what she could imagine, and it's the best kind of dopamine rush. The striations of rock look like the layers on a birthday cake. There's beauty and majesty and newness. It feels so far from Vista Summit, from her daily drive from her dad's house to the school, from her trees and her river and her sky. It feels like everything she used to dream about exploring as a kid.

It's dope as fuck.

When the sun is done exposing the colorful depths of the canyon, they all agree to walk along the paved South Rim Trail, even Hale in her three-inch wedges and ridiculous midi-dress. Logan insists on stopping every few minutes to take selfies of the four of them, and Hale doesn't even fight her on it. Joe is so content, he sings to himself as Hale pushes his wheelchair along. Odie tries to fight two elks in a field and has the best time of his life. It's the first time that everyone on the trip truly seems at peace.

The sun heats up quickly, and they're all drenched in sweat before 10 a.m. They have heat-protective booties for Odie, and Hale has enough sunscreen for everyone, but they still end up backtracking to the Yavapai Geological Museum just to get out of the heat for a bit. Joe reads all the informational posters aloud in his teacher voice, and Logan has never been so interested in rocks.

But once they're outside again in the excruciating heat, Joe turns red and the bad kind of sweaty. For once, Logan decides to be the responsible one. "We should go back to the hotel," Logan suggests as they attempt to huddle together in the shade.

"I agree with Logan," Hale says. "It's not safe out here for you. Or for this ridiculous dog."

Joe sits up in his chair and lifts his chin. "I don't need to go back to the hotel. I'm fine. Let's take the bus out to Hopi Point."

"I don't think—" Hale tries, but Joe cuts her off with a sharp glare.

"We came all this way. We're going to see as much of the Grand Canyon as we can."

They board a bus that's stuffed with other tourists, and thankfully, the driver doesn't question Odie's nonexistent service dog credentials. Joe is secured into a handicap spot, but Logan and Hale have to stand, Midwesterners in Zion National Park T-shirts crowding in on all sides. Logan reaches up for the handlebar, but there is nothing Hale-height to grab on to. So, without asking, Hale grabs on to Logan's arm with both hands.

The shuttle bus runs the length of the South Rim, taking them along bumpy and windy roads that make Hale squeeze her eyes shut. It stops at scenic points along the way, and Joe insists they get off the bus at Maricopa Point and again at Powell, each entrance and exit from the bus grueling for everyone involved. They spend most of the time standing in the direct sun waiting for the next bus to pick them up again, and by the time they reach Hopi Point, the sense of contentment has shriveled as badly as Hale's new sunburn.

They buy soggy sandwiches and eight bottles of water from the gift shop at Hopi Point, then let Odie shotgun two whole bottles before he collapses in some shade. Hale takes one bite of her questionable tuna fish and gags.

She puts a hand over her mouth. "I don't feel very well. I think I got motion sickness from the bus."

Her fair skin is currently as red as the canyon rocks. "I think you might have heat stroke, actually," Logan says, reaching over to press the back of her hand to Hale's forehead.

Hale clicks her tongue in disagreement, but before she can say anything else, she drops her sandwich in the dirt, grips her stomach with both hands, and takes off in the direction of the public restrooms.

"I'm so sorry," Joe says thirty minutes later when they're back on the bus. Logan manages to get Hale a seat this time, and she hunches over with her head between her knees. "I was stubborn," Joe continues. "I get so tired of being treated like I can't do anything, that I didn't consider what might be healthiest for everyone else."

"It's okay," Hale says to the floor.

But it's not okay. Hale throws up into the paper bag that held their bottles of water and has to get off the bus twice to use the bathroom. It takes almost two hours just to get back to the Gay Mobile, and by then Hale can barely walk.

Logan forces her to drink water, but it's useless. She can't keep anything down. Rosemary Hale—valedictorian, Teacher of the Year runner-up, Logan's lifelong arch nemesis—is experiencing humiliating gastrointestinal failure, and Logan can't even make fun of her for it because she looks so damn pitiful.

As soon as they're back at the hotel, Hale locks herself in the bathroom, and Odie collapses in front of the blasting air conditioner.

Logan fills him a huge bowl of water, then shifts to focusing on Joe. Inside Hale's medical bag are a dozen pouches of electrolyte powder. She pours some into a bottle of water and hands him some pills.

"I don't need to take that," he argues. "I'm not in pain."

"Joe." Her pit-stains have pit-stains, and she has no patience for his proud bullshit. "Your entire body is being eaten alive by cancer and you just spent all day traipsing around in the desert when it's 104 degrees outside. Don't make me shove these drugs down your stubborn-ass throat."

Joe takes the meds, drinks all the electrolyte water, and gets into bed like she demands. "I need to run to the market down the street to get some supplies for Hale. Are you going to be okay here by yourself for a bit?" Even as she asks, she's already reaching for the car keys.

"See?" Joe says before she's out the door. "I told you that you care too much about everything."

• • •

Joe and Odie are both passed out when she gets back from the store. The bathroom door is still closed, any sound coming from inside muffled by a gentle fan.

Logan bangs on the door. "Hale, open up."

"Go use the bathroom in the hotel lobby," Hale grunts back.

"Let me in."

"No!" Hale shouts. It's all for naught, because she forgot to lock the door, so Logan just opens it anyway. There are further screams of protest, and thankfully, for both parties involved, Hale isn't actively going to the bathroom as Logan pushes her way inside. She's sitting on the floor between the toilet and the rim of the tub, and she looks . . . *human*. Like she did last night when she cried.

Which is to say, she looks absolutely disgusting. Gone are the airs of perfect Hale, emotionless Hale, in-control Hale. Her hair is falling out of her braid in greasy chunks, and her skin is both horribly sunburned and somehow peaked at the same time. Her ridiculous wedges are tossed aside in the opposite corner of the bathroom.

"You can't be in here!" Hale croaks.

"Trust me, this isn't my ideal scenario either, Princess. The smell in this bathroom is truly something. But—" She pulls a Vitaminwater out of a reusable grocery bag. "You've got to try to get some liquids down."

"No," Hale says again, her head lolling to the side pathetically.

"Come on. I can only handle one stubborn invalid at a time, and Joe's already claimed that title."

"I can't drink liquids. I just can't."

"Of course you can. You're Rosemary Hale. You bend the universe to your will all the time. You're not going to let a little thing like vomit stop you."

At the use of the *V* word, Hale gags again. Logan steps deeper into the bathroom, until she's hovering over the piteous form of her teen frenemy. "You have to drink something. You're extremely dehydrated, and you're going to end up in the hospital if you don't."

"I'll just throw it up." Hale whines hopelessly. "I feel *awful*. I've never felt this awful before."

"Please," Logan begs. "Please drink."

Tears form in the corners of her eyes. "I-I just can't."

This is clearly about more than her heat exhaustion. Hale's anxiety is doing the talking again, which means pleading won't work. Logan thinks about Hale's brain, about that scared little girl, about how she used to help when it got like this. Then she puts down the grocery bag, pulls out her phone, opens Spotify, and presses play on an old favorite. The opening electronics fill the bathroom and Hale looks up at her with watery eyes and a confused mouth. "What—?" she starts, but the opening *hey, hey* clarifies all questions, and then Logan is doing the hand-mouth to the first "Bye Bye Bye."

"What's happening?" Hale asks, seemingly horrified by the pelvic thrusting. Logan is horrified too, both by the fact that she's not as limber as she used to be and by the fact that she's degrading herself to make Rosemary fucking Hale feel better.

They spent the entire summer after sixth grade watching MTV and memorizing the full routine to this song, filming their own music video on a camcorder in Logan's backyard, a boy band consisting of two girls. And for the rest of their friendship, without fail, nothing got Hale out of her head faster than watching Logan break out the old moves.

Except now, in this hotel bathroom, she just looks scared. And annoyed. "I have heat exhaustion! Why are you making things worse?"

Logan stomps her foot and punches her arm and does a body roll. "You know you love this."

The smallest smile cracks across Hale's chapped lips. "I really hate it."

But she clearly doesn't, and Logan commits to a full lip-sync for the second verse. Hale *almost* laughs. It turns into a belch, but Logan will take it.

"Okay, stop, stop!" Hale throws her hands up over her eyes when Logan goes for the crotch-grab and releases something that's distinctly chuckle-like in nature. "Fine, fine! I'll drink the Vitaminwater."

Logan is embarrassingly winded as she tosses Hale the drink. Hale lifts it to her dried lips and takes a cautious sip. Then, when she's certain it's not going to cause her stomach to explode again, she takes a full drink. "I can't believe you remember that dance."

Logan presses her back against the wall and slides down to the floor. "Don't lie. You totally still have the choreo memorized, too."

Her mouth curls into another smile, which she hides by taking a drink.

"Here. You need this." Logan hands her two Dramamine from a package she bought for thirty bucks, because national-park prices are criminal enterprises.

Hale obligingly takes the meds. "Why are you being so nice to me?" There's something about the sheer disbelief in Hale's tone that makes Logan feel sick to her stomach, too. "Last night, and . . . and now?"

"I have to be nice to you. You're absolutely wretched-looking."

"You know you love this." Hale attempts a little flourishing gesture at the dribble of puke down the front of her dress, and it's ridiculously charming.

Logan's stomach twists again. "And, well, because . . . I sort of feel like this is my fault."

"You gave me nausea from heat exhaustion?"

"I drove us to Arizona in June."

Hale takes another long drink. "Despite . . . all of this—" She gives another half-hearted flourish. "I don't regret coming here."

Logan stretches her legs out in front of her so her feet almost reach Hale's bare calves. "Wow. Your GI tract for the Grand Canyon."

Hale clicks her tongue in annoyance, but there's more life in her eyes now.

"Still. I'm sorry you got sick."

The bathroom goes quiet except for the hum of the fan. Hale is staring at her, motionless.

"What?"

"I-I don't think you have ever apologized to me before."

Logan snorts. "What would I need to apologize for?"

Even as she says it, she sees the long list of crimes against Rosemary Hale scroll through her mind. Those years in high school when she hurt Hale any chance she got, because it was easier than admitting how much she was hurting. Pranks on travel tournaments for Speech and Debate. The Fun-Noodle Incident that one summer they both took jobs as counselors at the same camp, before Logan drove Hale out of town for ten years.

And everything that's happened since she came back to Vista Summit: rude emails and tense department meetings and almost punching her in the face last winter when Joe convinced both of them to volunteer as Christmas elves at Evergreen Pines.

Rear-ending Hale's car.

Pushing her away because that is better than letting herself get close again.

Logan sighs. "I'm actually sorry for a lot of things," she confesses. Hale's expression softens and Logan holds up a preemptive finger. "Not for *all* the things. Some of them you deserved, but . . ."

Hale glances down at the half-empty plastic bottle in her hands and says nothing. Not *thank you*. Not *I'm sorry for the mean things I did too* or *I'm sorry I kissed you and then pretended like it never happened when we were fourteen*.

Finally, Hale opens her mouth. "Thank you for the . . . the Vitaminwater. I think it's helping."

Logan shakes off the disappointment. "Are you ready to try some saltines?"

Hale accepts the sleeve of crackers and nibbles at a single saltine like an adorably obnoxious squirrel.

"I do, you know," Hale says after she's gummed her way through three crackers. "Remember all the choreography."

Logan can't help but smile. "I know you, Hale."

Another saltine. Then: "Why do you hate me so much?" Hale asks in a small voice.

"Do you really want to go there?" Logan asks, sounding more tired than anything else. "Do you honestly want to rehash what happened at that pool party?"

Hale shakes her head. "I'm not asking why you hated me when we were fourteen. I'm asking why you hate me now."

A sarcastic answer gathers on her tongue, but for once, she holds it back. "Because—because you're so damn perfect."

Hale truly laughs then. "Perfect? You spend every minute of every day pointing out my flaws."

Logan adjusts herself against the wall. "That's because I'm insecure. Duh. You're so put together all the time, with your pantyhose and your heels and your tight skirts. Most of my clothes have bleach stains because I'm a thirty-two-year-old who doesn't know how to do her own laundry!"

Hale sits across the bathroom completely motionless, but Logan forces herself to keep going. Hale has been honest and earnest with her. She owes her this. "And you're so freaking brilliant, and your brain is like a flawlessly organized bullet journal, and you can just *do* executive functioning like a proper adult. Everything about you reminds me that I'm a total mess."

The fan hums in the tense silence that spreads between them until Hale finally speaks. "You're not a mess," she says quietly. "And I'm not all that put together. Hence the vomit." Hale flourishes again. "And you're not the only neurodivergent person in this bathroom. I also have ADHD, not that you've ever cared to notice."

Logan opens her mouth to argue, but she censors that impulse, too. She was wrong about Hale being straight. She's been wrong about a lot of things. "You have ADHD?"

Hale puckers her mouth indignantly. It's sort of cute. "I didn't get my diagnosis until a few years ago because I'm a woman, and because my ADHD doesn't look like restlessness or disorganization or blurting out. It looks like intense hyperfixations and overcompensating with perfectionism and poor emotional regulation."

"Oh" is all Logan manages to say.

"I'm medicated now, and in therapy, but before . . ." She stares down at the crackers in her lap. "It got sort of bad before."

Logan wants to push on this. She wants to force Hale to tell her everything, the way she used to do without prompting when they were kids. But she doesn't have that right, and Hale doesn't owe her anything.

"Do you want to talk about it . . . ?" she offers gently instead.

Hale shakes her head even as the words start coming out of her mouth. "Did I ever tell you my dad was an alcoholic?"

Logan's throat goes bone dry. "No. You didn't."

"Well, he was, at least for my whole life. It was how he self-medicated for his mental illness." Hale doesn't pause long enough for that revelation to fully sink in before she drops another bomb. "And I'm an alcoholic too."

Logan's brain spins its way through a catalogue of appropriate responses but gets stuck on slack-jawed silence.

Hale doesn't wait for her platitudes. "I started teaching English at an elite Manhattan prep school after I graduated from Columbia. The hours were grueling, the expectations were impossibly high, and the parents were vicious. But I was *good* at it. And my ADHD brain loves being good at things."

Hale smiles to herself, but there's something incredibly sad about it. "My brain likes to home in on one single thing to the detriment of everything else. Teaching became a hyperfixation for me. For three years I made it my whole life. I stopped going to therapy because I didn't have enough time, and I stopped feeding myself, stopped taking care of myself . . ."

She pauses for a moment. Logan can't stop staring at the clean soles of Hale's bare feet stretched in front of her. She thinks about those bare feet in the grass, running through sprinklers, kicked up on the front porch railing, burning on hot concrete as they walked home from getting ice cream at Rochelle's.

"And then I started drinking to cope with the impending burnout. I told myself that it didn't make me like my dad, that our situations were different, but I was lying to myself. I ended up losing too much weight for my body, and I had a nervous breakdown that landed me in the hospital," Hale finishes matter-of-factly. She crosses her legs at the ankle.

Those feet, in a twin bed next to Logan's.

"My mom paid for me to go to an in-patient clinic in central Oregon. That's where I got my ADHD diagnosis."

Logan briefly considers the way she sometimes dulls her own ADHD brain with alcohol.

"When I was healthy again, I learned about Joe's cancer and the job opening at Vista Summit, and I decided to just move back home. It seemed like the safest solution while I worked on staying sober and taking care of my mental health."

"Shit." Logan swallows around an unexpected lump of guilt and tries to think of something more meaningful to say.

Hale attempts a joke. "My brain does nothing in moderation."

Logan knows this. She always loved that about Hale's brain.

"See?" Hale smiles wanly. "I told you I'm not perfect."

Hale looks even *more* perfect to Logan in this moment, because for once she looks like a flawed human being. An uncontrollable deluge of emotions clog Logan's throat. It feels like heartburn but *worse*, because Tums can't cure her from caring about Hale. "I had no idea that's why you don't drink. That you . . . that you went through *that* right before moving home. And I—" Logan squeezes her eyes shut for a second. "I've been such an asshole to you."

"Aren't you always an asshole? Isn't that sort of . . . your thing now?"

"Ouch." She feels that one like a stab to the chest. A little over a week ago, Rhiannon Schaffer dumped her in an Applebee's and called her an apathetic asshole, and she refused to let it hurt her. But hearing it from Hale—from the girl who once knew her heart better than anyone—hits different. And it hits *hard*. Maybe because it feels more true. Even if Hale didn't have a mental health crisis and end up in rehab before starting at Vista Summit High School—even if Hale was the sanctimonious shithead Logan thought she was—she still didn't deserve the way Logan treated her. "True," Logan admits, "but rude."

"Sorry," Hale mumbles.

"No, it's—" she starts, before realizing she doesn't know what *it* is. "I don't really want to be an asshole anymore."

Hale lifts her head slowly so she's peering up at Logan through those ridiculously pale lashes. "You don't?"

Logan slides across the bathroom floor, and Hale quickly scrambles to pull her knees up to her chest before their bodies touch. "How about a friendship truce?" Logan sticks out her hand.

Hale eyes it warily. "A friendship truce?"

"Until Maine. I promise to try my hardest to be less of an asshole, if you promise to—"

"Be less rigid?" Hale rushes to fill in. "Less uptight? Less controlling? Less shrill?"

"You're not shrill, Hale. You're . . . passionate."

Her mouth puckers into a cat's butthole, and Logan can't help but laugh.

"And I was going to say, if you promise to be patient with me. And maybe call me out for my more rectally inclined behavior."

That almost makes Hale laugh. It sounds like just an indignant puff of air, but Logan knows. Her hand is still dangling in the space between them. Hale's frosty-blue eyes fix on that hand for a few seconds before she finally slips her small hand into Logan's. Her hand is clammy and gross, but they shake on it anyway. And Logan feels like maybe they managed to bridge something at the Grand Canyon.

The Grand Canyon to Somewhere East

Chapter Fourteen

ROSEMARY

"Come on, Hale! You can do it!"

"I-I can't."

"You can!" Joe cheers. "We believe in you! Throw it into the Grand Canyon!"

Odie barks three times in encouragement.

"What if . . . what if I've changed my mind?" Rosemary clutches the binder closer to her chest and glances out at the sun rising over the Desert View watchtower. "We . . . we can't *abandon the itinerary!*"

"Sure we can," Logan says breezily. "We're already two days and five hundred miles off course."

"*And I would drive five hundred miles and I would drive five hundred more,*" Joe sings in a Scottish brogue.

"And you said you wanted more detours," Logan reminds her.

A cool morning breeze ripples along Rosemary's bare arms, causing her skin to break out in goose bumps. Logan isn't wrong. She did, foolishly, say that. The surprise detour to Arizona was bad for their itinerary, but good in almost every other way. Except for the heat exhaustion.

The Vitaminwater and saltines helped a lot, but she still woke up the next morning feeling too nauseated to get back in the car. Logan insisted they take a rest day, which mostly consisted of lying around in the hotel room eating vending machine snacks and reading. Logan powered through multiple paperbacks. Joe slept a lot. Rosemary took several cold baths to help with the heat exhaustion and tried not to obsess over the feeling of Logan's hand in hers as they shook on their friendship truce.

And when Logan asked her if she would consider ditching the binder in favor of more spontaneous detours, she had said yes.

But now it's six in the morning, and they're saying goodbye to the Grand Canyon, and Rosemary isn't sure she can let go.

"I know you worked really hard on this binder," Logan says in her new, gentle, trying-not-to-be-an-asshole voice. "And I'm honestly in awe of your ability to craft a perfect travel itinerary."

Logan takes a cautious step closer to her. "How about this . . . ? You're still in charge of our daily schedule. You're good at planning stops for gas and meals and diaper changes—"

"Hey!" Joe interjects indignantly.

"And you'll have final approval over any and all detours. You just have to trust me a little. Can you do that?"

If Logan had asked for her trust a week ago, Rosemary would've laughed in her face, but now. She thinks about the Logan who tried to smooth her anxiety and the Logan who took care of her when she was sick. The Logan who apologized and owned her insecurities. The Logan who listened when she opened up about her dad and her mental health.

The Logan standing in front of her right now, trying to meet her halfway.

"I trust you," Rosemary says.

Logan's smile is wild and uncontained. "I knew she was still in there."

"Who?"

"The girl who carried around a list of places she wanted to see someday." Logan throws an arm around her shoulder. Rosemary takes in the view for a moment. The golden sweep of the Grand Canyon to the west, sun rising in the east, the pattern on Logan's tropical shirt. It's neon pink with yellow dinosaurs and orange palm trees, and it reminds her of the version of Logan who craved adventure, too.

"Fine!" Rosemary concedes. "We can throw out the itinerary for a few days. But then, it's the fastest route to Maine."

"Deal!"

"Maybe," Joe adds.

"Throw that thing into the Grand Canyon and let's roll!"

Rosemary takes a deep breath and holds the binder out in front of her. She turns toward the edge of the canyon.

"Whoa there!" Logan holds up both hands. "Throwing it into the Grand Canyon is a metaphor. This is a national park. You can't litter. Just stick the binder under your seat or something."

Joe hoots excitedly as they walk back to the van. Rosemary puts the binder under the passenger seat and Logan puts on her sunglasses with a smile. "Let's go see some cool shit."

• • •

They do see some cool shit.

Joe wants to see Mesa Verde National Park in Colorado, which is approximately a four-hour drive if they go straight there. But going straight there isn't the plan.

With Logan behind the wheel as they leave the national park, they pull over three more times on the side of the road to take photos of the gorgeous sunrise, then drive north to Horseshoe Bend to see a U-shaped red rock in the middle of aquamarine water.

They start to head east, and Logan asks to stop at every roadside attraction, because who doesn't want to see a giant stuffed buffalo? Rosemary agrees to most of the stops, and Logan buys her an iced coffee for her troubles.

They stop in the middle of nowhere to take a photo of real-life tumbleweed. They stop on the side of the road so Odie can bark at some majestic horses. They stop at a van with a cardboard stand that says, "Authentic Fry Bread $5."

Here, Rosemary protests. "We are not eating food served out of a sketchy van!"

"Trust me?" Logan pouts. In the sunlight, her hazel eyes look almost golden. She smiles, and Rosemary feels something lift in her chest. It's the same sensation she gets when airplanes take off: her own body, defying the laws of gravity.

And she does, so they do. It's the best fry bread she's ever tasted.

LOGAN

Hale is smiling at her from the passenger seat. They're basically crushing this whole friendship truce.

She rolls down the windows and watches Hale's braid get whipped around in the wind. Odie then climbs on top of Hale so he can stick his head out the window. "No, you dumb dog!" she squeals. "We're the same size! You can't sit on me!"

But he does sit on her, and eventually Hale stops fighting it. She even gives him the chin scritches he likes best. For the rest of the drive to Mesa Verde, Logan blasts her Gay Shit playlist, and Joe belts out every song, his face turned happily toward the fresh air.

"Come on, Hale. Sing with us!"

"I don't sing," Hale snaps. But then she starts bouncing her feet inside their heels, and Logan swears she hears her hum a little bit of Elton John.

• • •

It's dinnertime when they arrive in Cortez, Colorado, so they go straight to a hole-in-the-wall family Mexican restaurant with a small outdoor patio for Odie. It's the kind of place where the burritos are huge, and the margaritas are even huger.

As soon as they walk in the door, the hostess sees Joe and greets him in Spanish. Joe responds fluently, and it dawns on Logan that even though they've been in the diverse Southwest for a few days, this is the first time they've been somewhere that isn't predominantly white. Joe probably noticed this days ago. Hale, too.

Joe and the hostess chat amiably as she slowly guides them to the patio. As she sets down their menus, Logan catches the word *margarita* being tossed around in conversation.

Logan wants to order the biggest margarita to celebrate a successful day of detours, but she pauses when she notices Hale cautiously fingering the menu. She leans across the table so the waitress won't overhear. "Does it bother you?" she whispers. "When people drink alcohol around you?"

Hale looks perplexed by the question.

"I was going to order a marg, but I can abstain if that's easier for you," she clarifies. "Sober solidarity."

Hale's eyes go wide. "No one has ever asked me that before. But, uh, no. It doesn't bother me."

"Perfect! Then I'm getting the Muy Grande margarita. On the rocks, please."

Joe holds up two fingers to indicate he wants the same thing.

"It does bother me when Joe drinks." Hale raises her voice. "Because he knows it's against doctor's orders. It doesn't mix well with his meds!"

Logan adopts Joe's dramatic, pleading tone. "Rosemary, I'm dying whether I'm drunk or sober for it. Are you really going to deny a dying man this one small pleasure?"

"I don't sound like that." Joe frowns, and at the sight of his offended face wrinkles, Hale throws her head back and laughs, and Logan almost falls out of her chair in shock. It's a real laugh, one that shakes her shoulders and makes her blue eyes water in the corners—the kind of laugh that can only happen when you feel safe with the people around you. The thought makes Logan feel warm inside, even before she starts drinking her fishbowl-sized margarita.

"Joe . . . ?" Logan tries when he's halfway through his drink and tortas. "There's something I've been wondering . . ."

Joe's expression is soft and open. "Ask me anything," he invites with a huge margarita glass sloshing in his hand.

Logan leans forward. "Looking back at your life, do you have any regrets?"

She's not entirely sure where this question comes from, but in her happily buzzed state, she's suddenly desperate for an answer.

Joe burps. He's a true lightweight these days. "I try not to dwell on the past too much."

Logan pretends to study him through a monocle made up of her thumb and index finger. "Bullshit."

He burps again.

"You don't regret living in a crap town like Vista Summit for thirty years?" she presses.

"Or working sixty hours a week as a teacher?" Hale adds.

Joe contemplates this with a drunk man's seriousness. "I only have one regret in my life, and it's not teaching or living in Vista Summit."

Logan slams down her drink. "One regret! What is it?"

Joe tries to look dignified in his wheelchair at the head of the table, but the salsa on his chin diminishes the effect. "That's . . . personal."

Thankfully, Hale looks equally outraged by this evasiveness. "You never told us you have a regret! What is it?"

He shakes his head.

"I threw out the binder, and Logan is trying not to be an asshole," Rosemary argues like the debate champ she once was. "We're all making compromises here, Joe. Tell us!"

"I think I'll take this one to the grave, if it's okay with you."

"It's not okay with me!" Logan and Hale shout in perfect harmony. They turn to look at each other. And even though Hale is perfectly sober, she still bursts out laughing again.

They spend the rest of dinner speculating wildly about Joe's one regret. When they leave the restaurant, Logan feels warm and loose and floaty in a way that extends beyond the power of tequila.

The parking lot is dark as they walk to the Gay Mobile, and the sky above Colorado is speckled with stars. "The universe feels infinite tonight," she whispers as she looks up.

"Okay, no more margaritas for you," Hale teases. But for the first time in forever, Logan doesn't feel like she got drunk to outrun her busy brain. She feels at peace with her thoughts tonight.

Hale guides Logan into the passenger seat, helps Joe into the van, and drives them to Best Western, where the only available room has two queens. But when they get upstairs with all their things, Hale wordlessly puts her pillow on the bed next to Logan.

They share the bed, and Logan falls asleep to the sound of Hale's restless legs against the starchy sheets. Everything feels infinite tonight.

• • •

"Enough is enough!"

Hale glances up from where she's fiddling with the straps on her absurd gladiator-style wedges the next morning. "What?" she asks innocently, as if she's not performing bondage on her ankles.

"You cannot keep wearing heels in National Parks! I won't allow it!"

She scowls. "I don't recall you having any authority over what I wear."

"I'm seizing authority. This is a footwear coup." Logan stomps over to the two massive suitcases Hale packed and begins rummaging around for a different pair of shoes. "Shit biscuits, why did you pack so many pairs of heels?"

"Asshole violation!" Hale hops up from the bed and teeters over to her. "Please get your greasy sausage fingers off my things." She nudges Logan in the stomach with her elbow to shove her aside. "I like wearing heels!"

"Ew. Why?"

"Because I'm short, and when I don't wear heels, random strangers assume I'm a child." Hale bristles. "Besides, I like the way they look."

Logan considers this. "Okay, fair. But be honest. Were you comfortable wearing heels at the Grand Canyon?"

She makes her cat's asshole face before she finally admits. "No."

Logan continues rummaging through her things until she finally pulls out a pair of white sneakers that look like they've never been worn. "Ah-ha!"

Hale crosses her arms. "Those don't match my dress."

"Put them on." Logan insists, making the shoes tap dance in the air. "Put them on, put them on, put them on."

"Fine!" She snatches the shoes out of Logan's hands.

Hale spends the whole day in Mesa Verde three-inches shorter than normal and far more comfortable.

• • •

"What are you doing?" Hale asks after a long, sweaty day exploring the stunning Pueblo communities built into rocks.

"Taking my Adderall."

"But it's four in the afternoon . . ."

"I know, but I forgot to take it this morning, and if I don't take it now, I won't be able to go eat dinner or brush my teeth or follow very basic instructions."

Hale clicks her tongue. "Do you often forget to take your meds in the morning?"

"Hale, I often forget what I am doing when I am actively in the middle of doing it."

"You could put a reminder on your phone. That's what I do."

"Yeah, I've thought about trying that."

"Then why haven't you?"

"Because I have ADHD! Follow-through is not my jam."

The next morning, while Logan's loading their luggage back into the van, her phone chirps with an unfamiliar notification. She pulls it out of her pocket to find a push notification for a reminder on her lock screen. *TAKE YOUR MEDS, BOZO.*

"Why are you grinning at your phone like a dope?" Joe asks.

She shoves her phone back into her pocket. "Nothing. I wasn't. It was nothing."

Joe scrunches his face. "Was it porn?"

"Yes, Joe. I was watching porn at seven in the morning in front of my former English teacher while packing a car."

"Was it a text from a foxy lady?"

"Definitely not."

Hale emerges from around the corner of the hotel with Odie's leash in one hand and a full poop bag in the other. Today's dress is some pink, frilly disaster, but she's backlit by the early morning sun and the frills almost look like angel's wings.

"Whoever she is," Joe says in his wise and all-knowing voice, "be gentle with her."

Logan looks away from Hale's glow and reaches for her Adderall bottle. "There is no she."

• • •

"Okay, Joseph. Where to next?" Logan asks when the car is loaded and she's in the driver's seat, properly medicated and ready to take the first shift.

When her question is met with silence, she swivels in her seat to find Joe nervously pulling apart bits of a stale muffin from the continental breakfast. "Joe? What do you want to see next?"

"Bar Harbor?" Hale tries.

Joe throws the muffin at her.

"Don't hit me with cheap breakfast foods! I don't do spontaneous, and you hesitated!"

"I think we should go to . . . Santa Fe?" His voice lilts like this is a question.

"Are you sure?"

He looks like Hale the day she got heat exhaustion, but he nods slowly. "I'm . . . I'm sure."

Logan has never heard Joseph Delgado sound less sure of anything.

"Why Santa Fe?" Hale asks.

Joe stares out the window at the Best Western parking lot. "Because I've never been. And I . . . I should probably go." His tone is almost defeated.

Logan shoots Hale a look, but she shrugs in similar confusion. Hale's braid is looser today with a few strands already falling down around her face. Logan could easily tuck them behind Hale's ear if she wanted to.

She pushes on her sunglasses. "Then Santa Fe it is."

Cortez, Colorado to Santa Fe, New Mexico

Chapter Fifteen

LOGAN

The drive is breathtaking. She fell in love with red rocks in southern Utah, but heading south into New Mexico is even more beautiful somehow. It has never occurred to her that there were mountains in the desert, but these ones are even more magnificent than the ones back home. These craggy red mountains look molded out of sculpting clay and stretch their peaks up into an endless blue sky. There are trees—not as magnificent as the ones back home, but still—and they look lovely, dotted across the brown expanse of valley.

She drives, and the road seems to stretch out forever in front of her. The windows are down, and she's completely sober and still entirely free.

This is summer. This is what she needed. Wind in her hair and fresh air in her lungs and something new to look at. She keeps glancing over at Hale, whose braid is royally fucked now. Huge chunks of hair have fallen out in the wind, and they whip across her face. But Hale, being Hale, fights the wind, holding up her hands and batting away every rogue chunk of hair out of her face.

Hair keeps flying and Hale keeps fighting. Logan laughs wildly, and the sound drifts through the open window. "Just surrender to the chaos already!"

She makes a stubborn face, and in that expression, Logan sees the little girl who could never turn down a dare to jump off the tallest rock, to jump into the coldest lake. "Never!" Hale shouts. She cranks her window back up and manages to smooth her hair back down. "Driver's choice. What do you want to listen to?"

She smiles at Joe in the rearview mirror. "Let the dead man choose."

Joe has been weird all morning, sulking as they get closer and closer to Santa Fe. Hale stretches the extra-long aux cord into the back seat so Joe can plug in his phone. He cues up Van for the van. "Tupelo Honey."

Hale kicks off her heels and puts her feet up on the dashboard. Her toes jiggle in tune with the song. Logan swears she can hear her humming along.

She's as sweet as Tupelo Honey.

"Apt," Logan says to Joe in the rearview mirror.

Hale turns her head so Logan can see the smile on her pink lips. "Very apt."

"You can sing the song, you know," Logan tells her. "You don't have to just hum it."

Hale's smile falters. "I don't sing."

"We'll see about that."

ROSEMARY

For the last hour of the drive, Logan takes control of the music, and she oscillates between singing "Santa Fe" from *Rent* and "Santa Fe" from *Newsies*. At some point, Joe joins in, and Rosemary reaches for her AirPods.

"Come on, Hale," Logan goads. "Don't pretend like you don't know all the words." The 1992 film soundtrack version of "Santa Fe" starts playing, and Logan thrusts her hips against the seat belt like a young Christian Bale.

"Come on. Dance with me, Hale."

"I don't dance."

But she might if Logan asks again. Logan could always convince her to be brave, and with the wind whipping through her hair, she feels some of that recklessness. Rosemary feels fourteen years old again in the best kind of way.

Logan smirks. "We'll see about that."

• • •

Broadway show tunes promised them a Southwestern utopia, but when they pull into Santa Fe midday, it seems like nothing more than a medium-sized town with a very unified architectural theme in the middle of the New Mexico high desert. Even McDonald's is built in the Pueblo-style with brown adobe and smooth, rounded corners. After being in Mesa Verde, it seems . . . kitschy.

Logan follows signs to Old Town and parallel parks in front of a high-end shoe store. Old Town looks like an amalgamation of ritzy resort town and Disney's Frontierland, and everyone here is clearly an Instagram influencer. Women strut down the street lined with upscale boutiques in their boho chic dresses, gladiator sandals, and floppy hats.

"How do they all look so good?" Logan asks once they get out of the car. "It's tits-ass hot, and I've already got a rough case of swamp ass."

"What is swamp ass? Actually, no. Don't tell me."

She wrenches open the back door and sees Joe grimacing from where he's still strapped into his supine seat. "On second thought, I think I might just wait in the car. . . ." he grumbles.

"What are you talking about?" Logan throws up her arms. "You said you wanted to see Santa Fe!"

A sheen of sweat has broken out across Joe's forehead, and he dabs at it with his monogrammed handkerchief, the one with the wrong initials. *RSP.* "Yes, but I'm suddenly not feeling well."

Panic creeps into Rosemary's throat. "Do you have any chest pain? Brain fog? Numbness in your limbs?"

"Yes." Joe nods emphatically. "All of those things. Leave me behind."

Rosemary takes out the first aid kit and slides the pulse oximeter onto his finger, but his oxygen levels are fine.

"Bro." Logan shoves her sunglasses into her hair while Rosemary pulls out the blood pressure cuff. "You will die if you stay in the car. Right here and now. You can't leave dogs, babies, or melodramatic gay men in hot cars."

Joe swallows and his Adam's apple trembles ominously as he glares at Logan. "I don't . . . I can't do this."

"Do *what*?" Logan asks.

"Blood pressure is 96 over 52," Rosemary announces. "It's a little low, but—"

"We'll get him into the air-conditioning and get him some water," Logan says, pulling his wheelchair out of the car. "It looks like every other building in Santa Fe is an art gallery. Hopefully he'll start feeling better once he gets cooled down."

"No!" Joe fights it when they try to help him into the wheelchair. "No art galleries!"

Logan turns to Rosemary with a frustrated look on her face, but Rosemary hasn't the slightest idea what's going on, either.

"Okay," Logan concedes. "Let's sit down in a restaurant for a bit and get our bearings."

They find a lunch spot that accepts Odie's service dog status and order two Indian Tacos to share. After several glasses of water and some food, Joe looks less pale and sweaty, but his mouth is still twisted in an unhappy grimace. "Fine," he eventually says, "I guess we should go see some art galleries."

They pop into the nearest gallery after lunch, which is entirely photographs of the American Southwest printed onto glassware, and it doesn't seem to trigger any kind of emotional reaction in Joe. The next gallery is all paintings of the American Southwest on canvases the size of billboards, and the one after that features the American Southwest made entirely out of reclaimed wood. Joe keeps insisting they check out one more gallery, and Rosemary can't figure out why, which causes anxiety to begin fermenting in her chest.

After an hour, they pause on a bit of grass outside the basilica to give Odie some water and a break from his booties. The sun is oppressively hot, and Rosemary is starting to understand the meaning of swamp ass in a rather intimate way.

"Should we maybe . . . leave?" she tries. "Go find a hotel, or . . . ?"

"Heck no, techno!" Logan looks stubbornly confident despite the sizeable pit-stains on her pineapple shirt. "We don't leave until Joe says he's ready."

Joe makes several sounds of agony before he says, "Just a few more galleries. Let's head up Canyon Road."

They tiredly drag themselves past mud-brown luxury hotels, and giant parking garages meant to look like Pueblo dwellings, and row after row of cottonwood trees in bloom. Canyon Road is a narrow street composed almost entirely of galleries, metal and stone sculptures dotting the pedestrian pavilion. The short walk has them all damp with sweat, so they pop into the first gallery with a sign that reads, "Fur babies welcome, but all humans must be on a leash."

As soon as she steps into the Expatriate Gallery, a gust of air-conditioning hits Rosemary like a very pleasant semitruck, making every bare inch of skin erupt in goose bumps. She gasps with pleasure at the rippling cool, and Logan turns to shoot her a look, her perpetually parted mouth extra parted.

"What?" she asks, self-consciously patting down the sweaty baby hairs along her forehead.

Logan stares at her face for a beat too long before she finally tears away her gaze. "Nothing."

Then they're all distracted by the fact that Odie has devoured an entire bowl of complimentary dog treats by the door. "Sorry,"

Rosemary says to the gallerist who is glaring at the Pup-Peroni crumbs on Odie's snout.

The Expatriate Gallery seems to specialize in collections featuring artists from around the country, with landscapes of everything from Shenandoah to the Alaskan wilderness. It's a nice break from the inundation of local landscapes. Joe has stopped in front of a display labeled "The Gulf Coast," his hands frozen on the wheels of his chair, his eyes burning holes into a collection of paintings featuring pelicans, bayous at sunset, magnolias in bloom.

"These are lovely," Rosemary whispers as she comes to stand beside him. The paintings use color and texture in surprising ways, perspective often blurred, so you get the essence of a pelican instead of the actuality. There's some indefinable quality to the paintings that remind her of a Mary Oliver poem: sparse but resonate, an ode to nature.

"This collection is by a former local artist," the gallerist says in an accent that's vaguely European and distinctly fake. She looks like a gallery owner sent down from central casting. Big sunglasses pushed up into her flowing gray hair, a gauzy brown dress that sweeps the floor, bangles on both arms, a too-strong weed smell.

"His name is Remy St. Patin." She flourishes a bangled wrist toward the collection. "And these pieces are quite valuable."

"He . . . I mean, the artist . . . isn't local anymore?" Joe asks. His voice sounds distant even as his gaze is so firmly fixed on an impressionistic painting of two brown hands cupping the ocean as it escapes between the interlocking fingers.

The gallerist drops her gaze to Joe in the wheelchair, like she's noticing him for the first time. "You look very familiar. . . ." She studies Joe's sweaty face. "Have we met before?"

Joe shakes his head. "Probably not. This is my first time in Santa Fe. The artist . . . you said he used to be local?"

"He lived in Santa Fe for about a decade before he moved back to the Gulf Coast to take care of his aging parents," the gallerist explains. "He's a Black Creole artist who grew up in Mississippi."

Joe is still staring at the hands in that painting. "Joe . . ." Rosemary hedges. "Is this why you wanted to come to Santa Fe? Do you know this artist?"

Before Joe can answer, the gallerist snaps her fingers. "Yes! Of course! That's who you are!" She doesn't say another word but turns toward the register and beckons them to follow. They all do, a revived Odie leading the way. The owner disappears into the back and quickly emerges holding a frame wrapped in brown paper.

"St. Patin first emerged on the New York art scene in the early eighties, and we recently acquired a series of his early work. Mind you, they are nudes."

The gallerist carefully peels back the paper, untapping the Bubble Wrap beneath, until the painting is free. Joe seems to know which painting it is before she holds it up, because he suddenly covers his own eyes.

There, on a swath of canvas inside a gaudy frame, is a painting of a naked young man sprawled inside a bathtub, head leaning back against the porcelain edge, while his eyes remain fixed on the artist, staring at whoever is bold enough to look upon his nakedness.

Rosemary wishes she wasn't looking.

"Laura fucking Dern," Logan gasps.

"St. Patin did a series of paintings on this subject over the course of fifteen years." The gallerist points to the naked twentysomething in the painting. "Is this you?"

"Absolutely not!" Joe sputters.

But it absolutely is. There is something so distinctly *Joe* in those thick eyebrows and that tousled dark hair, Rosemary recognizes him instantly. The same single dimple in his left cheek, the same small birthmark just below his right ear. Broad shoulders and huge hands. He looks maybe twenty-five or so in the painting, his brown skin taut, his cheekbones high and proud, and his hair falling across his forehead in dark curls that look soft to the touch in the brush strokes.

Logan releases a low whistle. "Damn, Joe. You could fucking *get it*! You look like a flamboyant Oscar Isaac. And that is one glorious cock!"

"Logan!" Rosemary screeches. *Seeing* Joe's youthful penis is bad enough; they don't need to *discuss* it. "Please do not talk about his penis!"

"Please don't ever say the word *penis* again!"

Rosemary positions her body in front of the painting to block everyone's view. "Joe, did you know this painting of you existed?"

Joe looks like he might deny it's him again before his shoulders slump forward. "I consented to the artwork if that's what you mean. I knew these were out in the world somewhere."

"Can I please take a picture of this painting?" Logan already has her phone in position.

"Don't you dare!"

"Just one quick photo!" Logan begs.

Joe does a U-turn toward the exit. "Girls, we're leaving!"

Even Odie doesn't budge. Logan leans over the counter. "Out of curiosity, how much does the painting cost?" she asks in a low voice.

"We're listing it at fifteen hundred."

"That's a little more than I usually want to spend on porn. . . ." Logan winces and turns to Rosemary. "Wanna go halfsies?"

"It's not porn! It's art!" The gallerist clasps the painting to her chest. "It's a poignant play on the male gaze and a deconstruction of hypermasculinity and machismo!"

"Logan Maletis!" Joe says in his Teacher Voice. "Rosemary Hale! We're leaving! Now!"

Like scolded children, they promptly follow him out of the gallery, leaving behind the confused gallerist and the memento of a different Joe Delgado.

Chapter Sixteen

LOGAN

She can't believe she just stared down the barrel of Joe Delgado's giant dick and now he's outrunning her in a wheelchair through the streets of Santa Fe.

"Joe, wait! Let's talk about this!"

"There is no way we are ever talking about this. *Ever!*"

"But Joe!" Hale calls out. "This is clearly important!"

"It absolutely is *not*," he says gruffly. He's out of breath from hauling his dying ass away from his naked ass. "I just want to go back to the hotel."

"We just stumbled upon a naked painting of you from the eighties in New Mexico!" Logan huffs. "We should talk about it, Joe!"

"I don't want to talk about it." He reaches for his handkerchief again and frantically dabs his brow. Logan notices the letters stitched in purple thread for the first time. RSP. *Remy St. Patin.*

She looks at Hale, and it's clear she's made the connection too. "Is Remy St. Patin . . . someone from your past . . . ? A boyfriend, or . . . ?" Hale treads carefully over the words, but it's not careful enough.

"I said I don't want to talk about him!" Joe snaps. "Drop it! Please, girls."

"Come on, Joe," Logan coaxes, "we're on this death trip together, and if you have some long-lost love—"

"Logan, for once in your life, consider someone else's feelings and stop talking!"

Those cruel words decimate every ounce of feigned apathy Logan has, making her feel small and silly, the way her other teachers always had. The way her mom had, before she left. They all stand in awkward silence for a moment, sweating profusely on a Santa Fe sidewalk. "I know you have an incredible dick," Logan says as flippantly as she can, "but that doesn't mean you need to *be* a dick."

• • •

"I don't need help getting into bed tonight," Joe snaps once they've checked into their hotel and arrived at their adjoining rooms.

Logan makes a show of checking the time on her phone. "First of all, it's seven o'clock. And second, don't be a stubborn asshole. Of course you need our help."

"Not tonight," Joe mutters as he wheels himself over the transition strip between the room with two queen beds and his king-bed suite. The wheels keep getting stuck, but he keeps turning them with his wrinkled hands, unable to get himself over the hump. "Tonight, I just need to be alone."

"Fine." Logan throws her duffel violently onto her bed. "Have fun changing your own diaper."

Hale watches Joe struggle for another ten seconds before she loses her patience. She grabs the handles on his wheelchair and guides him into his room.

"I said I didn't need help!"

Hale pulls away her hands like the chair burned her. "You're right. I'm sorry. Will you please use the baby monitor tonight? Or keep your phone next to you so you can call if you need anything? And please don't try to walk on your broken foot. If you have another fall—"

"Enough, Rosemary!" Joe won't even look back at her. "Odie, come boy."

Odie lowers his head and glances at Hale, like he's asking her permission before he slinks into the king room with his angry owner.

"I hope he gets diaper rash," Logan grunts, tossing a pillow at the now-closed door between their rooms.

Hale pulls out a Tupperware of baby carrots from the cooler and begins taking the world's tiniest bites, like a bunny with generalized anxiety disorder. "I shouldn't have pushed him on Remy," Hale says, more to herself than Logan. "He said he didn't want to talk about it, and I shouldn't have pushed him."

Hale munches nervously and stares at a stain on the carpet. It's classic Hale, assuming she screwed up instead of realizing the other person is just being an ass.

"Don't do that," Logan says gently.

Hale looks away from the stain and blinks up at her. "Do what?"

"Don't burrow into your little self-blame hole. You didn't say or do anything wrong."

She keeps blinking, and Logan keeps fumbling her way through this attempt at friendship. "Joe was in the wrong, okay? Not you. You . . . you were great today."

She's overwhelmed by the urge to comfort Hale, to hug her or hold her close. She walks over to the bed where Hale is sitting and punches her in the arm like they're bros instead.

Logan grabs a hotel key and sticks it in her pocket. "Come on, Hale."

"Where are we going?"

"Anywhere but here."

She knows they can't actually leave Joe alone, but she also knows she can't sit around in another generic hotel room bedecked with tacky Southwestern art all night.

"First stop: the vending machines. Because carrots are not dinner." She snatches the Tupperware of carrots out of Hale's hands. "Second stop: the rooftop."

"The hotel rooftop? Are we allowed up there?"

"Definitely not. But how else are we going to see the sunset?"

• • •

This sunset is fucking bullshit.

Where does Santa Fe get *off*, having a sunset this magical? And when Logan is in such a profoundly crappy mood, too. "Can you believe this shit?"

Hale cradles her surprisingly robust collection of vending machine snacks. "I'm confused by your tone right now. . . ."

The roof of the hotel is clearly a popular hangout among the staff. They find a ratty couch facing the west side of the building, a few blankets, and a pile of cigarette buds inside an orange Home Depot bucket. The view is of the hotel parking lot, but it doesn't even matter, because she's looking up.

The sunset hasn't even properly started yet, and it's already gorgeous. In the distance, the mountains are silhouetted like charcoal drawings, the clouds painted periwinkle except for the fringe of yellow along the horizon. Logan throws herself down onto the couch and angrily opens a bag of Doritos. "Honestly, fuck this sunset. I can already tell it's going to ruin all other sunsets for me."

Hale lowers herself down beside Logan and dumps her snacks between them. "And you're . . . mad . . . about how beautiful the sunset is going to be?" she asks cautiously. As if Logan is another volatile landmine she has to tiptoe around tonight.

Logan sits up straighter on the couch and unsnarls her face as best she can. "It's not really about the sunset, and I'm not mad. Just kind of . . . hurt, I guess. By Joe's dickishness."

Hale relaxes into the couch a bit more. "He shouldn't have said that thing about you not caring about others."

"But I don't care, right? Isn't that all part of my assholish charm?"

Hale opens her Twix bar, and without a word, she offers half to Logan. Equally silent, Logan takes one of the Twix sticks. All those summer afternoons when they walked to the 7-Eleven, taking their Slurpees and candy back to the tire swing in Logan's front yard. Hale always shared half of her Twix.

"You care, Logan," Hale finally says. "You just don't want other people to know about it."

The cold desert evening creeps in around them, and Logan's skin prickles. It's been a long time since anyone but Joe made her feel so uncomfortably seen.

"Can you believe the sheer enormity of Joe's unwrinkled dick?" she says to break the silence.

Hale covers her face with both hands and groans. "Please, can we never discuss Joe's genitalia ever again?"

"It's the only thing I want to discuss from here to New England."

Hale peeks at her through her fingers. "You noticed the handkerchief too, right? The one he always carries around? The initials on it? Do you think that maybe Remy is Joe's one regret?"

"Maybe." Logan's throat feels strangely dry, and she cracks open her can of Sprite. In front of them, the sun sinks lower, and the sky explodes. Electric yellow at the horizon, then flames of gold, burnt orange, and bright pink lick the bottoms of the clouds. Everything burns radiantly.

"Do you have any major regrets?" Hale asks, so plainly, it takes Logan a second to arrive at the safest answer.

"Me? Are you kidding? I say at least ten regrettable things *a day*."

Hale tucks her legs beneath her and angles her body toward Logan's on the couch. "I mean, *real* regrets. Remy-level regrets."

She swallows another sip of Sprite. "My twenties are basically an orgy of regrets," she says, because she can't tell her the truth. That most of her regrets in life are about Rosemary Hale.

Logan regrets kissing her in that garden and giving away that small sliver of her true heart.

She regrets not kissing her sooner.

She regrets being so damn petty when Hale kissed Jake. She

regrets not telling her how she really felt. She regrets letting their friendship disintegrate over something as meaningless as a middle school kiss. She regrets that the kiss wasn't meaningless at all, at least not to her.

She regrets all the things she did in high school to stretch the chasm between them, and all the things she's done since Hale moved back.

But even with the friendship truce and the newfound closeness between them, Logan can't say any of these regrets out loud. It might . . . *change* things between them on the trip.

Or worse, it might change nothing at all.

"Okay, do you want to know what I regret, for realsies?"

Hale nods solemnly. "For realsies."

"I regret never leaving Vista Summit." Logan exhales and lets her confession float in the desert air between them. It sounds silly when she says it out loud, but it feels so heavy inside her all the time.

Hale stares out at the swirling sky, and Logan wonders if they're both thinking about all the summer sunsets they watched from her front porch. "Why didn't you leave?"

"I don't know," she lies. "A million reasons, but mostly . . . mostly because of my dad."

Hale turns so she can look at Logan fully. "Your dad?"

"You know how it was back then. He was wrecked when my mom left, heartbroken. For years after, he missed her. And I'm the only person he has! If I left him, I don't know . . . it feels like if I left it would mean . . . that I'm like *her*."

Logan takes another gulp of her soda to stop these humiliating confessions from pouring out. Hale always had this quiet understanding about her that made Logan spill her darkest secrets. "You know, I've never actually admitted that to anyone before."

Hale clicks her tongue to the roof of her mouth. "Really?" she asks. "Not even to your therapist? Because it seems like an obvious

byproduct of your attachment issues caused by your mother's abandonment."

Logan laughs. "Do I seem well-adjusted enough to have a therapist?"

"You should really get a therapist." Hale chews on her bottom lip.

"Oh, just say it!"

"Say what?"

"Whatever it is you want to say!" Logan throws a Dorito at her.

"I think your dad would be really sad to know that you aren't
living the life you want, to protect him."

Logan remembers her dad in the kitchen two weeks ago, practically begging her to go on this trip. "I don't even know what kind of
life I want to live," Logan grumbles.

Hale turns to look out at the sun as it spreads its colors like lava
across the sky. "I think that's my biggest regret," she says quietly.
Logan almost misses it over the sound of her own Dorito crunching.
"Not living the life I wanted. I regret that I stopped writing."

When Hale doesn't offer any further details, Logan treads carefully. "Why did you stop writing?"

"Writing isn't exactly a safe, stable career path."

"But you were *so good* at it!" she says with a little too much enthusiasm.

Hale used to conjure fantastical stories out of thin air like a
magic trick. She'd pick up a pencil and words would pour out of
her—stories about adventures and quests and romance. Stories they
would sometimes write together, a single pencil they passed back
and forth; stories Hale would read aloud by flashlight late at night
in excited whispers. It always felt like she was building a secret world
just for the two of them.

She shakes her head. "Being good at it doesn't matter. Plenty of
talented fiction writers never get published. And many writers who
do get published still have to work a day job. So, I switched my

major to education so I would always have a secure day job. And don't get me wrong"—she holds out a defensive hand and there's a smudge of chocolate on the pad of her index finger—"I love being a teacher. I love my students, I love creating an inclusive curriculum, and I love that I'm always learning. I don't regret teaching. But . . ."

"But teaching requires all of you," Logan fills in. "And it doesn't leave much time or energy to write an entire novel."

Especially not the way Hale approaches teaching. Hale cares too damn much. She strops around in her high heels and argues at staff meetings because she cares. She gets to work before everyone else and carries around papers to grade because she cares *so damn much*. Some of it is perfectionism, sure, but most of it is just Hale never learning how not to care. And unlike Logan, she never hides it, never fakes indifference or disguises her passions. She's impossibly brave. Always has been.

"No," Hale sighs. "It doesn't."

Logan thinks it's probably more than that. Hale always loved the self-contained desks and the bells and the rigidity of school. School was the place where she felt the most confident, the most comfortable with herself. Teaching seems like a perfect way to live in that safe routine bubble for as long as possible.

But writing . . . writing is chaos. It's creative and it's messy and it's uncertain. All things Hale hates.

"Though I guess now I have nothing but time. . . ." Hale says darkly down to her snack foods.

"What do you mean?"

"I—I got laid off."

"Wait, you *what*?"

Hale sits very still beside her as she factually recounts the story: "They're hoping to rehire me in the fall, but you know Vista Summit has never approved an education levy, so I don't know where the budget would come from, which means I'm currently unemployed."

Logan tries to think of an appropriate response, but draws a blank. Hale got *laid off*. No wonder she showed up at Logan's house with a giant binder, and no wonder her anxiety has been running amok all trip.

Logan tries to imagine school in the fall: no Hale sulking in the hallways, no Hale to torment at staff meetings, no Hale in the teacher's lounge or at the photocopier, her car always the last one in the parking lot each afternoon. Hale cut off from the thing she cares about most.

"Technically speaking, you already did it," Hale says, and Logan has no idea what she's talking about.

"I already did what?"

The sky burns for another minute before the sun vanishes completely, muting the palate to pretty pastels. The pastels project themselves onto Hale's pale hair. She looks like a living rainbow. "You already left Vista Summit," she says. "You left to go on this trip. You're away from your dad right now."

Logan snorts dismissively. "Yeah, but I call him every night while you're in the shower."

Hale cocks her head to the side like she's studying an inscrutable work of art in one of the galleries. "You do?"

"Yeah, just to check in and make sure he's okay."

Hale's neck looks like it's about to snap in half. She stares at Logan, and stares and stares. Then, she straightens and says, "I haven't called my mom once since we left."

That doesn't surprise Logan. She remembers all the nights Hale ate dinner at her house in middle school because her mom was always at work.

Hale shakes her head a few more times. "And you could never be like your mom, by the way." She says this like it's a plain, objective statement of fact, an incontrovertible truth. There's something about the quiet confidence of those words that takes root inside Logan's heart, like a gentle voice telling her it's not too late. She's not dying, and there's still time to live without regret.

Hale shivers and rubs her hands up and down her bare arms. "It's cold in the desert when the sun goes down."

"Here." Logan reaches for one of the blankets and attempts to drape it over Hale's exposed shoulders.

"Gross! I don't want some stranger's blanket touching my body!" she shrieks in protest, but she still allows Logan to wrap her up like a burrito in a southwest-patterned blanket that smells of weed. Logan wraps herself in it, too. A burrito made for two.

"Live dangerously, Rosemary. You're on an adventure."

"Ha!" Hale's hand bursts out of the blanket burrito so she can point a finger right in Logan's face. "You called me Rosemary."

Logan shoves her finger away. "No I didn't."

"You did!" She pushes herself up on her tucked legs so she's even closer to Logan, and they were already so close. *Too close.* Their bodies facing each other inside their snug burrito. Hale is two inches away, smelling like vanilla and peppermint and vending machine Cheez-Its. Her pale lashes and her pale cheeks, which have pinkened from the sun. Exactly four freckles have appeared beneath her right eye, and Logan's close enough that she could trace a route between them.

A route to a destination they can never reach.

"I knew you would slip up eventually!" Hale says smugly.

Logan stops staring at those freckles. "I did not slip up."

"You did. I have proof."

"Are you recording this conversation?"

Hale looks self-satisfied as she taps a finger to her temple. "The proof is up here. I know what I heard. Rose-mar-y." She stretches out the three syllables of her own name like a song. "You haven't called me that in years."

"Have you been keeping track?"

"Yes." Hale's smile shines prettily in the purple dusk. "I've missed hearing you say my name."

Logan swallows. She feels the way she did in Cortez, when the stars looked infinite and her chest felt looser than it had in years.

I've missed hearing you say my name. Leave it to Hale to say something so damn earnest.

Hale was always the earnest one when they were kids. While other people's brains told them to lie out of self-preservation, Hale's brain didn't have that protective hardwiring. She usually told the truth, even if it was too honest. So, it makes sense that they're touching knees and elbows inside a blanket, and Hale says something as ridiculously sweet as *I've missed hearing you say my name.*

Hale probably has no idea how that simple admission makes Logan feel.

Hell, Logan doesn't know how it makes her feel, except that she feels like her heart is a stupid dandelion puff about to float away in a dozen pieces. And she feels warm (probably from the blanket). And she feels like she's buzzing (probably from eating candy for dinner). And she feels like . . . like she could kiss Hale if she wanted to.

She doesn't want to kiss her, though. Instead, she twists her head so her mouth is directed toward Hale's left ear, and she says her name again in a quiet voice. *Rosemary.* She savors each delicious syllable on her tongue, and Hale inhales sharply. They're so close, and Hale would probably taste like Twix if she kissed her right now.

She thinks, maybe, Hale wants her to.

Hale tilts her head, and all Logan would have to do is lean in a fraction of an inch to take that pretty mouth in hers. One of them is breathing heavily, but Logan can't tell who. Maybe they're both breathing heavily, in unison, as Logan leans in and—

"Joe," Hale says, ducking her head out of what maybe (*definitely*) would have been a kiss. "We should really go check on Joe."

Logan yanks her head back, and the blanket loosens around both of their shoulders. Then Hale steps out of the blanket burrito entirely. Her bare skin looks pale and freezing, but she stands there like she can feel nothing at all. "I'm worried he's going to stubbornly try to sleep in his wheelchair when he realizes he can't get himself into bed," she blathers as she picks up their snack wrappers. "Don't you think we should go?"

"Totally." Logan clears her throat. "You're totally right. Let's go check on Joe."

A twinge of hurt tugs on her rib cage, but she shakes it off. She's not hurt. She's *grateful*.

Kissing Rosemary Hale would be the worst impulsive decision she's ever made twice.

Chapter Seventeen

LOGAN

Joe looks like death.

When Logan goes into his hotel room a little before seven in the morning, she finds him wide awake, lying completely still in the dark with his arms folded across his chest like a vampire in his coffin. She clicks on the light.

In the four years since his cancer diagnosis, this is the worst he's ever looked. Seeing him there in corpse-pose sends a spike of dread straight to her gut. He's dying, a voice intones in the back of her mind. This time, he's really dying.

She shakes off the voice and the dread. "You dead?" she asks flippantly.

"Only emotionally," Joe croaks.

She squats on the edge of his mattress and Odie bounces up from his spot at Joe's feet to enthusiastically lick her face. "Cause of emotional death?"

Joe tilts his head to look up at her. "Impossible to identify a single cause. There's the humiliation of knowing you girls saw my dick—"

"You know we change your diapers, right?"

"And then there is the deep regret over the way I reacted. The shame over how I spoke to you last night. . . . Logan, I didn't mean what I said, please believe me."

"I do. As a semiprofessional asshole, your little temper tantrum was farm league."

Joe blinks back unmistakable tears and reaches for his handkerchief. "I'm sorry, Logan."

He sounds beyond dejected. If she had to guess, she would say Joe didn't get any sleep last night, that he laid here thinking about Remy St. Patin and the painting and his guilt.

She is pretty sure no one slept last night. Hale audibly tossed and turned for hours until she finally surrendered, pulled out a notebook, and sat at the small hotel desk scribbling something by the glow of her phone.

Logan tried to breathe rhythmically like she was asleep while she was kept awake by her own cocktail of embarrassment, regret, and shame.

She almost kissed Hale last night.

Worse, she had thought Hale wanted to kiss her back.

And isn't that just a classic Logan move? Things are going well with Hale, so why not self-sabotage by kissing her?

She wishes she could tell Joe about the almost-kiss on the roof. He would call her a fuckboy, and they would laugh about her horrible life choices, and the almost-kiss would become funny instead of vaguely tragic.

But she can't talk to Joe about Hale, because Hale is currently walking into the room in a sheer, light pink sundress that makes Logan want to scream. Odie leaps off the bed when he sees her and jumps up so his paws are on her shoulders like he's trying to hug her.

At least Odie appears well rested.

"How are you feeling this morning?" Hale asks, hesitantly approaching the bed.

"I'm feeling very sorry, Rosie dear," Joe answers. "For myself, but especially about how I acted toward you. I was an asshole."

"No you weren't," Hale tries to reassure him.

"I was. Please forgive me?"

"Of course."

He breathes a sigh of relief. "Thank you, darling. And . . . And I think you were right. We should get this trip back on track. Take the direct route to Bar Harbor."

"Joe—" Logan starts, but he silences her with one pitiful look.

"I don't know what I was thinking, trying to extend the trip and make up for lost time. We should just . . ." He inhales sharply, then coughs twice into his handkerchief. "We should go straight to Maine."

Hale glances up from her side of the bed and meets Logan's gaze. She's all pale lashes and uncertainty. "If you're sure that's what you want, Joe . . ."

She's sure Hale is thinking the same things Logan is.

What about Remy St. Patin?

What about the painting? The handkerchief? The one regret?

And do they really want the trip to be over in four days? Does Logan really want to go back to Vista Summit and how things used to be with Hale? Will Hale even stay in Vista Summit if she doesn't work there anymore?

Logan isn't sure she can handle Hale driving away again.

"I'm sure," Joe says. "This is what I want."

Hale puts a hand on his shoulder. Her nail polish perfectly matches her dress. And her pale lips. And the soft pink of her cheeks.

"Okay, Joe." Hale squeezes his shoulder. "But do you think we could make one last detour before Maine?"

He opens his mouth to protest, but Hale cuts in.

"Come on, Joe. Trust me."

• • •

Breaking Bad lied to her.

Albuquerque, New Mexico, isn't a shithole. She thinks it's even prettier than Santa Fe. It has a quaint Spanish-influenced Old Town and beautiful tree-lined streets and staggering mountains every direction she looks. Logan is happy they get to see one more wonderful place before they spend the next several days driving on gray freeways.

Even though Albuquerque is technically west of Santa Fe, Hale convinces Joe to make a stop at something called Petroglyph National Monument using her favorite weapon, other than condescending tongue clicks: logic.

"It only adds an hour to our drive-time, and there's a great spot for us to get breakfast after. It's part of the Indian Pueblo Cultural Center, and they have authentic Pueblo dishes."

Joe can never resist good food, and he seems more willing to go along with the plan since it's Hale who's making it. Hale drives them to the Petroglyph Visitor's Center located in the suburbs just outside the main part of the city. It's not even nine yet, but they're hoping to beat the heat. Logan catches bits of Hale's impromptu lecture on the subject—one of the largest petroglyph sites in North America, hundreds of years old, of spiritual significance to the Indigenous people of the region. But mostly, Logan stares at Hale's mouth without hearing the words and wonders how Hale can act like the almost-kiss never happened.

But—Logan reminds herself—that's exactly what Hale did with their first kiss.

"I can take Odie for a walk to use the bathroom if you two want to go inside to get a trail map," Hale suggests, and before Logan can agree, she's bounding off with the dog and leaving Logan to get Joe out of the car.

He insists on wheeling himself up the paved path, even though he's already breathless and sweaty. "So?" he huffs, taking a break ten seconds into the journey. "Do you want to tell me what's going on with you and Rosemary this morning?"

"Do you want to tell me what went on between you and Remy St. Patin forty years ago?"

Joe narrows his eyes like he's cutting through her bullshit with a single gaze.

"Do . . . I mean . . . do things seem weird this morning? Between us?"

"I've never seen Rosemary volunteer to be on Odie poop duty before. . . ."

Logan kicks the toe of her Vans against a crack in the concrete. "I almost kissed Hale last night."

"Hot diggity dog!" Joe blurts with more enthusiasm than she thought he was capable of this morning. He holds up his hand like she's going to high-five him over it.

"No, not hot diggity dog. The dog is very tepid. Hale dodged the kiss."

Joe huffs, then continues his way up the path. "But you wanted to kiss her?"

"I don't know! It's all very confusing! Because I hate her, right? Except I also don't? And also, she's gay now, or was always gay, and she puked and wore sneakers and put a reminder in my phone, and now I feel like I'm back in middle school, desperate to find any excuse to touch her, analyzing every lingering glance, every word," she blathers on uselessly.

Megan fucking Rapinoe, being in love with her middle school best friend had been utter hell. She hadn't known it back then, obviously. They lived in a small town, and she had no framework to understand her confusing feelings for Rosemary. But then she kissed her during a game of Spin the Bottle, and all she could think about after was kissing her again.

And then Rosemary had kissed Jake McCandie right after their kiss in the garden, and the three years of confusing feelings suddenly made sense. She'd had a huge, fat crush on Rosemary.

Joe pauses on the path again. They've only made it halfway to the visitor's center. "Would it really have been such a terrible thing if you *had* kissed Rosemary?"

"Yes, because I will end up hurting her, or she will end up hurting me. Either way, kissing Rosemary ends in hurt."

Joe adjusts his wheelchair so he's facing out at the desert. The path is lined with indigenous plants and their adjoining plaques. He gestures to the closest one. "Did you know the prickly pear is my favorite plant? For parts of the year, it looks like any other cactus, but when it blooms—"

"I'm going to stop you right there. If this is the beginning of some metaphor that compares my sexuality to a blooming cactus, I will punch you in the tit."

Joe ignores her threat. "This one—the *Oputina ployacantha*— has sharp glochid, and if you get too close, it will poke you something fierce."

"*Glochid* is maybe the grossest word I've ever heard."

"But then the flowers appear after the summer rains"—he flourishes his hand toward the pink flowers—"and they transform into something achingly beautiful. And the flowers even taste sweet. Painful and lovely at the same time."

"Am I supposed to be the prickly pear?" she snaps. "Is Rosemary? Your metaphors are usually better than this, old man."

Joe reaches out, almost as if he could touch the prickly pear if it wasn't on the other side of a small fence. "Life is the prickly pear. It's always going to be a combination of beauty and hurt, no matter how hard you try to protect yourself from the hard parts. There is no way to avoid pain."

Logan stares at the pink blossoms flourishing in the heat. "I don't understand that metaphor at all," she lies.

"Hmmm . . ." Joe grumbles. "Well, I can't help but notice you started calling her *Rosemary*."

"She's been doing that accidentally!" Hale pops up beside them without warning, like a sunburned Jack-in-the-box. She's smiling, and she turns to look at the nearby plants.

"*Oputina polyacantha*," she says without even reading the little plaque beneath the cactus. "I love prickly pears."

ROSEMARY

She's on a trail in the desert, surrounded by hundreds of petroglyphs, and she can't even enjoy the rich history because of legs.

Specifically, Logan's legs. Peeking out beneath the hem of her overalls. Ten miles long, lean calves, bruises on her knees. Those legs brushing against Odie's black fur as Logan holds the leash.

Those legs pressed against hers under a blanket on a rooftop. The heat of them.

Rosemary squeezes her eyes closed. She almost kissed Logan last night.

Kissed.

Logan.

She can't remember the last time she kissed someone. Hell, she can't remember the last time she *wanted* to kiss someone, but on that rooftop, she wanted it so badly, it climbed into her throat like thirst. So, she almost did it.

How ridiculously unsafe that would have been.

But the shocking thing is how entirely safe she felt in that moment. They had talked the way they used to—honestly and openly, exchanging secret hopes and fears—and then Logan had wrapped them both up in a single blanket, so close they could share body heat and breath. Logan called her *Rosemary*, and it felt like someone yanked open a file cabinet in the very back of her heart and everything came spilling out.

Logan leaned in close, and Rosemary could've kissed her.

But if she had, there would've been no closing that file cabinet again. Her heart didn't do anything in moderation, either.

So, she swerved. Saved them both.

"This is hella cool." Logan points to an engraving of the sun knife on a rock, white against the dark stone. "These hieroglyphs are some cool shit."

"Petroglyphs," Rosemary corrects. The morning has turned muggy with purple and gray clouds on the horizon. Rosemary is sweating behind her knees, but that might have more to do with the crop top Logan is wearing under her overalls.

"Storytelling never ceases to amaze in all its forms," Joe says. Then he clutches his chest.

Logan laughs. "*Such* a melodramatic queen."

But Joe is still clutching his chest, and his mouth is twisted in a grimace of pain, and Logan stops laughing. "Joe?"

"I—" He tries to take a breath, but it's shallow and sharp. "I-I don't feel—" He tries and tries to catch his breath. Rosemary drops to her knees in front of him in the desert.

"What do you need?"

"It's hot out here," Logan says. "Maybe he just needs some water?"

Rosemary has Joe's water bottle out of the basket attached to the wheelchair before Logan finishes her sentence. Joe attempts to drink out of the bendy straw, but most of the water dribbles down his chin.

"Logan!" Rosemary clutches her own chest, trying to subdue the rising panic there. "I think there might be something seriously wrong."

"I'm sure he's okay. Let's try to calm down . . ."

She can't calm down because Joe keeps wheezing. Odysseus starts whining, and don't dogs have a sixth sense for when their owners are in trouble? "Joe! Please say something!"

"M-my . . . chest . . . It hurts . . . when I try to breathe . . ."

"We should call an ambulance!"

Logan doesn't argue. In a flurry of half-numb hands, Rosemary tries to find her phone. Her fingers feel disconnected from her body as she dials 911.

. . .

The wait for the ambulance is the longest fifteen minutes of her entire life. They manage to get Joe back to the parking lot before the paramedics arrive, and then they're both in the Gay Mobile, Logan behind the wheel, following the ambulance through Albuquerque.

Google Maps says the University of New Mexico hospital is eighteen minutes away, but they get there in ten, pulling up in front of the ER. They both jump out of the car to watch Joe get wheeled inside on a gurney. A nurse gives them directions.

"Only one of us can go into triage with him," Rosemary tells Logan.

"You should be the one to go," Logan says with a flippant shrug. "I know he's going to be okay."

Rosemary wants to shake Logan. She wants to scream at her. *You care. I know you care.*

Please, please, show me you care.

But instead she simply turns away from her old friend and hurries into the emergency room behind Joe.

Chapter Eighteen

ROSEMARY

"Gas."

Rosemary is beyond her emotional capacity from three hours in the UNM emergency room—and then another hour sitting in a waiting room after they transferred him upstairs—and she's certain that's why she has misheard the doctor.

"Excuse me?"

"Joe isn't having a heart attack," the young Indigenous doctor tells them. "He just had gas."

Logan snorts into her strawberry milkshake. "Gas?"

"Yep! Something he ate clearly didn't sit with him, and he got heartburn and gas pain. But we gave him some simethicone and a laxative, and he was able to have a bowel movement, so he should be right as rain."

Rosemary fixates on the doctor's gold name tag. "Sonny Summers," it says. Like all the name tags at UNM, it lists the doctor's pronouns and tribal affiliation below that. "They/Them. Acoma Pueblo."

She's not sure what comfort she's hoping to find in those etched letters, but she stares and stares until the words finally come. "That . . . this can't just be gas."

Dr. Summers frowns. "This is good news. Your dad is going to be fine. But given the aggressive nature of his cancer, we want to keep him overnight for observation, just to be safe."

"He's not our dad," Logan says after another slurp of her shake. Rosemary is confronted by the indifferent expression on Logan's face.

The doctor nods, even though they're clearly confused about the dynamics between these three people. "I was surprised to hear Joseph is on a road trip, given the severity of his condition. We found calcium deposits in his lungs, and I'm not sure further travel is what's best for him."

"It's not," Logan says. "But it's what he wants."

The doctor cuts their gaze between Rosemary and Logan. "I'll give you some materials on our palliative care options just in case," they say. "In the meantime, you're both welcome to go back and see him."

At that, the doctor turns away and swipes their badge against a keypad into a back room.

"I told you he was fine," Logan says. She has her feet kicked up on a waiting room coffee table next to the *Highlights* magazines, and she takes another obnoxious sip of her almost-empty milkshake, and it's like the last few days never happened. It's almost as if Logan never began peeling back the layers of her apathetic mask. This is the flippant, smirking, asshole Logan, and Rosemary needs to get the fuck out of here right now.

She's out of her chair before she knows where she's going. Her angry legs take her to the bank of elevators, but when she presses the call button, and an elevator doesn't immediately open, she takes the stairs instead.

"Hale! Stop!"

She doesn't stop, even as Logan shouts at her in the middle of the hospital. Her body is on autopilot until she makes it out into the parking lot where the purple clouds from earlier have amassed into a gnarled tangle overhead.

It's raining, she realizes, as it begins to soak through her dress.

"Hale! What are you doing? Where are you going?"

"Away from you!" Rosemary calls over her shoulder as she weaves through the parked cars, trying to remember where they left the Gay Mobile. Thunder grumbles in the distance.

"Wait, are you mad at me or something?" Logan shouts behind her.

Rosemary wheels around. "Of course I'm mad at you!"

Rainwater has already drenched Logan's hair and it's plastered against her confused face. "Why?"

"Because Joe was in the emergency room, and you went to the cafeteria for a milkshake!"

The milkshake in question has disappeared, thankfully, probably in a trash can on the way outside. "I was hungry! We didn't have lunch!" Logan raises her voice over the pounding rain and thunder. They've finally arrived at the van.

Rosemary's throat already feels hoarse when she screams again, "You reverted back to your asshole self when it really mattered. You're allowed to admit you care, Logan!"

She can't see Logan's expression through the rain, can't even be sure Logan heard her. This isn't like Pacific Northwest rain, with its incessant light spitting. The desert is weeping huge, hot drops that soak her skin and blur her vision.

"What does that mean?" Logan asks, all pretenses of friendship gone from her tone.

"Joe could've died, and you acted like it didn't matter!"

"You can't die from farts!"

Rosemary takes a step closer to Logan so she can stare up into those eyes. And then the bastard reaches for her sunglasses. "Don't you dare put those on! It's raining right now! You don't get to hide behind your sunglasses or your indifference!"

Rosemary doesn't want to have this conversation with her own reflection in Logan's sunglasses; she wants to say this to Logan's face. "You know what? I'm glad I didn't kiss you last night. Because you would've pretended that didn't matter, either. That's what you do. You run away from anything real."

Logan's eyes narrow. "You . . . you were going to kiss me last night?"

Rosemary rubs rainwater out of her face and takes another step forward. "It must be exhausting, never letting yourself feel anything!"

Now Logan surges forward. "Just because I don't catastrophize about everything doesn't mean I don't feel anything!"

"Bullshit."

Logan barks out a single laugh like a bullet. "Ha!" Rain drips into her open mouth.

"You can't even accept that Joe is dying. You refuse to let yourself feel the impending loss!"

"We're going to lose him, Rosemary!" Logan screams. "Why would I want to feel that?"

"Because!" Rosemary throws her hands toward the sky. "Because some people are worth the hurt!"

"Like you?" Logan asks. The words crack like thunder. "Is that what this is really about? You're just hurt that I didn't kiss you last night?" she asks in her asshole voice. "Did you consider that maybe I just don't feel that way about you?"

Rosemary grabs the front of Logan's overalls. She wants to punch her in that arrogant, uncaring, milkshake mouth.

She kisses her instead.

Because *that* will show her.

Rosemary kisses Logan Maletis in the rain outside an Albuquerque hospital, and dammit, she tastes like strawberries. Logan's mouth is wet and soft, and Rosemary grips her overalls tighter, trying to keep them both upright.

Logan lets them fall, and they stumble backward until Rosemary collides with the back of the Gay Mobile.

In the chaos, their mouths come apart, and now Logan is staring down at her with those fire eyes again. She has her pinned to the van, trapped, breathing angrily. And then Logan kisses her again.

Rosemary fucking knew it.

It's nothing like that innocent, exploratory kiss when they were fourteen. Rosemary still has handfuls of Logan's wet clothes, and she pulls her against her own body, pulling them both back harder against the van. Logan grabs Rosemary's hips and pushes herself away, teasing her. Rosemary begs for more with her tongue against Logan's closed lips. In punishment, Logan bites Rosemary's bottom lip before she relents, opens, and it feels like there is nothing between them at all when Logan's tongue touches hers.

It's how she always imagined kissing adult Logan would be. (And she had imagined it, hadn't she? So many times.) There's nowhere for Logan to hide her feelings in the nonexistent space between their bodies. It's a kiss like arguing. Like passion and stubbornness.

A kiss like mutual surrender.

LOGAN

Rosemary fucking kissed her.

Hot diggity dog, indeed.

Joe almost died today, but as long as she keeps kissing Rosemary against the Gay Mobile, she doesn't have to think about that. She *can't* think about it. Because *Rosemary* is kissing her. With tongue. With her whole body.

Logan isn't letting go. For the first time in her life, she doesn't need an excuse to touch her childhood crush. She just gets to do it, and she takes full advantage. She starts with her thick, wet braid, then traces the anxious tendon down the column of her throat. Collarbones and ribs and the surprising softness of her hips. Down the backs of her thighs, up the hem of her dress.

They're in a hospital parking lot, but she's dry humped in worse places.

She knows this is going to end in hurt, but for the moment, she doesn't care. Because Rosemary kisses like she does everything, with precision and perfection and so much care. With just enough restraint to make Logan absolutely feral over nothing more than a kiss.

This. This isn't *just* a kiss.

She thought Rosemary would kiss like they're in a Jane Austen novel, but she kisses her like they're in a Jane Austen *movie adaptation*.

A demon from hell begins to roar at them, and Logan and Rosemary come apart in a scramble of squelching limbs and confusion and regret. It's Odie. He's thrashing against the back window of the van, barking for his freedom. Poor dog. Logan had no choice but to leave the car running and the AC on when she went inside the hospital for news, but Odie still looks traumatized.

Rosemary looks traumatized, too. She still has rain clinging to her pale lashes and her bottom lip is plump, already swollen. Logan feels a surge of triumph. She did that. She made Rosemary Hale lose control.

Rosemary smooths down the hem of her soaking dress. "Well, I think I proved my point."

"What point was that?"

"That you do feel something for me, whether you're willing to admit it or not."

Logan laughs in the rain. "Oh, I definitely feel *something* for you."

Rosemary puckers that swollen mouth into her cat's-asshole face, and Logan just wants to kiss her again. They're still standing there, still staring at each other. Odie barks again.

"We . . . we should go check on Joe." Rosemary attempts to compose herself, but the evidence of the kiss is still written all over her blush.

"We definitely should," Logan agrees.

The anxious tendon in Rosemary's neck sticks out, and Logan hopes this isn't her last chance to touch that spot.

"Joe," Rosemary repeats.

"Joe," Logan says. She will find a way to touch that tendon again.

• • •

"Gas, huh?" Logan smirks as she flops onto Joe's hospital bed beside him.

"We will never discuss this again," he says grimly. Then he cranes his head to eye Logan beside him before he stares at Rosemary hovering on his other side.

"Why are you both wet and guilty-looking?"

Chapter Nineteen

ROSEMARY

"I'm going to come," Logan moans. "Seriously, I'm about to orgasm."

Rosemary kicks her under the table. "Could you not? We're in public."

Logan obscenely licks a glob of green chilies off her finger, and Rosemary does not think about kissing her yesterday. Not even a little bit. "I can't help it. This is a sexual eating experience."

They're eating brunch at the Pueblo Indian Kitchen that's part of the cultural center in Albuquerque. Joe insisted they drive here straight from the hospital, since Rosemary had been so excited about it as part of their detour. But if she'd known Logan would make such pornographic noises while eating her Rancheros de Albuquerque, Rosemary might have protested the decision. Rosemary tries to focus on her Pueblo pie, but it's . . . distracting.

Logan unleashes one last toe-curling groan, then throws down her cloth napkin to signal the end of her meal. "I think it's time to address the elephant dick in the room," she announces as she rubs her belly contentedly. She then reaches into the backpack at her feet and pulls out the nude painting of Joe. Slams it down on the table in the middle of the crowded patio.

Joe chokes on his atole. Rosemary is equally disoriented to find herself reunited with Joe's penis.

"How . . . ?" Joe tries. "How did you get that?"

"We have our ways. Which is to say, we bought it over the phone before we left Santa Fe," Logan answers with an equally distracting wink at Rosemary. "And the gallerist kindly delivered it to our hotel room."

"It was fifteen hundred dollars!"

"And worth every penny on the credit card I'll never pay off," Logan sings.

"And you've been carrying that around in your backpack?"

"Where else would I keep a naked painting of my English teacher?"

"We?" Joe clutches his chest and gasps. "You said *we*! Rosie, my favorite, please tell me you had nothing to do with the acquisition of this art?"

She gives him a pitying look. "I had to."

"Honestly, if I had a nude where I looked this good, I would want it preserved in the Smithsonian."

"I died, didn't I?" Joe closes his eyes and does a pantomime of the sign of the cross. "I died in that hospital, and now I'm in hell."

"Joe." Rosemary grabs his shoulder. "We have to talk about Remy St. Patin. He was clearly very important to you."

Joe visibly flinches at Remy's name. "He . . . he didn't mean anything to me."

"False." Logan jabs a finger at the painting. "Exhibit A: you're semihard in this painting."

Joe waves his hand. "Enough about my dick. Put that thing away."

Logan slowly places it face down on the table.

"Exhibit B: you still carry around his handkerchief."

Joe shifts nervously in his chair. "Okay, fine. *Fine.* I'll tell you about Remy. I-I should've just told you about him in the first place."

Logan makes a smug *go ahead* gesture. Joe takes a deep breath.

"Remy was . . . a man I once knew," he starts specifically.

"In the Biblical sense, clearly."

His pain grimace appears in the corner of his mouth. "He was my . . ."

"Lover?" Logan guesses.

Joe heaves a sigh proportional to Logan's badgering. "I was going to say that he was my one regret."

Rosemary glances over at Logan to find she's already glancing at her. Her eyes look like honey in the morning sun.

Rosemary pulls her gaze away.

"We lived together, in Bar Harbor, for five years," Joe continues, "but we met long before that. At NYU in '81. My junior year of undergrad. I was a good Catholic boy back then. I was living the life my parents wanted, even though I'd moved across the country to escape them. I went to mass every Sunday, I was active in the on-campus ministry, and I was even dating a good Catholic girl named Alma Ortiz."

Rosemary tries to picture twenty-year-old Joe: Bible tucked under his arm and a girl's hand in his. Nothing feels right about that image.

Joe keeps talking, and his voice begins to take on that rhythmic quality she associates with his lectures. "Alma was from New Orleans, and my family lived in San Antonio at the time. Junior year, we decided to carpool home for the holidays. The plan was for me to stay with her family for a few days, and then my brother would come to pick me up on Christmas Eve and take me home. Alma had a Pontiac station wagon, and to help cover the cost of gas, we put up one of those bulletin board ads offering to drive other students who lived along the way. Remy was the only person who answered."

"Like in *When Harry Met Sally?*" Logan asks.

"Yes, exactly like that, except my girlfriend was there too. But Remy . . ." Here Joe pauses. Sighs. "He was the prettiest boy I'd ever seen, and I felt this immediate need to know him, to impress him. We talked the whole drive, about Cervantes and Márquez and Goya. Audre Lorde and Angela Davis. About being brown and Black in a place like NYU, navigating spaces that weren't meant for us. About Freire, and artists we loved. He showed me his sketchbook, and I showed him my poems. In his presence, I felt like I was transforming into the person I was always meant to be. I . . . I loved him instantly."

Rosemary forces herself not to look at Logan, not to think about friendship and kisses and becoming your truest self around someone who makes you feel safe.

"When we arrived at Remy's parents' house in Ocean Springs, Mississippi, I broke up with Alma and I stayed with Remy instead."

Logan whistles. "Joe, that's a *brutal* way to break up with someone. And this is coming from me, the king of brutal breakups."

Joe looks entirely unapologetic. "Alma was comfortable. Remy was real."

Absolutely not. Rosemary will not look at Logan.

"It was the most perfect week of my life. I spent the holidays with his family, sleeping on the floor of his childhood bedroom. Remy's parents knew he was gay, and they just . . . loved him anyway. That was such a miracle to me."

"What about your parents?" Logan asks gently.

Joe takes a bite of his porridge and swallows. "Alma's father called my father to tell him what happened, what he . . . suspected. My brother never came to pick me up for Christmas."

"Joe, I'm so—"

"No sorrys, Rosie darling." Joe offers her a wan smile. "I chose what I chose, and I knew choosing Remy would come with pain. I chose him anyway."

She can't help it any longer. Rosemary looks at Logan, and *oh*, the ache of yesterday's kiss floods her bones. She's fourteen again, tasting that popsicle mouth. She's thirty-two, and that mouth is a strawberry milkshake. If she kissed her right now, would she taste like homemade tortillas and green chilies and Pueblo pie, like sugar and spice? Like something real?

Yesterday, kissing Logan in the rain felt like writing when the words were good. It felt like everything inside her was clicking together, instinct and art melding in her fingertips, like *that* was the thing she was put on this earth to do. Write stories and kiss Logan Maletis.

"Remy and I moved in together as soon as we got back to New York," Joe says, pulling Rosemary out of her own thoughts. "I came out to our small circle of friends. I stopped going to church. My parents wouldn't talk to me, but I didn't care. We were young, idealistic artists living on the Lower East Side. We thought nothing could touch us, until everything did. Remy was my first . . . everything."

"You were an artist?" Logan asks with that pouty mouth Rosemary can't stop staring at.

"Poetry. That's what I studied at NYU. After undergrad, I got a job teaching at a Waldorf school to support myself while I did open mic nights and poetry readings. On the weekends, we did drag shows, making just enough money to cover the cost of submissions to magazines that might publish my work. Remy waited tables to pay the rent and painted every other second of the day. We lived above a Middle Eastern restaurant, and the apartment always smelled like falafel and turpentine, and I truly thought we would never stop loving each other."

The words fall out of his mouth in that musical voice he used as a teacher, and Rosemary feels like she's listening to him read a poem she knows will rip her heart out in the end.

"So, what happened?"

"The AIDS crisis happened."

Logan's tan face goes visibly ashen across the table. "Remy . . . he didn't . . . *die*, did he?"

"No," Joe answers, "but so many of our friends did. It was

everywhere, all the time. The specter of death. I felt like I was choking on the air I breathed on the way to work." The tears come quickly to Joe's eyes, and then they're in Rosemary's eyes, too, as she absorbs his hurt. Joe hasn't publicly cried over his prognosis in the last four years, but here he is, sobbing now at the memory of everything he lost. She's always known there are parts of Joe's queer experience she will never fully understand as a white woman, but she'd never allowed the true horrors of what he lived through to sink in.

"Remy was always the fighter, and he got involved right away. Attended Act Up meetings, went to protests, got arrested—so completely desperate to get the government to care that we were dying. He always coped with tragedy by turning outward to those around him, to people he could help. I coped by turning inward."

He shakes his head like he still carries guilt over such a valid reaction to the sheer terror of an epidemic of that magnitude.

"I never wanted to leave our apartment. I stopped writing poetry. I sat on the couch watching *Mary Tyler Moore* reruns, wishing I could live in the version of America I saw on TV. I was so consumed by the fear of losing Remy that I started losing him while he was still right in front of me."

Rosemary looks at Logan. She looks and looks and looks. There's nothing unfeeling in that expression now.

"I needed to leave the city for my mental health, and I convinced Remy to move even though he wanted to stay. We found a small cottage in Maine that I could afford with the money I'd saved from teaching, and we lived there, in a safe little bubble, for five years. They were beautiful years, close to the sea and mountains and trees. I got a job teaching English at the local high school, and living in Maine, Remy could afford to paint full-time. I wanted to believe we could be happy like that forever. Drinking coffee on our front porch while we watched the sunrise, wine at sunset. But . . ."

Joe sighs again. Rosemary looks.

"But Remy never wanted to leave the city, where we could be

close to the art scene and the queer community, and I could tell I was holding him back. He wanted a life of adventure, and I wanted a life that was safe. I kept trying to end things, but we'd been together for fifteen years, and Remy couldn't let go. So, one day, I packed up all my things and I moved as far away from Bar Harbor as I could, without telling him. I left a note and just . . . disappeared."

"That's how you ended up in Vista Summit?" Rosemary asks in a hushed tone. Tears drip down her chin, and under the table, Odie puts his head on her lap. She starts to shove the dog away, but there's something comforting about the weight of him, the feeling of his silky fur beneath her fingers.

Logan violently pushes aside her own tears with the back of her hand. "Wait, did you say you used to do *drag*?"

Rosemary fixes all her attention on Joe. "And that's your one regret? Leaving him?"

Joe stares out at the parking lot of the Pueblo Indian Kitchen. "I regret the *way* I left."

Rosemary uses Odysseus's ears like a stim toy, stoking back and forth to soothe herself from the secondhand heartache.

"I was so convinced that I was going to lose Remy eventually that I hurt him before he could hurt me."

Now they're both looking at Logan. She squints, like the sun is in her eyes, and shoves her sunglasses onto her face.

Joe keeps staring at Logan anyway. "I took away his agency and made the decision for him. And I regret that very much."

"Have you told him that?" Rosemary asks.

"I haven't spoken to him since I left. It's been thirty years."

"Are you fucking kidding me?" Logan screams. Several other patrons turn to glare. "Pick up the damn phone and call the man! Tell him you're sorry, and you still love him!"

"I-I'm not . . . still in love with him."

"Oscar fucking Wilde, then what was that entire Nora Ephron bullshit you just spewed at us?"

Joe stares down at his half-empty bowl. "I wouldn't even know how to find Remy after all this time. . . ."

"Because the internet doesn't exist?"

Rosemary already has her phone open. "Remy St. Patin . . ." She ticks her nails against the screen. ". . . owner of the Heather on the Hill gallery, 1224 Government Street. Ocean Springs, Mississippi."

Logan picks up her napkin just so she can throw it down on the table theatrically. "That's it! Next stop: Mississippi!"

"Absolutely not."

"Absolutely *yes*!" Logan jumps up from the table. "Rosemary, grab the dog and the leftovers. We're going to find Remy St. Patin."

"Logan!" Joe pleads.

"Joseph!" Logan pleads back.

"Joe," Rosemary says. "You brought us to Santa Fe. You dragged us around art galleries. You wanted to find him."

Joe meets her eyes, and she sees a new level of vulnerability there. He's so . . . *human*, this man she's immortalized. He loves and he fucks up and he regrets. He makes mistakes and makes amends. "This is your death trip. Do you really want to have regrets when it's over?"

He considers this, his head tilted toward the warm sun. "I really did look fantastic in that painting, didn't I?" Joe wonders in visible awe at himself.

Rosemary holds his gaze. "You were the prettiest man I've ever seen."

Joe's lip quivers a bit in response before he squares his shoulders. "No regrets," Joe grumbles under his breath. Rosemary contemplates whether she'll be able to say *no regrets* at the end and mean it. "Okay. Let's go to Mississippi."

Logan punches her fist toward the sky. "Fuck yes! To Mississippi."

"You girls want some *Tuesdays with Morrie* advice?" Joe says when they're all back in the car. "Here it is. Take more nudes while you're young."

Albuquerque, New Mexico to Ocean Springs, Mississippi

Chapter Twenty

LOGAN

There is the small matter of Mississippi being three states and one thousand miles away.

Logan expects Rosemary to panic, or at the very least, pull out her printer and diligently remake the itinerary at this abrupt change in plans. But when they stop at the Four Winds Travel Center for gas and snacks, Logan pulls Rosemary aside to check-in on how she's feeling and is mystified by her apparent calm.

"You're sure this detour is okay?" Logan asks softly, bartering for Rosemary's truth.

But Rosemary looks determined. "We *have* to go to Mississippi. For Joe. Besides, it is, technically, getting us closer to Maine."

Logan doesn't argue with her logic. She just gets in the Gay Mobile and drives.

A little before noon, they cross the border into Texas. And western Texas kind of sucks.

It's all flat fields and giant billboards with statements that are either aggressively pro-Jesus or anti-teacher. She didn't know anti-teacher billboards were a thing, but apparently everything *is* bigger in Texas, including hatred.

The other drivers on I-40 East do not seem to like the Gay Mobile, and they make this known with car horns and middle fingers. A woman at a gas station waits outside the bathroom to corner Logan to tell her that the homosexuals stole the rainbow from Jesus.

"Time for gay shit," Logan says when they get back in the car.

"Let's not be any gayer than is strictly necessary," Rosemary squeaks from behind the wheel. They're all feeling on edge.

"It's my playlist. Called 'Gay Shit.'"

She plugs her phone into the aux and presses shuffle. The first song to come on is "Mamma Mia"—the film version beautifully sung by Meryl, obviously. When Logan was a tween, Antonio would put on his original ABBA records, and they would all dance around the kitchen to this song. Rosemary would dance, too, swaying her arms and bobbing her head.

Logan glances over at her in the driver's seat. No swaying. No head bob. Just Rigid Rosemary, clearly wishing Texas wasn't sure a big state.

"Have you ever wondered why this song is such a bop when the lyrics are actually a major bummer?" Logan asks the car.

"Lyrical dissonance," Rosemary answers.

"Huh?"

"When the lyrics don't match the music, that's what it's called," she explains with her back erect over the wheel. "On the surface, the song sounds happy, but if you listen closely, it's actually heartbreaking."

"Comedy and tragedy always go together," Joe says during the dance-break. "Prickly pears, Logan. Prickly pears!"

Logan shakes her head. "I think all songs should be bops."

Hale turns her head just enough to side-eye her. "I like lyrical dissonance. Some people are really good at acting like everything is fine even when they're falling apart inside."

With that pointed comment, Logan cranks the volume on the song until it's so loud, they can't even hear the honking, and both her and Joe sing at the top of their lungs.

For the first time since they crossed the border, Logan notices the impossible blue of the northern Texas sky, the way it stretches on forever over the undulating fields of brown. There is immense beauty here, despite everything else.

• • •

They stop in Amarillo for lunch. It's a cute, Western town on Route 66. But the real draw is a place called the Big Texan steakhouse: an enormous yellow building with an ox statue and a sign that says, "Yes Everything's Bigger 'n Texas."

"No," Rosemary says, eyeing the kitschy monstrosity through the windshield.

"Yes!"

"We just ate a huge breakfast!"

"Uh, like four hours ago . . ."

"Joe literally ended up in the ER with heartburn from eating food like this!"

"You promised we would never speak of that again!" Joe is already unbuckling himself. "And I'll get something healthy. Like chicken."

Rosemary winds herself up to argue, then deflates like an old balloon. "Fine. Whatever. I'll wait out here with Odie. Can you just get me a salad?"

"Rosemary. The Big Texan is no place to order a salad."

The Big Texan is a saloon-style restaurant with a balcony over-looking the dining area, and oh-so-many animal heads mounted on the walls.

"Wanna share a seventy-two-ounce steak with me?" she asks Joe as they get in line to order at the counter.

"No, I'm ordering fried chicken."

"I guess I'll just have to share it with Odie, then."

"Did you and Rosemary have sex?"

"*Jesus!*" Logan screeches, completely caught off guard by the non sequitur of all non sequiturs. "You can't ask me that in a BBQ line!"

"Did you?" Joe presses, staring up at her with that intense stare.

"No! What the hell, you perv?"

Joe slowly rolls himself forward in line. He's clearly still recovering from his health scare. "Sorry, but I'm getting . . . vibes."

"There are no vibes."

They get to the counter and order. Logan snatches up the small flag with their number on it and sulks over to a table. "When would Rosemary and I find time to have sex? We both slept in your hospital room last night!"

"I happen to know you've had sex in some very creative places."

This is on her, really, for choosing to talk about her sex life with an old man. "Well, I haven't had any creative sex with Rosemary Hale, okay?"

"Good." He gives a curt nod of approval.

"*Good*? You wanted to fist-bump me when I almost kissed her."

Joe considers this as a man wearing an absurd cowboy hat shouts something at the table next to them. "Rosemary isn't like you," he finally says when they can hear each other again. "Sex would mean something to her."

Logan feels like she's been stabbed by the overabundance of spurs in this restaurant, because the implication is clear: sex means nothing to Logan. Rhiannon's words come back to taunt her. *Apathetic asshole who doesn't care about anyone or anything.*

"Damn, I get it," she says as flippantly as she can. "Rosemary is sweet and earnest, and I'm a slutty fuckboy."

Joe tries to reach out to grab her hand. She's already pulling away. "That isn't what I meant at all."

"It is basically what you said, though."

"Then I'm sorry." Joe doesn't give up easily, and no matter how hard Logan tries to put distance between them at this table, Joe keeps wiggling forward in his chair until he can reach her. "I love every damn hair on your head, young lady. Even the slutty ones."

Logan studies the serious expression on his lined face. "You . . . you've never said you love me before, Joe."

"Then I have two regrets in this life," he says, fiercely clutching her hand. "Of course I love you. Why else would I have wanted you on this trip with me?"

Logan blinks rapidly. Her dad is the only person whose ever said those words to her. She is not going to cry inside the Big Texan. She's fucking not. "We didn't have sex, but we did . . . kiss. At the hospital yesterday."

Joe breaks into a grin. "I knew it!"

"You did not."

"I knew it was only a matter of time," he clarifies smugly.

"I'm not sure it . . . *meant* anything. It was kind of a weird, angry-horny kiss."

"Did you want it to mean something?" Joe is still holding her hand, and she honestly can't remember the last time someone did that.

"No," she snaps. "Maybe. How should I know?"

"Here's an idea: Why don't you try *talking* to Rosemary about the kiss?"

"Ew. No way."

He sighs heavily, like Logan is the cause of the calcium deposits on his lungs. "You're not teenagers anymore. It's time for the two of you to have a big-girl conversation about your relationship."

Their number is called loudly into a microphone, and Logan hops up from the table, grateful for the excuse to walk away. Three giant bags of food are the perfect emotional shield.

"This salad is all iceberg lettuce," Rosemary complains when she sees her meal.

"I tried to warn you."

Rosemary pouts down at the Styrofoam clamshell container in her lap. "And is that . . . *ranch* dressing?"

"Here." Logan opens her crate of steak and puts it on the center console of the van between them. "We can share my meal. It is large enough to feed all of Texas."

Rosemary scoots in close and hesitantly reaches for the plastic fork. She scoops up a bite of mac and cheese, and Logan watches as the fork tines linger against her pink lips.

And yeah. They need to have a big-girl conversation.

Chapter Twenty-One

ROSEMARY

Logan was right about the salad, but she's wrong about Dallas. She insists they can breeze through Dallas and keep pushing onward toward Louisiana before they stop for the night. Never mind that Joe is exhausted and sleeps off and on for hours while digesting his absurd portion of fried chicken. Never mind that Odie is losing his little doggy mind from being trapped in the car all day and keeps trying to climb onto their laps while they drive.

Never mind that it's getting late, and she keeps accidentally staring at Logan's mouth while she sings Kylie Minogue and Miley Cyrus.

"We should stop when we reach Dallas," Rosemary says for the tenth time.

Logan is bouncing behind the wheel. "We can keep going. I feel good! I think we can get as far as Shreveport tonight!"

"And I don't think it's safe to drive in the dark when we're all tired," she points out. Logan just bops up and down to the music while she drives eighty miles per hour down the straight, never-ending freeway. But then she looks over at Rosemary, and her frantic demeanor changes.

"You want to stop in Dallas?" Logan asks, like she's really hearing her for the first time.

"Yes. Please."

Logan reaches over and places a hand on Rosemary's shoulder, just for a second. The briefest flutter of fingertips on bare skin. "Okay. Then we'll stop in Dallas."

They don't make it there until after nine o'clock. Their hotel for the night clearly caters to business travelers with its bluish mood lighting and sleek, chrome finishings. The hallways smell like cheap cologne and *man*, and if she didn't have a headache before, she certainly does now thanks to the Courtyard by Marriott.

And, of course, when they reach their adjoining rooms, they find two king beds, one in each. Twelve hours ago, spontaneously driving to Mississippi seemed like such a romantic idea, but now the exhaustion of the day has caught up with her, and all she can think about is the uncertainty of where they're going and what's going to happen next. Rosemary cries a little in secret as they struggle to get Joe situated in bed, and then she cries a little more openly once the door is closed between their adjoining rooms.

"Shit sticks," Logan says when she sees Rosemary crying on the edge of the king bed. "Are you okay?"

Logan reaches for a box of hotel tissues on the desk and awkwardly outstretches them toward her. "No. I'm tired and maybe hormonal and generally overwhelmed by *everything* that's happened in the past twenty-four hours! Thinking Joe was going to die, and the emergency room, and the kiss, and learning about Remy and driving to Mississippi . . ."

Logan hovers awkwardly with her tissues. "The kiss?"

Rosemary reaches up for a tissue and blows her nose. "Yes, Logan. The kiss. I can't just shove it aside like you apparently can."

The cardboard tissue box collapses between Logan's clenched hands. "I haven't shoved it aside. I've been thinking about it all day." The hotel room becomes stifling quiet. "Did the kiss, uh . . . mean something to you?"

Rosemary squeezes her eyes shut, takes four deep breaths, and forces the words out. "Kisses always mean something to me. Yesterday's kiss meant something to me, and our kiss eighteen years ago meant something to me."

Logan slowly lowers herself to the bed beside Rosemary, both hands still choking the tissue box. "But you kissed Jake McCandie right afterward. Eighteen years ago, I mean."

Rosemary can't believe Logan even remembers that. "Of course I did! I was fourteen, and it was 2005, and I had just kissed my female best friend, who made a joke about it and *ran away* afterward. I was having a . . . a gay panic. I kissed Jake because I thought . . ." Another four breaths. "Because I thought it might make me forget how much I liked kissing you."

The hotel room becomes quiet again. The only noise is the compression of the cardboard in Logan's hands. "Someone was coming," Logan grumbles down at the carnage in her lap.

"What?"

"I didn't run away because I didn't like the kiss. Someone was coming, Jennifer, I would guess, since that's when the rumors started going around that I was a lesbian." Her tone is bitter now. "And the only way I could prove their taunts didn't hurt me was by coming out before I was ready. By reclaiming the word they used to try to hurt me."

Someone was coming. In Rosemary's teenage brain, it had been so much easier to believe Logan only kissed her to prove a point. That's what her insecurity told her. That's why she stopped talking to Logan after that. That's why she spent years in a relationship with a boy who didn't understand her, to protect her from the rumors that hurt Logan and to protect her from her own true feelings. That's why it took her so long to understand what her heart really wanted.

Logan detaches one hand from the tissue box and places it carefully on Rosemary's leg. Just above her knee. In the place where her dress has slid up to reveal bare skin. "I liked the kiss, too," she confesses, her voice barely above a whisper. "It . . . it meant something to me."

Rosemary doesn't know what to do with that information. Sure, it happened when they were kids, but Logan is also here now, with her hand on Rosemary's thigh. Her long, tan fingers against pale skin. The *heat* of her. Logan's skin has always run hot, like she's summertime personified. But Logan is made for summers. For sleeping in and staying out late to stare at the stars. For endless days with nothing to do—days where doing *anything* becomes possible. Logan is sunshine and adventure and freedom and the month of July.

Rosemary is September. A new planner and sharpened pencils and outfits laid out on her bed the night before. Raised hands and right answers.

They never made sense as friends, and they don't make sense together, but here they are. On this road trip together. With Logan's hand on her leg. Once, in sixth grade, Logan convinced her to climb out on a fallen oak tree above the river, and Rosemary feels like she's balanced unsteadily on that tree branch right now.

"Did the kiss in Albuquerque mean something to you?" she ventures. She might fall off this tree branch. Or she might fly.

Logan springs off the bed and paces fitfully for a second, before she marches over to the hotel desk where a now-cold box of pizza sits, the leftovers from their earlier dinner. She flips open the box, stares down at the slices like maybe they'll save her from her own feelings in this moment.

Then, without turning around to face Rosemary again, Logan tells the box of pizza, "It meant everything to me."

LOGAN

As she often does in emotionally vulnerable moments, Logan shoves an entire slice of pizza into her mouth.

The pizza is cold and congealed, but at least it buys her some time after her catastrophic confession. She can feel Rosemary's eyes on her as she chews, and all she wants to do is go back over to that bed. She wants to grab Rosemary by the shocking curve of her hips and taste that pink mouth again. She wants to claim that tongue, to consume her. She wants to kiss Rosemary like she's making up for twenty years of not kissing her, ever since that night in the garden when a kiss woke up parts of Logan she didn't know existed.

Thankfully, pizza is a great boner killer, and it stops her from doing anything impulsive.

She can't kiss Rosemary with food in her mouth—can't touch her with greasy fingers—and Rosemary would never kiss her after eating sausage, anyway. That, combined with the inevitable cheese farts and heartburn from the tomato sauce, and it's a perfect sex shield.

The pizza also prevents her from *saying* other silly, reckless things. Like about how Rosemary broke her fourteen-year-old heart.

Pizza is the best! All hail pizza.

"Well, shit," Hale says when the pizza-induced silence has gone on for too long. And there's something so charming about that single swear word in Rosemary's prim mouth that Logan almost sticks her greasy fingers all over her anyway. "I didn't think you were going to say that."

Logan swallows a painful hunk of crust. "I didn't think I was going to say that, either."

Rosemary smiles and looks down at her hands in her lap. She's so earnest, so genuine, so unafraid of showing how much she cares. Her fingers twist a simple gold bracelet around her right wrist. Her pale lashes flutter against her blushing cheeks and fuck it. There's not enough pizza in the world.

Logan steps closer to the bed and stands in front of Rosemary's legs. She towers over her, so Rosemary has to crane her neck to look up.

"Can I kiss you again?" she asks quietly. They're close enough for quiet.

"Not with pizza sauce on your face."

Logan doesn't break eye contact with Rosemary as she swipes the corner of her mouth with her thumb. "How about now?"

Rosemary smiles like she wishes she could stop, but her mouth keeps spreading across her entire face, lighting her up from the inside out. "You're so gross."

Logan overtly wipes her pizza-grease fingers down the front of her overalls.

"Seriously disgusting. Is this really how you've seduced all those women?"

She's not thinking about all those other women right now. She's only thinking about Rosemary on this bed, in this hotel room where they're completely alone. Logan opens her legs, so her knees are bracketing Rosemary's knees, and she bends down so her mouth is pressed against the shell of her ear. "Rosemary." All three syllables, her lips brushing the earlobe until Rosemary shivers like she did on that rooftop in Santa Fe. She scrapes her teeth along that anxious tendon and growls, "Can I please kiss you again?"

Rosemary abruptly grabs Logan by the waist, and Logan half expects Rosemary to push her away.

She pulls her forward with a violent tug instead, just like in the hospital parking lot, and Logan loses her balance. She tumbles awkwardly onto the bed, and there is a chaotic moment of limbs and confusing intentions until Rosemary's pink mouth finds hers. And then there's those soft lips and that hot tongue, claiming and consuming and kissing like it matters more than anything else in the world.

Logan has kissed dozens of people, but somehow kissing Rosemary feels like the first time, every time.

Maybe because none of those other women she kissed were ever really kissing *her*. They were kissing an idea of her. A warm body across a crowded bar. Long legs and big breasts. A pair of willing hands and an eager mouth. A rumored good time. An ex of an ex, or a friend of a friend, who would fuck you behind the bleachers at a

Roller Derby bout, or go down on you in the bathroom at a Thorns game, and wouldn't care if you ghosted after.

Those women never chose Logan *for Logan*. Because they didn't know Logan. She never let anyone truly know her.

But Rosemary fucking Hale. Rosemary *knows* her, knows the absolute worst parts of her—her recklessness, her assholishness, her selfishness, her indifference—and she's kissing her anyway. Rosemary kisses her like she wants her. Singularly. Individually. Rosemary kisses like they're thirteen, not watching each other change into pajamas at every slumber party. Like they're fifteen, enemies who are incapable of staying away from each other, constantly stuck in each other's orbits.

Like they're twenty-eight and seeing each other for the first time in a decade.

Like they're rewriting the history of their first kiss.

Logan is completely unspooled, unmoored, as Rosemary kisses her deeper.

There is a heady push and pull between them, like tug-of-war with their bodies. Logan loves it, and she grabs Rosemary's hips and rolls them over, so Rosemary is on top of her, straddling her, pinning her to the hotel duvet.

It's a graceless fumble of hands. Rosemary's: in Logan's hair, gripping the front of her T-shirt, sliding down over her breasts, sliding up under the shirt, cool fingers on her stomach.

Logan's: on Rosemary's hips, on Rosemary's thighs, higher and higher until fingers find the edge of cotton underwear beneath her dress. So many other people, and Logan has never been this turned on by only the friction between their clothes and a mouth on hers.

So many women, but Logan has never kissed any of them the way she's kissing Rosemary. Because she knows Rosemary at her worst, too—condescending and controlling and so terrified of being flawed—and she still wants to kiss her. Individually. Singularly.

Logan's pretty sure she's always wanted to kiss Rosemary. The pantyhose and the heels, that puckered mouth and those tongue clicks. That supercomputer brain and that anxious tendon and the thoughtful way she approaches everything. She made an entire binder for this trip because she cares about Joe so fucking much, and Logan is pretty sure that if she let her, Rosemary would care about her that way, too.

"Virginia fucking Woolf," Rosemary gasps and she rips her mouth away. She drops her forehead onto Logan's shoulder and tries to breathe, and Logan laughs. It comes out high-pitched and girly, the way she used to laugh, back when none of her laughter was ironic.

Rosemary is still on top of her, breathing heavily. Her face is flushed, her mouth puffy, her hair messy, and Logan wonders what it would feel like, to make Rosemary completely lose control.

Chapter Twenty-Two

ROSEMARY

She feels completely out of control.

Her body doesn't feel like hers; it feels like a sentient being that's come to life for the first time and completely hijacked her brain. Every inch of her crackles with electricity and she's overwhelmed by a deranged urge to physically weld herself to Logan.

It's uncharted territory. She's terrified. She's . . . aroused? She's mostly confused.

At least Logan looks equally ruined. She's still beneath Rosemary, and her pupils are huge, even as her eyes have become heavy-lidded, only half-open. Logan's mouth is curled into a lazy smile that's so goddamn sexy, Rosemary would scream if not for Joe on the other side of the wall.

Has she ever found someone sexy before? And why oh *why* does the first person have to be Logan Maletis?

Logan lifts one of her extraordinarily deft hands and traces her fingertips softly down Rosemary's bare arm. That touch turns her into a shivering, mewling mess.

"There are other things I could do to you," Logan says in a raw voice. It's not the asshole voice, and it's not her gentle voice. It's something new, something Rosemary has awoken from her. That thought makes her ache everywhere. "Other dead queer authors whose names I could make you shout at the ceiling . . ."

That offer is enough to bring Rosemary's brain back online, to make her remember where she is and what she's doing and why she absolutely cannot do it.

She scrambles off Logan and starts sputtering incomprehensible excuses. "I'm tired" and "we shouldn't" and "Joe."

"Whoa! Whoa." Logan sits up quickly. "It's okay, Rosemary. We don't have to do anything else. There's no pressure at all. I may be a fuckboy, but I'm also a fan of enthusiastic consent."

The problem is that Rosemary couldn't be unenthusiastic if she tried. "Sorry," Rosemary mumbles.

Logan shakes her head. "No sorrys. You have nothing to be sorry about. I'm the one who got carried away with her horniness. I'm sorry I made you uncomfortable."

"It's not that I . . . I mean, I want . . . um . . ." She has no idea how to do this, how to *talk* about it, when she's spent more of her life trying so hard not to think about it.

But Logan isn't mad. She isn't mocking her. And what Rosemary really wants is to tell her. "I'm not . . . like you. When it comes to sex."

Logan smiles, but it's different than the lazy one before. "Not slutty, you mean?" she asks jokingly, and Rosemary realizes this is the smile Logan uses when she's pretending not to care.

"I don't think you're slutty. Unless you want to be slutty?" Rosemary has no idea if slutty is a good thing or bad thing these days. "But I've never had sex. Like, at all."

The smile vanishes entirely. "Oh. So, you and Jake never . . . ?"

"Definitely not. We were each other's beards. You do know he came out his freshman year at UW, right?"

Logan's mouth hangs open. "*Never* never, then?"

Rosemary rushes to explain herself before Logan rushes out of the room in horror. "I don't really date or think about dating very often. And sex has never felt that important to me, so I just haven't prioritized it. Which probably sounds really weird . . ."

"Not weird at all," Logan says, not rushing anywhere. She's still sitting right here with Rosemary. "Maybe you're asexual. Or aromantic. Or both."

"Maybe . . ." she says. She's looked into other labels for the way she experiences attraction, but none of them give her the same sense of rightness she found with the word lesbian. She knows she doesn't experience sexual attraction like other people, but she's pretty sure she does experience it.

"It's okay that you don't want to have sex with me," Logan reassures her with a real smile. It shows the entirety of her crooked teeth. Rosemary is obsessed with those teeth, that mouth, and the possibility of this moment.

"The thing is . . . I think I do want to have sex with you."

"Oh," Logan says again.

"Oh," Rosemary repeats.

They sit in silence for a minute until Logan finally speaks. "I have an idea. . . ." Her smile turns devilish. "Would you take a nude photo of me?"

• • •

Rosemary sits uneasily on the closed toilet seat and watches Logan turn on the hot water in the bathtub.

"A nude . . . ?"

"Yep," Logan says as the bath begins to fill. "*Tuesdays with Morrie* demanded it."

Rosemary barks out a little laugh at the ridiculousness of Joe's life advice. "And you're going to listen?"

Logan shoots her another devilish grin, and this one sends an anticipatory tingle through her limbs. "If you want to. You're in control here. Just how you like it."

Rosemary doesn't fully understand what she means.

Logan seems to sense her confusion. "Is it okay if I take off my overalls?" she asks, and Rosemary nods slowly.

Logan unfastens the buckles, and Rosemary is mesmerized by the way her jean overalls wiggle down over her hips, then slide down her long legs.

"Can I take off my shirt?"

Rosemary nods a little faster this time. Her instinct tells her to look away as Logan pulls the tank top over her head, but she fights that urge and lets herself stare. Orange sports bra and tan skin. Fire on fire. The thirst is back in her throat as she understands. Logan is handing Rosemary complete control over whatever happens in this bathroom.

"Can I take off my sports bra?" Logan asks with an impish grin.

Rosemary swallows. Nods once. Then she nearly loses consciousness in the absence of that sports bra. Logan's large breasts hang low on her chest, like two perfect teardrop diamonds, and her areolas and nipples are both a darker brown that contrasts her olive skin. Acres and acres and acres of skin.

Logan tugs at the waistband of her TomboyX black briefs. "Can I take my underwear off?" she asks quietly.

An ache begins to build in Rosemary's lower stomach. She wiggles uncomfortably on the toilet seat. But she's nodding. She never stops nodding.

The black underwear is gone, and instinct wins out, forcing Rosemary to look away from the thick curls between Logan's legs. "Ha-have you ever, uh, taken a nude photo before?"

"I've never taken a nude that's only for me," Logan answers as she lowers herself into the steaming tub. "Do you want to grab my phone?"

Rosemary takes the phone off the ledge of the sink and crosses the bathroom to the tub. Each step is a mix of agony and anticipation.

"You're going to have to look at me if you're going to take my picture, Rosemary," Logan says gently.

Rosemary takes a deep breath and allows herself to look. Logan's long, lean limbs are sprawled out in the small tub the way Joe's were in the painting, one leg thrown over the edge. Her head is tilted back at an indolent angle, and Rosemary has no idea what to do with herself. Logan is naked and making blazing eye contact, like she's daring her to look away. Rosemary wants to look away and can't. She's never seen a naked woman in real life (outside a locker room), so visceral and imperfect and sweet.

Everything goes wobbly, and Rosemary *needs* to jump in that tub with her and wrap herself up in those wet arms and legs.

She raises the phone and takes a picture. The lighting is terrible, but Logan still looks like fucking Aphrodite.

Logan looks away from the phone, and Rosemary takes another picture of her in profile, then another. She takes a dozen photos. The longer Logan is stretched out naked in front of her, the more comfortable and safe Rosemary starts to feel, even as the ache pulsing through her grows more intense. "Let down your hair," she orders.

"I think I like being controlled by you." Logan reaches for the hair tie tangled in her bun, her back arching as she does this, her breasts heaving out of the water. Her dark, wild hair falls out, fans around her. Rosemary keeps snapping pictures. There's something about seeing Logan through the phone screen that gives her permission to stare. She stares and stares, tries to capture that perfectly imperfect body, this perfect moment, just the two of them.

"Is it your turn?" Logan asks.

Rosemary lowers the phone away from her face. "I-I don't know . . . I've never taken a nude photo before."

"I assumed." Logan stands up and the water whooshes all around her. Without bothering to dry off, she steps out of the tub, dripping onto the floor with abandon.

"Here." She holds out her hand, and Rosemary passes her the

phone. She knows this is the moment she's supposed to undress, but she can't make her arms move.

"You don't have to, Rosemary," she says in that same gentle voice. It sounds the way seeing a lighthouse must *feel* to a ship that's desperate for safe harbor.

"I want to," she says. And she does. Rosemary wants to consider her body as something other than the meat canister that carries around her brain. She wants to feel as confident and sexy as Logan looked in that bathtub. At the end of her life, she wants tangible proof that she was once brave enough to bare everything to someone else.

So why are her teeth chattering with nerves?

Logan's slick body moves closer. "Do you want me to undress you?"

Rosemary looks up into those lighthouse eyes and nods. Logan's wet hands take the hem of her dress, and Rosemary raises her arms like a small child. But there's nothing childish about the way it feels when Logan tugs her dress up over her head. Her skin prickles, goose bumps rising up and down her limbs.

"I-I'm not as sexy as you," Rosemary whispers as Logan studies her matching bra and panties.

"You're the sexiest thing I've ever seen," Logan says with perfect sincerity. Then she comes around Rosemary's back. She unfastens the clasp on her A-cup bra and slowly glides the straps down Rosemary's arms until it falls to the floor with her dress.

"My boobs are small enough to fit inside a martini glass," she blathers. "With room leftover for the martini."

"How dare you?" Logan gapes. "I love your huge knockers."

Rosemary laughs until Logan makes her stop with those damn hands. The hands circle around Rosemary's waist, her fingers wandering closer and closer to Rosemary's nipples. Logan leans down behind her and plants a kiss right on her bulging stress tendon. "Is this okay?" Logan murmurs against her throat. Rosemary makes an animalistic sound of consent.

Logan circles her, comes around in front of her, and kneels. "You've also got this shocking *ass*."

Logan bites her lip as she coaxes Rosemary's underwear down her hips.

"I know I look like a prepubescent boy."

Logan stares up at her naked body in blatant *awe*. "Who told you that?"

"*You* have told me that. Several times."

The hands are cupping her ass. "I've always thought you're sexy, Rosemary. Will you let me make you feel sexy?"

Words are both her profession and hobby, but they've completely escaped her at this moment. All she can do is nod. *Enthusiastically.*

Logan takes Rosemary by the hand and leads her to the edge of the bathtub. Rosemary dips in one toe, then quickly submerges herself. "How's the temperature?"

"It's a little cold," Rosemary admits as she tries to hide herself in the water. "But it feels good. I was—" She coughs. "A little warm."

"Did I make you hot?" Logan tilts her head to the side with feigned innocence.

"Oh, shut up and take my picture already!"

"You need to pose for me first."

She attempts to situate herself for the photo, but every part of her body feels stiff and foreign, exactly like a meat suit disconnected from her brain.

"Relax, Rosemary," Logan whispers. "Think about new calligraphy pens, bullet journal stickers, the smell of warm lamination."

"Oh, fuck you!" she snaps, but she also relaxes a bit, her shoulders easing under the surface of the water. Logan raises the phone and takes a photo. She feels herself stiffen again.

"I can delete that if you want. Or you can delete it yourself if you don't trust me."

"I trust you," Rosemary says automatically. "How does the photo look?"

"Sexy as hell," Logan growls.

For the first time in her life, she *feels* sexy as hell. "Take another one."

LOGAN

She knew seeing Rosemary naked would do something weird to the fourteen-year-old part of her brain. She knew that letting Rosemary take a nude photo of her would feel vulnerable and scary, and she knew that taking photos of naked Rosemary would feel exciting in that way all reckless things were exciting to her.

But Logan isn't even remotely prepared for what it feels like when Rosemary says *I trust you.*

Just like that. No pause, no hesitation. Rosemary *trusts* Logan to have these nude photos on her phone, and it's the most intimate thing that's ever happened to her. It feels like she's stripped down deeper than her clothes, like Rosemary has seen all her sinew and bone, and still finds her beautiful.

"What are you thinking about?" Rosemary asks as she throws an arm up over her head like Rose posing in *Titanic.* Logan takes another photo.

"I'm thinking about how this might be the best impulsive decision I've ever made."

Rosemary giggles as she poses with a hand on her soft thigh. She opens her legs a little wider, and Logan's whole body floods with lust. She moves up and down the length of the tub, taking photos from different angles, getting ridiculously turned on by the sight of Rosemary unabashedly feeling herself.

"Let your hair down."

Rosemary undoes her braid, and Logan can barely contain herself at the sight of pale hair over pale shoulders. In this moment, there is nothing icy about Rosemary's blue eyes. They look like the desert sky—endless and open and full of new things to explore.

"Can I join you?" Logan croaks. She sounds nervous.

Rosemary doesn't seem aware of Logan's sudden anxiety as she shifts in the tub to make room. It's too small for both of them, and Logan struggles to pretzel her long legs in place as water sloshes over the rim. But Rosemary moves her legs to one side, and Logan stretches hers out on the other, and their bodies lock into place like puzzle pieces in this hotel bathtub.

They sit across from her, hair down and bodies bare.

Rosemary wets her lips with her pink, pink tongue. "So. What now?"

Slow, Logan reminds herself. Rosemary deserves someone who will go slow with her, someone who will make her feel safe. "Will you touch yourself for me?"

Rosemary reacts like Logan asked to fist her. "What? Why? No!"

Slow. Gentle. Safe. "Do you touch yourself when you're alone?" she asks softly.

Rosemary lapses into a brief coughing fit. It's maybe the cutest thing Logan's ever seen. "Uh, yes, I . . . um . . . I do masturbate."

Logan pauses for a beat until Rosemary's blush fades a bit. "How do you masturbate? Do you watch porn?"

Rosemary scrunches her nose. "I've tried, but it doesn't really work for me. The characters never spend any time getting to know each other first. I think I need to believe the characters are emotionally connected before they get to the smutty stuff, otherwise, I just . . ." she trails off, but Logan fills in the blanks. Sex means nothing to Rosemary if it means nothing.

"So, not porn. What do you use when you masturbate?"

"My . . . imagination," Rosemary answers, and Logan wishes she could leap across this bathtub and kiss her right now. Of course Rosemary doesn't need anything but her beautiful brain to get aroused. She wonders if Rosemary ever writes her fantasies down, if there is ever sex in her wonderful stories.

"And my hand," Rosemary adds. "My imagination and my hand."

Logan grips the edge of the tub to force herself not to lunge. *Slow. Safe.* "Will you show me?"

Rosemary freezes. Beads of water drip from her hair down her slender throat, and Logan would give anything to see that perfectly polished hand slip between those pillowy thighs.

"I want you to show me how you pleasure yourself," she says earnestly. "I want to know how to make you feel good."

Rosemary's desert-sky eyes go wide. "You want to watch me masturbate?"

Logan nods and says, "Fucking yes," and she sounds too eager, too nervous, too everything.

Rosemary brushes her hair out of her face and her mouth crinkles into its familiar puckered shape, that pattern Logan knows by heart, like a road she could drive in the dark, always finding herself safely home again.

"What if I do it with you?" Logan runs a hand across her own breasts, down her stomach, her skin prickling with sensitivity like it hasn't in years, since those early sexual encounters when she hadn't yet learned to guard her heart. Logan slides her fingers between her legs, and she has to bite down on an immediate gasp.

Rosemary mirrors her actions, so tentative as her fingers inch closer to her smooth vulva. She touches herself, then cringes in embarrassment. Logan closes her eyes while Rosemary gets more comfortable with herself, and when she opens them again, Rosemary has two fingers moving in slow circles around her clit. She releases the sexiest fucking sound Logan's ever heard. Before Rosemary can feel embarrassed again, Logan whispers, "I loved that sound. Please, Rosemary. Let me hear you."

Rosemary gasps again as she begins touching herself more vigorously. She becomes unguarded, uncensored, and completely unafraid.

Logan watches every stroke like it's a choreography she needs to memorize. She sinks deeper into her own touch. She barks a string of curses, letting every joyful "shit" and "fuck" and "motherfucking clit sucker" fly free, which makes Rosemary laugh wildly. Rosemary loses a little more control, the occasional *yes* escapes her mouth. Then Rosemary's free hand clutches her breast. She pebbles her own nipple between her manicured fingers, and Logan is probably going to die.

Rosemary's head is thrown back, her teeth biting down on her full, bottom lip. The pale column of her wet throat. The tremor in her chest. The absolute glory of watching Rosemary "Binder" Hale come undone. Logan can't handle it. She looks as open and free as the girl from the summertime woods, and Logan is overwhelmed by how much she wanted Rosemary back then and how much she wants her right now.

Rosemary opens her eyes and catches Logan's gaze. Blue eyes burning, she holds her stare without losing her rhythm, two feet away, riding her own hand toward climax. "Rosemary," she pants. "Can I please finish you?"

"Yes," Rosemary whispers back without hesitation.

Yes, yes, yes.

They shift. More water sloshes out of the tub, and they laugh as Rosemary tucks herself between Logan's legs, back to chest. Logan kisses that beautiful throat, and Rosemary cranes her head back so she can capture Logan's mouth. Kisses her deeply, desperately, as Logan slides two fingers back under the water.

Logan touches Rosemary exactly like she touched herself. Two fingers, massaging around her clit. And Rosemary grips Logan's thighs and clenches her toes against the water spout. Rosemary's ass is pressed firmly against her, and she feels herself still coiling, too. Tightening and building and almost breaking.

It's never felt like this. She's let so many other people into her bed and into her pants. Some she loved when she was young, even if they couldn't love her back. Some who loved her, even if she had completely closed herself off from caring.

But *this*. Logan feels like someone threw open all her windows and doors, dragging the furniture into the front yard. There is nothing left to hide behind, no part to play. She cares. She cares so damn much, it might destroy her.

She bites down on Rosemary's neck and wishes she could consume her.

Rosemary comes apart with her back arched, her toes clinging to the faucet, and her mouth on Logan's. She comes in a fit of curses and gasps, holds on to Logan ferociously through the tremors Logan teases out of her until she's boneless in Logan's arms. Until she feels like hers.

Rosemary doesn't give herself time to fully recover before she's sloshing around again, angling herself so she can get a hand between Logan's legs. She's too eager, too far to the right, but it doesn't matter. Logan uncoils completely from nothing more than a single finger on Rosemary Hale's right hand.

ROSEMARY

She can't just go to sleep. She maybe won't sleep ever again. She has the entire infinite sky in her chest and the taste of Logan on her tongue.

When Logan falls asleep in a damp pile of sheets, Rosemary slinks over to the small hotel desk. She moves the pizza and sits in the chair, still completely naked, and starts writing on the hotel stationery.

Chapter Twenty-Three

ROSEMARY

"Are you really going to eat a shrimp po'boy at ten in the morning?"

Both Joe and Logan look at her from across the table like that question is the most ridiculous part of this little tableau. Logan has her po'boy suspended midair in front of her unhinged jaw, and Odie is halfway in her lap, ready to catch any falling shrimp. "Why wouldn't I?" Logan asks before cramming the monstrosity into her mouth, remoulade sauce dripping down her chin. And for some inexplicable reason, Rosemary finds the whole thing very attractive.

She imagines Logan's mouth wrapped around a moan of pleasure, her fingers grazing her own skin across the bathtub . . .

Maybe it's not so inexplicable.

Rosemary banishes all sexy shrimp thoughts and turns to Joe. "Really, Joe. For breakfast?"

"Rosemary, I'm dying," Joe snaps. "I'm not sure how many times I have to tell you this. And if I'm going to be dead tomorrow, then I absolutely need to eat this shrimp po'boy."

"You aren't going to die tomorrow." She rolls her eyes, and then she hands him an extra napkin. Joe chomps down on his po'boy with slightly less vigor than Logan, but his eyes still go wide in his wrinkled face.

"Best po'boy ever, right?" Logan asks through a full mouth.

Joe swallows. "Better than any po'boy I've had in New Orleans. The perfect last meal." Then they're both stuffing their faces again.

Joe got them up early this morning and said nothing about the state of their damp, rumpled king bed. Rosemary was too tired to be subtle. She didn't sleep at all—she'd been too wired, too awake, too filled up with Logan to know what to do with herself. So, she wrote while Logan snored. She wrote until her eyes became too sore and too heavy to keep staring at the white paper in the dark hotel room. And even when she finally got into bed, she still couldn't sleep. She lay there beside Logan, counting her own heartbeats and Logan's exhalations.

They left Dallas before six in the morning. Texas sunrise is almost as beautiful as New Mexico sunset: pinks, blues, and yellows stretched out across a never-ending sky as they drove east. Rosemary took the first shift, and as she drove through the quiet of the morning, she couldn't wrap her mind around how the outside world appeared relatively unchanged while her world had been flipped upside down.

She'd had sex. With Logan Maletis.

Sex had never felt like a goalpost or a major life event she needed to reach. It was never an item on her to-do list. It didn't matter to her the way it seemed to for everyone else, and until she kissed Logan in the rain, she wasn't sure she would ever have it.

But then Logan gave her total control, made her feel safe, made her feel sexy. She gave all her trust to Logan, and Logan showed her a version of sex that felt like emotional connection. Like a really good conversation on the front porch watching the stars.

And now. Now, she doesn't entirely know how to *be*. She doesn't know what any of it means to Logan. Or what it means to her. They were best friends, and then they were high school enemies; they spent ten years apart and four years hating each other. The friendship truce and feelings.

Where do they even stand now? What are they to each other? And where do they go from here?

She might be spiraling a bit.

Joe insisted they stop in Shreveport, Louisiana, and he directed them to a restaurant in what appeared to be an old auto repair shop. A man in a fedora greeted them and introduced himself as the owner. Then, when he saw the Gay Mobile parked outside, he smacked his thigh and loudly declared in front of all the Shreveport locals—"I'm queer too! Queers get the special discount!"

Rosemary nervously glanced around the restaurant, but none of the locals batted an eye at the owner's antics. They got fifteen percent off their order, and Rosemary felt some kind of way about this gay man in the Deep South who owned a popular small business and was unapologetically himself.

"I-I've changed my mind," Joe suddenly announces over breakfast. "I don't think I can go to Ocean Springs."

"Why? What's wrong?"

Joe blots his mouth with a napkin. "I-I don't want him to . . . to see me like this."

Rosemary reaches for him across the table. "You're beautiful, Joe."

"Oh, fuck you! I look like a man who is *actively* dying. I have liver spots, girls. *Liver spots!* At sixty-four!"

"You look like a man who has *lived*," Rosemary insists. "And Remy will have aged, too."

Under the table, Logan reaches for her. It's just a hand brushing against her leg, then settling itself on her knee.

"Yes, but he probably aged like a Black Harrison Ford. I want him to remember the version of me that was young and lithe and wrinkle-free, with a fully functioning cock."

Rosemary coughs and reaches for her coffee. Logan squeezes her knee. The pressure of her fingers makes Rosemary feel safe, and she's struck by an old impulse. She wishes she could undo the last eighteen years, stitch her and Logan back together, until they become one person with two heartbeats like they were as girls.

"What if he doesn't remember me?"

"You were together for fifteen years," Logan says plainly.

"And everyone who has ever met you remembers you, Joe."

"But . . . but what if he's married?"

Rosemary keeps her voice gentle. "Then you'll be so happy for him and you can say your final goodbye knowing he lived a full life."

"And then, when we're alone again, we'll reassure you that you're so much prettier than his ugly-ass husband," Logan adds.

Joe is unconvinced. "You don't know his husband is ugly-ass."

"I don't know his husband *exists*."

Joe stares down at his shrimp po'boy, his expression one of absolute agony. "I don't want Remy to know about the diapers."

"The good news is you don't have to lead with that."

"Gay men aren't supposed to get old," Joe mutters.

Under the table, Rosemary puts her hand over Logan's, lets their fingers loosely thread. "Then how lucky is it that both you and Remy did?"

Joe exhales dramatically. "Fine," he relents. "Onward to Ocean Springs."

LOGAN

She fucked up.

As a rule, she's usually fucking up something most of the time. But on the Logan Maletis fuckery scale, this is an eleven. Out of ten. This is kissing-your-best-friend-at-a-pool-party level of fucked.

This is having sex with Rosemary Hale in a hotel bathtub fuck-boy behavior.

Logan grips the steering wheel and tries to come to terms with the fuckedupness she's created.

She's had sex with people she shouldn't have in the past. Monogamous married women who were still in the closet; a few of her friends' ex-girlfriends; once, the parent of a student. Logan doesn't feel any shame about those hookups, though. As long as sex is between two consenting adults and all boundaries are respected, Logan doesn't let shame anywhere near her sex life, even if the sex is reckless or impulsive or borderline self-destructive. She likes sex, and she isn't ashamed of that.

But sex with Rosemary is a whole new level of bad behavior. It was Rosemary's first time. And there were *feelings* involved. And now Logan *cares*.

She closes her eyes and tries not to think about Rosemary writhing in the water, about her hesitance and the way she eventually unfurled. About her blush and her willingness and the way she *felt* in Logan's arms.

Sex with Rosemary hadn't felt like fuckery. It felt like having the bud of a prickly pear flower without the barbs. All beauty, no pain.

"Are your eyes closed?" Rosemary screeches. Logan's eyes fly open in time to see Rosemary grab the wheel and yank it toward her, pulling the Gay Mobile out of the neighboring lane. "You can't close your eyes! You're driving!"

"Shit! Sorry! Sorry!" Reality slams into her right before they slam into a semitruck. She takes back the wheel and forces herself to focus on the road, on Van Morrison singing "Crazy Love," on Odie barking frantically from the back.

This—this is why sex with Rosemary Hale is fuckity fucked, no matter how good it felt in the moment. Because Logan is going to hurt her. She will close her eyes when it matters and sideswipe a semitruck. Metaphorically speaking.

Logan can't be trusted with someone else's feelings.

• • •

The rest of the way to Ocean Springs, Joe practices what he's going to say to the long-lost love of his life, and Rosemary and Logan take turns helping. They're on the freeway that cuts right through the middle of Louisiana. The landscape changes from brown fields and sagebrush to thick, green swamp along the side of the freeway. Giant live oaks dripping with Spanish moss, magnolias and fan-pines and kudzu, everything drooping like a Dalí painting. Rosemary is the one who teaches her the names for all these new trees, her polished finger pointing out the front window excitedly.

They stop again in Baton Rouge to switch drivers and end up getting lunch at a place called Coffee Call. It's in a strip mall, but the café has clean white walls with blue accents, and they apparently have the best beignets in town. They serve their powdered sugar out of a huge trash can, which is all Logan has ever wanted in life.

"Po'boys for breakfast, beignets for lunch . . . I think we did this backward," Rosemary says with powdered sugar all over her face.

"You look like you just performed oral sex on a Belgian waffle."

Rosemary blushes. She delicately tongues the corner of her mouth. "Is that better?"

"Come here, Hale." Logan grabs a napkin and swipes the sugar off Rosemary's chin, the tip of her nose, her cheek. "Can't take you anywhere, I swear . . ."

Rosemary licks her lips and blinks those long, pale lashes. "Did you get it all?" Rosemary asks.

"Hard to tell when your skin is the same color as the powdered sugar."

Joe, who's been quiet on his side of the table, suddenly looks at Rosemary and Logan. "Dammit, you girls had sex, didn't you?"

• • •

As she pulls the Gay Mobile into Ocean Springs, Mississippi, Logan realizes she has no idea what day of the week it is. She asks Rosemary, who looks equally befuddled. "Tuesday?"

"The day of my humiliation!" Joe languishes.

"Oh, it's Monday." Rosemary sounds pleasantly surprised as he checks her phone. Everything has been a blur since the Grand Canyon, excitement and exhaustion converging to smear the trip into an indistinguishable series of events. Have they been on the road a week? A month? And in the name of Shay Mitchell's triceps, how the hell did they end up in the Deep South?

"It's five o'clock," Rosemary announces.

"In what time zone?"

Rosemary squints. "Eastern? Central? One of those two. Anyway, the gallery closes at six, so we should hurry."

As they drive through the streets of Ocean Springs, she notices how different the Gulf Coast feels from everywhere else they've been so far. The whole town is flat and low to the ground. It isn't only the lack of mountains or hills or literally any incline that makes it feel this way; the buildings themselves are hunkered down, as if the entire town is always braced for an incoming storm.

Downtown Ocean Springs is quiet and quaint on first impression, and Logan parallel parks the van a block from the gallery. She turns around in her seat, and Joe touches his jowly chin. "How do I look, girls?"

"Like a man with a fully functioning cock," Logan answers.

"Are you ready, Joe?"

"Absolutely not." Joe sighs. "But are we ever ready to face our greatest mistakes?"

Logan climbs out of the van, and holy shit. It's like stepping into a dishwasher at the end of the heated dry cycle. Her sunglasses immediately fog, and she pushes them into her hair. She yanks the back door of the van open. "It's as humid as Joe's sweaty underpants out here."

"And why does it feel like the sun is punching me in the face?" Rosemary demands as she pries the collar of her dress away from her throat.

In the five minutes it takes to get Joe out of the car, Logan sweats through her T-shirt. Rosemary has beads of sweat along her hairline, and her cheeks are bright pink. "How do I already have swamp ass?" she curses, and Logan smiles at the knowledge that she got prim Rosemary Hale to say *swamp ass*.

Logan pushes Joe's wheelchair over the uneven, inaccessible side-walk while Rosemary keeps a firm grip on Odie's leash. The dog finds it critical to pee on the trunk of every Magnolia tree between the van and the gallery. The Heather on the Hill is sandwiched be-tween an antique store and a brewery, the brick facade painted white with purple flower accents. Heather.

"No dogs." Rosemary points to a sign in the window. "I'll go sit on that bench in the shade with Odie."

"No, wait!" Joe reaches for her. "I want the nice one!"

"*Hale* is the nice one?" Logan screeches.

"Odie likes me better," Rosemary says simply. "Sorry, Joe, but Logan will be with you. You can do this. Just like we practiced in the car."

"He might not even be here," Logan attempts to reassure him.

A bell jingles when Logan shoves a reluctant Joe through the door of the Heather on the Hill gallery. The whole place is bathed in natural light, creating a glowing path inside. Logan barely has time to take in the art on the walls before a man at the front counter raises his head to greet them, and it's Remy St. Patin. Logan just *knows*.

Partly because the man looks like a Black Harrison Ford. She can tell he was gorgeous in his youth, and he's still gorgeous, in a hot dad sort of way. His dark eyes look rimmed with liner, his lashes are full, and his smile is easy. He is short and weedy, whereas Joe is tall and broad, and Logan can perfectly imagine how beautiful they must have looked together all those years ago.

But Remy has also aged. Gracefully, yes, but aged all the same, like Joe. There are lines around his eyes and mouth, a receding hairline that pushes his close-cropped black curls halfway back his forehead. There's something altogether droopy about him, like the branches of Southern trees.

"Welcome in today, folks!" He beams until his eyes fall upon the customers in question. Then his entire face changes, until he looks twenty years old, somehow, the way he probably did that day he plucked a ride-share flyer off a college bulletin board. Remy's face brightens as he steps out from behind the counter. He's wearing a pair of paint-stained corduroys and a Henley.

"Oh God," Joe mutters. He releases an anxious belch just as Remy St. Patin comes to stand in front of them.

"Joseph." Remy smiles. "I've been waiting for you."

Rock fucking Hudson. Logan is swooning. The confidence of that statement, delivered in that Creole accent, is a siren song.

Logan waits for Joe to follow this up with an equally suave response like they practiced.

"I wear adult diapers!" is the first thing Joe says to Remy. Not suave at all. He wasn't supposed to lead with that.

Remy stares at Joe with unbridled awe and rubs a callused hand along his jaw. "Okay . . . Are the diapers the reason it took you thirty years to come see me?"

Logan balks at the directness of this question. She feels like she's witnessing the boldest, most fearless man in the world. She doesn't know what to do with herself. Joe clearly doesn't, either. "No, the diapers are new. Because I'm dying."

Remy presses a hand to his chest. "I'm very sorry to hear that," he says. "But I'm so glad you chose to find me before that happens."

"Well, we were in the area," Joe lies. "We . . . we were in the area, and we had some extra time, so we thought we would pop in and check out the gallery. Heather on the Hill. After . . . ?"

"That Van Morrison song you always loved, yes. I named this place for you."

Damn. The fearless honesty. Logan can't imagine being that reckless with your own heart.

"You . . . you named it for me?" Joe stammers.

Remy nods. "I did. I wanted you to be able to find me. When you were ready."

Joe chokes on his tongue. "Well, uh, I did, I suppose. And congratulations on opening your own gallery. It's beautiful. But like I said, we were just in the area, and now we need to get going."

"What?" Logan blurts, but Joe is already angling his wheelchair back toward the door.

"Don't argue with me on this one, Maletis," he hisses in panic. "Just go. *Go!*"

She obeys, grabbing his wheelchair and shoving him out the door.

"Joe!" Remy calls behind them, but they're already outside, and Joe is shouting, "Go, go, go!"

So they go.

"What happened?" Rosemary yells as she runs over from the bench, but Logan and Joe are running too, jostling over the uneven pavement. Odie, naturally, thinks this is a game, and keeps twisting his leash around Rosemary's legs.

"No questions!" Joe bleats. "Just go! Go! Back to the car!"

They get back to the van, which has warmed to a cool one-hundred and fifty degrees in this heat, and Logan refuses to put Joe inside to cook. "What the hell just happened?" Logan demands. She's sweating *everywhere*. How has Ocean Springs uncovered new parts of her body that can ooze moisture in just twenty minutes?

"Was Remy not there?" Rosemary pants.

"No, he was there. And he hasn't aged a day."

Yes he has, Logan mouths to Rosemary.

"He was there, and he's still so . . . so—" Joe bursts into tears. Big, wet, hacking sobs that take over his whole body. "What am I doing here? Coming back into his life just to die? How fucking *selfish*."

Without a word, Rosemary hands Logan the leash and she wraps both arms around Joe, hugging his as tightly as she can. "It's not selfish," Rosemary reassures him quietly, "to want to say goodbye to someone you love."

Joe clings to Rosemary, and for Fletcher's sake—she *is* the nice one. "I'll hurt him again," Joe whimpers. "I can't come back into his life only to destroy him."

Logan tries not to think of her own fuckery, her own future hurt. "Maybe he's okay with being destroyed," she tries. "Maybe he knows it will be worth the hurt. Prickly pears and all that."

Rosemary looks up at her and their eyes meet on this sweltering sidewalk, and Logan feels the urge to cry too. To be comforted.

I've been waiting for you, Remy had said. Logan wonders what would have happened if those had been her first words to Rosemary when she moved back to Vista Summit. That day in August when she found out about Rosemary's return during teacher training days, when Rosemary was standing in the library with the other new staff members, wearing a polka-dot dress. *I've been waiting for you.*

What if she'd admitted that she'd looked for Rosemary during every holiday in college, at the Safeway and at Rochelle's, every blond head on Main Street belonging to her?

"Can we please just go?" Joe asks.

"Sure, Joe," Rosemary coos. "We can go."

"Let me cool down the van first." Logan jogs around to the driver's side and climbs into the sweat sauna, but when she turns the key in the ignition, nothing happens.

"Joe!" a voice calls from down the street. Logan doesn't need to look up through the windshield to know it's Remy. She tries to start the car again, and again, nothing.

"Joe! Wait!" Remy reaches them on the sidewalk, and Logan feels a deep emotional pull to watch this. She gets out of the van.

"You're really leaving?" Remy seems nonplussed by the thirty-two-year-old woman practically in Joe's lap, but Rosemary still scrambles into a standing position.

"Yes," Joe manages with snot all down his face. "We have plans."

"We don't have any plans," Logan corrects. Remy turns to face her for the first time, and the sincerity of those dark brown eyes is paralyzing.

"I'm Remy St. Patin." He outstretches his hand.

"Logan."

Remy squints at her like he's trying to find an answer in her face. "His . . . daughter?"

"Holland fucking Taylor, *no*. His former student."

Remy seems to find this even more troubling.

"We both are," Rosemary blurts. "Hi, I'm Rosemary."

"Hi, Rosemary."

Joe sits there in a disheartened pile of his own sweat and tears, but when Remy looks down at him, it's clear that he still sees the Joe from the painting.

"Were you really in the area?" Remy asks him.

Joe sniffles. "Sort of. We were in Albuquerque."

"Oh, so only twelve-hundred miles away. Practically just around the corner," Remy teases. "What were you doing in Albuquerque?"

Joe can't find the right lie, so Logan answers. "We're on a death road trip, driving Joe from Washington to Maine."

"Washington to Maine . . . and you're now on the Gulf Coast?"

Rosemary shifts awkwardly in her sweat-stained dress. "We're sort of just letting the journey tell us where we need to go."

"And you needed to come here."

It's not a question. It's a statement of incontrovertible fact, delivered in Remy's calm, confident voice.

"And who's this?" Remy asks when Odie begins vigorously licking his crotch. He bends down to scratch Odie's ears, and now everyone is under the spell of Remy's charm.

"This is Odysseus. My cancer dog."

"Cancer." Remy is now at eye level with Joe. "Where?"

"Everywhere, now. It started in my pancreas."

Remy looks away from his dying ex, and his eyes land on the logo on the side of the van. "This is quite an interesting choice of vehicles for a cross-country road trip." Remy smirks. "Are you, Joe?"

"Am I what?"

"Still a queer cuddler?"

Joe barks out a mucus-filled laugh, and finally, he smiles up at

Remy. He looks transformed. Thirty years younger. Joe from the nude painting. "It's been a while since I've had someone to cuddle, to be honest."

"We could fix that," Remy offers, and Logan blushes from secondhand horniness.

It's a little too much AARP-level sexual tension for her taste. "I hate to block some geriatric cock, but we have a slight problem. The Gay Mobile won't start."

"Who are you calling geriatric?" Remy scowls. "I'm sixty-three and not ordering off the senior menu quite yet, thank you."

Logan thrusts her thumb at the van. "Good for you, but we still need a mechanic. And"—she checks the time on her phone—"I think we might be stuck in Ocean Springs for the night."

Remy once again responds with unruffled calm. "I have a friend with a shop just up the street. I can give her a call and have her tow the van," he offers. "And y'all can come back to my place for the night."

"Oh, no!" Joe flusters. "We couldn't possibly impose on you like that!"

"My ingrained Southern hospitality has to insist. It wouldn't be an imposition at all." Remy looks at Joe like he's the sole glittering star in the night sky. "It would be a chance for us to get caught up."

And Joe looks two seconds from taking off his underwear and throwing it in Remy's face. He clears his throat. "Uh, okay. If you don't mind."

"Mind? Joseph, having you in my house after thirty years would be an honor."

Logan looks at Rosemary in her yellow dress. What would it be like, to be so unafraid of your own feelings?

"Okay, Remy." Joe smiles, surrenders. "Okay."

Chapter Twenty-Four

ROSEMARY

"The good news is, you can buy shrimp at this auto repair shop."

Rosemary glances up from her plastic waiting room chair and sees Logan strut back from the front counter. "How is that good news, exactly?"

Logan doesn't sit down in the vacant chair next to Rosemary but leans sideways against the nearest wall. "It can't be bad news. Frozen shrimp next to the spark plugs sounds like a good omen to me."

It sounds like a terrible omen to Rosemary. Remy's mechanic friend is a gruff, butch white woman named Gladys, who seemed personally offended that they'd already driven the decrepit Gay Mobile three thousand miles and intend to drive it another two thousand to Maine. She also seemed shocked the van hasn't collapsed from beneath them before this.

"What did Gladys say?"

Logan sighs and shoves her sunglasses up into her tangled bun of hair. She looks exhausted, and Rosemary wonders if maybe Logan didn't sleep much last night either. "She said it's probably just the dead battery, but she wants to run a full diagnostic. They're closing now, but she promised to get to it first thing tomorrow."

"Of all the places to break down, I suppose we lucked out."

Remy had helped them transfer all their belongings into the back of his truck, and then he drove Joe and Odie back to his place with the promise that there was room enough for everyone to crash. For some reason, Logan is being weird about the whole thing.

"The Gay Mobile will be fine," Rosemary tries to reassure her. "I'm fairly certain that beast will outlive us all."

Logan taps her foot against the linoleum. "Are we sure we can trust this *Remy* character?"

"Remy? The impossibly handsome artist who talks like mint juleps taste and clearly still loves our Joe?"

"Yeah. Like, what if this is all just some big elder scam, and Remy just wants Joe's money?"

"An elder scam that he planned even though he had no idea we were coming . . . ?"

"Maybe . . . it just doesn't add up, right?" Logan crosses and recrosses her arms, then continues talking like a film noir detective. "Who is that excited to see an ex? Joe left him after fifteen years with nothing more than a note. Probably broke his heart. And he's just . . . happy to see him? Just like, *I named my gallery after you and I've been waiting for you forever?*"

"Was that accent . . . Australian?"

"I don't buy it." Logan shakes her head. "No one is that open with their heart."

Rosemary stares up at the heavy bags under her eyes and the snarl of her bushy eyebrows. She wants to reach out for Logan, but she doesn't know how. "I-I thought it might be nice to give Joe and Remy a little privacy, so I found us a place to get dinner that I think you'll love."

Logan frowns. "We're just going to leave Joe *alone* with a stranger? How do we know Remy isn't turning Odie into a fur coat as we speak?"

"You do know *101 Dalmatians* isn't based on a true story, right?"

• • •

Ocean Springs is the kind of place where your auto mechanic kindly offers to give you a ride to dinner after she closes the shop. Gladys has a rusty old pickup, and they sit three across in the cab, with Rosemary straddling the gear shift. Gladys plays Brandi Carlisle the entire fifteen-minute drive.

As the pickup crunches over a gravel parking lot, a huge sign becomes visible in the dark: "The Shed Barbeque & Blues Joint." Above the name is a giant, winking pig welcoming them into his warm embrace.

"What the hell is this place?" Logan asks her. "It looks like your personal nightmare."

"But it looks like your dream."

They thank Gladys the mechanic and head toward the pig sign. The restaurant is a collection of low-slung wood buildings with tin roofs—*literal* sheds—and the line to order is out the door. There is a giant list of all the awards they've won for their barbecue and the Food Network shows they've appeared on. License plates hang from the rafters inside and kitschy signs cover the walls, and it's just the kind of tacky Americana shit Logan loves. Still, her weird mood persists, even as she orders a giant platter of beef brisket.

"Are you sure you're okay?" Rosemary asks when they find themselves at a picnic table outside.

Logan takes the plastic utensils out of their sleeve. Rosemary can't believe she's about to eat a meal that's served with wet wipes. Logan stares down at her towering mountain of food, then jerks her gaze back to Rosemary. "We had sex last night."

Rosemary's first bite of macaroni salad turns to stone halfway down her throat. "And . . . that's why you're in a bad mood?"

"Yes," she grumbles. "Wait, no. Not like that. Shit. Sorry. Hayley fucking Kiyoko—that's the greatest thing my lips have ever touched." She's not talking about last night; she's talking about her first bite of beef brisket. "Hurry, try your pulled pork."

Rosemary hesitantly obeys and gathers a bite with her plastic fork and knife. "Eleanor fucking Roosevelt!"

"See!"

"Holy hell!" Rosemary shovels in another forkful of saucy, tender meat into her mouth. "I truly might orgasm from this pulled pork."

"Right there with you," Logan agrees with a moan. Her hazel eyes have lightened again, and for a few minutes, their communication is limited to exchanging tastes of their food while making sex noises, emphatically pointing at the biscuits, the fried okra, the mac salad.

Rosemary delights in the way her stomach expands into the waist of her dress. Logan has barbecue sauce all over her face, and Rosemary wishes she had the confidence to wipe it off, the way Logan had done with the powdered sugar earlier.

"So, um," Logan eventually says. "The sex . . ."

Delights are short-lived. "Yes . . . ?" Rosemary isn't sure what Logan wants here. A play-by-play debrief? A Yelp review? A solemn vow that they'll never speak of it again?

"I-I should've checked in with you first thing this morning," Logan says sullenly. "I should've asked how you're feeling about what happened and made sure you're okay, but I've been in my own head about it. I'm sorry."

Rosemary crosses her legs under the table, then uncrosses them, then rubs the side of her heel against Logan's calf, because if she doesn't touch this other woman immediately, she might explode. "How are *you* feeling about the sex?"

Logan stares down at the carnage of her plate. "I feel guilty, Rosemary."

Rosemary breaks contact with Logan's leg. "How come?"

"Because it was your first time, and I'm"—Logan lifts her arms, then lets them fall back to her sides—"a fuckboy."

The plastic fork slips out of Rosemary's hand and clanks dully on her tray. Right. Of course.

Rosemary should have expected this. Last night felt like something special, for both of them. Like they were both peeling off the carefully crafted layers they show to the outside world to reveal the rawness underneath. Watching Logan touch herself, she could almost see the years of feigned apathy and indifference and guardedness dissolving into the water. Or she thought she could.

But here they are twenty-four hours later, and Logan is insisting she's still that careless fuckboy. That whatever Rosemary thought they shared in that tub was an illusion.

"You have nothing to feel guilty about." Rosemary sits up straight and tries not to feel foolish. "I didn't hook up with you under the delusion that it would actually mean something to you."

Logan's expression jars. "Ouch."

"What? I'm alleviating you of any misguided guilt over plucking my delicate flower, or whatever. I wanted to have sex with you, and I thoroughly enjoyed myself. You're very good at it." She can't believe how detached she sounds right now, but that's the efficiency of her emotional filing system. As soon as she feels a twinge of heartbreak, her brain shoves it down on instinct. "And now that we got it out of our systems, we can just move on."

"Good," Logan says, but it doesn't *seem* good. She violently stabs at her brisket like she's trying to murder it all over again.

"You still seem upset. . . ."

"Astute observation. I wonder if it's because you just implied that I'm an unfeeling, promiscuous himbo, and that you just used my body for sex?"

"What? That isn't what I said!" Rosemary finds herself unintentionally raising her voice.

"It's basically what you just said."

"You said you felt guilty about having sex with me, and I was only saying what I thought you wanted to hear!"

"The fact that you think *that* is what I wanted to hear makes me even more furious!"

Rosemary smacks her hands against the table. "How? You're the one who calls yourself a fuckboy! I don't want you to feel like you owe me anything just because we had sex!"

"Maybe I want to owe you something!" Logan screams back at her. "I don't feel guilty because we had sex! I feel guilty because I know I'm going to hurt you! But maybe—maybe I want to *try* not to. Maybe I want to try to be something with you."

Rosemary snaps her mouth shut as the dust settles in the wake of that statement. Her brain struggles to process what's happening, like a frozen computer, and she has to give it a second to do a whole system reboot. By the time she's back online and aware of her surroundings, Logan is staring at her with a miserable expression. "I—" she starts.

"Excuse me?" A blond man has appeared at the edge of their table. He's wearing a salmon-colored polo shirt and khakis. "I'm sorry to bother you, but I'm over there trying to have dinner with my family, and y'all are having a very loud, very *adult* conversation, and I'm wondering—"

"I'm going to need you to back the fuck up, homophobe!" Logan erupts, both hands braced on the picnic table like she's ready for a fight.

The khakis man intensely furrows his brow. "My family is right over there—" He points one table over, and when Rosemary follows his finger, her gaze lands on a South Asian man with glasses giving her an uncomfortable wave. "That is my husband, sitting with our kids."

Two toddlers are also staring at her, while a newborn screams in horror from inside a stroller.

"Fuck," Logan says when she realizes her mistake.

"Your family is very beautiful," Rosemary chokes out in utter humiliation.

"I don't care if you're girlfriends or ex-girlfriends or . . ." He awkwardly tries to puzzle out their relationship but can't understand what he's witnessing. *That makes two of us, buddy.*

"I just wanted to see if you could perhaps stop shouting the word 'sex' quite so loudly?"

"Seems like a fair request," Logan squeaks.

"We should go." Rosemary stands up with her tray.

"We're going," Logan adds.

The khaki man blusters at them some more.

"Sorry!"

"So, so sorry!"

They take turns apologizing to everyone they pass until they're standing under the pig sign again. Logan looks at her, horror-stricken, and Rosemary can't help it. She bursts into laughter, lets it bubble up like a fizzy LaCroix, her whole body shaking with it. Logan stares at her for an awkward heartbeat, and then she starts laughing too. Rosemary has to reach out for Logan's shoulder to keep herself upright as tears start streaming down her face, and for a few minutes, under the stars and sheds, it feels so easy, so simple, like it used to when they would laugh wildly as girls.

But then Logan puts a hand on Rosemary's waist, and they both stiffen at the contact, and the fight from before comes rushing back in.

They aren't girls anymore, and nothing is simple.

Chapter Twenty-Five

LOGAN

The thirty minutes they spend outside the Shed while waiting for their Uber driver are some of the worst moments of Logan's life.

Rosemary sits on a stump in the parking lot, her head turned away from Logan. And Logan is kicking around gravel with the toes of her Vans like a dejected Dennis the Menace. She can't believe they got into a fight about having sex and got shamed into leaving barbecue heaven.

She can't believe she told Rosemary she wants to *try*. What does that even mean?

Her stomach twists with a feeling she can't quite place. Dread? Fear? Beef brisket–induced indigestion? The pain only intensifies during the dark drive to Remy's house.

Remy St. Patin lives in a squat brick house in a neighborhood filled with squat brick houses lit up with harsh streetlamps. The Uber driver pulls up to the house, and the passenger side of the car dips toward the curb. Logan carefully maneuvers herself out of the back seat, and as soon as her feet make it to the ground, her Vans squelch into mud, and her toes get wet through her socks.

"What the fuck is this? A swamp gutter?" she shouts, standing in some kind of irrigation ditch. There are no sidewalks at Remy's house. It's just a road, and then swamp. And the swamp is somehow Remy's front yard?

Mississippi is a wild place.

Rosemary blazes up to the front door where Remy has left them a note and a spare key on a little café table by the door, out in the open for anyone to find. Rosemary reads the note aloud as Logan trudges along with her wet toes.

"'Welcome, Rosemary and Logan! Thank you so much for letting me spend some alone time with your Joe tonight. We've gone to bed early, but I've made up the guest room for you. I wasn't sure if you ate dinner, so I put some andouille jambalaya leftovers in the fridge for you. Please help yourselves to anything else you might need. My home is now your home. See you in the morning!'"

"Is this man some kind of saint?" Logan snaps.

The outside of the house isn't much to look at, but the inside is as beautiful as his gallery. The walls are bold colors—vermillion and terra cotta and burnt orange—and they're covered in artwork. Remy has gorgeous built-ins that are actually stuffed with books, not soulless tchotchkes from Pottery Barn. Plush rugs and eclectic furniture that all perfectly complement the space. Odie is curled up on a mustard couch, but he leaps down as soon as he sees Rosemary so he can come assault her with kisses.

They quietly make their way through the small ranch until they find the guest room, and for fuck's sake: there's once again only one bed.

There are also sage-green walls and white linens and a surplus of soft-looking pillows. The room smells like calming lavender, and Remy has left a stack of fresh towels on the edge of the bed with two mints on top, like a fancy hotel, and now Logan is crying. Big, embarrassing-ass tears.

Rosemary closes the door with a muted snick. "Logan, what's wrong?"

"I don't fucking know!" she blubbers uselessly.

Rosemary is already by her side, helping her sit down on the bed. Then she reaches for a box of tissues on the dresser and hands them to Logan.

"God, are these Puffs with lotion?" she cries into the soft tissue. "Why is this man so damn perfect?"

"A nose in need deserves Puffs indeed," Rosemary tries awkwardly.

Logan snorts, and snot flies out of her nose. Thank God for the Puffs.

"What is your deal with Remy?"

Logan wants to be able to put it into words, but her brain feels like eight high-speed trains with no brakes all going in different directions. "He just . . . you didn't see him, in the gallery, but he . . . he was so happy to see Joe."

Rosemary moves uneasily in front of her. "That seems like a positive thing."

Logan shakes her head. "He wasn't bitter at all. He harbored no visible resentment toward Joe for leaving. He wasn't angry or cynical. He was just . . . open."

"Which is . . . bad?"

"Yes it's bad! Because I could never be like that."

Rosemary tentatively sits down next to Logan on the bed and she puts a hand on her thigh. It's such a small gesture of comfort, but it feels enormous inside Logan's body. And that's the problem with her ADHD brain. If she lets it feel one thing, it will feel all the things, all the time. It doesn't do moderation either. Every emotion is always at eleven, which is why it's easiest not to feel anything at all.

But she already feels so much for Rosemary. She always has.

"I think you could be like that," Rosemary says quietly, her hand so soft on Logan's leg.

Logan blows a giant raspberry.

"Do you think maybe we could try to have a grown-up conversation for once?"

Logan doubts it, but for Rosemary's sake, she tries. "When my mom left me, and I became so bitter and cynical. I'm so afraid of anyone ever leaving me again, so I always leave first. I walk away from friendships and girlfriends and anything remotely real."

Rosemary threads her arm through Logan's and pulls them closer together on the bed. "I know you do," she whispers. "I was there, remember? I saw what your mom did to you."

Logan closes her eyes and sees an image of eleven-year-old Rosemary, saving her from the grief and loneliness after her mom left. "I try so hard not to care too much about anything," she confesses as she opens her eyes again. She looks down at the small woman clinging to her side. "But I've never been able to stop caring about you."

Rosemary props her chin on Logan's shoulder and glances up at her with so much cautious optimism in those blue eyes. "Never?"

Logan snorts unattractively. "In case you haven't noticed, I've been Prince Zuko–level obsessed with you for the better part of twenty years."

Rosemary frowns. Logan wants to trace the unhappy lines of her face, brush them away like powdered sugar. "You've *hated* me for almost twenty years."

"Exactly! I cared about every little thing you did! I couldn't stop obsessing over you. You were always there, even when you weren't. You . . . you've always been in my orbit, like the world's most irritating moon. But I didn't hate you. Not really."

Rosemary sits up and tucks a strand of hair behind her ear, and that sweet gesture is enough to push Logan to keep spilling all her secrets. "I love the way your mouth puckers like a cat butt when you're thinking really hard, and the way you click your tongue when you're trying to censor yourself. When we were apart, I missed your stories and the sound of your voice and the way you never made me feel like I was too much. I missed dreaming with you. You're so passionate, and you care so damn much, and you fight for what matters, and I never should've made fun of your binder, because that's how you show people you love them. And Joe is so lucky to have your love."

Rosemary's mouth goes full cat's asshole, and Logan has spent her entire life wanting to kiss that puckered mouth. "So . . . you're saying you . . . *like* me?"

Logan laughs at the utter disbelief in her voice. "Yes, Rosemary, I like you. I like you very much."

Rosemary shakes her head like she can't quite believe it, and Logan has a horrible thought. "Wait. Do you *hate* me?"

"I wanted to," Rosemary confesses. "I *tried* to. Hating you always seemed so much safer than the alternative."

This small confession feels like a huge miracle. Logan has been such an ass, and still, Rosemary doesn't hate her. Still, she finds room in that secretly huge heart to care.

"The sex last night . . . it felt different for me," Logan tells her. "Or maybe it wasn't even about the sex. It was all the non-sex parts. Talking to you and teasing you. *Seeing* you and letting you see me. When you opened up to me about your romantic history. The intimacy of it, and the way you let yourself love your body in that tub."

"I might be new to the whole concept," Rosemary says nervously, "but I thought those things were all part of the sex?"

"They aren't usually for me," she says.

"Oh." Rosemary's mouth relaxes. Logan still wants to kiss it. "What did you mean earlier, at dinner? About trying?"

Logan's stomach turns, and she's not sure if it's from excitement or in absolute horror over what she's about to say. "I mean, I like you, and I think you like me. So maybe we should just . . . try to do this."

"Do what, exactly?" Her eyelids flutter against her cheek, and

Logan can't believe she ever convinced herself she hated this lovely woman.

"Be in like with each other," Logan tries. "And just . . . do things that people who like each other do. I know I'm a fuckboy, and that I have a history of hurting people, but maybe I want to try not to hurt you."

Rosemary is still and silent, and the stomach flutter is definitely horror.

"I mean, if you're even interested in something like that. I guess I don't know if you even want a romantic relationship. Not that this would have to be a *relationship*, but, um—"

"Logan," she says quietly. Rosemary reaches up and touches two fingers to Logan's lips. And then she kisses her again. Their mouths meet, and a thousand feelings roar to life in Logan's body. Longing and tenderness. Safety and security. Nostalgia. So much fucking *hope*.

This kiss is pure sweetness, like an adolescent kiss in a garden.

When Rosemary pulls away, Logan feels like she'll never be able to breathe. Rosemary reaches toward the stack of towels on the edge of the bed and grabs the mints on top. She pops one mint into her mouth and hands the other to Logan. "Eat this," she orders. "You taste like beef brisket."

Logan giggles hopelessly. She sort of loves it when Rosemary bosses her around, so she eats her mint, and Rosemary starts kissing her again with the same slow, steady sweetness. These aren't the kind of kisses Logan is used to. Kisses as foreplay. Perfunctory kisses before the real action, Logan between some gorgeous, anonymous woman's thighs.

But Rosemary might be the most gorgeous woman she's ever seen. And she's kissing Logan for kisses' sake, kissing her like the kisses matter in and of themselves. As if she wants and needs nothing more than soft mouths and gentle tongues.

And Logan kisses Rosemary like she fucking cares.

ROSEMARY

There is something mildly humiliating about waking up as the baby spoon. She feels little and vulnerable with Logan's chest against her back, Logan's arms around her shoulders, Logan's leg over her legs, like she's a fragile Russian nesting doll.

She wants to roll away and pretend like she never enjoyed being swaddled by another human. But she can't.

Because the feeling of Logan's body this close to hers is too delicious. Logan has enveloped her entirely, and Rosemary wants to melt into her body, form a covalent bond between their atoms until their one entity.

Which is . . . a lot. Especially for day two of a maybe-relationship.

"Are you awake?" Logan grumbles against the back of her neck.

"No."

"You are; I can hear you thinking."

"You cannot."

"You think very loudly."

Rosemary huffs and rolls over so they're face-to-face in the cage of Logan's limbs. She's about to say something snarky, but she's arrested by the sight of Logan's groggy morning face, so close, so all she says is, "Hi."

"Hi," Logan says back.

They lay there for a moment, just staring into each other's eyes, until she starts to feel embarrassed by all of it. "We should get up and check on—"

"Joe!" Logan shouts as the door to the guest room flies open. Logan pulls the blankets over both of their bodies. "Don't you knock?"

Joe wheels his way into the bedroom, and the second Rosemary sees his face, she knows coming here was the right choice. Because Joe is smiling the way he used to, before the diagnosis and the chemo and the years of hoping and hurting. Joe looks like his old self. "It's almost ten o'clock," he says, "and you know I'm not a patient man."

Remy stands behind Joe in a billowy linen shirt that's unbuttoned

enough to reveal his chest hair, and even though Rosemary isn't usually attracted to men, she's a bit attracted to him. Remy seems to
transcend sexuality. Like Taika Waitaki.

"I made brunch," Remy adds, "But I'm very sorry if we're interrupting something."

"You're not," Rosemary says quickly.

Beneath the sheets, Logan's bare foot rubs against Rosemary's
leg and she shivers. "I mean, they *could* be interrupting something."

Rosemary turns to find Logan grinning mischievously. Wild
hair and tired eyes and a little drool crusted into the corner of her
mouth. There are too many feelings inside Rosemary's chest for her
to contain, and the most overwhelming urgent is her need to be
touching Logan absolutely everywhere.

"Give us a couple more minutes, actually."

• • •

Somehow, while they were sleeping in, Remy managed to run to
the grocery store, come home again, and prepare a generous brunch
spread, replete with homemade biscuits and gravy, country potatoes, scrambled eggs, and shrimp grits (not made from the auto mechanic shrimp, Logan checks). Rosemary has a giant mug of coffee
with chicory, and they eat in a conservatory-style room behind the
kitchen, with sunlight streaming in through the glass walls and the
AC running to keep them cool.

"Gladys called and left a message this morning," Logan tells
everyone as she heaps food onto her plate. "She said the Gay Mobile
just needed a new battery, so as soon as we go pick it up, we're good
to get back on the road."

Joe shoots Remy a nervous look, and Remy reaches out for his
hand and clasps it on top of the table. "Remy and I have only just
started reconnecting," Joe hedges. "And we were talking this morning, and we wanted to ask if perhaps we could stay in Ocean Springs
one more day. I think we could all use a day out of the van. Odie

certainly needs it—" In the backyard behind them, Odie is climbing a beech tree in an attempt to eat a thoroughly unthreatened egret chilling on a branch out of reach.

"Do you think that might be okay?" Joe is looking directly at Rosemary. "If we stay one more day? I know we're behind schedule, but—"

Rosemary looks at Joe and Remy's intertwined hands. "Of course we can stay."

Remy sighs happily and stares at Joe like his presence at this table is a miracle that could only be explained by the divine.

"Fuck yes we can stay," Logan consents. "You dudes need more time to bump butts."

"We won't *bump butts*," Remy corrects in his luscious Creole accent. "But the Ohr-O'Keefe Museum of Art in Biloxi is wonderful, and I would love to take Joseph there this afternoon."

Rosemary perks up. "I've heard amazing things about that art museum! I'll just need to take a shower before we leave."

Remy and Joe exchange another secret glance. "Well, I was thinking it could just be Joseph and me. I want to take him out on a date."

She slumps back in her chair. "Is that safe? Do you think you could get him in and out of your truck by yourself? And we need to be careful. He shouldn't be in the direct heat for too—"

"Rosemary, I'm not an invalid child in a Victorian novel! Please don't talk about me like I'm not here."

"Sorry, Joe, but I want to make sure you'll be okay."

"He'll be okay," Remy says, and he looks at Joe like *he* is the miracle. "I can take care of him."

LOGAN

"Maybe we should go on a date too."

Rosemary is standing by the front window, watching Remy and Joe pull out of the driveway in the truck like an anxious parent. "Hmmm?" she says, fiddling with the bracelet on her wrist.

Logan swallows down some of her pride. The word *date* feels strange in her mouth, and she can't remember the last time she asked a woman out on an earnest, honest-to-God date. College? Shit . . . high school? But this isn't just some woman. It's Rosemary Hale, and she's freshly showered with her clean hair back in its signature braid and another crisp summer dress clinging to all those subtle curves, and there is no reason for Logan to pretend she doesn't care.

"Rosemary," she repeats. "Will you go on a date with me?"

She turns away from the window, and her sunburned cheeks have deepened with an adorable blush. "A date? You want to take me on a date?"

"Yes. I really do."

Before he left for the art museum, Remy helped Logan pick up the Gay Mobile. Now, with Odie in the back seat, Logan drives them out to Biloxi Beach, where they put their toes in the Gulf of Mexico. They drink nonalcoholic piña coladas served inside a pineapple with a flamingo-pink umbrella garnish while Odie chases birds, and they lay out on a blanket they found at Remy's, at least until the heat becomes unbearable. And on the beach, they talk, the way they used to.

Logan asks about Yale and Columbia and the private school, and Rosemary tells her she doesn't know who she is if she's not a teacher anymore.

"Then maybe this is the chance to find out," Logan offers. "It seems like as long as you've been teaching, you haven't been able to have a life outside of it."

Logan tells Rosemary about the girls in college who broke her heart, and the girls who came after, the ones Logan never let get too close.

Rosemary has first-date horror stories that make Logan laugh, and first-date tragedies that make Logan want to cry. Mostly, she wants to punch every queer woman who didn't appreciate Rosemary. She wants to punch herself, too.

Sweaty and sun-kissed by late afternoon, they get dinner somewhere that serves half-priced oysters on Tuesdays and allows Odie to eat with them on a patio. They keep talking: about the dreams they let go and the adventures they never had; about Rosemary's dad and Logan's mom; about their past together and their years apart.

After dinner, they drive out on a dirt road until they find a place where they can park the Gay Mobile to watch the sun set over the bayou. Logan hoists Rosemary up so they can sit on the hood, side-by-side with their backs to a dirty windshield.

Rosemary takes out her phone with her free hand and cues up Spotify. "Steal My Heart Away" by Van Morrison.

"Apt," Logan whispers.

"I thought so too." Rosemary reaches out and takes Logan's hand, winds their fingers together slowly and thoughtfully. Rosemary's hand is small and smooth, but it somehow fits perfectly in her large, rough one.

She can't believe this moment exists.

Holding hands. Listening to Van. Watching everything go orange and hazy.

Van croons about the heather on the hill, and Logan closes her eyes and inhales the scent of vanilla and peppermint that is Rosemary. Her pink polished toes in her wedge sandals and dripping live oaks reflected on the glassy bayou, the sky a creamsicle dream. Sun and sweat and Odie lying in the dirt like nothing could ever bother him.

A symphony of frogs and birds, and the beautiful bayou, and her voice asking, "Do you want to dance with me?"

She waltzes Rosemary around in the dirt, dips and twirls her, until Rosemary's laughing like a rabid hyena. Then Rosemary stands on her tiptoes to hook her hands around Logan's neck, because they really shouldn't fit together, and they sway long after the song stops playing, long after the sunset is over. Swaying in the headlights like a country song.

This moment. Logan didn't know she could have moments like this.

Chapter Twenty-Six

ROSEMARY

One more day in Ocean Springs quickly turns into two, and Rosemary finds herself sprawled out on the mustard-colored couch midafternoon with her paperback copy of *Emma*, feeling totally and shockingly relaxed. Logan is on the other side of the couch reading Akwaeke Emezi, her bare feet in Rosemary's lap.

The house is quiet except for the whorl of the air conditioner and Odie's steady breathing as he sleeps on a patch of cool floor. Remy set up two easels in the conservatory so he and Joe can paint the birch tree in the backyard side by side, and she hears the occasional low murmur of their voices, but otherwise, everything feels frozen in time.

Or maybe time doesn't exist here at all. There is nothing to do, nowhere to be. Logan's here, and she could stay like this forever. She woke up in Logan's arms again this morning.

Rosemary turns the page in *Emma* even though she isn't really reading. She knows what's happening in the story, anyway. Knightly is scolding Emma; Emma is lashing out.

She turns another page and slowly arches her body closer to Logan's, pressing herself against her legs.

Logan nudges her in the stomach with her toe. "What are you thinking about over there while you pretend to read?" she asks over the top of her own book.

Rosemary aches for closeness. "I'm thinking about how I like being here with you."

Logan waggles her eyebrows. "You wanna make out?"

Rosemary tosses *Emma* aside. "Very much so."

They make out on the mustard couch for over an hour. There is really nothing else to do.

• • •

Two days in Ocean Springs turns into three. Logan and Rosemary get up early to take Odie for a walk before the heat and humidity set in. When they get back, Rosemary helps Remy prepare brunch. He teaches her the right way to prepare grits and gives her his biscuit recipe, and she learns a little bit more about his life while chopping veggies.

She learns about how his father was the one who taught him how to cook and his mother was the one who taught him how to paint. He moved back to Ocean Springs ten years ago to help take care of his parents, and they ultimately died only two days apart, because they could never stand spending more than one night away from each other.

He talks about opening his gallery five years ago, though his assistant manager is running things for the time being so he can be here.

She learns that Remy had been a true activist during the AIDS crisis. He'd been there for the protest at St. Patrick's church. He'd used his art to raise awareness about what was happening when the world didn't care. After brunch, they watch *How to Survive a Plague* and find Remy in the background of an Act Up meeting.

Remy takes down an old shoebox and shows them photos of Joe in leathers at Pride, Joe in drag, Joe smiling in the sunshine at

Coney Island, wearing a neon-pink mesh top. All Rosemary can see is the fact that Remy kept a box filled with photos of Joe for thirty years.

She learns Remy's had many boyfriends, but only one Joe. He spent a year painting in rural Vietnam, another year hiking the Pacific Crest Trail. He briefly joined an artist commune outside Sedona before he settled in Santa Fe, where he fostered rescue dogs. He'd summited six mountains, including Kilimanjaro, and he'd traveled to Paris and Peru, Lagos and Auckland and Johannesburg, but he still looks at Joe like he's better than the sunrise over Machu Picchu and the Eiffel Tower lit up at night combined.

"Damn, I wish I could travel like that," Logan says that night while they're playing Scattergories. Remy is walloping them, and the English teachers are all on the verge of revolt.

"Why did you move around so much?" Rosemary asks without Logan's tone of jealousy.

Remy considers his answer. "Well, I wanted to see *cool shit*," he answers in clear mockery of Logan. "But I think I was searching for something, too."

"What?"

His eyes shift to Joe. "A place that felt like home."

Rosemary looks at Logan.

• • •

On the fourth day in Ocean Springs, Remy takes Joe on another date after brunch. It's a brief adventure, and Joe comes home exhausted but alive. Not merely with lungs that can still breathe and a heart that can still beat, but with a glowing sense of aliveness.

While they're gone, Rosemary logs on to a virtual therapy appointment with Erin for the first time in weeks. She tells her therapist about the detours and the difficulties of the trip, but she also tells her about Logan. About what they're doing and what it means and what it says about Rosemary's sexuality.

"You don't have to have all the answers right now," Erin tries to reassure her.

But they both know there is nothing she fears more than uncertainty.

After learning more about Remy, Rosemary feels like she's starting to learn more about this new version of Joe Delgado, too. Not just Joe the Poet and Joe the Drag Queen and Joe in the pink mesh tank top. But also, Joe who used to want to be a writer. Joe who always had ink stains on his fingers and stayed up until two in the morning writing his poems, until Remy dragged him to bed so he could teach the next morning.

The Joe who lived by the click-clack of typewriter keys and the sting of rejection letters. Joe, who gave up on that dream to become a full-time teacher. He'd been in her life for twenty years, but she had no idea they had this in common.

Rosemary thinks about the uncertainty of her job and the chaotic pages she's written in the middle of the night at random hotels, scraps of a story about two girls who go on a magical quest with a wizard to save the world. And just like that, she starts writing again, during warm afternoons, when everyone naps, or while Joe and Remy work on a puzzle together at the kitchen table. She takes those chaotic words and types them on her laptop, then reorganizes them into something cohesive.

Suddenly, the words start coming easier than they have in years. At night, Rosemary and Logan sit cross-legged on their bed, and Rosemary reads her the new pages from the day aloud. Logan sits perfectly still, enraptured by the words, no matter how shitty they are.

"It has to be shitty," Logan tells her. "It's a first draft. Isn't that the rule of first drafts?"

She hadn't thought of these words as a first draft. "I guess."

Logan plays with the drawstring on her basketball shorts. "Sometimes, I think I'm still a shitty first draft."

Logan asks probing questions about the story, gives a few suggestions about the beginning, and it feels like they're girls again, passing a single sheet of paper between them to create new worlds.

"I think I might be a shitty first draft too," Rosemary confesses as they're falling asleep.

Logan scoots closer to her in bed. "I think you've been rewriting yourself bit by bit this entire trip."

• • •

Rosemary doesn't know what day it is, but Logan has made mint juleps, and Remy's built a fire in the pit out back, and they're all staring up at the stars while being devoured by mosquitos. In the south, the mosquitos are the size of birds, and the birds are the size of Cadillacs, and somehow, Rosemary doesn't even care.

"If we'd stayed together . . ." Joe wonders aloud. "If I hadn't left, and we'd stayed together long enough for marriage equality to pass, do you think we would've gotten married?"

"Absolutely," Remy answers. No hesitation at all.

"Hmm . . ." Joe keeps staring at the stars. "I thought so."

Rosemary's nonalcoholic julip sweats in her hands.

"What about you two?" Remy points a finger at Logan, then Rosemary.

"Marriage seems a tad premature," Logan answers coolly, but her hand is in Rosemary's, and they're both looking up at the stars.

• • •

In the middle of the night, someone shakes her awake. "Rosemary! Come on, get up! We've got to go!"

She bolts upright. "Joe. Is Joe okay?"

"Joe is fine," Logan hisses excitedly. "Come on."

Logan clicks on a lamp, and Rosemary blinks as her eyes adjust, slowly registering that Logan is fully dressed. "Where are we going . . . ?"

"You'll see. Follow me."

Logan's vibrating on her restless frequency, her limbs jangling with wild recklessness. There are limitless possibilities when Logan is in this mood, and Rosemary is pretty sure she'd follow her anywhere. She gets out of bed and gets dressed.

They sneak out of the house and drive the Gay Mobile to a quiet, completely empty beach. "What are we doing?" Rosemary tries again as they fumble their way across the sand toward the dark ocean.

Logan kicks off her shoes. "I want to go skinny-dipping!"

"Seriously?"

"Yes!" She tugs off her T-shirt and her bra, and Logan's breasts look pearlescent in the moonlight. Rosemary needs to see every inch of her—every acre of her exposed skin. "Remember? When we talked about going to Europe together after college? We always said we'd skinny-dip in the Mediterranean!"

"This is the Gulf of Mexico," Rosemary points out. But she remembers the bathtub, and trusting Logan, and feeling safe. She starts to strip, too. Soon they're both completely naked under a big sky, and there are acres and acres and acres of Logan. How could Rosemary ever see anyone else when Logan Maletis takes up so much space in her field of vision?

The warm air is thick against her bare skin, and Logan reaches for her hand. Leads her into the Gulf. The ground is pure silt, and Rosemary feels the world slip out under her feet with every step. They wade out up to their shoulders, tread water, facing each other. Logan's face is ethereal. She takes up so much space inside Rosemary, there's no room for all these feelings. She has to send some of them outside her body.

"I like who I am with you," she blurts.

Logan treads water in front of her. "What do you mean?"

Shit, what does she mean? She came on this trip with no intention of changing or *relaxing*, yet here she is, bathed in moonlight with a woman who kisses her like she cares. "I mean . . . if I've been rewriting myself on this trip, it's because of you. Like this! We're skinny-dipping right now! I never thought I was capable of skinny-dipping!"

Logan laughs. "I always knew you were capable of it. But also . . . I'm sorry if I made you feel like you need to change."

They both quietly tread water, arms circling around their bodies, forcing a distance between them. "But I'm rigid and uptight and controlling," she says, emboldened by the safe distance between them.

"You're methodical and organized and a boss-ass leader," Logan corrects. "I never could've done this trip without your binder and your planning and your ability to think ahead. You keep us moving forward, and it's because of you that Joe is getting the death trip he wanted."

They're surrounded by water, but Rosemary's mouth has gone completely dry. "Thank you, Logan."

"But . . ." Logan's arms move in slow circles. "The Rosemary I knew as a kid also liked to take risks."

Rosemary frantically kicks her legs under the water but tries to look calm where Logan can see her above the surface. "Risks are . . ." She searches for the right word. "Risky." She cringes.

Logan is silent, but in the fragments of moonlight, Rosemary can see the hurt tugging at the corner of her mouth. She wants to give Logan more than evasive answers. She wants to give *more* of herself. "My dad, Malcolm . . . did I ever tell you how he died?"

She shakes her head.

"It was an overdose," she hears herself say, even though the words feel detached from her mouth. "He struggled with mental illness his whole life. Undiagnosed, of course, because he didn't believe in therapy. He self-medicated to deal with it. Alcohol, then opioids, because he had a bad back."

She's already so tired from treading water, so tired from unearthing the things she's buried in the deepest parts of her. Logan—who has always known her better than anyone—knows how tired she is without Rosemary saying anything. She swims a little closer, wraps an arm around Rosemary's waist, and helps her stay afloat. Their faces are so close, she switches to whispering. "Growing up, my dad always told me our brains worked the same way. We saw the world in similar ways. When he was healthy, he was an artist, too. Kept a pottery wheel out in a shed in the garden. And when he died—" She chokes on the story. It feels like a tennis ball has lodged itself in her throat, and she can't swallow around it.

"When he died," Logan repeats in a low voice, "you thought you had to always play it safe to avoid becoming him."

The hazel of Logan's eyes is too intense, too *seeing*. Rosemary looks down at the black surface of the water. "I am like him. I got unhealthy, and I coped by self-medicating."

Logan wraps her slick legs around Rosemary's, tilting her body so all her weight is resting on Logan. She doesn't even have to tread water, but she keeps circling her arms anyway. "I'm going to say the same thing to you that you said to me in Santa Fe. You're not like your dad. Because you do believe in therapy. Because you try so damn hard all the time."

Rosemary finally stops fighting and lets herself rest against Logan's body.

"You're allowed to be a flawed person, Rosemary. You're allowed to take risks and make mistakes."

"It doesn't feel that way sometimes."

Logan murmurs in understanding. "I get that. But I need you to know something, Rosie." She melts a little, hearing that nickname in Logan's coarse whisper. "Your brain is the most beautiful thing about you. And I'm including your soft ass in this list."

She barks out a laugh and breaks the quiet tension of the moment.

"I'm serious," Logan deadpans. "Your brain is an asset. Not a liability."

And that's when Rosemary stops laughing and starts kissing her. She kisses her like they weren't just talking about dead dads. Or, maybe, she kisses her like they *were*. She kisses her like she unearthed something important about herself, and Logan didn't run away.

Logan tangles around her even more as she kisses her back just as fiercely. She's weightless, drifting in the circle of Logan's arms. "Acres and acres and acres of you," Rosemary mutters.

Chapter Twenty-Seven

ROSEMARY

"I'm bored," Logan declares one hazy, lazy afternoon.

Much to her apparent chagrin, no one responds. Joe and Remy are working on their puzzle, while Van Morrison sings about how these are the days from the record player. Rosemary has her laptop on her thighs, and she's writing all the imperfect words.

Apparently frustrated that she didn't get more of a reaction, Logan throws her paperback across the living room. "I said, I'm *bored*."

"I'm not sure what you want me to do about it," Rosemary answers without looking up from her laptop.

"Joe!" she shouts. "I'm bored!"

"Boredom is a sign of a lazy mind," Remy calls back from the kitchen.

"Or a neurodivergent one!"

"Hmm. Fair point." Remy comes to stand in the threshold between the kitchen and the living room. "What's the cure?"

Logan languishes on the couch like she's fainted and needs to be revived. "I don't know. It's a deep-seated boredom, and it's filled my bones with lead and my brain with worms."

Joe rolls into the living room behind Remy. "It happens to be the Fourth."

"I don't want to celebrate the Fourth of July." Logan shudders. "America is being a shady bitch, and I'm not going to her birthday party."

"What about a different sort of party . . ." Remy teases with an impish smile.

Logan perks up like Odie when someone picks up his leash. "What kind of party?"

He waits for a beat, and Logan wiggles in anticipation. "An underground amateur drag show, perhaps?"

Logan turns her hands into paws and starts panting.

"Are drag shows illegal in Mississippi?" Rosemary asks.

"Not yet. But we do tend to get fewer protesters and bomb threats if we keep these things hush-hush."

"Where is this clandestine drag show?"

"At a church out in Pascagoula."

The house goes quiet for a moment. Then: "A secret, underground, Fourth of July amateur drag show *at a church*?" Logan repeats slowly.

"It's a good church," Remy says. "One where they truly love all of God's children."

"Well, then, I'm in!" Logan shouts.

Remy turns to Joe. "What do you say? Can Rita Morenhoe handle one last ride?"

Joe's expression flits from horrified, to hopeful, to elated, to crushed all within the span of a few seconds. "I-I couldn't possibly . . . I-I don't have any of my stuff anymore."

Remy's eyes twinkle. "Lucky for you, I think I might have something that will work."

And that's how they all end up agreeing to go to an amateur drag show on the Fourth of July.

• • •

Rosemary is too embarrassed to admit she doesn't know what a drag king is, but when Logan steps out of a Goodwill dressing room in a three-piece suit, she decides drag kings are her new favorite thing.

"Drag is all about playing around with gender," Logan says as she eyes herself in a dressing room mirror. "Breaking and bending the cis-heteronormative rules. So let's play."

Logan puts together an outfit for herself with effortless finesse, repurposing donated (and often heinous) items into something new. "How are you so good at this?" Rosemary asks in awe.

"Halloween is my Christmas. I've been training for this my whole life."

Unfortunately, Logan is momentarily stumped when she discovers there are no men's suits in a women's size x-small at the Ocean Springs Goodwill. "Have you ever dressed in drag before?" Logan asks after she's overturned half the store.

"I think you know I haven't."

She taps her chin and considers. "Okay, but have you ever looked at an actor and thought *I wish I looked like him.*"

Rosemary's mind immediately flashes to those middle school sleepovers where they watched *Grease* over and over again. John Travolta with those tight pants and loose hips, winning over Olivia Newton-John. "I guess as a kid I wanted to look like Danny Zuko, kind of . . ."

Inspired, Logan takes off and emerges moments later with a child-sized leather jacket from the boy's section. She finds a plain white T-shirt, a pair of boyfriend jeans cuffed at the bottom, and black boots that also once belonged to a ten-year-old boy, probably. When Rosemary steps out of the dressing room in the ensemble, Logan whistles triumphantly. "There he is. Danny Zuko in the flesh."

Rosemary catches sight of herself in the mirror and does a double take. She doesn't look like herself, or like any version of herself she ever thought she could be. She looks like some badass fifties greaser, like a rebel without a cause.

Logan finishes off the look by tucking the T-shirt into the jeans and securing them with a black belt. She steps back and admires her handiwork. She bites down on her lip and groans rather obscenely for Goodwill. "Damn. I cannot wait to take these jeans off you tonight."

Happy Birthday, America.

Back at Remy's, Logan secures her thick hair underneath a hilarious wig that makes her look like she's wandered off the set of *Bonfire of the Vanities.* She even bought an old pager to clip to the front of her trousers. For Rosemary's hair, they use unholy amounts of gel and slick it back with a comb that Logan slides into Rosemary's butt pocket when they're done.

Using Rosemary's makeup, Logan gives herself impressive stubble. Rosemary is heavy-handed with the eyeliner, and then they're both fully transformed.

Joe's record player is blasting "Dancing Queen," and Remy is fixing whiskey sodas when they enter the living room.

"Not Remy," he declares as soon as he sees them. He adopts an exaggerated French accent. "Je suis Madame La Tush." And then, La Tush shakes her tush before passing Logan a drink and pulling her into a twirl at the same time. Remy's drag persona looks like a slutty Marie Antoinette, complete with an elaborate powdered wig, white face powder over his dark skin, and rosy cheeks. There are even star stickers in the corners of his—*her?*—eyes.

Her lips are bright red, her fishnet stockings are white, and her heels are four inches high. The slit in the front of her poofy dress must require some intense tucking.

"You boys look fabulous!"

"So do you!" Drag King Rosemary says in a low timbre she's decided to try out, because why not? She's someone else tonight, like a character she's invented in one of her fantasy novels.

Madame La Tush can-cans to the end of "Dancing Queen," and Logan shouts over the music, "Where's Joe?"

"She needed a minute to herself before joining the party," La Tush says. "Now, who are you, sir?"

Logan cocks her chin. "The name is Chad. Chad Van Dyke."

Remy hoots. "Love it! And who's the new member of the T-Birds greaser gang?"

"Um . . ." Rosemary has no idea how to come up with a drag name.

"Danny Zukblow?" Logan offers.

La Tush shakes her head. "Manny Zuko? Kinhickey?"

"James Dick? Like James Dean, but you know. Dick."

"Too crass and unoriginal," La Tush declares with a head shake.

"Maybe I'm . . . *Rebel Without a Cock*?" Rosemary squeaks.

La Tush and Chad Van Dyke both lose their shit. "Yes! Rebel! Work it!" The madame snaps her fingers three times. Rosemary has no idea how to "work it," but tonight, she's Rebel. And Rebel gyrates his hips to the next ABBA song without overthinking it.

Logan cackles and Remy shouts "All tens for Rebel," before a small cough from behind them renders the living room silent.

It's Joe, sitting in his wheelchair.

Except, it's not Joe. It's Rita Morenhoe. And she's wonderful.

Her hair is a brown crown of curls spilling down her back and framing her face. Her makeup is all earth tones, with shimmery brown eyes and clay-colored rouge, plum lipstick. But the dress is the main attraction: iridescent sparkles that dance like a disco ball and low-cut in the front with her perky breasts lifted majestically.

She's smiling.

"Hot diggity dog, Rita!" Logan hoots. "You look incredible! How do you feel?"

Rosemary can see Joe beneath the wig and makeup, and he's positively glowing. "I feel beautiful," Rita says. "One last time."

"I'll cheers to that!" Logan holds up her whiskey and after everyone takes a drink, Logan goes into the kitchen and fills a low-ball glass with sweet tea for Rosemary. They take photos in character: Rebel leaning against the doorframe with his "whiskey" and a prop cigarette. Chad Van Dyke adjusting the knot of his tie. La Tush in Rita's lap.

Remy and Joe rework their old choreography to accommodate Joe's wheelchair, everyone dancing to the ABBA record, including Odie.

Then Odie is crying as the rest of them load into the Gay Mobile. Rebel is behind the wheel and Chad cues the Gay Shit playlist, and when they're driving down the highway listening to Cher, Rosemary rolls down the window to let the sticky air hit her skin. Even though she didn't drink, she feels drunk on this strange night already.

Drunk on the possibility of disappearing into this new persona, of becoming something she never dreamed of. Tomorrow, she'll probably put on heels again, because she likes wearing heels. But tonight, she's Rebel, and there are no rules.

The church in Pascagoula looks like any of the other churches they've seen on every street corner in the South. It's a large, white wooden building with a giant cross in front. But there, next to the entrance and lit up by spotlights in the grass, is a line of old doors, standing upward, painted in the colors of the progressive pride flag.

When they get Joe out of the car and Remy back in his heels, Logan reaches for Rosemary's hand, and they walk like that through the seemingly ordinary church parking lot.

It's not until Remy leads them around the back that signs of the extraordinary start to appear. The thrum of a bass. Glitter on the walkway. A white feather boa hanging from a low branch on a beech tree. At the back door, a butch biker asks for the password.

"Willi Ninja," Remy whispers, and then they're in a giant basement with a stage erected on the far end. There are a dozen tables throughout the room, but most people are standing. A few drag queens gather around the makeshift bar, sipping martinis and flirting with the young man who's playing bartender. A group of college students hover in one corner, looking both excited and out of place. A queer couple in street clothes is kissing in the middle of the dance floor. Close to the stage, people have clustered around to watch a queen do a gut-wrenching rendition of Celine Dion.

Logan goes to the bar to get a round of drinks and Remy takes Joe to an empty table, but Rosemary just stands there, mesmerized by the performer onstage. She's a large Black queen with a silvery wig and a sequined dress, and Rosemary knows it's lip-syncing, but she puts her whole heart and soul into it. In this church basement in Mississippi, she *becomes* Celine Dion. For the length of this song, she gets to be someone else too.

When the song ends, everyone claps and catcalls for Celine, and she takes several proud bows. Rosemary claps the loudest, caught up in the buzz of this supportive community. How could this ever be illegal?

There's a hand on her lower back. "Hooked already?" Logan asks close to her ear. She's got another glass of dark alcohol for herself and a ginger beer with lime for Rosemary. "She was so *amazing*," Rosemary gushes.

"Is this your first drag show?"

Rosemary nods, and for some reason, that answer earns her a kiss. Logan stoops down and pulls her in close. "I can't wait to see Rebel up there," Logan purrs in her Chad voice.

Rosemary wants to protest—she doesn't sing, doesn't dance—but she stops herself. She has no idea what Rebel will do tonight.

At the table, Remy and Joe are whispering, but it stops as soon as they join them.

"Welcome, welcome, welcome!" someone calls out from the stage, and Rosemary turns in her chair to see a king dressed like John Wayne, using a microphone to hype up the crowd.

"Gladys!" Logan grabs Rosemary's leg under the table. "MJ fucking Rodriguez, it's frozen shrimp–selling, Brandi Carlisle–loving *Gladys*!"

Rosemary looks again, and it is the auto mechanic who fixed

up the Gay Mobile. Remy shouts over the noise when he sees their shock. "I told you we are friends!"

"For those of you who are new to the Gulf Coast Amateur Drag Show, this is a chance for the untested queers, sissies, and missies to take the stage. But fair warning: our judges are a bunch of jaded bitches, and they will eviscerate you. Let's get those bitches up here. Please welcome to the stage Girl George, Miss Maybell, Madame La Tush, and Deena Diva!"

The room erupts in catcalls and applause as Remy and the other three judges take the stage. There is a round of rehearsed trash talk between the judges, while Remy leans in and whispers something to Gladys. Then Gladys is back at the mic. "All right, my beautiful children, it sounds like we have a fresh young king ready to make his Gulf Coast debut. He hails from—well, from a teeny town no one cares about, so we'll just say he's from Portland!"

"Maine?" Someone shouts from back by the bar.

"No, the other one." Gladys pretends to expectorate into a spittoon. "This Wall Street bro will steal your life savings and your wife. Please give a huge Mississippi welcome to Chad Van Dyke!"

Logan flies out of her seat in mock outrage, pointing at La Tush onstage. "Did you do this?"

Madame La Tush blows a kiss, and Logan makes her way up to the stage with a cocky swagger. Rosemary's heart thumps in her chest as Logan forgoes both the steps and the wheelchair ramp and leaps her way onto the stage instead. There are probably only fifty people gathered in this church basement, but that's still a paralyzing number of witnesses. But Logan—who has nothing prepared and, quite frankly, no musical talent to speak of—is grabbing the mic like it's nothing. She stands in the center of the stage beneath three glowing spotlights, and she smiles like the crowd is already hers. It probably is.

"Hey, y'all," she says in a sultry drawl. "Thanks for that warm welcome."

The group of college girls cheers spiritedly. Logan looks like a masc god up on that stage, so of course every sapphic in the room is losing their mind. Rosemary is losing hers, too, even as the rest of her body riots from secondhand nerves.

"This song might seem like an odd choice for a ladies' man like me, but I want to dedicate this performance to someone very special." Logan points directly at her from the stage. "Rebel Without a Cock. We used to sing this song together when we were young, but I would always switch the boy to girl in my head."

Rosemary feels like her heart is beating outside her body, like it's been put in an airless jar for everyone at Amateur Drag Night to examine. Because the song Gladys cues up is "She's in Love with the Boy" by Tricia Yearwood.

Rosemary gasps, and Joe reaches out for her hand. The guitar and piano kick in, and onstage, Logan is doing some sexy head bob, but in Rosemary's memory, Logan is wearing an oversized T-shirt as pajamas, singing this song into a hairbrush; she's in the backyard holding a camcorder, directing a music video to this song; she's on that front porch swing, sharing one set of headphones, staring at the stars to this song.

The lyrics start, and Logan dramatically lip-syncs. She begins with a slow-ballad performance, eyes closed, hand to heart. But as the song picks up, Logan switches to a full-on interpretive dance. It's horrible, but it's also so damn funny, no one seems to care about her lack of coordination. By the chorus, everyone is screaming the lyrics along with her. Because obviously, all the Mississippi queers know Tricia Yearwood.

Rosemary laughs so hard, she forgets about her twisting stomach and exposed heart. And then, when Katie and Tommy are at the Tastee Freeze in the song, Logan leaps off the stage, shimmies her way to Rosemary and Joe, and drops to one knee at "Tommy slips something on her hand."

Logan pantomimes proposing to Rosemary, and Rosemary's brain knows this is all part of the charade, but the rest of her doesn't get the memo. Her jar heart nearly explodes.

I would always switch the boy to girl in my head.

She's in love with the girl.

Logan finishes the performance with a triumphant knee-slide across the stage, and the room erupts in a standing ovation.

She has to distract herself from the overwhelming surge of feelings. "I . . . I see why you did drag," she says to Joe, still staring at Logan onstage where she's taking an absurd number of bows.

Joe watches her too as he talks. "Growing up, I was relentlessly bullied for being effeminate, a sissy, a wuss, a *funny boy* as my dad used to say. It wasn't even because they thought I was gay. I just wasn't *man* enough. I was too sensitive, too quiet, interested in the wrong things."

Onstage, three of the judges are holding up 10s, except Deena Diva, who's flashing a 7. In response, Logan starts doing a striptease to win her over, naturally. Rosemary's attention shifts back to Joe. "But when I dressed up as Rita for the first time, I felt like I was taking all those names they called me and claiming them as my own. The femininity that had made me inadequate in the real world made me a showstopper when I performed in drag. I learned to love myself onstage."

Joe's shimmery eye shadow catches the light. "I haven't been to a drag show in over thirty years. Drag shows were supposed to be a place where we were safe. A place where we could escape their hate and love ourselves. But they don't want us to love ourselves, not even behind closed doors. And that's hard for me because I love safety."

"So do I."

Rita's fake nails dig into Rosemary's hand as she squeezes. "I know you do, Rosie. That's why I'm telling you. Some things are more important than safety."

Chapter Twenty-Eight

LOGAN

She's in love with the girl?

What the hell was she thinking?

She *wasn't* thinking, that was the problem. Two whiskey-sevens with Remy and a Pendleton neat from the bar, and she'd surrendered herself to the bubbly, dizzying joy of being in a queer space. A church basement full of queens young and old. Joe transformed and Rosemary in a leather jacket.

That jacket. She should've known better than to dress Rosemary like this. As much as the pencil skirts and the nylons and the heels drive her absolutely wild—and they do, dammit—nothing prepared her for Rosemary in a leather jacket and a white T-shirt and jeans. Rosemary with a fake cigarette dangling from that anxious mouth.

Logan has been hoisted by her own horny petard.

And then she went onstage and sang that song from middle school summers. She confessed the truth.

I would always change the boy to girl in my head.

This is a disaster, and it's all Remy's fault.

Remy with his cute-ass house in this cute-ass town they can't seem to leave. It's like the land of the Lotus Eaters in *The Odyssey*:

they've all drunk the sweet Ocean Springs nectar and they've been lured into a sense of complacency. This is a road trip. They shouldn't stay in any place for too long; they should keep moving at the same pace as Logan's restless mind.

But instead, they've stayed. And it's been *nice*.

She's never had someone she can comfortably relax with as an adult, but on warm afternoons, all she wants to do is sprawl out on the couch with Rosemary, napping and reading while she types away on her laptop. She's never enjoyed silence with another woman. Her short-lived relationships have always been frenetic, packed with activities and passion and sex, and they've always burned out with equal force.

And it's not that there isn't passion with Rosemary. But there's also grocery shopping. There are days they go to Rouses and wander the aisles with a list from Remy for the night's dinner. There are long conversations where Rosemary asks her questions like she genuinely wants to know the answers, like she wants to *know* her.

Women never want to get to know her. That's not the *point* of her.

Logan is long legs and big boobs, a fun time, always down for a party and a good fuck.

But Rosemary. Rosemary just wants to hold her damn hand and read chapters of her book aloud and look at her like she's doing right now in this tacky church basement. Her blue eyes shining like sapphires and her expression so open, it makes Logan dizzy.

She finally finishes her exit from the stage and approaches the table where those blue eyes are watching her. "What a rush!" she announces, throwing herself down in a chair. "I legit feel like I just snorted a bunch of coke and fucked over the middle class."

Her joking comment does nothing to diminish the intensity of Rosemary's stare. "You were incredible."

Her face warms, and she pulls her blazer off, throws it over one shoulder. "Did you like it?" she asks, aiming for flippancy again.

But fucking Rosemary. She's so earnest as she replies, "I loved it, Logan."

Love. Logan had used that word, hadn't she? In the song? She'd confessed to loving Rosemary back when they were girls.

And she had. Before she understood what love was—what losing it could truly mean—she let herself love Rosemary Hale.

Back onstage, a young kid death drops as a song comes to a screeching halt, and the room goes wild, giving Logan a reprieve from those eyes. "Give Miguel a *hand*," Gladys insists into the microphone, and Rosemary puts her fingers into her mouth and whistles for the kid.

"All righty, folks. Up next, we have a very special one-night only reunion tour for a pair of New York dames."

Joe stares at the stage in open-mouthed horror, and Logan forgets about Rosemary and the word *love* entirely. "I think I'm going to be sick," he mutters under his breath.

"Please welcome back to the stage, Madame La Tush and Rita Morenhoe."

"You don't have to do this if you don't want to," Logan reassures him, but they've already cued ABBA, and Remy is already moving toward Joe, beckoning him with the crook of his finger. Joe begins rolling himself toward Remy, caught in the enchantment of this siren. Remy helps Joe onto the stage using the ramp, and then Rita is front and center, under the spotlights where she belongs.

The lyrics begin and La Tush and Rita immediately fall into old choreography. They're singing "Mamma Mia" as a duet, moving their older bodies in their younger synchronicity, except they both make modifications for Joe's wheelchair. And Joe looks magnificent. Triumphant. *Alive*.

That's the true allure of the Ocean Springs lotus flower: it has made them all forget how this road trip is going to end. Here, under these lights, Joe seems like his pre-cancer self, and it's so easy to believe that he and Remy will have a happy ending.

The crowd is on their feet, clapping and cheering, and there's something about the instant camaraderie of this moment that over-whelms Logan's chest. There's so much love in this church base-ment, it's pressing down on every inch of her.

"He's perfect!" Rosemary shouts into her ear, and Logan turns to see Rosemary is crying openly as Joe dances onstage, loving him fiercely, like she's forgotten she's going to lose him.

Logan grabs her by the waist and tugs her close. Their mouths meet even as Rosemary is still saying something about Joe. She catches up quickly, and her hands grip Logan's suspenders, pulling their bodies flush as they stand. And this kiss—it feels like the un-wavering acceptance of a room full of queers, like a good hug and a warm voice in her ear saying, "Welcome. I see you. You're safe here."

"Rebel," Logan says into Rosemary's ear. "Will you please sing to me?"

Rosemary looks up at her, eyes fierce and free. "I thought you would never ask," she responds in a confident purr, and Logan feels every pro-tective barrier in her body disintegrate at the feet of this woman.

Joe and Remy are both back at the table before Logan registers the song has ended. "Sing for us, Rebel!" Joe slurs, drunk on happi-ness and martinis he snuck when Rosemary wasn't looking.

Without hesitation, Rebel struts his way toward the stage, and Logan screams so loudly, she misses what Rosemary says when she first grabs the microphone.

"I only know one song I can confidently sing by heart," she tells the room. She leans close to Gladys to give her the title, and then Gladys turns to the laptop to cue it.

"The instrumental version, please," Rosemary teases into the mic. And Logan witnesses the exact moment that Rosemary fully becomes Rebel: she shakes out her limbs, then straightens into someone taller and prouder, somehow. It's not her usual rigid pos-ture, but something self-assured and sultry. Logan doesn't realize the song has started until Rosemary draws the mic to her mouth and growls, "I hate the world today."

It's "Bitch" by Meredith Brooks, and Rosemary isn't lip-syncing. It's her real voice, and it's the most beautiful siren song she's ever heard.

"Elton fucking John," Joe cries. He latches on to Logan's arm with his fake nails. "Did you know Rosemary can sing?"

Logan doesn't take her eyes off Rebel in the spotlight. "I did."

Sing-alongs with Olivia Newton-John while watching *Grease*. Singing all of "Bye Bye Bye" when they filmed the backyard music videos. Sleepover nightmares that woke Logan up with missing her mom and Rosemary singing her back to sleep. Like so many things, it's a talent Rosemary buried when it didn't fit into her image of who she is.

But Rebel hasn't buried anything. He sings the first verse with restrained breathiness, then bursts out at the chorus, screaming that he's a bitch, he's a lover.

Logan can't look away. She can't *breathe*. Rebel stamps his foot and belts the chorus, and all Logan can think is, *I'm so epically fucked.*

"So take me as I am," Rebel sings in that thick, raspy, holy voice. "This might mean you'll have to be a stronger *wo*-man."

And that's it. Logan is going to jump off the ship into dangerous waters for this brave woman. She's going to chase this siren song all the way to her demise. She let herself care, and now she cares so much, she'll never recover, never again be able to hide behind her mask of apathy. But she doesn't have the faintest idea how to love fiercely or freely.

"Here you go, kiddo," Joe says, handing her a handkerchief. She's crying, apparently.

Rebel finishes the song, and Logan is so absorbed, she almost misses the way the audience has flooded the stage for Rebel. Logan wants to run to Rosemary, too, but she waits until the judges all hold up their 10s, waits for her to move through the crowd back to their table, sweaty and beaming and beautiful.

Rosemary is an unguarded heart and eyes of pure fire, and Logan feels like she can't catch her breath. She reaches for Rosemary's hand. "Can we get out of here?" she whispers.

Rosemary takes her hand and guides her through the crowd toward the door.

• • •

Logan steps into the cool night desperate for air, but the night isn't cool at all, isn't comforting. They're in Mississippi, where it's humid as balls and the air always feels too close. Encroaching. Suffocating.

Logan loosens her tie, but it doesn't help.

Fireworks fill the night sky with explosions of color and sound. Logan is exploding.

"What's the matter?" Rosemary asks when it's just the two of them outside the church. "Are you okay?"

"No." Her lip quivers. She is going to start crying again. "No, I'm not okay."

Rosemary's skin shimmers in the moonlight, and another firework lights up the confused expression on her face. "Damn. Was my singing that awful?"

"What? No! You were amazing. You were . . ." *everything*. "It's me. It's just . . . me."

Rosemary steps closer, and Logan wants to meet her halfway. She wants to be comforted and cared for, but she doesn't know how. Logan falls back away from her.

"Take a deep breath. Whatever you're feeling right now, it's okay." Rosemary's voice still sounds like a song. "Let yourself feel it. I'm here. You're not alone."

"But I always end up alone. In the end." The sky riots all around them. "We've been drinking Remy's lotus, and you're a siren, and I am going to drown in you."

"You're confusing your *Odyssey* metaphors."

"That's not . . . that isn't the point."

Rosemary takes another step forward. "What is the point?"

Logan takes another step back. "The point is that I . . . *like* you. So much."

Rosemary takes ten more steps forward, keeps moving forward until Logan runs into a crate myrtle bush and can't step back anymore. "Yes, we've already established this. I like you too," she says, and she reaches up to cup Logan's face in her hands. "So, so much."

"But *why*?" Logan cries. "You like safety, and I'm the opposite of safe. I'm a thousand red flags cobbled together in the shape of a woman. I'm great in small doses, but I'm not the woman people stick around for. I'm the prickly pear, and I'm going to poke you. I won't want to do it, but my glochids are just trying to protect me."

Rosemary pulls Logan's face down, low enough that she can brush a kiss on her forehead. "My prickly pear, you're safe with me. You can stop working so hard to protect yourself."

The sweetness of it overwhelms her, and she kisses Rosemary in the dark. "I want to," she says into Rosemary's mouth. "I want to be as brave as you. But I don't know how to do any of this."

Rosemary kisses her back, and it feels like fire, like there is something burning between their bodies. Rosemary tastes like freedom and kissing her is the river Lethe. It erases her memory of her panic and her fear, her conviction that this will end with her hurting. It makes her forget everything but Rosemary's sweet words and pretty smile and perfect mouth.

They're making out in a church parking lot as fireworks decorate the sky above them, and it's cheesy as hell.

For tonight, she's going to let herself be cheesy for Rosemary Hale.

Chapter Twenty-Nine

LOGAN

She wakes up to sirens.

As her eyes flicker against Rosemary's silk pillowcase, she thinks the sirens are in her head. A product of too much alcohol. Flashes of last night's revels ticker tape across the back of her eyelids.

A leather jacket. A song. Fireworks and singing, *She's in love with the girl.*

Alarm bells in her brain scream *stop* and *slow down* and *protect your goddamn heart, you fool.* Still, she reaches out for Rosemary in their shared bed.

But Rosemary isn't there.

And the sirens—they aren't inside her head.

Someone cries out. Logan throws herself out of bed, gets tripped up in the sheets as she stumbles into the hallway. Her heart whooshes in her ears, because the crying is coming from Remy's room at the end of the hall. She walks toward it as if in a nightmare, the hallway growing longer with each step.

It isn't . . .

It couldn't be . . .

Joe.

He's laid out on the bed, the blankets all thrown back. When she sees him, she thinks he's okay. Because his cheeks are bright with color.

But Rosemary is on her knees on the bed beside him, leaning over him, pushing up and down on his chest.

Joe's cheeks aren't bright. It's the last remnants of his drag makeup, not washed completely away.

It's Remy who's crying out—"It's not working!"

"Keep using the bag valve mask!" Rosemary orders, and Remy fastens a plastic suction mask over Joe's mouth and squeezes the bag with his hand as tears stream down his face. Rosemary interlaces her hands and presses down on Joe's chest.

Odie is at the foot of the bed, watching the scene, whimpering, like he knows something they don't.

And Logan is frozen by the bedroom door, watching, thinking *no, no, no.*

It's gas. Farts. It's just gas again.

No no no.

Maybe she's saying *no* out loud, because Rosemary turns toward her. Her eyes aren't ice and they aren't fire. They're some third element, hard and faraway and completely in control. "Logan," Rosemary says. "Go let the paramedics in."

Logan is still asleep. She must still be sleeping. Rosemary isn't even dressed. She's on the bed in a pair of white cotton underwear and one of Logan's tropical shirts thrown haphazardly over the top, her boobs exposed to Remy and Joe. Awake-Rosemary would never do that. This has to be a dream.

This has to be a nightmare.

"What happened?" Logan hears herself ask.

"H-he . . . he was gasping for air." In Remy's eyes, there is nothing but panic. "And then he just . . . stopped breathing."

"The paramedics!" Rosemary shouts. "Show them inside!"

There are paramedics at the front door, a fire truck is parked in the swamp gutter. A gurney. For a body.

"Where is he?" someone asks.

Logan leads them to Remy's room, clears a path as they go. One paramedic takes the bag valve mask from Remy. Rosemary slides out of the way, closing the tropical shirt over her chest. It's the shirt with all the cacti on it. They look like prickly pears.

And this isn't how it's supposed to go. It's supposed to be *Rosemary* who breaks her heart, not Joe. Not right now.

"What happened?" a third paramedic asks. He has a gentle hand on Logan's shoulder. She gets the impression he's been asking her this for a while.

"I-I don't know what happened."

The paramedic nods, and Odie whines and whines.

"We went to a drag show last night," she tells him, because she's not even sure what's relevant at this point. "He danced and sang. He was alive last night."

The paramedic nods again. "Why don't you go get dressed?"

She looks down and realizes she's naked, too.

"Is he dead?" she asks the paramedic. His hand is still on her shoulder.

• • •

Joe isn't dead.

It's still dark outside when Rosemary climbs into the back of the ambulance clutching Joe's hand.

Remy is crying too hard to drive, so Logan gets behind the wheel of the Gay Mobile and shuts off all tears, all feelings. She puts on her sunglasses, even though there's no sun, and she drives them both.

The hospital is across the street from the Rouses grocery store, which means she's seen it a dozen times without registering what it is. They park close to the ER. A woman at the check-in counter tells them Joe has been admitted, but they can't see him yet. Logan feels untethered to her body.

Now they're moving him to a different floor. A different nurse comes to lead them through ghoulish, fluorescent hallways toward a waiting room.

The hospital is larger than it looks from the outside, the halls all designed in an undulating blue meant to mimic ocean waves. It's probably supposed to be comforting and calming, but it reminds Logan of sirens. Drowning. It reminds her of the sea Joe wants to be beside when he dies, and the fact that they brought him to the wrong one.

Rosemary sits in the waiting room with perfect posture in the cacti shirt and sweatpants, and Logan feels an overwhelming urge to be hugged and held by her. She needs Rosemary's voice telling her it will be okay. She needs to crawl into Rosemary's lap and cry, and she needs to be the baby spoon, and she needs Rosemary to stroke her hair and rub her back.

It's all going to be okay.

Rosemary is busy providing a list of all of Joe's medications to one nurse, his complete medical history to another. Somehow, amid all the chaos, Rosemary remembered to grab her binder, the one she didn't actually throw into the Grand Canyon. She really did come prepared with everything.

Logan and her neediness sit on a plastic chair across the room.

Remy is gaunt and silent beside her as the hours pass. Every time a doctor or nurse appears, they go straight to Rosemary. Logan catches snippets of the updates through the brain fog.

"Breathing, but oxygen levels are low. . . ."

"Calcium deposits on his lungs . . ."

"Moving him out of the ER . . ."

". . . on fentanyl now . . ."

". . . oxygen levels increasing, but there's fluid in his lungs . . . waiting for the oncologist to make her rounds before we move forward with treatment, but . . . DNR . . . power of attorney . . . the beginning of the end . . ."

In-between updates, Rosemary sits down in her chair a million miles away.

"He can't die here," Logan says into the silence.

She can't see Rosemary's expression behind her medical mask, but she can see her eyes. Immovable. Unnerving.

"Odie isn't here. And he doesn't have his blanket, or his record player . . . He can't die without those things. We promised."

Sometime around noon, the oncologist enters the waiting room. She's a tall, broad-shouldered Black woman with box braids and a statement necklace that reminds Logan of fireworks. "Joseph is stable," she tells them. Unlike all the other harried doctors and nurses, she sounds genuinely relieved. "We got his oxygen levels back up, but he's still having some trouble breathing, so we're going to keep him on a BiPap machine for twenty-four hours and monitor his progress. There is a procedure we can do to remove some of the fluid from his lungs that might prolong his life, but we don't have to talk about that right now. Y'all probably want to see him. He's asleep, but sometimes, it helps patients to have their loved ones near, even if they aren't aware of it."

Logan takes a true deep breath for the first time all morning. Not dead. He's not dead. Not yet.

But he could have been, and Logan is suddenly haunted by the ghosts of all her reckless decisions. Allowing Joe to eat fried chicken and shrimp po'boys. Smoking weed with Joe on their hotel balcony during their rest day at the Grand Canyon, getting drunk with him in Cortez. The detours and the days in the sun, pushing Joe to his physical limits. She got bored and took him to a drag show, and now he's in the hospital and it's her fault. *My fault.*

It feels like the walls of the waiting room are closing in on her, like she's the one gasping for breath.

Rosemary pivots in her white sneakers to face Logan. Her glacial eyes have melted into two pools of relief. Logan wants to run to her. She wants to run away from her. They should have stuck to her binder, her itinerary, her careful planning. *My fault. My fault.*

"Will you go see him with me?" Rosemary asks in a timorous voice that makes Logan's heart crack down the middle. Logan will hurt Rosemary, like she hurt Joe. She'll ruin everything.

She's going to lose Joe. Lose Rosemary. Lose everything. And she doesn't know how not to care.

My fault my fault my fault.

She wants to walk down the hospital hallway with Rosemary, but she finds herself walking back toward the exit instead. Leaving first, before she can be left.

• • •

Logan is dry heaving into a parking lot trash can when Remy finds her. He puts a hand on her back, but she can barely feel it, barely register the sensation through the tingling numbness that's overtaken her body.

She keeps trying to expel the contents of her stomach, but nothing comes up. Remy rubs circles on her back.

"Do you know what I need right now?" he says in a gentle, soothing voice.

Logan moves away from the trash can. "What?"

"Whataburger."

She thinks about walking away from Joe when he's hooked up on those machines, inches away from death. She thinks about walking away from Rosemary when her unguarded heart must be breaking. She's selfish and self-sabotaging. Unfeeling and unloving. An apathetic asshole. Like her mom.

She doesn't deserve Joe or Rosemary. She doesn't deserve anything good. She hates herself in this moment, but she looks at Remy and says, "Yeah. Burgers."

That's how she ends up in the Whataburger drive-through in the middle of a panic attack.

She's fully numb, and she barely registers the drive down Belleville Boulevard and into the fast-food parking lot. When they roll up to the window, Remy orders enough fries, burgers, and small unsweetened teas to feed an army before turning to her. "And what are you having?"

Logan leans closer to the open driver's-side window. The thought of food makes her empty stomach heave again, but she has the vaguest notion that it's lunchtime. That food might help ease the jitters. She orders a fry, burger, and large Coke.

"What the fuck is this?" she asks five minutes later when Remy passes along her drink.

"Your large Coke."

"This isn't large." She can't even wrap her hands around the cup and the absurd sight of it yanks her out of her fugue state. "Why would anyone want two gallons of soda?"

"This is clearly your first encounter with Southern fast-food sizes."

"Why didn't you warn me?"

"I thought you wanted a large!" Remy yells back at her. For the first time since she met him, he sounds irritated. "I didn't want to shame your food choices!"

"Whoa. Are you okay?"

"Of course I'm not okay!" Remy slams his open palm against the steering wheel as he pulls away from the window and into a parking spot. "None of this is okay!"

Logan watches as his hands curl around the wheel and squeeze. "I thought you never got angry," she says.

"I am angry," he says, but he only sounds sad. "Joe walked out of my life thirty years ago like we meant nothing, and now he's walked back into it just so he can leave again. I'm really fucking angry." Remy takes a deep breath and swipes one hand over his face. "And I'm hurt. I'm heartbroken. I love him so much—I never stopped loving him. But I'm so mad at him, and I feel guilty for being mad because he's going to die."

He starts to cry, and for a moment, Logan doesn't know what to do. But then she thinks of Rosemary, and she simply reaches out. Places her hand on Remy's shoulder and lets him cry.

"How can I be so happy that I had the chance to say goodbye and so goddamn furious with him for coming back into my life just to fucking die?"

She wants to be able to comfort him, but she doesn't even know how to comfort herself. "Because life is a prickly pear," she tries. "It's always going to be beautiful and painful."

Remy smiles softly at her. "You sound like Joe."

They both sit in silence for a moment while Remy dries his eyes on a Whataburger napkin. "You should eat your lunch," he eventually says. "Before it gets cold."

Logan reaches into the bag. Her burger is the size of a hubcap. "This is the most ridiculous thing I've ever seen!" And somehow, the comically large food makes her burst out laughing, and then Remy is laughing too, and maybe crying again. They both laugh-cry so hard and so long, they can't even see each other over the Gay Mobile's center console.

Chapter Thirty

LOGAN

By the time they get back from Whataburger, the hospital has moved Joe again. This time, he's on the second floor. When they step off the elevator, there's a blue wall in front of them, words painted in white.

And I think to myself what a wonderful world.

Their arms are full of Whataburger, and Remy insists on feeding every nurse on Joe's floor before he goes to see Joe himself. "Are you coming?" Remy asks, reaching out a hand to Logan so they can go into Joe's hospital room together.

She wants to be there for Remy. She wants to be there for Rosemary, who must be so lonely at Joe's bedside. She wants to be there for Joe. But she can't make her feet move toward that hallway.

Logan waves away Remy's hand. "Actually . . . I-I should go home and check on Odie. He's been alone all morning, and I'm sure he's scared."

Remy doesn't break eye contact. "When you're ready, Logan."

She's not sure she'll ever be ready. This was always a death trip; death was always going to be the destination. But Logan has been taking detours and scenic routes, like the right highway might spare them from it.

She drives back to Remy's in a daze and finds Odie lying by the front door like he's waiting for Joe to come home. A vat of Coke sloshes around in her stomach as she puts on his leash and takes him outside.

She's sweating after a few steps through the neighborhood, and Odie is walking cautiously, like he can't quite trust the enjoyment of the outing. Without realizing it, Logan is suddenly holding her phone.

She's pressing the favorites button in her contacts.

"Chicken!" Her father shouts after two rings. "How are you?"

His cheerful voice and the sound of music in the background feel jarring. She imagines him dancing around the kitchen with his spatula, and then she's crying again.

"Logan?" he says gently but seriously. She wants to reassure him that everything is okay, but nothing is okay, and all she can do is put one foot in front of the other and sob into the phone. "He's going to die, Dad."

Her dad is silent on the other end except for the sound of a slow, steady exhale.

"I don't . . . I can't . . . I haven't been able to accept that he's dying and now he is. I don't want him to die."

"No," her dad says. "I know you don't, my Chicken."

"It is going to hurt like a punch to the tit."

"It is," he says.

"It . . . it's going to hurt like it did when Mom left."

"It will," Antonio echoes quietly. "It has to. Joe is *worth* that hurt."

"You don't understand, Dad," she blathers into the phone, but the truth is, she doesn't understand, either. She doesn't know why it's so hard for her to let in that hurt. "I . . . I don't know how to love halfway," she reasons aloud. "I don't know how to care just a little bit. If I let myself care at all, I'm going to care with every ounce of my being. And if I do that, and I lose them, it will hurt like hell."

She's not sure if she's talking about Joe or Rosemary or both of them. The sun is blinding and she can't see a thing.

"And . . . and I don't know how to hurt halfway, either," she continues. "I don't know how to feel anything in moderation."

There is no silence on the other end this time. "Ah, but Chicken," her dad says immediately. "Your big feelings are one of the most beautiful things about you."

• • •

It takes her twenty-four hours to go see Joe.

Rosemary doesn't leave his bedside once over the course of that first day, and Logan finds a million excuses not to see his bedside at all. She has to take care of Odie. She has to go get dinner for Remy and Rosemary. She has to get Joe a change of clothes.

Someone needs to run to Rouses for supplies.

Someone needs to make sure the gallery is still doing okay.

Someone needs to get a good night's sleep.

She doesn't sleep well, though, and when she gets to the hospital midmorning on Monday, she finds Remy waiting for her next to the Louis Armstrong quote. "He's awake," Remy says, throwing his arms wide around Logan. He smells like bleach and stale coffee, and he holds Logan as tight as he can against his chest. "They were able to take him off the BiPap machine, and he's talking and everything. Rosemary is with him now."

Logan immediately cycles through her excuses, but then she learns that Joe's first order of business after regaining consciousness was to tell Rosemary she smells like dirty feet and order her to go to Remy's, shower, and sleep. Remy got the same marching orders.

Logan sees Rosemary as she passes through the waiting room. She looks pale and exhausted, with bloodshot eyes and purple bags under them, her hair is stringy and unwashed, still loaded with the gel they used the night of the drag show.

Logan wants to reach out to her, but Rosemary won't even look at her. She brushes right past.

With Remy and Rosemary gone, someone has to go sit with Joe.

• • •

"You look like shit," she says from the doorway to his hospital room. In bed, Joe turns his head slowly toward her and his eyes go wide.

"No! Nurses! Not her!" He reaches for the call button. "Nurses! Help! Not the mean one!"

Logan rolls her eyes. "That must be one hell of a fentanyl patch."

"I'm sorry." Joe blinks up at her. "Who are you?"

"You're a riot," she deadpans, and he hack-laughs wetly. It sounds like he's drowning from the inside out.

She throws herself down in the chair pulled close to the bed. The blanket is beige and pulled up over his herringbone hospital gown. His skin is even beige-ier. He both is and isn't Joe. His eyes are their usual rich brown, but glassy, a little vacant. Easily drifting in and out of focus. His skin is drooping more prominently around his jaw line. And there's that pinch in the corner of his mouth that suggests he's in pain, though he'd never admit it.

"I really thought you were dead," she tells him.

A spark alights in his eyes before he says, cavalierly, "Just give it a few more days."

Logan refuses to start crying this early in the visit. "Well, you can't die here, okay? It's not on the itinerary, and you know how Hale gets."

"Is she *Hale* again?"

She truly doesn't know. And then, quite predictably, she's crying again. "Joe, I'm so, so sorry. This . . . it's all my fault."

He begins to protest, but she cuts him off with the argument that's been spiraling through her head for the last two days. *Pushed you, detours, pretended it wasn't real.*

"My sweet girl," he says in a tired voice. "None of this is your fault. I was always going to end up here."

She tries to blink away her tears, but they're coming too quickly. She wants to hide them behind her sunglasses. She wants to push them away and pretend like nothing ever hurts her. But her dad is right. Joe is worth this hurt. "I told myself you wouldn't," she confesses. "You said you were going to die, and I waved it off. Refused to acknowledge it. I pretended it wasn't happening because I didn't want to feel any of it."

"I know," he says.

"Then why did you pick me to take you on this trip?" She realizes she's shouting at a dying man—that she's forcing Joe to console her when he is the one in the hospital—but she can't quite stop herself. "I'm the worst person to be with you at the end, Joe. I don't take anything seriously, I avoid all negative feelings, I'm a fuckboy—"

"You're not a fuckboy."

"I am! I don't know how to care about other people, and I don't know how to let people care about me."

Joe swipes away her tears with his thumb. "You care about me. So much."

She laughs. "Yeah, and look where that's got me. When you die, it's going to fucking destroy me."

Joe uses what little strength he has to push her feet off the bed. "Good. It should destroy you. If nothing can destroy you, Logan, then what's the point?"

She stares at the beeping monitor. A lifeline. Oxygen reduced to a number.

"The detours and the shrimp po'boy and the days I spent laughing with you—that was the beauty I wanted before the pain of dying. I want you by my side when I die because I know you'll make it as beautiful as possible. You always find joy and wonder in the world. It's one of the many things I love about you."

"I love you too, Joe," she manages through the hurt and tears. She leans in close and props her chin on his shoulder. He winces, and she pulls back. "Does it hurt?"

He presses a hand to his heart. "Dying hurts so much. But I want you close."

She carefully climbs up onto the bed, tucking herself against him as gently as she can. "Are you scared, Joe? Of dying?"

"I'm only scared of dying in beige." His eyes are starting to droop and the words come out slowly, without their intended comedic effect. "Yes. Yes. I'm scared."

"How can I help, Joe?"

The pain meds must be kicking in because his words begin to slur. "Just . . . please don't leave me again, okay?"

Logan snuggles her face against his chest so he won't know she's crying again. "I won't, Joe. I promise."

His eyes slide closed, and Logan takes out her phone and cues the right song, letting the soft sound fill the hospital room.

Have I told you lately that I love you?

Ease my troubles, that's what you do.

His pain grimace dissolves into a genuine smile. "Apt," he says.

"Very apt," she agrees.

"You had to, Logan," he says, half-gone. "You had to come on this trip. You see that, right?"

Logan lets herself quietly cry as Joe falls asleep to Van. She watches his chest rise and fall like he's a newborn baby, counting the distance between each breath.

ROSEMARY

On the drive back to Remy's, she feels like she's waking up from two days in bed with a fever. Everything that's happened since the ambulance feels hazy and unfocused, as if she weren't fully conscious for any of it. Now, she's re-emerging, and she's disoriented by the world outside the car windows.

Has Ocean Springs always been this ugly? Flat and unvaried, chain restaurants and chain stores blending into the cracked concrete and humid, gray sky. A few days ago, Ocean Springs felt like a magical bubble, but now, it will be the place Joe dies. It's the place where her relationship with Logan dies, too.

When they step inside the house, Odie is right there, curled up in a ball and waiting for Joe. And then Rosemary is on the floor, too, crying for the first time since the hospital. She wraps her arms around Odie and coats his black fur with her tears. She releases all of her emotions, and Odie absorbs them, and Remy just lets her cry in the entryway for as long as she wants.

Eventually, the tears run dry, and both Rosemary and Odie get into the shower. Beneath a stream of scalding hot water, she feels the last two days seep out of her.

The terror and adrenaline of hearing Remy cry out—of bursting into the bedroom to find Joe unconscious, maybe dead.

The instinct to repress all her feelings and worries and fly into problem-solving mode. To have control over the uncontrollable.

Sitting in the ambulance with Joe, holding his hand while the paramedics poked and prodded his body like it was already a lifeless cadaver, telling herself not to think about it, *forcing* herself not to feel.

The hours of uncertainty in the waiting room and the relief when he was stable. Turning toward Logan because she could finally let herself feel. She wanted to hold Logan and be held as the feeling overtook them both.

And then Logan walked away. Logan *left* her.

Rosemary cries in the shower as she washes Odie with her expensive vanilla shampoo and tries not to feel the way she did in that moment, watching Logan's back recede down a long hallway and realizing she was completely alone in her feelings.

She should've known Logan would walk away eventually. That's what Logan *does*, and even though they had a few magical days in Ocean Springs, it doesn't mean Rosemary is an exception to Logan's rules.

Rosemary should've expected it and was blindsided all the same.

But she packaged it all up, filed it all away, and forced herself to stay in control for every minute she spent beside Joe's bed.

She cries again when she gets out of the shower and sees her ruined reflection in the steamy mirror. She cries again when she steals one of Logan's big T-shirts and wears it as pajamas instead of her sleep dress.

And when the last of her tears are purged, she realizes she's absolutely starving. Rosemary pads out to the kitchen with Odie at her feet and little regard for her pantlessness.

Pants don't seem so important when your favorite person is dying.

In the kitchen, she finds Remy sitting at the table and staring at the half-finished puzzle. It's late, and the world outside is dark.

"I'm sorry for interrupting," she whispers into the quiet.

Remy looks up from the puzzle and manages a small, sad smile. "You're not interrupting. I've been waiting for you."

He rises slowly from his chair. "I've put the kettle on for some tea and made sandwiches."

There's suddenly a turkey sandwich in front of her, and she almost starts crying again in joy. They sit across from each other at the table and eat their sandwiches in silence. When that's done, Remy clears their plates and returns to the table with two mugs of peppermint tea.

Rosemary wraps her hands around the warm mug. "I'm awful. It's been complete hell for the past two days, and I haven't even asked how you're doing."

He takes a slow, deliberate breath. "You're not awful, Rosemary. And I'm doing terribly. How else would I be?"

"I'm sorry."

He takes a small sip of his steaming tea. "I suppose that's the cost of loving someone . . ."

She lapses into uncomfortable silence and stares out the kitchen window into the dark backyard, but all she can see is herself reflected back to her. "I'm not sure it's worth it."

Remy's eyes feel heavy on her. "I've felt that way, too, at times, especially since y'all showed up here."

She glances down at the fingers curled around her too-hot mug. "And what did you decide?" Under the table, Odie comes and puts his head in her lap. He always knows when she needs him most. She strokes his ears in that familiar, comforting pattern, trying to self-soothe the chaos inside her.

"I don't know yet," he says after another sip of tea. "Ask me again after he's gone."

Rosemary strokes Odie's ear over and over again. "Logan is gone, and I don't think it was worth it at all," she says, and she feels an immediate stab of guilt for bringing up Logan when Joe is dying.

"Logan is still here."

The tea is finally cool enough for Rosemary to take a sip. "She walked away from me at the hospital. When I needed her most, she just walked away."

She strokes and sips and strokes. "And that's her whole deal. She runs at the first sign of anything real, and I was so naïve to think she might stick around for me."

"Was I naïve, for believing Joe would come back to me one day?" Remy asks, and Rosemary has no clue how to respond to that.

Remy clears his throat. "Let me ask you something: What do you gain by being in control all the time?"

She's startled by the question. "Oh, you know. Safety. Security. A false sense of order in a chaotic world. The reassurance that I won't end up in rehab again."

Remy nods and sips. "But what do you *lose* by being in control all the time?"

She stares down at the fragmented image of the abandoned puzzle and thinks about seeing the Grand Canyon at sunrise and the stars over Mesa Verde. About nude photo shoots and dancing in headlights. A Google Doc with ten thousand words and the boring life waiting for her in Vista Summit. The *lonely* life, without inti-

macy or connection, where she comes home to plants and a lamination machine, and only confides in a mother who can never meet
her emotional needs.

"Joe will never be able to finish this," she says as she picks up a
single puzzle piece and turns it over in her hands.

"Should we finish it for him, then?" He adjusts his chair so it's
closer to the table, and Rosemary does the same.

"We should."

She holds the piece beside the completed picture on the box: the
gray ocean breaking against jagged rocks. Rosemary's piece is part
of the stormy sky. She slots it into place. One by one, they put the
pieces where they belong, until it's after midnight and the puzzle is
finished. Until they're both crying over all the things Joe will never
see come together.

Chapter Thirty-One

ROSEMARY

"I don't want it!"

"Stop being such a stubborn ass!"

"It's my ass!" Joe shouts from his hospital bed. "I get to be stubborn about it if I want to!"

"The problem is that other people care about your wrinkly ass, and this is the least you can do for us!" Logan shouts back.

"I'm sorry, Logan, but my death isn't about you."

"You made it about me! About us! Will you please talk some sense into him?" Logan wheels around and looks at Rosemary directly for the first time in four days. They've been alternating shifts with Joe, passing each other like ships in the night, only existing in the same room whenever it's time for this fight.

Rosemary massages her temples. The combination of hospital disinfectant, fluorescent lighting, and screaming has her feeling overstimulated and anxious and so very tired. Logan's hazel eyes aren't helping, either. "Joe, please. Just get the procedure," Rosemary begs in her exhaustion.

Joe reaches for the call button and presses it. "Nurses! These cretins are trying to prolong my life against my will!"

Dr. Rutherford, the oncologist, walks over to the call button and turns it off with her usual unflappable calm.

"Can we try discussing this like rational adults?" Remy suggests. "And *quiet* adults?"

Logan has turned to Dr. Rutherford, her last hope. "Please tell him he has to do it."

"Unfortunately, I cannot do that. . . ."

"Fine! You gave Hale power of attorney, so she'll just sign off on the procedure for you!"

Dr. Rutherford clears her throat. "That's not how power of attorney works."

"You need to have the liquid removed from your lungs, you fussy little fuck!"

"No, I don't!"

Rosemary keeps rubbing her temples like they're Dorothy's ruby slippers, and eventually, they'll take her away from all this death and fighting. They've been having this argument off and on for the last three days. It's always the same: Dr. Rutherford tells Joe he needs to have the fluid removed from his lungs using a procedure called thoracentesis. Joe demands to be checked out of the hospital instead. Logan yells at him.

"Joe, *please.*" Rosemary finally drops her hands away from her face. "Please. Don't put this on us. If you don't have the thoracentesis procedure, the end is going to come quick. And it's going to be painful. Please don't put us in the position to watch you suffer."

"I'm not going to suffer. They'll give me the good end-of-life drugs. I'll be as high as a fucking kite, just like I planned."

"And what about Maine?" she asks.

"We're still going to Maine," he says confidently.

"I don't recommend traveling to Maine in your condition, Joseph. . . ."

"I'm sorry, Doc, but I have to," he says in a barely there whisper. That's the thing about the yelling. It never lasts for too long. Either the pain gets to be too much, or the meds kick in and he falls asleep, or his oxygen levels drop and they switch into life-saving mode instead.

The end is going to quickly come no matter what they do.

"I'll have home hospice when I get to Bar Harbor," Joe barters with the doctor. "Remy has already arranged everything." He licks his dry lips. On instinct, Logan grabs his water bottle and holds the bendy straw to his mouth. Logan's screaming never lasts long, either. It always dissolves into this: caring for Joe the best she can. It makes Rosemary's heart hurt.

"You promised me, girls," Joe croaks. "You promised me you wouldn't let me die in beige."

Rosemary turns to look at Logan, and Logan looks back at her, and Rosemary feels the same rush in her gut. The desire to hold and be held. "Fine," Logan finally says, her shoulders slumped in defeat. "Fine. No beige, old man. A promise is a promise."

"I'm not getting the procedure," Joe says, one last time. "And I want to be discharged."

Dr. Rutherford clears her throat. "There are just a few things I'd like to go over with you in the hall, then." The doctor directs this statement to Rosemary, but Logan steps in.

"Let's step outside," Logan says, and she looks at Rosemary one last time before they leave. Rosemary is so grateful to be spared another conversation about the logistics of death, she almost weeps.

"I need to call home hospice back," Remy says, pulling out his phone, and then he's gone too and it's just her and Joe.

"You understand, don't you? Why I don't want this procedure?" She sits down on the edge of his bed. "I do."

"Thank you, Rosie," Joe croaks. "Thank you."

She can't accept his thanks for letting him die, so she just sits there in silence, staring at his beige blanket.

Joe suddenly shifts in bed. "I have something I've been meaning to give to you." He points a finger at a manila envelope sitting on one of the chairs by the window. It wasn't there before; Remy must have brought it from the house. She climbs off the bed to fetch it. It's heavy in her hands, nothing but the word "Rosemary" scrawled across the front in Joe's loopy script.

She returns to the bed. "What is this, Joe?"

He shakes his head. "Just open it."

So, she does. A huge stack of papers slide out into her hands.

No, not just papers. Her papers. Her writing. Newspaper articles and essays and poems she sent him during undergrad. Short stories and random chapters of almost-books. He kept it all. All of her words gathered together in a neat little stack. It's like a box where a mother might keep every macaroni necklace and handmade Mother's Day card. She doesn't know if she should be flattered or slightly terrified she has a dying stalker.

"Joe . . . ," she says hesitantly. "What is all this?"

"You think it's weird I kept it all these years," he surmises simply by studying her expression, and Rosemary isn't terrified at all. No one knows her better than Joe. "But I was always so proud of you and your brilliant work, Rosie. You reminded me so much of myself. That love of words. That passion and care. You loved writing, my girl."

She stares down at the stack. He kept her work because he was *proud.* Years of considering Joe a replacement father, and she never once wondered if he might see her the same way: as a replacement daughter, a token from the path in life he didn't choose.

She flips through the pages one at a time, remembering each assignment she finished days early, and the sense of pride she felt at every perfect grade. She remembers the stories she stayed up all night to write. All of her words chosen with love and care and *joy.*

At the back of the stack is a single sheet of stationery. White with a blue border and the words "From the desk of Joseph Delgado" stamped on the bottom. She gave him that stationery pad as a gift for his sixtieth birthday, only two months before the diagnosis. On that single piece of stationery, is a short note.

I kept it all for when you're a famous author one day.

"You . . . you weren't going to give me this until after you died, were you?" she muses.

"No, but I thought you might need a little . . . encouragement, these days. Some inspiration to go after the things you love."

She stares at the years of work she threw away because safety was more important than love.

What do you lose by being in control all the time?

Ocean Springs, Mississippi to Bar Harbor, Maine

Chapter Thirty-Two

ROSEMARY

Eight days after Joe was admitted to the Ocean Springs hospital, they leave for Maine.

"Are you sure you don't want to come with us?" Rosemary asks Remy one last time on his front lawn Sunday morning. It was one of the many surprises of the past few days: Remy isn't coming with them to Maine. He and Joe decided this was the goodbye they wanted.

"I'm sure." Remy's smile is unreadable in the early morning light. "We've had our happy ending."

Logan hangs herself out the passenger-side window. "You had *multiple* happy endings from what I could hear." She removes her sunglasses and winks at him.

"Logan Maletis, I will miss you very much." Remy edges toward the swamp gutter so he can plant a kiss on Logan's cheek. Rosemary has to turn away from the gesture. Eight days, and she and Logan still haven't talked about anything but Joe's medical care and the semantics for getting him to Bar Harbor.

They haven't talked about what happened at the hospital when Logan walked away, they haven't talked about what was happening before, when it felt like they were building something new and beautiful between them. They haven't touched each other in eight days; they've barely looked at each other. It's like it used to be back in Vista Summit: constantly circling each other, colliding but never connecting.

Rosemary's not sure how she'll survive losing Joe when she's already grieving losing Logan.

Remy interrupts her morose thoughts when he hoists a giant red cooler in through the open side door of the van. "I packed y'all a tomato pie for lunch, along with some fried chicken and potato salad for dinner. And a peach cobbler for dessert, of course. There are also meals for you girls to freeze when you get to Bar Harbor. Jambalaya, a batch of biscuits with my homemade gravy, and a week's worth of okra soup with shrimp."

"Auto mechanic shrimp?" Logan asks.

"As demanded, yes, I got it from Gladys's, though I will not be held responsible for the gastrointestinal distress caused by this choice."

"It will be worth it." Logan adjusts her sunglasses back over her eyes.

Rosemary reaches up and pulls Remy into a clumsy hug. "Thank you, Remy. I promise we won't starve."

He kisses both of her cheeks, and she knows *this* is his love language: feeding people, even when he's hurting. She holds on to him longer than she probably should.

"I'll be seeing you soon," Remy whispers into her ear before he finally pulls away. "And one last thing."

He jogs back to the front porch and grabs a package. It's a flat rectangle wrapped in brown paper, clearly another one of his paintings. "This is for you, mon chéri."

Remy sets the package on the back seat next to Joe. "Now, don't you open this until you get to where you're going. I want you to hang it on the wall in the living room of that old cottage."

It's unclear if Joe can hear his old lover. If he can understand. His eyes flutter open and closed, but they're unfocused. Un-Joe. The hospital gave him one last fentanyl patch for the drive, but even with it, the pain of loading into the van was almost too much.

Remy cuts his gaze to Logan. "Will you make sure he's alert when he opens it? I really want him to see it."

Logan gives a salute. Remy half climbs into the van to kiss Joe's dry lips. "I'll be seeing you soon too, my love."

Joe's eyes are closed when he responds, "But not too soon."

Remy visibly holds back his tears, for Joe's sake. "Not too soon. I promise."

He closes the side door. Odie wails from the back seat, then jumps into the front to sit on Logan's lap so he can wail some more. Remy reaches through the window to scratch his ears one last time. Rosemary is already in the driver's seat, putting on her own sunglasses to mask her tears.

Then she pulls away from the swamp gutter, away from the brick house where she was so happy and so sad, and away from Remy St. Patin.

"The South sucked anyway," Logan says through her own phlegmy tears as they get back on the highway. "Dragonflies the size of seagulls? Who needs it?"

"And mosquitoes the size of dragonflies," Rosemary adds. "And the goddamn swamp ass."

"Lady fucking Gaga," Logan splutter-sobs. "The swamp ass. Being outside is like swimming through a vat of gumbo. And it smells like ball sack."

"And why is there always a Dollar General right next to a Dollar Tree? Come on, Mississippi, that's just bad urban planning." Rosemary chokes on a sob. She doesn't want to cry right now—not about Joe and not about Logan. She wants to see the road in front of her. She wants to drive away from this place as fast as she can. "And the food is terrible. I'm still digesting most of it."

"There are no mountains, no hills, no elevation at all. It's just *flat*. And the live oaks with Spanish moss aren't even *that* beautiful."

They both know it's one of the most beautiful things they've ever seen.

"And the people weren't even *that* nice."

Rosemary thinks about Remy and Gladys and Dr. Rutherford. Of all the queens at drag night who cheered for Joe as he danced in his wheelchair.

"And the sunsets were mediocre at best."

Rosemary thinks about that evening on the bayou, the perfect sunset and the perfect feeling of being in Logan's arms.

Rosemary clicks on the blinker and pulls over onto the shoulder of I-10 so she can cry until they're ready to move forward again.

LOGAN

Twenty-six hours.

That's how long it will take them to get to Bar Harbor.

Twenty-six hours *straight* of driving, because it's too painful for Joe to get in and out of the van. Twenty-six hours of looking over her shoulder, hoping Joe is still alive. Twenty-six hours trapped in a van three feet from Rosemary Hale, switching drivers every few hours. Remembering what they had and struggling to figure out how to get it back. *If* she even wants to get it back.

Falling apart was inevitable, wasn't it? They were playing house in Ocean Springs, but Logan was always going to find a way to fuck it all up. She was always going to push Rosemary away.

Through the rest of Mississippi and most of Alabama, Logan pretends everything is normal, like this is still any other day in their road trip across the country. She cues a playlist and DJs the best songs, dancing with her upper body, turning around to ask Joe things like, "Best party anthem of the early-aughts?"

Joe never responds, but Odie always whines like he's trying to answer for Joe. And Odie is probably a Kesha stan.

She pulls Rosemary into inane conversations about vanity license plates and the abundance of Waffle Houses that are missing letters from their signs. She eats three of Remy's biscuits for breakfast and stares out the window at the changing landscape once again. Goodbye, crepe myrtle and crabgrass. Goodbye, magnolia trees. Goodbye to the place where she let herself be open and vulnerable with Rosemary Hale. Goodbye to the place where she lost her.

In the next twenty-six hours, they will pass through ten states, all places Logan's never been. She presses her forehead to the warm glass and feels a brief flare of sadness for all the things she won't see along the way. They'll pass it all by at sixty miles per hour, a blur of green trees and freeway walls until it gets dark.

They pass a rusted tractor turned over in a field of cotton now, and it strikes Logan as the loneliest thing she's ever seen.

She'll be back, she decides. She'll return to the South (just maybe not in July). She'll visit all the places from here to Maine, some day. Now that she's seen some of the world, she's hungry for all of it. Too hungry to stay in Vista Summit forever.

She laughs to herself, and her breath fogs up the window.

"What?" Rosemary asks.

"Joe was right," Logan admits. He's asleep in the back seat, still out of it from the fentanyl.

"Joe is always right," she says. "What was he right about this time?"

"I had to go on this trip."

ROSEMARY

She's never been more miserable than she is in Alabama.

Losing Joe is going to hurt like hell, but losing Logan when she's still *right here*, an arm's reach away behind that steering wheel—being next to Logan but not being allowed to touch her—is a kind of grief she isn't prepared for. Like trying to mourn a ghost who won't stop haunting her.

Joe is going to die, and they're going to return to Vista Summit, and it will be like they never held each other in moonlight in the Gulf of Mexico.

In Montgomery, they get onto I-81 North, and Rosemary puts on the end of the *Persuasion* audiobook. Logan doesn't protest, and at one point, Rosemary looks over to catch her tearing up.

"Are you okay?"

Logan sniffles. "I get why you read this straight shit. It's a really good book."

Outside Chattanooga, they stop at a dog park so Odie can run around. She sits on a bench, forcing herself to eat cold tomato pie, thinking about all the unused pages of her binder. The things she prepared for that never happened, and all the things she never could've predicted. She tries not to think about how every minute brings them closer to Bar Harbor and further from each other.

The Southwest and Remy and the drag show. Falling for her. Letting her walk away.

"I've been thinking about Odie," she says while the dog chases birds around the open field.

"What's there to think about?" Logan asks. Her Tupperware of tomato pie is completely empty.

"I've been thinking about what happens to Odie *after* . . ."

She doesn't say *Joe dies*. They never really say it, not fully, not aloud. The Gay Mobile is parked right behind them, the side door open, the baby monitor connecting them to Joe. "Someone will need to take the dog," she says down to her still-full portion of tomato pie. "I-I know it took me a while to warm to him, but I think I should do it. I should take him."

"You don't have to do that," Logan says quickly. "I can take him."

"No, no. You live with your dad, and you don't want to sign Antonio up for that."

"But you have intense cat energy."

"Yes, but for some inexplicable reason, he likes me better, so I should—" On cue, Odie races over and thrusts his head onto Rosemary's lap, pushing the pie onto the ground. She obeys the tacit command and scratches him behind the ears.

"It's not so inexplicable," Logan says quietly. Rosemary doesn't know what to do with that comment, so she lets it blow away in the Tennessee summer breeze.

She presses her face into Odie's fur. At least she won't lose him.

LOGAN

"You need to eat something," Logan tells Rosemary in a McDonald's parking lot in Roanoke, Virginia.

"I'm not hungry," Rosemary snaps, which is proof that she is. She sits in the back seat next to Joe, wringing a wet paper towel into his mouth, so he'll drink *something*.

"Have some fried chicken." Logan outstretches a nugget.

Rosemary swats it away. "I'm definitely not hungry for fried chicken."

Logan isn't particularly hungry for fried chicken, either, but she forces herself to take one listless bite after another because this is their dinner stop. Because she needs to keep her energy up. She needs to take care of herself so they can keep taking care of Joe.

Rosemary has had four iced coffees and maybe three bites of tomato pie all day. "Come on, Rosie. We're not even halfway, and I can tell you're fading. Please eat."

"Don't call me that!" she snaps again. She sounds like old Rosemary. Like the woman who would read her for filth in a staff meeting, like the woman who crashed into her car and still chewed her out, just to feel in control of something.

"Please," Logan tries. "Take care of yourself."

Rosemary's face twists into a sneer, and then she stomps out of the van and across the parking lot. She disappears into McDonald's in an angry huff. Odie makes distressing noises that mirror Logan's distressing thoughts the entire time she's gone.

Fifteen minutes later, Rosemary flies out of McDonald's just as quickly as she went in, clutching a brown to-go bag in one hand and a half-eaten double cheeseburger in the other. She houses the rest of the burger before she even reaches the van. Face blotchy from crying and a dollop of ketchup in the corner of her mouth, and she looks like herself in this moment. The version of herself she unearthed over the course of this trip.

"I'm sorry," Rosemary says. "I was hangry, and tired, and you—"

Logan cuts her off. "It's okay. Why don't I drive a little longer so you can sleep?"

Rosemary takes a deep breath like there's more she wants to say. Whatever it is, she exhales and eats a McDonald's french fry instead of saying it.

"Okay. Thank you."

Logan puts her sunglasses back on. "What are friends for?"

ROSEMARY

Is that what they are now? *Friends?*

As they drive out of Roanoke, she blasts "Bitch." She belts it out so loudly that the volume of her own voice drowns out all the other thoughts in her head. No room for fear or grief or sadness. No space to miss Joe or Logan while they're still right here. Only room for Meredith Brooks.

The song ends, but she puts it on repeat, so it starts again and again, and she sings until her voice goes hoarse.

Logan is behind the wheel, and she's singing, too.

LOGAN

She'll sing this song for however long Rosemary needs. She'll scream the lyrics until she has a splitting headache if that gives Rosemary some peace.

ROSEMARY

They watch the sun go down behind the Blue Ridge Mountains, and how can anything be that beautiful when Joe Delgado is dying?

"I want to come back here," Logan says, watching the colors spread across the sky.

"Me too," Rosemary whispers.

"Me, three," Joe croaks from the back, suddenly awake. "Next summer? Let's take another road trip."

Odie barks in agreement.

LOGAN

Somewhere in eastern Pennsylvania, Joe starts aspirating. His breathing becomes a staggered, choking, wet rattle.

Everything is dark beyond the Gay Mobile. There is nowhere to pull over, no service lights as far as her eyes can see.

Rosemary clicks on the car light, unfastens her seat belt, and climbs into the back. She leans over Joe and tries to clear his mouth with a gloved hand. Then she crouches back there all the way to New York, squeezing the hand pump valve in a perfect rhythm, helping Joe catch his breath. Logan steals glances in the rearview mirror.

"Not yet, old man," Rosemary whispers. "Just a little farther to go."

Logan repeats those words as she hunches over the steering wheel. *Just a little farther to go.*

Her physical pain surpassed her emotional pain two states ago. Everything *hurts*. Her wrists from holding the wheel. Elbows and shoulders and the back of her neck.

Her right knee hurts from keeping it in one position, pressing down on the gas pedal. Her hip flexors. Her lower back.

It's a good thing she never cared too much about her ass, because it broke back on the New Jersey Turnpike. All she can do is hunker down and focus on the few feet of dark road illuminated by her headlights in front of her.

Just a little farther to go. She counts the passing minutes in mile markers. She recites every song from *Rent* in her head.

Joe is more alert once his airways are clear, and Rosemary falls asleep curled up next to him, Odie tucked under her other arm.

"How much farther?" Joe croaks.

"Just a little farther, Joe. Just a little farther."

He goes quiet, and she goes back to counting mile markers.

"Is this hell?" he eventually asks.

"No, this is Connecticut."

ROSEMARY

She dreams she's a puppet master, like in that scene from *The Sound of Music*. A wooden stage with her above it, pulling strings to make the puppets dance. *Lay ee odl lay ee odl lay hee hoo.*

Except the strings have all been cut, so her wooden puppets aren't listening to the commands of her fingers, running around on their own accord. They are leaving her stage, and she is yodeling all by herself.

"Rosie."

Something brushes her shoulder, and she finally lets go of her grip on the strings.

"Rosemary. Wake up."

She blinks away, sees a bright white light. Gas station lights.

Then Logan's face comes into focus above her. She looks terrible.

"I'm so sorry, but I can't drive anymore."

Rosemary tries to sit up, but Odie is pinning her to the back seat. "Where are we?"

"Massachusetts. Please. I'm so tired. I just can't."

"Right. Okay."

Rosemary pees inside a Cumberland Farms with her eyes only

half-open, then zombie crawls her way to the register to buy a Monster energy drink and two packs of Ding Dongs. She'll ride a processed sugar rush through New England.

When she gets back to the van, Logan is already snoring next to Joe. He's vaguely conscious, enough so that he gives Rosemary a droopy version of his smile and says, "Maine doesn't even matter, Rosemary. This does."

She doesn't know what to do with that comment, either.

LOGAN

She wakes up to a smell.

She hasn't slept nearly enough, there's a crick in her neck, and something in the van smells like poop.

Her first thought is cows. Her second thought is Odie.

But then Joe groans deeply and in an unmistakably GI-upset kind of way.

Logan bolts upright.

"Rosemary, something . . . happened . . ."

Joe groans again.

ROSEMARY

There is poop everywhere.

It's five in the morning in a Dunkin' Donuts parking lot in Portsmouth, New Hampshire, and everything is literal *shit*. It's been almost twenty-four hours, and she's reached the delirious stage of the journey.

"How could you possibly poop this much?" Logan shouts with her tank top pulled over her nose like a mask. "You haven't eaten anything!"

Joe responds with a few guttural sounds that vaguely resemble *fuck you*.

Logan gags. "It's like when an infant has a blowout, and you just burn the onesie and move on."

"We will have to burn the Gay Mobile."

"My dignity," Joe wheezes.

"You've got none left. Rosie, I'll lift, and you remove the diaper."

"*You* remove the diaper!" Rosemary shouts back.

"You're not strong enough to lift him!"

"I just got poop on my foot!"

"Odie, no! Don't eat that!"

"If you don't want Odie to eat the poop, don't put the dirty diaper on the floor of the van!"

"Where else should I put it?"

"Outside!"

"In a Dunkin parking lot?"

"Better than *in the van*!"

"God, how is he so heavy? He's already a corpse."

"I can't see to wipe him. Can you shift your phone?"

"You missed a spot. There, on his upper back."

Cough. "Please." Joe coughs again. "Kill me now."

"Is there a bag to put his poopy T-shirt in?"

"Absolutely not. Throw it into the parking lot."

Cough. Cough. "Kill me. Just kill me, girls."

As Rosemary runs across the Dunkin' Donuts parking lot toward an orange garbage can holding a dirty adult diaper and some poop-stained clothes, she thinks *I went to Yale and Columbia.*

I was Valedictorian, class of 2010.

Perfect SAT scores. Scholarships. Washington State Teacher of the Year. Finalist, but whatever.

None of it matters. Every accolade is inconsequential now. Every day that she got to work in the dark and went home in the dark amounts to nothing. The weekends she worked, wearing her busyness like a badge of honor. All the essays she got back to her students faster than the other teachers, all the extra professional development seminars, the conferences, the tireless attempts to be bulletproof. Test scores and gold stars and every little thing that she tries to control, and none of it can protect her from having human diarrhea between her toes at a Dunkin' Donuts. Because ultimately, she doesn't have control over anything.

The puppet strings were never attached. Life was always going to be beautiful and painful in equal measure.

"Why are you muttering to yourself about puppet strings?" Logan asks when she's back at the van.

"I have no control over anything," Rosemary laughs.

She feels drunk.

She feels weirdly and gloriously free.

Joe is going to die. There is no secret medical trial that will save him. No third-act miracle coming their way. Absolutely nothing she can do. So, she frees herself from the burden of responsibility. It's not her fault. All she can do is clean up the shit when it comes.

"I want to write a book," she tells Logan.

"Can we clean the poop off our hands first?"

Another deranged laugh emerges from Rosemary's throat. It's hilarious. Or maybe it's tragic?

The early morning Dunkin' employees take pity on them, and Rosemary washes her feet in the bathroom sink, then orders herself the largest iced coffee possible.

The van still smells like poop, but they drive with the windows down. As they finally cross the state border into Maine, they get to see the sunrise over the Atlantic out the passenger side of the car. Everything is beautiful and painful.

Except the Dunkin' iced coffee. That tastes like actual shit.

LOGAN

Dunkin' has the most magnificent coffee she's ever tasted.

Rosemary is behind the wheel, and she oscillates between laughing at nothing and crying at everything. She seems a few mile markers away from a total mental breakdown.

But the sunrise is in her hair as it whips in the wind of the open windows. Logan wants to sleep, but she doesn't. She watches Rosemary come into full light instead.

ROSEMARY

Bar Harbor, Maine.

At nine o'clock in the morning on July 12, they finally arrive. It only took them a month. She laughs at the thought.

And then she's crying again, because this—this pretty little resort town in northern Maine—is where it all ends.

"Hang in there, Rosie," Logan orders as she uses her phone to navigate them to a small, Cape Cod–style cottage by the sea. "You can sleep soon."

Rosemary tries to keep it together until she pulls into a gravel driveway. There's already a white van with the words *Mount Desert Home Hospice* painted on the side.

Rosemary turns off the engine for the last time. Then, she falls out of the van like a lifeless ball of clay. Somehow, Logan is already there by the driver's-side door, waiting to catch her.

A burly white man with a full auburn beard wearing scrubs appears in front of them, pushing a gurney. He looks like he belongs on the cover of a romance novel about lobster fishermen. "I'm Nurse Addison," he grunts by way of greeting. Rosemary has no idea if Addison is a first name or a last name.

"I'll be overseeing Joseph's medical care," Nurse Addison explains as he effortlessly lifts Joe out of the Gay Mobile and onto the gurney. Rosemary is only vaguely aware of the fact that Logan is still holding her upright.

"And I'm Guillermo," says an equally large man in bright floral scrubs. "Mr. St. Patin hired me to assist Nurse Addison until Mr. Delgado passes. Let's get everyone into the house."

The *house* in question looks like it hasn't been touched since the eighties. Nurse Addison puts Joe into a hospital bed he's set up in the living room, and Guillermo leads Logan and Rosemary upstairs to two bedrooms separated by a shared bathroom.

Separate bedrooms.

Logan deposits Rosemary into a drafty bedroom with maroon carpet and vomit-colored walls. The bed is rickety, sharp coils digging into her back, but she doesn't even care because it's a bed. Odie climbs up next to her and curls himself into a tight ball against her side. Logan turns to go find her own room.

Everything is beautiful and painful.

Rosemary stares at the ceiling as tears roll sideways down her temples. The shower whooshes to life on the other side of the wall.

Rosemary should shower, too. Rosemary should *sleep.*

Instead, she rolls over and studies the room. A dated dresser with a built-in vanity. A dormer window with a desk tucked into the nook. And on the desk, a typewriter. Joe's old typewriter.

She drags her body over to the desk and sits down on the wobbly wooden chair. Out the window, she can see green trees. Sunshine. The ocean.

There's a stack of aged printer paper, almost the same color as the walls, in one of the desk drawers. It takes a few minutes to figure out how, but eventually, she feeds a sheet of paper into the typewriter, her index finger punching an experimental key. The letter *L* appears on the paper with a forceful clack.

She hits another letter. Then another. A word appears, then a sentence, then a paragraph. In a delirium, Rosemary writes a random scene from her new novel. The old wizard who took the heroes on the quest is dying, and they're rushing to get him to the nearest inn before it's too late. . . .

Half-asleep and practically unconscious, Rosemary types and types, feeds in new pages, and fills them up. She doesn't know how to delete on the typewriter, how to go back, so she only goes forward, deeper and deeper into her own grief, thinly disguised in a fantasy world.

"Rosemary." A calm voice. A soft hand on her shoulder. "You need sleep."

She looks at the slew of pages in front of her. She looks at Logan behind her, hair wet, eyes tired.

"I can write a little longer," she says.

Logan shakes her head. "The typewriter is loud. Please. Come to bed."

She lets herself be led back to the rickety bed, lets Logan climb into the bed beside her, wrap her up in limbs that are better than any blanket.

With Odie against her stomach and Logan at her back, Rosemary finally falls asleep.

Bar Harbor, Maine

Chapter Thirty-Three

ROSEMARY

According to her phone, it's 7:37 when she wakes up, but that tells her very little. She has no idea if it's morning or evening, and the muted light coming in through the curtains isn't helping.

There is a quilt over her body. This is a mattress beneath her. She's alone in this bed, but she remembers falling asleep wrapped up in Logan's arms. Maybe she dreamed that part.

The rest of the room comes into sleepy-eyed focus. The carpet and the puke-colored walls and the window. The desk with the typewriter and all her pages.

She climbs out of bed, out of the room, down the stairs. And *oh*. It's evening. She's facing a wall of windows that look out at the Atlantic Ocean during golden hour, and the view is so spectacular, she almost forgets everything else.

"Rosemary," a hoarse voice says, and she turns away from the golden hues and calm water.

Joe.

He's in a hospital bed in the middle of a living room with floor-to-ceiling bookshelves and a giant stone fireplace, eclectic art, and outdated technology. He's raised up just enough that he can see her standing there at the base of the stairs. His brown eyes are open and alert.

"Joe!" She catapults herself toward him, reaches for his papery hand. "You're awake!"

He grunts and holds her hand back.

"I was shocked when he woke up before you."

Rosemary turns and sees Logan sitting sideways on a threadbare reclining chair, her legs spilling over one arm. Rosemary didn't dream it. Those legs were definitely wrapped around her in her sleep.

Their eyes meet, and Logan offers her a brief smile before her gaze drops down to the mug of tea in her hand. Rosemary becomes aware of clanking in the kitchen, and then one of the nurses— Guillermo, she thinks—comes into the living room with another mug of tea.

"Thank you," Rosemary says when Guillermo wordlessly pushes the warm mug into her hands. "I'm Rosemary, by the way."

Guillermo shoots Logan a look in her reclining chair. "I know" is his only response as he shifts to tidying the medical supplies beside Joe's bed.

"Are you the hospice nurse?"

"No, that's Nurse Addison," Guillermo clarifies. Then, he gently adds: "I work for Mount Desert Home Hospice, but I provide wrap-around palliative care. I'm here to make Joseph and you girls as comfortable as possible through the end."

The lumberjack lobster fisherman appears out of nowhere again and extends a beefy hand toward Rosemary. "I'm Nurse Addison," he says in that same gruff, romance hero kind of way. "I'll come by three times a day to check on our patient." Then Nurse Addison *winks* at Joe as he reaches for a tablet to record Joe's vitals.

Joe *blushes*. Not dead yet, then.

Rosemary squeezes his hand tighter. "And how often do you come by?" she asks Guillermo.

"Always," he answers. "Any time you need me. I can stay overnight so you girls can sleep if you want. Or I can take the day shift with him. I live ten minutes away, so I can be here whenever you need me. I'm here to take care of you, so you can take care of him. Being a caretaker is so very hard."

Still half-delirious, Rosemary decides she's a little bit in love with Guillermo.

"Speaking of, are you hungry?"

Rosemary's stomach feels like the Grand Canyon. "Um, a little . . ."

Guillermo makes a *tsk* sound and heads back to the kitchen. "I'll heat up some okra."

"Ah, hell yes!" Logan hoots. "Give me all that auto mechanic shrimp!"

Nurse Addison slides his stylus back into the breast pocket of his scrubs. "Our Joe seems to be in good health, all things considered. The fentanyl seems to still be helping with pain management, but if it gets worse, I can give him some morphine when I come back in the morning. Does that sound okay, Joe?"

Joe blushes again. Nurse Addison squeezes Joe's shoulder, and Joe positively melts.

Once the nurse is gone, Logan whistles. "You old horn dog."

"Joe." Rosemary scoots even closer to his bed. "How are you?"

Joe licks his chapped lips, and Rosemary reaches for a small pink sponge and tries to wet his mouth. "I'm . . . ," Joe starts, then stops. He starts somewhere else entirely. "We made it to Maine, Rosie."

She leans in and kisses his forehead. "We made it."

• • •

The first few days in Bar Harbor fall into an easy rhythm. Nurse Addison arrives at the cottage at five in the morning sharp, when the view through the front windows is still moonlight and mystery. His arrival wakes up either Rosemary or Logan—whoever fell asleep beside Joe's bed the night before. If it's Rosemary, she asks Nurse Addison a dozen questions about Joe's condition, but Nurse Addison's answer is always the same: "He's still alive."

He's not here to cure Joe. He's here to make him comfortable.

Nurse Addison leaves and Guillermo arrives to make coffee and change Joe's diaper, his catheter. He gives him a spot bath, if he wants it, and rubs his feet when they start turning gray from lack of blood flow. As he completes these tasks, Rosemary drinks her coffee on the front porch while the sun rises over the Atlantic Ocean. Logan often joins her out there in the cold, her perpetually bare legs covered in goose bumps.

After coffee, Logan takes Odie for a walk, and in the evening Rosemary does, and in-between, that dog weasels his way onto the hospital bed with Joe, even though there's no room for him.

Logan reads Joe Mary Oliver poems and his favorite novel, *One Hundred Years of Solitude*. Rosemary writes at her window upstairs, and then brings the pages downstairs to read them aloud to Joe after each session. Forward and forward and forward she presses into the story. She might write the whole thing before he's gone.

For some reason, baseball is always playing on the old, wood-paneled TV, even though none of them care about sports. Guillermo feeds them Remy's food, and when they start running out of that, he brings them his mother's homemade tamales and his father's pozole. Rosemary has no idea if this is part of his job, or if he does it simply because he cares.

Sometimes, Rosemary falls asleep in the reclining chair and wakes up to find someone put a blanket over her.

Rosemary writes and Logan reads and Joe sleeps and sleeps and sleeps.

No one says anything about their long-term plan, but Rosemary knows that both she and Logan are here until the end.

LOGAN

"Who is that handsome son of a bitch?" she asks when she gets home from a morning walk with Odie to discover Joe sitting up, eyes wide open. Rosemary's feeding him reheated grits. He *smiles*, and Logan feels her heart stretch out in her chest, like its waking from a weeklong hibernation.

"More like decaying son of a bitch," Joe manages, and his smile turns into a gas grimace.

Rosemary sets aside the grits. "Someone is in very good spirits this morning."

"It sounds like the perfect morning to open your present from Remy, then." Logan snatches up the gift-wrapped frame from the corner of the living room.

"Yes!" Rosemary beams. It's clear she's turned the optimism up to eleven, for Joe's sake. "Great idea!"

"Let's see what your *lover* gave you!"

Joe doesn't have the dexterity to tear the paper, so Rosemary helps as Logan holds it up in front of him. The paper falls away, then the Bubble Wrap, and then they're all staring at another nude painting of Joseph Delgado.

At first glance, it's just like the one from before: Joe, in a bathtub, looking boldly at the artist. But this isn't twenty-five-year-old Joe. It's sixty-four-year-old Joe. This is the same Joe that's in the hospital bed in front of her. The Joe who is dying. And he's absolutely beautiful.

Remy has rendered him magnificent, like an ancient redwood tree, the wrinkles around his eyes as deep as grooves in the bark.

No, he's the Grand Canyon: lines and cracks and crevices cut into a mesmerizing pattern by time and nature. The soft, vulnerable skin drooping from his forearms. The sag of his barrel chest, the puckered skin around his stomach, his thin legs awkwardly folded into the tub. Every part of him looks majestic and perfect, and Logan is crying.

This is love. Love is seeing perfection in every flaw. Seeing every flaw as a miracle because it belongs to the person you care about most. Love is saying, *yes, still. Even after all these years.*

Every brush stroke contains awe and reverence, a love letter to a gay man who grew old, and the miracle of Joseph Delgado. Remy painted Joe with wonder.

"Wow," Rosemary whispers, also with wonder. "It's you, Joe."

Joe laughs, then coughs, then cries. The Joe in this painting isn't staring at viewers with the cocksureness of his younger self. He's staring at them with a desperate plea in those brown eyes. *Live*, he seems to beg. *Live as much as you can.*

Logan clears her throat. "You look like that Johnny Cash song. 'Hurt.'"

"I look like Johnny Cash?" Joe wheezes.

"No, you look the way that song *feels*," she tries to explain. "Like a nice, long cry."

Rosemary snatches up the painting and flies out of her chair. She moves like a woman on a mission, marching over to the wall beside the TV. She removes a painting of a lighthouse and on the bare nail behind it, she hangs the nude portrait of Joe. She adjusts it, then steps back to study it for a second. Rosemary looks pleased with herself, and the sight of her makes Logan's newly awoken heart ache.

Logan wishes she could find a way to paint all of Rosemary's perfect flaws, all the things Logan was wrong about.

Rosemary's not rigid. She simply knows what her brain needs. She's not controlling. She's organized and thoughtful, and she always wants things to be perfect for the people she loves. She's not condescending. She's just usually right, always the smartest person in the room. And she's not that scared little girl who lost her dad. She's the bravest person Logan has ever met. Brave enough to try to be her best self. Brave enough to care.

She cares about Logan. Or she did, back in Ocean Springs. She couldn't hide that at all. The way Rosemary nuzzled herself into Logan each night, like a perfect baby spoon. The way Rosemary would tilt her head up toward Logan without even realizing it, asking for a kiss. The way her eyes softened when Logan touched her, like she couldn't quite believe she was letting herself lose control with someone else.

Logan loved being that someone.

She thinks she could get back to that, if she could find a way to show Rosemary how much she cares.

ROSEMARY

She adjusts the painting of her naked former English teacher one more time.

There. It's perfect.

Rosemary takes a step back and appreciates the sight of it on the wall, on display, where it belongs.

"Girls," Joe says from the hospital bed. "Come here. I need to tell you something."

Rosemary turns around and catches Logan staring at her intently. Their eyes meet across the dated living room, and for a second, she lets herself enjoy the alchemy of those hazel eyes. Slowly, Rosemary crosses the room and sits on the edge of the bed next to Odie.

"Something to, uh, confess . . ." Joe carries on.

"Oh, please, Joe, don't divulge your sins to us," Logan whines. "Twenty years of idolizing you, and it might destroy me if I find out you don't recycle or you voted for Reagan."

Joe laughs. "Don't worry, I'm going to hell with my sins. This is . . . this is about the cottage."

Rosemary takes in the scuffed hardwood floors, and the Formica kitchen countertops and ancient appliances. The big windows and the front porch with a view. "What about the cottage?"

Joe asks for his water, and he takes a long drink through his bendy straw before he can continue. "I-I couldn't part with this house, even after I left Remy and Maine. Remy moved out shortly after I did—the neighbors told me—but I didn't want to sell. I convinced myself that I kept it because it was a good investment—" He coughs for a moment, and Logan helps him drink more water. "But the truth is, I just couldn't stand the idea of parting with it."

Rosemary looks at the nude painting on the wall and understands. Thirty years did nothing to dull the love Remy and Joe had for each other, and he kept this house like keeping a shoebox of old letters, a memento of that love.

"And it *was* a good investment," Joe continues. "I own this house outright. The mortgage is paid off, and home values have increased considerably since I bought it."

"I can only imagine," Logan says slowly. Rosemary doesn't have to imagine. She looked up this cottage on Zillow the day after they arrived. Three bedrooms and an ocean view in a resort town near Acadia National Park? It's worth just under a million, even with all the updates it needs.

"Do you need us to help you sell it?" Logan asks. "Clean it out for you? Whatever you need, we'll do it."

"Yes, of course we will," Rosemary adds. "We'll help take care of the house."

Joe's shoulders relax against his pillows. "I'm glad to hear that, girls. Because it's yours."

Rosemary gapes at him for a moment, not understanding his words. "Wait, what?"

"I left the cottage to both of you," he says slowly. "That . . . that's what I'm trying to tell you."

Rosemary jerks her head up to look at Logan and sees her own shock mirrored back to her. She tries to put her confusion into words. "You . . . you left us . . . *a house?*"

"Yes. That's why I wanted the three of us to come to Maine, together. Because I'm giving you this house."

"Queen fucking Latifah, Joe! You can't give us a house!"

Rosemary is stunned into silence. "Joe." She manages when she finally finds her voice. "Logan's right. You can't leave us this house."

"Who else would I leave it to?"

"Leave it to Remy!" Logan insists. "Damn, that man had to deal with your dramatic bullshit for half a lifetime. This is the *least* you can do for him."

Joe shakes his head. "I talked to Remy about it, and he doesn't want the cottage. He agrees with my choice."

"Was this always your plan? To bequeath us your eighties sex cottage?" Logan pinches Joe's side, and he yelps.

"I am *dying*. Stop hurting me!"

Rosemary starts rubbing her temples. This all feels like too much. Twenty minutes ago, Joe was smiling, and she was feeding him grits. She wants to go back to *that* moment, where she could pretend like everything was okay for a little bit longer. "You . . . you left us this house . . . ? To . . . to share?"

"You're both equal owners, yes." Joe looks at Logan, and Logan looks away. "The house will be yours, to do with it what you want. Sell it, or . . . live in it."

"Live in it?" Logan sounds disproportionately outraged at this suggestion. She stands up so quickly her chair topples over. "Joe, we can't move to Bar Harbor, Maine! Especially not *together*."

Logan flails her arms indignantly, and Rosemary feels her heart crack open all over again. She looks out at the view. Ocean and trees and so much sky. A typewriter under a window and a dog to walk on the beach and quilt that could be big enough for two, if they were snuggled close together.

Joe huffs. "Fine, then sell it. Use the money to build the kind of life you really want for yourselves." He points a gnarled finger at Logan. "Get the fuck out of Vista Summit!" He swivels accusingly toward Rosemary. "Don't go back to teaching! The layoff is a sign it's time to take a risk! Write your book, my darling girl. You only get one life, and it goes by too quickly to spend time waiting for what you want. Have adventures! See cool shit!"

Rosemary feels the pressure of her tears pushing on her sinuses. It's too real. It's all feeling too, too real. He's going to die, and he left them this house, and her anxiety is deafening.

Logan chokes on a sob. "No *Tuesdays with Morrie* shit!" she shouts. "You promised!"

"Logan. My stubborn, reckless, impulsive Logan." Joe is crying now, too. "There has to be a little bit of *Tuesdays with Morrie* shit at the end. Surely you know that."

Logan shakes her head and refuses to hear him.

"I know you think your impulsivity is a flaw, but it's a gift," Joe insists. "Life is too short. You've got to jump in with both feet."

Logan keeps shaking her head, keeps crying. Rosemary wants to reach out for her. She wants to hold her and be held. She doesn't want to go through this alone.

"I lived my life trying to avoid hurt and pain, and I ended up with pancreatic cancer at sixty. You could both guard your hearts for another thirty years, and you will still experience all the same hardship. We're never truly safe. That's *life*."

Rosemary knows that he's talking about them. About their relationship. About the adventure of loving Logan Maletis. Perhaps this entire road trip was all just an elaborate excuse for Joe to cosplay Emma Woodhouse and force the two of them together.

But Logan is already pulling away. She shoves out of her chair and pivots, all set to run away, like she always does, and Rosemary has her answer. Loving Logan isn't worth all this hurt.

Logan makes it to the foot of the stairs before she stops her angry stomp. She turns back, marches to Joe's bedside again, and throws herself back down in the chair. "I said I wouldn't walk away again," she says bitterly. She shifts in the chair like she's being held there against her will. "So, this is me staying."

"Thank you," Joe says to her.

"Thank you," Logan says back. She sounds pissed about it. "Thank you for leaving us this place."

"Thank you both." Joe reaches out for both of them, takes each girl by the hand. "For agreeing to drive a dying man across the country. You understand now, don't you? Why it had to be both of you girls?"

There's a long stretch of silence before Joe speaks again.

"Watching the two of you grow up was the coolest shit I witnessed in this life."

Chapter Thirty-Four

ROSEMARY

The next morning Joe's health declines again. He's feverish and half-asleep. He can't speak, except to mumble incoherently in Spanish. He groans in pain and throws off his blankets, then shivers miserably. Three times he attempts to get out of bed. One time, he falls onto the floor and they have to call Nurse Addison to help get him back into bed without hurting him.

They position Joe's bed so he can stare out the wall of windows whenever he's awake. Guillermo makes cup after cup of tea. Van Morrison spins into silence on the record player. Someone is always by his side.

On the fourth day of this, Guillermo comes into the living room to give Joe a bath, and Logan finds Rosemary standing on the back porch, staring out at the ocean. "How are you holding up?" Logan asks, leaning against the railing beside her.

Rosemary turns just enough to see the exhausted bags beneath Logan's eyes, the tightness in her crooked mouth, the tension in her eyebrows. Neither of them is holding up well. "I just got an email from Miller. It looks like they won't be able to hire me back. I officially don't have a job for the fall."

Logan's hand moves closer, and for one hopeful moment, Rosemary thinks she might reach out for Rosemary's hand. But she doesn't. "I'm really sorry, Rosemary. I know what that job meant to you."

Rosemary turns completely toward her. "What did it mean to me? Because I'm suddenly not so sure."

"You care so much," Logan answers instantly. "You care about the future of education and literacy, and you care about your students more than any teacher I've ever met."

"I do," she agrees. "But do I care about myself?"

"What do you mean?"

"It's like you said in Ocean Springs. Teaching is my whole life, and I don't know how to have a life outside of it. I . . . I had therapy yesterday, with Erin."

Logan is quiet as she waits for Rosemary to continue, her gaze fixed on the water. They haven't had a real conversation in weeks, and Logan hasn't done anything to regain her trust, but Rosemary still wants to talk to her about this.

"I'm good at teaching, and sometimes, I think I've kept doing it because I feel like it's what I owe the world. Joe saved me, and I feel like I should pay it forward. I mean, how can I walk away from a job where I'm making a difference in the lives of teenagers who need me?"

"You don't owe anyone anything," Logan cuts in. "And if you think about teaching that way, you're just going to burn out."

"I know," she says quietly. "That's what I'm starting to realize."

When she read the email from Miller, she didn't feel devastated like she thought she would. Instead, she kept thinking about Joe. About safety and adventure. About what she loses by being in control all the time. She takes four deep breaths. "I think I want to keep the cottage," she tells Logan.

Logan frowns. "And turn it into an Airbnb?"

"No. I want to keep it and live in it." She's not sure when she came to this realization, but it feels like she's speaking some deep truth from a hidden place inside herself. "And I think you should live in it with me."

Logan finally tears her gaze away from the ocean. "Are you serious?"

Rosemary wishes she knew how to be anything other than serious. "I think I want to stay here for a while. Sell my condo, live off my savings and finally write a book like I always dreamed of doing. I could sit at that desk in front of the window looking out at the sea," she continues, the image crystalizing so beautifully in her mind. "I could write it all on Joe's old typewriter."

"You absolutely should, Hale!" Logan says, unable to contain her excitement. "You're such a good writer, and this new story *needs* to be told."

Rosemary flinches at the sound of her last name in Logan's mouth. *Hale* is just another way Logan keeps Rosemary at a distance, and Rosemary wants to protect herself from this new, incoming hurt.

But it's like Joe said. She's going to hurt no matter what, and she doesn't want to be like Joe and Remy. She doesn't want to find Logan again in thirty years when it's already too late. She doesn't want to leave things unsaid. "And I think you should stay here with me," she says again.

Logan takes a step back. "You want us to live in this cottage together? *Why?*"

"Well, for starters, because you hate Vista Summit," she says coaxingly. "And because I want you here. With me."

Logan eyes her suspiciously. "Why?" she asks again.

Rosemary takes a deep breath and imagines herself accessing that wellspring of truth she's kept buried inside her for so long. "Because I'm pretty sure I'm in love with you."

She feels instantly lighter as those words float in the space between them. Because even if Logan takes those words and uses them against her, she said something profoundly true without fear of the pain that will come after.

"You're . . . pretty sure?" Logan asks cautiously.

Another deep breath. "I've never been in love before, but I'm pretty sure it feels like this. Kisses that feel like waking up. Touches that feel like dreaming. Love is finding someone who helps you re-write the story of yourself."

Rosemary waits for Logan to take another step back. She waits for her to run away. But she doesn't. Logan doesn't move or speak or breathe.

"Actually, that's not entirely true," she corrects. "I have been in love before. With you, back when we were kids. It just took me a long time to recognize my feelings for what they were. But I loved you then, and I fell back in love with you now, and I'm not ready for things to go back to how they were before."

All at once, Logan is moving and speaking and breathing heavily. "You don't love me," she says sadly. "This is grief talking. Joe is dying, and the entire world is falling apart, and you're trying to find something to cling to in the wreckage. But it's not me. It shouldn't be me."

"Why not?"

"Because I'm not the woman you fall in love with!" She pushes herself away from the railing and paces in a tight circle across the porch. "I'm a fuckboy, remember? I'm everyone's fun time and no one's forever! Hell, even my own mom couldn't stick around for me."

"Logan, that's not true—"

"It is! Don't cling to me, Rosemary. Because I'll fuck things up. I'll disappoint you. And you'll get bored of my whole schtick sooner rather than later!"

Tears prickle in her eyes, and she's not sure if she's crying for herself or for Logan. "I could never get bored of you."

Logan stops pacing. "Don't love me, okay? I'm not worth it."

She sees Logan through her tears, but she doesn't see a callous fuckboy. No, she sees an eleven-year-old girl with bruised knees who just lost her mom and blamed herself; she sees the little girl who didn't understand her own brain, the girl who thought no one else would ever understand her brain either, the girl who pushed everyone else away. The girl who kissed her in the garden and pretended it didn't matter because she was so afraid of rejection.

Hurt first, so she'll never be hurt at all.

Leave first, so no one ever leaves her.

Careful, not careless.

"You are worth it to me," Rosemary says with all the conviction she can muster. Logan's warm legs under the blankets, her loud laugh and her sharp eyes and the way she can completely envelop Rosemary in arms like Bubble Wrap, so nothing can ever hurt her. "And I won't leave you. If you decide to stay."

"I-I don't want to leave you either," Logan chokes out. "But . . . but I need a minute to think, okay?"

"Okay," Rosemary says. And then Logan does leave.

• • •

Rosemary wakes up the next morning with her neck cricked against Joe's shoulder, the imprint of his wool cardigan against her cheek.

Guillermo hasn't arrived yet, but the kitchen smells like fresh coffee. "Hey," a voice says, and Rosemary realizes there's a hand on her shoulder. Logan is hunched over her, fully dressed. The world is still dark.

"There's something I need to go take care of," Logan explains in a whisper. "I'm going to leave for a little bit, but I'm not *leaving.*"

It's four-thirty in the morning, and Rosemary doesn't really understand, but she says okay.

Logan gives her shoulder a squeeze, then she bends lower and plants a kiss on Joe's forehead. "Please don't die while I'm gone, old man."

Joe grumbles in his sleep, like he does understand.

Chapter Thirty-Five

LOGAN

She leaves the cottage before sunrise, and she's already on her third Dunkin' coffee when she enters the White Mountain National Forest. She drives too fast on the twisty, tree-lined highway, fueled by iced coffee and misplaced hope.

She's not even sure what she's hoping for, but her racing middle-of-the-night thoughts convinced her she will find the answers in Vermont.

It's just her and Van Morrison and the pressing need to push forward, to understand a piece of herself that doesn't make any sense. The piece of herself that's so afraid to *feel*. The piece of herself that's so afraid to be loved.

Logan thinks about Joe and his detours to see cool shit and his *Tuesdays with Morrie* advice. She thinks about him returning to Remy, even when it was hard.

She thinks about Remy and his open heart, about what it would feel to love like she's never been hurt, even when she's secretly hurting.

She thinks about Rosemary and . . .

And it hurts too much. The way Rosemary looked standing on

the porch yesterday when she said she wanted to keep the cottage—the way she looked when she told Logan she loved her. She was *relaxed*. Her mouth wasn't puckered and her jaw wasn't clenched and her neck tendon wasn't bulging. Her face was open, soft, and easy. Her body moved elegantly, like every part of her was in harmony.

Maybe for the first time ever, Rosemary looked completely at peace with herself.

But Logan. She poked, like she always does. She used her prickliness to keep Rosemary at bay, even as her heart bloomed inside her chest like flowers on a cactus. No matter how much she wanted to, Logan couldn't let Rosemary get close, because all she ever does is hurt people.

Rosemary said she loves her, but how could anyone ever love someone as damaged as Logan?

• • •

It's a little before noon when she reaches Burlington. The sky is marble-blue, and she follows North Avenue out along Lake Champlain. Logan has had the address memorized since she was fourteen, back when she always hoped to see it stamped in the upper-left-hand corner of every piece of mail.

She's not sure what she expects to find at the address, but she isn't prepared for a mansion on the lake near an expansive green park. Trees and water and sky.

It never occurred to Logan that maybe her love of wide-open spaces is genetic.

She doesn't hesitate once she arrives. She's out of the car and ringing the doorbell before she can second-guess her impulsivity. Jumping in with both feet.

An old Greek man in pristine tennis whites answers the door. Logan recognizes him from Facebook photos. Yiannis Doukas: CEO of Doukas Beverages and her stepfather. A man she's never met.

Despite Logan's unshowered, caffeine-fueled state of grief and exhaustion, Yiannis clearly recognizes her, too. His expression shifts from overt surprise, to understanding, to sadness.

"Is she here?" Logan blurts. It's only as the words come out that she remembers it's a Thursday, and her mom could be at work. Or, judging by the size of this house, at one of her various nonpaid positions on the boards of local charities. Or pilates.

"She is, but—" Yiannis starts. At the same moment, a voice calls out, "Is that my Amazon delivery?" and Logan is shocked to discover she recognizes it from late-night lullabies and even later-night screaming matches with Antonio.

And then Logan sees her over Yiannis's shoulder, rounding a corner into the foyer. She's dressed in expensive-looking athleisure wear, her dark brown hair streaked with caramel highlights that cascade down her back in perfect barrel curls. Even at almost-sixty, she's as beautiful as Logan remembers, getting tucked into bed at night, gazing up at that face.

"Hi, Mom," Logan says from the front porch.

Sophie looks horrified at the sight of her daughter, and whatever hope Logan harbored during her seven-hour drive here, crumbles at her feet. Sophie's eyes dart around the foyer like she's searching for an escape hatch, and *that* Logan absolutely inherited. Her need to avoid feelings, to duck out of every serious conversation before it starts, must be halfway coded into her DNA.

"Why don't you come inside?" Yiannis offers with a friendly smile, opening the door wider. Logan steps inside, and Sophie shakes herself out of shock.

"Is everything okay, Logan?" she asks with some semblance of maternal instinct.

"Yes," she answers automatically. Then, she laughs at the absurdity of it. "Actually, no. Nothing is okay. Someone very important to me is dying, but that's not why I'm here."

Sophie struggles to look natural in her own home. "Then why are you here?"

The walls of the opulent foyer are lined with photos of her half-siblings, and Logan can't stop staring at the two statuesque teens with her olive complexion and her sharklike eyes and her pouty mouth, assuming she'd had access to orthodontia. Her siblings are carbon copies of her, but with a different socioeconomic status. She presses her finger to a photo of them on a sailboat. "I don't even know how old they are," she says.

Yiannis answers. "John just turned twenty, and he's a sophomore at Amherst. Phoebe is eighteen and graduated from high school in June. She's off to MIT here in a few weeks."

Two perfect, academic superstars. Logan drops her hand from the frame.

"Can I get you something to drink?" Yiannis offers. "We have sparkling water, seltzer water, tonic water, wine—"

"Why are you here, Logan?" her mom interrupts. And Logan sees herself in her mother's utter lack of tact.

"I just want to talk, Mom."

Sophie blinks erratically like she's still searching for a way out.

"And wine sounds great."

• • •

Like every Greek dad she's ever met, Yiannis foists as much food on her as she can stomach. And Logan can stomach quite a lot. The "snack" he prepares to accompany the wine includes freshly made spanakopita, cold slices of lamb, Greek lasagna, pita with tzatziki, and baklava for dessert. Logan ravenously eats all of it, letting the food soak up the caffeine while Yiannis makes small talk.

How's your dad?

How's teaching?

Are you still living in Vista Summit?

What brought you to New England?

Do you want to hear more about your wunderkind half-siblings, who are richer, prettier, smarter, neurotypical versions of you?

Sophie simply studies Logan like she's some fascinating new species on display at the zoo until Yiannis is convinced that Logan is truly full. Then, he gives himself a generous pour of the retsina and makes a clumsy excuse to leave the kitchen.

Sophie and Logan are alone with only a breakfast bar between them.

"Oh, just ask me!" Sophie practically shouts into the silence.

Logan slowly sets down her wine. "Okay . . . why did you leave, Sophie?"

Her mother bursts into tears. "I'm sorry." She chokes through a dramatic sob, reaching for a cloth napkin. "I'm so, so sorry."

Logan finds herself entirely unmoved by her mother's crying. She didn't come here to assuage her mother's guilt about abandoning her. "I don't need you to be sorry," she says. "I just want to know why."

Sophie blots at her eye makeup. "Because I wasn't happy!"

"Being my mom?"

"What? No!" She comes around the breakfast counter and sits on the stool next to Logan. "I was unhappy with your dad. We wanted different things out of life. Your dad was content with a small life in Vista Summit, with the same small Greek community we grew up in, with doing the same thing every day, with never leaving. I needed *more*."

"And you found your big life in Burlington, Vermont?" Logan seethes. She didn't come here to be angry with her mom, either, but she finds the emotion readily available to her.

"Yiannis and I *traveled*!" Sophie explains. "We've seen the world together! We spent six months sailing around the Aegean, homeschooling the children on deck. You haven't seen Naxos until you've seen it in early spring."

"I've never seen Naxos at all. Or anywhere else in Greece." She feels her bitterness grow, and she realizes it was never hope that drove her here. It was fury. "So, I was part of that small life you hated?"

"Of course not!" Sophie puts a hand on Logan's thigh. "It had nothing to do with you!"

Logan yanks her thigh away and laughs. "Of course it had something to do with me. You *left* me. You made me believe I was easy to leave!"

She fumbles through some half-baked lie. "I-I tried to take you with me, but your father wouldn't let me!"

"Yeah, I'm sure you fought *really* hard for me. Tell me, Sophie. Did my dad stop you from ever visiting? From flying me out to see you? From taking me on one of your family trips?"

Logan already knows the answer to these questions, but she revels in the way each one lands on her mother's facial expression like an emotional slap. Antonio Maletis spent years trying to protect Logan from the truth about her mother: that Sophie Haralambopoulous was selfish and self-centered, reckless with the feelings of others, and terrified of ever looking inward.

And the worst part is, in trying to avoid ever feeling the pain of her abandonment again, Logan became just like her mom.

"I was eleven years old, and you left me! You made me feel like I was too much *and* not enough. You made me believe no one would ever stick around for me."

Sophie's bottom lip quivers.

"Oh, stop that! You're not the victim here, and the least you can do after twenty years of pretending I don't exist is to listen to me!"

Her mom's pouting stops instantly, almost like it was never real in the first place.

"When I started my period in seventh grade, I used *leaves* as pads because I was too embarrassed to talk to Dad about it. My ninth-grade English teacher had to teach me how to use a tampon. And it's fine! I didn't need a mom. I had Dad, and I had Joe, and they were more than enough. But sometimes, I wanted *you*. When I kissed my best friend the summer after eighth grade, I wanted to talk to *you* about it, but you weren't there, and since then, I've never been able to trust that anyone will stay."

Sophie blinks again. "Who's Joe?" Like that was her only take-away from Logan's speech.

"He's someone who chose me, and he's dying. But because I'm so afraid of being abandoned, I can barely acknowledge what's happening. And then there's Rosemary"—just her name is a vicious tear through her blooming heart—"and for some deranged reason, she loves me, but I don't know how to let her love me. I don't know how to let anyone get close because I'm afraid they will hurt me like you did."

"Well." Sophie presses her lips together in a thin, mean line. In that gesture, Logan doesn't see herself at all. "I guess I'm to blame for every single problem in your life. You're welcome. Now you don't have to accept any responsibility for your actions. You can just say it's all my fault for being such an awful mom!"

That comment reverberates through Logan's chest. She hasn't used her mom as an excuse—she knows that. But she hasn't let herself heal from what happened, either—has refused therapy and help— and maybe in some ways, that's the same thing. She let this woman's cruelty control her entire life, but the truth is, Logan's been in control the entire time. She doesn't need to understand why her mom left in order to let herself be loved; that's a choice she can make. And she's finally ready to make it.

The French doors open and two girls step inside from the back patio. "Mom? Is everything okay? We heard yelling," asks the girl who Logan places as Phoebe. Only this Phoebe doesn't look like a perfect Greek daughter ordered from a catalogue. Real-life Phoebe's dark hair is shaved on one side, with purple streaks through the rest. Nose ring, ankle tattoo, a crop top and a pair of high-waisted shorts, her hand threaded through the other girl's. This Phoebe looks *exactly* like Logan at eighteen.

"Everything is fine," Sophie responds with a calculated air of nonchalance. Heaven forbid her new daughter knows about the old one.

Logan turns to her sister. "She's a real fucking piece of work, isn't she?"

Phoebe rolls her eyes. "You have no idea."

Sophie loses some of her cool. "Phoebe! Go to your room!"

"You queer?" Logan asks bluntly, gesturing to the hand-holding between these two girls.

"Duh," Phoebe says with a Gen-Z monotone. She appraises her older sister with a critical stare. "Are you?"

Logan is wearing overalls with a sports bra and her dino tropical shirt over the top like a coat. "Duh."

Phoebe cocks her head to the side. "You're my sister, aren't you? The one no one ever talks about?"

Despite all the evidence of Sophie's coldness and callousness, this still hurts. "Yeah. I'm that sister."

Logan grabs a fistful of baklava for the road and shoves it into the front pocket of her overalls like it's a Joey pouch for future emotional eating. "It's nice to finally meet you," she says to her sister. "You seem cool. Maybe we can chat sometime."

She doesn't say anything else to Sophie.

She's already gotten all that she's going to get from this reunion.

• • •

When she gets back out to the Gay Mobile, she feels amped up, restless, torn between needing to sob and wanting to hysterically laugh. She finally confronted her mother after all these years, and her mother just . . . sucked.

She climbs into the driver's seat but doesn't start the van. Logan has to do something with herself before she sits still for the seven-hour drive back to Bar Harbor.

What she *really* wants to do is call Rosemary. She wants to cry to Rosemary and laugh with Rosemary and hear Rosemary matter-of-factly say something like, "So your mom is a bitch. What else is new?"

But she can't call Rosemary. She has no right to, not until she's ready to figure out exactly what she needs to say to make things right. Katharine fucking Hepburn, how can she ever make it right?

She holds her phone in her agitated hands and scrolls past

ALISON COCHRUN

Rosemary's contact repeatedly, until she spots a different contact a few names below that. *New Science Teacher, winky face.*

Logan jumps out of the Gay Mobile and presses the call button as she marches toward the park. Rhiannon Schaffer answers on the second ring. Logan is immediately word-vomiting into the phone. "I am so, so sorry for the way I treated you. I was an asshole. Worse than an asshole. I was *Satan's* asshole after he's eaten Taco Bell. And I'm not calling to ask for forgiveness or anything!"

There's a sound of protest on the other end of the line, but she plows on both in the conversation and in her walk to the park. "I acted like our relationship didn't mean anything because I was scared, but that doesn't make it okay." She takes a deep breath as her lungs strain from the exercise. "I should've worked through my attachment shit before we started hooking up, and before I hurt you, and I'm just really sorry."

"Who is this?" Rhiannon asks innocently.

"Ouch. Okay, I deserve that."

The call is silent for a minute, and Logan wonders if there's a chance Rhiannon truly doesn't remember her. Logan finds a bench and sits down under a slice of shade.

"Whatever." Rhiannon huffs. "Thanks for the apology, asshole."

Logan smiles into the phone. "You're welcome."

"And you didn't really hurt me. I knew what I was getting myself into with you."

She winces. "Right. The apathetic asshole who doesn't care about anyone or anything."

Rhiannon groans. "I really said that to you, didn't I? I—I'm sorry, too. That was a shit thing to say, and it isn't true anyway. No one cares about their students as much as you do," she says genuinely. Logan looks up at the sun cutting through the branches on a maple tree. "You care about being a good teacher. You care about nineties pop country a little *too much*. You care about your dad. And everyone in Vista Summit knows how much you care about Joe Delgado."

She lets this list wash over her as she takes a bite of baklava from her overalls' front pocket.

"I was just bitter because you didn't care about me," she finally confesses, and Logan feels the hurt in her voice through the phone.

"For what it's worth, that wasn't about you. I didn't let myself care about anyone."

"I know." A tenuous silence stretches between them before Rhiannon suddenly says, "I want you to know that I had a lot of sex this summer. With some incredibly hot people. People who were *way* hotter than you."

"I'm very happy for you."

"Thanks. Now. Please never call me again."

Rhiannon hangs up, and Logan stares at her black phone screen. She sees her wild-eyed reflection staring up at her, and all at once, she knows what she needs to do to make things right.

She needs to show Rosemary how much she cares.

Chapter Thirty-Six

ROSEMARY

Rosemary didn't think she could ever wish for Joe's death, but that was before she learned what death *is*. Its recursive nature, its prolonged process. Its pattern.

Joe continues to decline. Logan returns in the middle of the night from her mysterious adventure, and she tells Rosemary to go upstairs for a proper night's sleep. But Rosemary is too afraid to leave Joe's side.

Nurse Addison comes by the next day and tells them it's the end, that they should say their last goodbyes. So they do. They observe nighttime bedside vigils, Rosemary leaning against Logan's shoulder saying, "This is it. Tonight's the night." Holding his hand until morning. Holding each other's hands despite everything.

Then small miracles. His vitals get better. He wakes up and his breathing steadies. He holds down water or Jell-O or mashed potatoes. He goes a day without needing morphine. He smiles. He tells a joke. His brown eyes come into focus. He says, "my girls," and squeezes their hands back.

But he never actually gets *better* better. He's still in pain, his lungs are still full of fluid, his whole life is still confined to one bed.

He's never going to get better. They're all here trying to help him let go. But Joseph Delgado is strong and stubborn until the bitter end.

One night, after Guillermo has gone home, it's just her and Logan. "What do you think he's waiting for?" Logan asks.

Rosemary clutches his hand tighter. "I think he's scared."

"Of death?"

"Of finally surrendering control."

Two days later, Rosemary watches Nurse Addison take his vitals, and then shouts, in a fit of tears and rage, "You can go, okay! I give you permission, you proud, proud man. You can go!" She sobs into his chest for hours.

That same day, Logan asks Guillermo while he prepares dinner: "What percentage of your patients die?"

"All of them," he answers plainly. "That is my job."

"How do you deal with it? Watching all those people die?"

"It's an honor," he says, "to be there for someone at the end."

The next morning, when Guillermo arrives at the same time as Nurse Addison, he has a copy of *One Hundred Years of Solitude* in its original Spanish tucked under his arm. He doesn't make coffee or tea; he sits by Joe's bed and reads him Márquez the way he was meant to be read, and Joe is alert enough that he weeps. Even Nurse Addison stays to listen, comes back again and again for more chapters, while Rosemary prays for the end.

• • •

"Logan is up to something," Rosemary tells Joe the next morning as she sits beside him with her coffee. His eyes are glassy from the morphine, but they're open.

Logan is banging around upstairs, and Rosemary glances at the ceiling. "I'm not sure *what* she's up to, but it's something."

The banging started as soon as Logan returned from her unexplained day away. Given Joe's health, Rosemary moved her suitcases and the typewriter downstairs so she could always be with him, but Logan keeps disappearing upstairs for hours at a time, emerging for meals and to check on Joe, occasionally going on mysterious errands and returning with mysterious bags.

Rosemary asked her what she was doing, but Logan simply said she needed to take care of some things. And Rosemary has been too preoccupied with Joe to press beyond that cagey response.

"You know what she's doing, don't you?" Rosemary asks a barely conscious Joe. And she swears the man smirks at her.

Joe is awake and alert for most of the day, so Rosemary takes Odie for an extra-long walk that evening, two miles down the beach, then up the access stairs and two miles back through town. They both need the exercise and fresh air.

When they return to the cottage, she finds Joe asleep with Guillermo next to him watching baseball. There's a stack of empty cardboard boxes by the front door, and there's a toolbox on the kitchen table. "What's going on?"

Before Guillermo can answer her, she hears Logan shout from upstairs, "Rosie? Are you home? Get up here!"

Something thumps upstairs, like Logan is dragging something heavy across the floor. Maybe a dead body. Or the baggage containing all her abandonment issues.

"Rosie!" Logan calls out again before Rosemary can speculate any further. She unhooks Odie's leash and he bounds up the stairs after the sound of Logan's voice. Rosemary follows.

Logan's wails aren't coming from her own bedroom, but from Rosemary's, the one she hasn't entered in over a week. Odie whimpers at the closed door. Rosemary pushes inside her bedroom, except . . . it's not her room. Not the version of this room she's slept in for the last few weeks. Nothing is where she left it.

"What . . . ?" she starts, but she can't fully form the question, her eyes fluttering around the room, unable to focus on any one thing.

The maroon carpet is gone, and in its place are light oak floors, rubbed smooth with age. The vomit-colored walls are somehow a calming blue. The rickety bed is now a thick-looking mattress with a minimalist white headboard. The quilt is still there over crisp white sheets. The ancient dresser has been cleaned, and the top is lined with plants. She spots a pot of mint, an aloe plant, birds of paradise, camellias. A philodendron like the one she has back home. A cactus with yellow flowers. Prickly pear.

"Where . . . ?"

She is paralyzed in the doorway. A cream rug on the floor, framed photos and prints of the places they've been this summer on the walls, drawers with label-maker stickers on the front and the label maker itself sitting on top next to her laminating machine.

"When . . . ?"

Under the window—*her* window—is a white desk, and on that white desk is her typewriter next to a stack of new paper. In front of the desk is—"Shit, is that a Herman Miller desk chair? *How?*"

Rosemary tries to take in the transformation as a whole, but it feels like she's stepped through a wardrobe into her version of Narnia, which includes office supplies and house plants, clean lines and cool tones, Odie already curled up on the bed, and Logan in the middle of it all, a burst of chaos in a room of precision and order.

Logan has paint in her hair and on her overalls and a little bit on her cheek, too. Her knees are red and ruddy, and she's sweaty and exhausted-looking and smiling.

"Surprise!" Logan says.

"How?" Rosemary asks again. And, "*Why?*"

"I can answer some of those questions!" Logan balances excitedly on the balls of her feet. Rosemary notices the weathered toolbelt secured around her waist and the wild glint in her hazel eyes.

"What." Logan sweeps her arms widely. "I revamped your room into a Rosemary-approved writing space. Because you said you want to stay."

Stay. Rosemary looks at the desk, the typewriter, the plants . . .

"As for where I got everything," Logan continues, "well, believe it or not, these floors were under the heinous carpet when I started peeling it up. The paint I got from Lowe's, along with most of the furniture."

"Is there a Lowe's in Bar Harbor?"

"No clue." Logan hops in place. "I got all this stuff at the Lowe's in Burlington, Vermont."

"You drove to *Vermont*?"

"Yes, but not for the Lowe's. I went to see my mom. And it turns out, my mom is kind of a dickhead."

"Of course she is," Rosemary replies, half in shock. So *that* is where Logan went during her day away. "You didn't need to go to *Vermont* to learn that."

Logan stares at her for a heartbeat, then bursts out laughing. "I thought you might say something like that. But I did need to go to Vermont. I-I needed to confront my bullshit mommy issues." Logan brushes the unwashed hair out of her eyes. "And wouldn't you know it? Sophie leaving was never about me at all. It was about her being a selfish twat."

"I did know that. No decent person would ever leave *you*."

Logan looks at Rosemary the way she looks at shrimp po'boys, and Rosemary feels a tug in her chest. *Oh*, she loves her. She loves her so, so much. It had been easy to push those feelings aside for the last few days and focus on Joe, but now it all comes back to life inside her. She told Logan she loved her on that porch, and Logan told her she needed to think about it.

"I was eleven, Rosie. How could I ever understand it wasn't about me?" Logan shakes her head like she's easily shaking away the memories that haunted her for so long. "Vermont was illuminating, to say the least, but you asked *when* I did all of this, and the thing is, I've been working on it since I got back. I haven't really slept much."

"Logan!"

"I know, I know! Definitely an ADHD manic productivity binge."

She waves her hands around like she's not *still* manic. "But I had this whole epiphany, and I don't want to keep using what Sophie did as a reason to never care, because I do care. I've always cared about you. And I love you, and I made you a writing room. So that's *why*, I guess."

Rosemary still doesn't understand what's happening, but she takes a step closer to this frantic chaos tornado with blue paint on her cheek. "You . . . you love me?"

"I did and I do and I always will," Logan says plainly.

Rosemary disintegrates into stardust and swoon at those words.

"I should have said that two days ago. I should have said that *twenty years* ago," Logan rants. "I loved you when we were girls. Even when I was too young to understand what love is, my heart still loved you on instinct. Loving you was like breathing. My body just knew what to do, even when my brain was still a primordial hormone soup."

Rosemary temporarily forgets how to breathe.

"And when I kissed you in that garden—" Logan touches two fingers to her bottom lip as if she can *still* feel that kiss there. "It was the best moment in my first fourteen years on this earth, but I didn't know how to trust that good things could happen to me, so I acted like it was a joke."

Rosemary inhales a staggering breath. "Logan," she manages, "you don't have to explain. We were teenagers. We both had soup brains."

"I *do* have to explain," she insists emphatically, "because I need you to know that I spent ten years seeing you on every street corner, wondering when you would come home to me. The day I saw you at teacher training, I should've told you the truth: I'd been waiting for you."

Rosemary wants to laugh. "Waiting for me? We kissed *one* time."

"Twice, actually. But it was never just about the kiss. You were half my heart."

She can't look directly at Logan, can't handle the intensity of those hazel eyes. But there's nowhere else in this room she can look that doesn't overwhelm her with feelings. "You made me a writing room," Rosemary says softly.

"You deserve it," Logan insists with more affection than Rosemary can handle, too. "You are the most passionate, bravest person I've ever met. When you love something, you love it wholly and unapologetically. When Joe asked us to take this trip, you didn't even hesitate. I want to be more like that."

Rosemary finally bridges the gulf between them. "I can't believe you did this for me."

"Oh!" Logan flails again. "There's one more thing!"

Logan rushes over to the desk and picks up a white, two-inch plastic binder, just like the one Rosemary prepared for this trip. Logan hands her the binder. "What's this?"

"I could never plan an itinerary like you, and I could never paint you like Remy painted Joe, but . . ." Logan trails off as Rosemary opens the binder. There's a title page with the words *All the Things I Love About Rosemary Hale* written across the center. Rosemary's head swims and swirls as she reads the labels on the binder dividers.

Her Personality.
Our History.
The Way She Makes Me Feel: Part I.
The Way She Makes Me Feel: Part II.
Her Ass (and Other Attractive Features).

Logan finally finishes her thought. "But I wanted to find a way to show you how much I care about you. And I figured someone should make a binder for you."

Eventually, Rosemary will read every word on every page of this binder, but right now, she allows it to drop to the floor with a thunk, and she rushes to Logan, throws her arms around her. Holds her and is held.

"I care about you so fucking much," Rosemary says with every ounce of certainty she has. "And I love you too."

"Yeah?" Logan asks, like she still doesn't know, like she still doesn't get it. As if Rosemary could ever stop caring about this glorious disaster of a woman.

"I did and I do and I always will."

Logan chokes on a sob, and Rosemary reaches up to wipe away her tears. Then Rosemary stands on her tiptoes and kisses Logan without caution or hesitation. Because even if this ends in hurt, Logan is so fucking worth it.

• • •

The next morning, Joe sees them through the open window, kissing on the front porch while they drink their coffee and watch the sunrise.

"I take it the HGTV Hail Mary worked?" he asks haggardly as they come back inside. He's alert again, even as his mouth twists in familiar agony.

Logan grins at her, and Rosemary reflexively grins back. Joe is dying, and they're so in love, and it's beautiful and painful all at once. "It did," Rosemary confirms. "I love my new writing room."

Joe exhales and allows his tired eyes to close. "Finally. Now I can die happy."

Chapter Thirty-Seven

LOGAN

The end finally comes. Rosemary is still on her walk with Odie, Guillermo is tinkering in the kitchen, and Logan is holding Joe's hand. Tonight is the night. She can feel it.

He hasn't had water in three days and his chest barely moves with each shallow, ragged breath. Over the weeks, Logan has learned you can only say goodbye so many times, so she presses her forehead to his and says, "Let go, Joe. You can let go now."

He coughs like he wants to argue, but he hasn't said real words in over twenty-four hours. "We're going to be okay. I promise. You can let go." She kisses his wrinkled temple. "Rosemary and I are going to be okay. You've given us so much, Joe. You raised us right. Trust that we are going to be okay and let go."

She starts to cry. Guillermo goes quiet in the kitchen. Then, she hears his receding footsteps and the sound of the patio door opening and closing.

Logan is alone with Joe now. "You win, you crusty old hag. I'm in love with Rosemary, and she's in love with me, and we're going to figure out how to be happy. Here, I think. In this cottage. If she'll let me stay with her."

He doesn't move in his hospital bed.

"Isn't that what you wanted, you manipulative diva? You wanted me and Rosemary to live in this cottage like you and Remy did? Make a new life here, next to the ocean and among the trees?"

Tears dribble all the way down her chin. "That's what you wanted, and now you can give up the damn ghost, okay? We're going to be fine. We're going to move into this house, and I'm going to sub for the local school district, and Rosemary is going to write her novel and sell it and make tons of money so I never have to work again. We'll take hikes with Odie and we'll swim in the ocean and we'll travel. We'll travel the whole fucking world. Is that what you need to hear?"

She can't catch her breath. She lets out a sob, but there's still something sharp in her throat. "I'll be healthy, okay? I'll always take my meds and I'll find a therapist. I'll eat vegetables, and I'll let Rosemary love me. I'll become okay with the painful parts, and we'll be okay."

It's a stabbing feeling, like a trowel digging down into her esophagus. She's choking on the pain of *this*—her true last goodbye.

"We'll be okay." She buries her face in the crook of his neck. "I promise we will be okay. You can let go."

ROSEMARY

When she and Odie arrive back at the cottage from their walk, the sun is starting to set. Inside, she finds Logan tucked into Joe's side, sobbing. She thinks *it's happened*, and she's surprised to discover her first feeling is relief. That his suffering has finally ended.

Joe isn't dead, though. Not yet.

Rosemary goes to his bedside and wraps her arms around Logan. "Tonight is the night," she says. It's not a question. It's a certainty deep in the pit of her stomach.

"Tonight is the night," Logan repeats through her tears.

They wait.

Nurse Addison comes by every four hours to administer more

morphine. Guillermo makes thirty cups of tea. They put on baseball, they put on music, and they wait as the world goes dark.

Rosemary falls asleep for a few hours, and when she wakes up,
Logan is still sitting upright in her chair on the opposite side of the
bed, still holding Joe's hand.

"Do you remember the first day of freshman year, the first time
you walked into his classroom?" Logan asks her.

His brightly colored scarf, the rainbow flag, the way he said,
"Welcome, my children," as if they were his, instantly. His to teach
and to protect. His to love, no matter what.

"I do remember, yes."

They spend the rest of the night telling stories about Joe and
sharing memories. Reading *Romeo and Juliet* as a class. Debate tournaments out of town, hours in a district van while Joe curated the
playlists, the first time they saw him eat Taco Bell and realized he
really was human after all.

Eating lunch in his classroom. A safe space where they didn't feel
judged.

The emails and the phone calls after they graduated. The feeling
of always having an adult who believed in them.

At four in the morning, Joe wakes himself up with a terrible coughing fit. They try to turn him onto his side to clear a pathway to his
lungs. They squeeze droplets of water into his mouth from the pink
sponge. Tonight is the night, and they try to make him comfortable.

They adjust the bed so he's sitting up a little. He's facing the wall
of windows and even from here, they can all see the stars.

Joe doesn't sleep again, but he's not awake, either. His eyes stay
open, but they're not really his eyes.

The sky begins to shift from black to purple, from purple to dark
blue. Joe manages to lift his hand off the bed just enough to point
to the windows.

"It's almost morning," Rosemary says.

Joe makes a choking sound and points again. Rosemary knows it probably means nothing—he's not really here—but she has to make sense of these last moments. "The ocean? The patio? The sunrise? What, Joe?"

He uses his last ounce of energy to jab his finger once more.

"I think he wants us to take him outside so he can watch the sunrise," Logan translates.

"But we can't."

But they do.

Logan moves all the furniture out of the way. They unlock the brakes on his bed and guide it slowly and carefully toward the sliding glass door. Guillermo helps them seesaw the bed over the raised tracks of the sliding glass door, and out onto the patio.

They position Joe so he has a full view of the sun beginning to rise over the ocean. Rosemary grabs his Pendleton blanket and positions it over his legs. Logan drags out the record player and cues up Van Morrison. "Someone Like You." As apt as ever.

They grab two chairs. Logan on the left, Rosemary on the right, each holding one hand. Odie is always there, curled up at Joe's feet.

The orange rims the horizon, lighting up the clouds, turning the purple and blues into textured bruises. It gets lighter. More orange, the smallest dusting of yellow. The blues are now violet, the purples now a luscious pink.

Rosemary watches Joe watch the sunrise, and for a moment, she does see him in those brown eyes. He opens his mouth. "So many colors," she thinks she hears him say. But that's probably not possible. Joe closes his eyes.

"So many colors," Rosemary says.

The sky continues to lighten. She counts the distance between Joe's breaths, then stops. For the last few minutes, she closes her eyes and chooses to remember the version of Joe from the first day of ninth grade, Joe from the original bathtub painting, Joe from the Grand Canyon, so full of awe.

His grip loosens in her hand. She chooses to remember the feeling of him squeezing back.

Chapter Thirty-Eight

LOGAN

That's how Joe dies.

So many close calls, and then it's like flipping a coin. One minute he's watching the sunrise.

Flip. And he's gone.

Odie starts whimpering at the foot of his bed.

The sun keeps rising, keeps spilling its lush colors across the sky, but Joe isn't here to see it anymore.

Most people die in beige rooms. But Joe . . . he dies in technicolor.

He dies as the sun rises over the Atlantic on the patio at the cottage by the sea. He dies on his own terms, and Logan feels the tension go out of her like the tide. She's awash with relief. He's not in pain. He's not suffering. He finally let go.

But the tide comes back in, like it always does, and Logan is suddenly filled with anger and grief and heartbreak. The frantic, restless need to push, to run away, to do something reckless. To do anything to escape the incoming hurt.

She looks at Rosemary quietly crying on the other side of Joe's body. Logan wants to go to her, to wrap her arms around her so they can ride out this pain together. She wants to run, wants to be as far away from this moment as possible.

She releases Joe's hand and grips the arms of her chair. She holds on as tight as she can, like if she just never let go of this chair, she can weather this new storm.

Her grip slackens. She could outrun this pain.

She stands up.

She looks down the beach, at the infinite escape disappearing in the distance.

She turns to Rosemary, and she goes to her, and she wraps her arms around her. And they weather the storm together.

ROSEMARY

Death is a to-do list.

After weeks of dying, Joe is now dead, present tense, and Rosemary is overwhelmed by all the things they need to do. She can't just sit here crying in Logan's arms. She's already wasted too much time.

How much time? She has no concept of it, but the sun is at a forty-five-degree angle overhead, and every muscle in her body aches. There's no time for this.

They need to call Nurse Addison so he can come declare the time of death.

They need to call the funeral home to come pick up the body.

They need to choose an urn because Joe wants—*wanted*—to be cremated.

There will be paperwork to sign, and Rosemary needs to sign it.

There are things to do, and Rosemary starts to get them done. She puts her feelings aside and takes control of the death.

She has to call Remy.

She has to call Joe's brother in Houston.

She has to call her mom, and Logan's dad.

She has to write an obituary for the Vista Summit newspaper.

She needs to write a Facebook post for all his friends.

She needs to write an Instagram post for all his former students.

She needs to keep doing things and keep in control.

There goes his body. Here is the catalogue of urns. They're almost as expensive as coffins. She points to the cheapest one, a wooden box. It looks almost like a binder.

She must keep going, keep moving, forward and forward and . . .

"Stop, Rosie. Please stop."

Logan's arms are around her again. They're standing in the kitchen, but Rosemary can't remember why she came in here. Logan squeezes her so tight, feeling floods her numb body. Terrible, painful feelings.

"Thank you for taking care of things," Logan says in a low whisper. "Thank you for always being organized. But right now, I need you to be with me."

Rosemary hugs Logan back.

"There is no way around the pain," Logan tells. "We've got to go through it. Please go through it with me."

They're on the kitchen floor, and Rosemary isn't sure how they got here, but they're holding each other while they sob.

"It has to hurt," Logan is saying. "Joe meant too much for us to pretend it doesn't hurt."

Rosemary doesn't need to tackle the to-do list right now.

In this moment, on this kitchen floor, all she has to do is feel this excruciating pain.

LOGAN

After two planes, a train from Boston to Portland, a bus ride from Portland to Bangor, and an awkwardly silent hour-long drive in Nurse Addison's van from Bangor to Bar Harbor, Remy arrives at the cottage by the sea at five in the morning the day after Joe's death.

Logan and Rosemary are already awake to greet him.

His linen shirt is unwrinkled, and Rosemary cries into his chest when she sees him.

Remy cries too, until he sees the nude painting on the wall, and a smile breaks through the tears. "As it should be."

The cottage feels strange without Guillermo and Nurse Addison and Joe and all the medical equipment. Logan can't stand being inside, so the three of them drink coffee with chicory on the patio and watch the sunrise.

"Did he tell you about the cottage?" Remy asks.

"Yes," Logan says, her eyes fixed on the purples beneath Rosemary's eyes, the reds of her cheeks from another night of crying. But Logan was there, under the quilt just big enough for two, her arms wrapped around Rosemary. "We've decided to stay here. At least for a while."

Remy takes a long sip of coffee. "I decided it was all worth it," he tells her. "In the end." Logan doesn't understand.

Rosemary blinks away more tears and looks at Remy. "I decided that too."

• • •

The next day, the crunch of gravel beneath tires signals another arrival. It's her dad, and he's out of his rental car before it's shut off, launching himself at Logan and pulling her into a tight hug.

It's been almost ten weeks since she's seen him, and she doesn't realize how much she missed him until his arms wrap around her. She lets herself collapse against him because she doesn't have to be strong for her dad. She doesn't have to take care of him. She just gets to be comforted.

"You're different, Chicken," Antonio says one evening as he takes a sip of his beer.

Logan kicks her feet up on the railing of the patio. "How so?"

Her dad glances out at the water. Sunset isn't quite as magnificent as sunrise, but Logan still measures the days by witnessing both. It's Wednesday. Her dad has been here for two days, and they managed to give a face lift to the upstairs bathroom in that time. Logan installed the new plumbing. Her dad picked out the new vanity. He accepted this is how she needs to process Joe's death. By fixing up the place he loved.

"You just seem . . . *settled*," Antonio tries. "Settled in your body. Like your feet are planted here. Less Chicken-like."

Logan holds her sweaty beer bottle in both hands. "I saw Mom."

"Yikes. How did that go?"

"Fucking awful. But also . . . good, in a sense. It was never really about me, was it?"

"No, Chicken. It was always about her."

The label on her bottle begins to peel, and she picks at it. "I'm thinking about . . . maybe . . . staying here?" There is no maybe about it, but she doesn't know how to tell her dad she's choosing to leave him like Sophie did. "In Bar Harbor? For . . . I don't know. For a bit."

"I figured," he says. "You don't update a bathroom for nothing."

"That would mean . . . moving out . . ."

"Yes, it would."

She rips off a slice of label, the wet paper sticking to her fingers. "How would you feel about that . . . ?"

"Thank Shay fucking Mitchell," her dad says, and Logan chokes on an unexpected laugh. "It's about goddamn time. That's how I feel about it."

"But I—" Tears sting her eyes, and she grabs the arm of her chair, forcing herself to stay in this pain. "I always felt like, if I left you, it would . . . it would be like I'm Mom."

"Oh, my Chicken." Her dad gets up from his chair and comes to kneel in front of her. "You are nothing like your mother. And you've got to get the hell out of my house."

She laughs again, and the sound settles in her chest. "Thanks, Dad."

He reaches up and gives her a noogie, like they're both twelve. She shoves him away and sloshes a bit of her beer onto the patio. "Oh, I see. My childish behavior comes from *you*."

"Oh yes. You've always been *exactly* like your dad."

"Dinner's ready," Rosemary says, poking her head out the sliding door. She hasn't cried in seven hours. Logan is keeping track.

Rosemary smiles wanly at Logan, then pops back inside.

"You love her? Like, for realsies?" Antonio gestures to Rosemary's receding figure through the glass.

Logan sighs. "For realsies."

Chapter Thirty-Nine

ROSEMARY

On a Thursday, they have a funeral.

They don't call it that, though.

No, Joe left clear instructions for his "Death Party," just like he always had a clear vision for his death trip. Rosemary doesn't fight this one.

Logan carries camp chairs and a portable speaker, and Rosemary has a bag of s'mores fixings in one arm and his ashes in the other, as they walk down the trail to the beach.

Antonio builds up a bonfire, and Remy makes sure everyone has a whiskey-seven for the toast. Nurse Addison is there too, with Guillermo. Logan holds her whiskey-seven the highest as she says, "To Joe's next great adventure."

She starts crying, and then they're all crying around a bonfire on the beach.

"Some party," Antonio announces after honking his nose into a handkerchief.

For a long time, the six of them sit in silence, staring at the flames. Sipping their cheap beers. Thinking about Joe. Rosemary thinks about how only Joe could bring together such an odd assortment of people.

That's what he did. He brought people together.

• • •

Only Rosemary and Logan spread his ashes. They wade out into the water, hands linked, the ashes inside the wooden box from the funeral home. The waves lap against her calves, then her knees, until she's submerged all the way up to her waist. Everything goes numb from the cold, but Joe wanted to swim in the Atlantic one last time. Logan's hand is still in hers.

Logan extends the box toward Rosemary and she pulls off the lid. It's so strange to think a man like Joe could be reduced to nothing more than a pile of dust inside a plastic bag. But he's more than his remains. He's in every mile they drove to get here, in every word Rosemary writes, every click of her typewriter keys. In the cottage Logan is fixing up with her own restless hands.

Joe lives in every student he's ever taught. As expansive and incontrovertible as the ocean.

Rosemary lets go of Logan's hand long enough to reach for a pinch of ashes. She feels the legacy of Joe against her palm before she sprinkles the ashes into the water. Logan does the same. Just a pinch, taken away by the waves.

Tears blur her vision as bit by bit she releases him.

"This isn't Joe," Logan says, staring at the ashes swirling around their legs. Rosemary knows she's crying too.

"It isn't *all* of Joe," Rosemary corrects. Because it is part of him. The part of him who wanted to return to this place where he lived with the love of his life. The part of Joe who loved this cottage and these trees. The Joe who loved Rosemary and Logan best of all and wanted them to be as happy here as he was once.

Rosemary takes the plastic bag—just a trace of ashes circling the bottom remains—and tips it over, the rest spilling out in a streaming ribbon.

It doesn't feel like an ending. It feels like a middle, continuous and unending, like the crash of these waves. Again and again, they pound against the shore.

"Goodbye, Joe," Logan says quietly. Dipping her hands into the water, she washes the last of him from her fingers. The final ashes dissolve and float away and are carried out with the tide. Again, and again.

Logan takes a deep breath, and Rosemary watches her lungs expand with air through her tropical shirt. The one with flamingos on it. She wades closer, and when Rosemary kisses her, Logan tastes like tears and sunlight and salt water. Part of Joe will always live in Logan, too. In the way she teaches and touches the lives of her students. In how much she cares. In her fight and in her compassion. Rosemary kisses her as the waves lap around her thighs.

"I love you," Rosemary whispers against Logan's wet throat.

She reaches out for Logan's hand again. And again and again. Rosemary tugs them along, deeper into the surf, until the waves lap around her shoulders. She counts to three, and as a wave rolls in, she plunges beneath it, feeling the cool water envelop her.

When she pops up again, she's laughing. She can't help it. Even better, Logan is smiling fully back at her.

Rosemary shifts her body so she's floating on the top of the water. "Race you?" she smirks, stroking her arms in preparation for the coming wave. Logan does that competitive grimace Rosemary loves so much. They both kick their legs as the wave approaches, and when it comes, Rosemary feels herself buoyed above the wave, floating on the crest all the way back to the sand.

Of course, she wins.

"Best two out of three," Logan argues as she spits salt water out of her mouth.

They wade back out into the depths, and they ride the waves back to shore. It's beautiful and it hurts like hell when they land on the scratchy sand, and Rosemary feels completely and utterly out of control.

They go again and again.

Next Summer

Bar Harbor, Maine to Vista Summit, Washington

LOGAN

"What is *that*?"

"What?"

Logan points to the offensive object in question. "That. Is that a binder?"

Rosemary clutches the binder-shaped thing tightly to her chest. "No."

"I can see it, Rosie. That's a fucking three-ring, two-inch son of a bitch. We agreed this trip would be spontaneous!"

"It's just research," she says, slipping the binder into the passenger seat. As if that settles things. "Just some information about possible routes and interesting stops and clean hotels and places to get gas and—"

Logan frowns, but she's not actually upset. She can't wait to see what Rosemary has planned for them. Still, Rosemary tries to reassure her. "We can have structured spontaneity!"

"You packed the laminating machine, too, didn't you? And . . . oh God, not the label maker!"

"You love my label maker." She comes in close, and there's that vanilla and peppermint, now mixed with salt water and something woodsy Logan associates with the cottage by the sea. Tree bark after rain and spring flowers in bloom. Cedar and soil. Something impossible not to love.

Rosemary presses herself up on her tiptoes and kisses Logan's cheek. "You just focus on your part of the packing, Pear."

Logan puffs out her cheeks, set to argue, but the air goes out of her at that term of affection. *Pear*. Rosemary started calling her that sometime after Joe's funeral.

Rosemary is *very* aware of the effect of this word. Logan is always *Pear* when the garbage needs to be dragged to the curb for pickup or when the grass is looking a little long or when there's a particularly nasty spider in the shower. She is never *Pear* when her dirty towel is left on the bathroom floor or when she brings home mountains of student work to be graded and takes over the entire kitchen table. She's definitely not *Pear* when she blasts music from Joe's old record player and sings along too loudly during Rosemary's writing time.

But sometimes, she is Pear when they are curled up under the single quilt they share, trying to stay warm through Maine's winter. Sometimes she's Pear when they shower together or when Logan does that thing with her tongue Rosemary really likes. Sometimes, she is absent-mindedly Pear in the produce section at Hannaford, when Rosemary needs help reaching something on a high shelf. And sometimes, she is Pear when they're hiking in Acadia or camping in Nova Scotia or taking weekend trips to Portland or Providence, when Rosemary is so overcome with awe, she forgets to guard any part of her heart.

And in those moments—in *most* moments with Rosemary—Logan forgets to guard her heart, too.

There are still mornings when Logan wakes up convinced it will all be yanked away. There have been arguments that she was sure would be their last. Sunrises that felt too good to be true. So many instances when Logan was too much—too loud, too chaotic, too messy—that she was waiting for Rosemary to walk out the door.

But Rosemary never does. Every day, Rosemary proves she's too stubborn to break a promise. She never walks away, and Logan is learning not to push thanks to the inner child work she's doing with her new therapist.

Logan hunches over to lift the giant cooler and waddles toward the open side door of the van to slide the cooler onto the floor of the Gay Mobile. Odie takes this as his signal to load up. He barks twice, then jumps onto the back seat, sitting upright like he expects Logan to fasten his seat belt.

"Odie!" Rosemary snaps her fingers. "Bed."

Odie gives her his otter-eyed look of innocence before he resettles himself in a dog bed Rosemary's propped up to keep the seats clean.

Logan grabs the rest of Rosemary's luggage—her personal cooler of bottled iced coffees and LaCroix, two rolling suitcases, a reusable grocery bag of snacks, her silk pillow, a white-noise machine, a literal *hat box*—and loads it into the trunk. She reaches for a black suitcase, and then almost falls forward from the weight of it. "What the hell is this?"

"My typewriter," Rosemary says like it's obvious. "Just in case the mood strikes and I need to write something down."

"You couldn't do that on your laptop? Or the notes app on your phone?"

Rosemary deposits one bag into the truck. It's full of *towels*. "You know I prefer to write on my typewriter. It stops me from editing as I go. Keeps me moving forward."

Logan does know. She knows the sound of clacking typewriter keys as well as she knows the sound of the ocean, the sound of Odie snoring at the foot of the bed. The typewriter keeps Rosemary pushing forward into the unknown.

And Logan almost throws out her lower back loading it into the van because it also connects them both to Joe.

They have a road trip emergency kit and a basket of muffins from Nurse Addison and a small vial of what remains of Joseph Delgado, those few ashes they didn't send out to sea. It's 3,265 miles on the direct route between Bar Harbor and Vista Summit, but they have no intention of taking the direct route.

Maybe they'll swing through Vermont. Yannis has reached out a few times and tried to lure Logan back with the promise of cheese. They'll probably go to Massachusetts to visit her siblings, John and Phoebe, whom she's been getting to know. Phoebe wants to take them to her girlfriend's show in Boston (she's a bassist, of course), and John wants to take them to the Emily Dickinson Museum in Amherst.

They'll definitely head down to Ocean Springs to check in on Remy. Rosemary wants to see the Outer Banks and Logan wants to see the Blue Ridge Mountains, and they both want to discover all the things they don't yet know they need to see.

They have six weeks before Logan has to be back in Bar Harbor for teacher training days at Mount Desert Island High School.

They have six weeks before they have to return to the real world. Six weeks of adventure and freedom and seeing cool shit. Six weeks to get lost together.

Logan slams the back door of the van and prays that the Gay Mobile can handle another cross-country trip. She walks around and finds Rosemary still standing by the passenger door, clacking her pale pink nails against her phone screen. Some things never change. "I'm so sorry, princess," Logan teases. "Is all my packing disrupting your crucial screen time?"

"Sorry, sorry," Rosemary mutters, even as she's still typing furiously. "It's my critique partner. They just emailed me their notes on the current manuscript, and I want to make sure I reply before we're officially on vacation."

Logan smiles. Some things do change, though. Like Rosemary saying sorry when her hyperfixated brain makes her a less-than-attentive partner. Or Rosemary using that miraculous brain to write the first draft of an adult fantasy novel in six months, entirely on Joe's typewriter.

Like Rosemary willingly taking six weeks off from book revisions and prepping query letters to take a trip back home to see their parents.

Though Logan isn't sure that Vista Summit really is *home* anymore. They went back for a Celebration of Life for Joe at the high school when they packed up the rest of their things and drove the Toyota Corolla to Maine. They flew back for a week at Christmas. The rest of the year was spent at the cottage by the sea.

But Bar Harbor isn't really *home*, either. At least, it's not their forever home. Logan's not really sure where they'll end up long-term.

Rosemary finishes her email and slides her phone into the pocket of her dress. "Okay, sorry. I'm here. I'm present. Hi."

Logan slides across the gravel in her Vans. "Oh, hi." Her arms snake around Rosemary's waist and pull that familiar scent as close as possible. Their mouths meet in the middle and *this*. This is definitely home. This waist and this mouth and these moments.

"I actually made a playlist for this trip." Rosemary sounds exceptionally proud of herself as she effortlessly boosts herself into the passenger seat and starts fiddling with the aux hookup.

"Excuse me, but you're encroaching on my territory." Logan swats her hand away. "If you don't need me for playlists, then what am I even contributing to this relationship?"

"You can reach the high cupboards in the kitchen and you kill all the spiders."

"That's it?" Logan deadpans. "You only keep me around because I'm tall and slightly less afraid of spiders than you?"

"No, Pear, of course not." Rosemary leans over to massage her shoulder. "You're also really good at cunnilingus."

"I'll take it." Logan pushes her sunglasses into her hair and backs out of the gravel driveway. "But just to clarify, we are going to listen to audiobooks on this trip, too, right? Because I downloaded *Emma* and *Pride and Prejudice*."

"Yes. We can listen to Jane Austen." Rosemary cues up her playlist, and the first song is from the *Mamma Mia 2* soundtrack, one of their favorite cozy, movie Sunday watches. It's the title track. "Good choice," Logan admits begrudgingly.

"Here we go again," Rosemary says, sticking her feet up on the dashboard.

Logan stares at her legs and her nonsensical shoes, the way her toes bounce up and down in rhythm with the song. "I don't think this time will be anything like last time."

"Oh. I almost forgot." At a red light, Rosemary reaches into the pocket of her dress and pulls out the vial of ashes dangling from a blue piece of yarn. She leans forward and hooks the yarn around the rearview mirror so that Joe's ashes hang between them like a good luck charm.

Logan touches her fingers to the dangling vial. "We'll take lots of nudes," she says seriously. "For Joe."

"For Joe," Rosemary agrees with a solemn nod.

Logan raises an eyebrow. "Should we start now?"

The light turns green. Rosemary takes down her hair and flicks the scrunchie at Logan. The windows are open. Her pale-gold hair whips around her face, but she doesn't try to contain it again. Doesn't try to control it. Rosemary laughs as her hair covers her eyes, and Melissa fucking Ethridge, Logan never thought a moment like this would be possible.

"I love you," Logan says, simply because she was thinking it. And there is no point in pretending not to care anymore.

Rosemary pushes her hair back and smiles. "I love you, too."

Logan pulls on to the 3 heading north and turns to Rosemary again. "Out of curiosity, what is in that jumbo binder of yours?"

Rosemary hoists the binder up into her lap. "I'm so glad you asked, Pear. You remembered to pack your passport, right?"

Logan nods slowly. Her brand-new passport is tucked safely in her fanny pack.

"Perfect. Because I already booked a room at Chateau Frontenac in Quebec City for the night. I thought we could stroll around the old city, and I can practice my French and you can eat patisserie, and then there's a waterfall we can hike out to tomorrow, and—*what?*" Rosemary blinks at her from the passenger seat. "Sorry. Was that too much?"

Logan can't help but smile. "Nope. That was just enough."

She pulls her hair out of its bun and lets it get tangled in the wind, too, as they drive onward.

Acknowledgments

Back in September 2021, when I first told my agent that I wanted to write a sapphic road trip rom-com about death, I personally hadn't experienced much death in my life. I'd lost my paternal grandfather a few years before, and that first encounter with true grief had been brutal to be sure. Still, I went into the idea for this book with a naïve detachment from the subject matter.

Sadly, the day after I pitched this book to my agent, a dear friend, Missy Ryan, died from breast cancer. I spent three weeks in Ocean Springs, Mississippi, with my friend Meredith in the wake of that loss as she cleaned out her mother's house. The heaviness and grief of that experience left an indelible mark, as did Missy. And so I hope with Joe's story, I've honored Missy and the town she called home in some small way. Thank you to Meredith, for letting me be beside you during that time. Thank you for introducing me to Whataburger and auto mechanic frozen shrimp, and for allowing me to tell this story.

In 2022, I also lost both of my maternal grandparents. We were extremely close, and I feel their absence every day. But I'm grateful for that hurt and what it says about the impact they had on my life. I'm grateful that my grandpa got to read my debut novel before he passed. He secretly told my mom it wasn't for him, but then he gave the book to every single old lady at his assisted living facility to read. At the celebration of life, people came up to me and asked if I was the romance author granddaughter, and I'll never get the chance to tell him what that meant to me.

Thank you to my mom and aunts, for showing me what it means to be a caretaker. And thank you to every health care worker who treated my grandparents with dignity in the end.

Thank you to my agent, Bibi Lewis, for immediately jumping on board when I said "rom-com about death." Thank you to my editor, Kaitlin Olson, for everything you did to turn that seedling idea into a novel.

It truly does take a village to publish a book, so thank you to everyone at Atria who had a hand in making this book possible, but a special thanks to Megan Rudloff (always), Ifeoma Anyoku, Jolena Podolsky, Stacey Sakal, Sarah Horgan (for the gorgeous book cover of my dreams), Nicole Bond, and Liz Byer. Thank you to my beta readers and sensitivity readers, but especially Ellie Mae MacGregor, who went above and beyond to make this book suck a little less. And Andie Sheridan and Timothy Janovsky, who always try to make my writing suck less.

Thank you to my sister Heather for taking the research road trip with me. Thank you to my dad for instilling an early love of both road trips and Van Morrison in me. Thank you to my dog for being the inspiration behind Odie. Thank you to my therapist for coming in clutch with that ADHD diagnosis. Thank you to my Adderall. This book literally could not exist without you.

Thank you to every queer student who trusted me with their coming out over the course of my teaching career. I left the classroom, but I never wanted to leave you.

Thank you to my author friends and my Bookstagram friends and everyone in the romance community who has shown me support and made writing books in my pajamas slightly less lonely.

Thank you to my family and my dearest friends (you know who you are). None of this would be possible without your love. And biggest thanks to Michelle, for sustaining my joy with cute videos of your daughter when the writing got rough.

Finally, and most importantly, thank you to my wife for her medical expertise and for constantly asking when she could read the book. You are my favorite adventure.

About the Author

Alison Cochrun is a former high school English teacher and a current writer of queer love stories, including *The Charm Offensive* and *Kiss Her Once for Me*. She lives outside Portland, Oregon, with two giant dogs, her small wife, and too many books. You can find her online at AlisonCochrun.com or on Instagram as @AlisonCochrun.

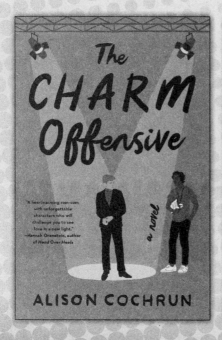